THE HURRICANE PARTY

Klas Östergren was born in Stockholm in 1955 and is the author of several novels, including the Swedish cult classics *Gentlemen* (1981) and *Gangsters* (2005). A leading star of Sweden's literary scene for nearly three decades, he has won countless prizes, among them the Piratenpriset and the Doblougska Prize from the Swedish Academy. Östergren is also an esteemed translator, playwright and scriptwriter. His many memorable translations include works by J.D. Salinger, the collected works of Ibsen, and numerous British playwrights, such as Nigel Williams, Ted Hughes and Harold Pinter. He now lives with his family in the seafront town of Kivik in southern Sweden.

Praise for Klas Östergren's *Gentlemen*

'An exuberant, complicated thriller and literary tour de force . . . The unravelling of the mystery is extremely compelling and highly imaginative.' Kate Saunders, *The Times*

'An amusing, vivid depiction of a romantic era in post-war Sweden.' *Herald*

'A modern Swedish classic.' *Financial Times*

Myths are universal and timeless stories that reflect and shape our lives – they explore our desires, our fears, our longings and provide narratives that remind us what it means to be human. *The Myths* series brings together some of the world's finest writers, each of whom has retold a myth in a contemporary and memorable way. Authors in the series include: Alai, Karen Armstrong, Margaret Atwood, AS Byatt, Michel Faber, David Grossman, Milton Hatoum, Natsuo Kirino, Alexander McCall Smith, Tomás Eloy Martínez, Klas Östergren, Victor Pelevin, Ali Smith, Su Tong, Dubravka Ugrešić, Salley Vickers and Jeanette Winterson.

THE HURRICANE PARTY

KLAS ÖSTERGREN

Translated from the Swedish by Tiina Nunnally

CANONGATE

Edinburgh · London · New York · Melbourne

Published by Canongate Books in 2009

I

Copyright © Klas Östergren, 2007
English translation copyright © Tiina Nunnally, 2009

The moral right of the author and translator have been asserted

Originally published in Sweden as *Orkanpartyt* by Albert Bonniers
Förlag in 2007

First published in Great Britain in 2009 by
Canongate Books Ltd, 14 High Street,
Edinburgh EHI ITE

www.meetatthegate.com

Lines from 'The Dry Salvages' by TS Eliot are reprinted with
the permission of Faber and Faber Ltd

The publisher gratefully acknowledges subsidy from the
Anglo-Swedish Literary Foundation towards the production of
this book

The publisher gratefully acknowledges subsidy from the
Swedish Arts Council towards the production of this book

British Library Cataloguing-in-Publication Data
A catalogue record for this book is available
on request from the British Library

ISBN 978 1 84767 258 2

Typeset in Van Dijck Regular by Palimpsest Book Production Ltd,
Grangemouth, Stirlingshire

Printed and bound in the UK by CPI Mackays, Chatham ME5 8TD

This book is printed on FSC certified paper

That the future is a faded song, a Royal Rose or a
  lavender spray
Of wistful regret for those who are not yet here
  to regret,
Pressed between yellow leaves of a book that has
  never been opened.
And the way up is the way down, the way
  forward is the way back.

T. S. Eliot

A Major Second

The power went out a few minutes before three in the afternoon. The sky filled with heavy rain clouds, and the whole city went dark.

Hanck Orn was sitting in his living room listening to the organ concert broadcast from the Cathedral. Then came the power outage. The subsequent silence and the darkness that followed first aroused annoyance and irritation, only to modulate immediately into another sort of darkness, which in a larger context would last far into the future, perhaps for the rest of his life.

He would later say as much to his few acquaintances. 'My entire existence has gone dark.' It sounded bombastic and pretentious, coming from him. But those who understood the nature of the circumstances were willing to overlook it.

The concert had been performed in the church for generations. Lately the notes had expressed a descending interval; those in the know speculated whether it might be moving towards a cadence and, if so, what it might portend. But even those amateurs who simply heard the notes were seized by the development and awaited the next tone with anxious anticipation, discussing and speculating. Peculiar systems for calculating the probable changes were touted at every bookmaking agency. Experts and interpreters who had predicted the right notes became famous and were considered oracles.

Hanck rarely participated in this form of gambling. The

notes themselves were enough for him. They could transmit a power that seemed beneficial, although he often wondered whether it was captivating or liberating or possibly both.

Regardless of how you look at the world, and no matter what you choose to call the powers that be, you can never ignore what is called the 'magic of events'.

It's part of the human equation, the rhythm of the heart, the pulse of the narrative, the way things take shape whenever a story begins; expectations are awakened and with them the sense that at some time the whole thing will have to come to an end.

He had been leaning back comfortably in an easy chair. The tone was the same as the last time he listened, several days earlier. A warm, pure note. It was a G.

A G that could peel away and push aside all those things that you otherwise went around thinking about, all the worry chafing in your subconscious, things that were talked about in the city, old ailments, new epidemics, money, the daily bread, and of course everything that a father might ponder with regard to a son, the dangers that await a boy in this world.

The tone was powerful, absolute, and soaring, clear and open. It could be speaking about anything at all. Or it might be saying nothing, if that was what you preferred. It was simply there, a solid pillar of sound, strong and stable enough to support the considerable weight of the listeners' expectations.

One of the premises was that at any moment, at any time whatsoever, it could be replaced by another, either higher or lower tone; along with the memory of the old one it would express an interval, give a hint of a larger pattern, a thought, a narrative that was on its way somewhere, a movement which you could follow step by step.

There were people in the city who had lived a long life and who had listened to the organ as often as they could, and yet had missed each and every shift in tone. For his part, Hanck had ticked off quite a few. He could even associate a decisive event in his life with a certain interval: a major second.

Now, on this rainy day, no such thing took place. Yet he had remained sitting in that armchair for several hours, spellbound and absorbed. Maybe because nothing was happening.

Part of the nature of this magic is that it can erect boundaries, at times sharp and high and difficult to breach. Those affected may appear to be prisoners of the course of events.

It's a common experience for a person to find himself drawn into a development which even at an early stage points in an undesirable direction, perhaps straight to hell, and later, when the catastrophe becomes a fact, you remark: 'I could feel it from the very beginning . . .'

Now this may seem both comforting and gratifying, since most hells become tolerable whenever the person who has ended up there can say: 'What did I tell you?!'

Entire cultures have vanished as the prisoners of events, marching in step towards their own downfall, as if blinded, turned towards another existence, absorbed in a vision of something other than what is at hand.

What is called human freedom has nothing to do with turning to magic to influence the forces of destiny; rather it's a matter of breaking the magic.

As in the case of misfortunes or deeds of valour, when physical and spiritual faculties are put to the test, a total sense of presence occurs, a state that may be regarded as alienating and in hindsight might be described in this way: 'It seemed totally unreal . . .'

Misfortunes are dated, assigned a precise place in time and space and preserved as distinct events until they've cooled and hardened and taken on a manageable form; then they're set out in a clearing where wind and weather wear away what is unique, leaching away the pain and making them less personal. Gradually they become incorporated into a larger expanse of experiences, where they allow themselves to be told as one story among all the others. What once broke the magic can now restore it.

The essence of the misfortune has been vanquished, art has altered the bookkeeping, entering a debit among the assets. The tragedy has lost its effect; it can be illuminating and instructive or may simply present an entertaining tale in the glow of the fire in the evening.

The misfortune that struck Hanck Orn does not need to be further specified in terms of time and space, or set aside to cool down and become manageable. From the very beginning it had already taken on features reminiscent of the classical tragedies.

He'd been having a good day up until three o'clock. It was largely like any other day, and he would later recall everything he had done, down to the smallest detail, the way people like to go over a series of events in the hope of finding an explanation or seeing some sort of meaning, and whether things could have been different, not as senseless.

His days usually started in the same way. As soon as he awoke and climbed out of bed, he would go over to the window facing the street and pull aside the curtain to get some idea of the weather. If the sun was shining he might open the window and stick out his head and look towards Vinterplatsen, where the big monitor displayed information about the current temperature and weather conditions.

When it was raining, on the other hand, he would get an idea of what sort of rain it was. Sometimes it was a risky business to stick out his head since a good deal of the precipitation, especially at the start of the rainy season, was downright harmful to the eyes.

He had a son. Every time he admonished the boy to protect himself from the sun or the rain, he could hear his own mother's voice saying: 'Never go out bareheaded!' Her nagging had been just as fruitless as his own: 'So what's wrong with this hat, anyway?!' It seemed part of normal life to repeat such phrases of concern. That's how he preferred to view it, that it sounded equally persistent, that a certain feeling automatically found its expression, that it was the children who had once taught the adults what love is.

It was a fine and quiet drizzle that was falling on this occasion. The rainy season had been going on for a while, and the festivities that took place at the start of the season had given way to ordinary days of wetness.

Hanck Orn was not a particularly old man, yet he could still recall when the rain festivals in the city were no more than informal merrymaking at various locations staged by immigrants, mostly the second- and third-generation Flemish, who comically enough had come up with the idea of welcoming the rain.

Soon the celebration had grown, acquiring its own ceremonies, and by now it consisted of official holidays and festivities that were inaugurated by representatives of the Administration. Naturally that should have signalled an end to the fun when what was once spontaneous was taken over by those who believed that they represented the common good. But the power of the torrential rain was considerable, and it seemed to induce a resistance to attempts at taming or regulating anything.

People did precisely what they liked when the rain came, even though at first the downpours were filled with all manner of harmful substances. After a few days they became less dangerous, the layers of air were rinsed out, the city's dusty, dirty streets were flushed clean after many months of oppressive and stagnant heat. The rain brought with it a liberating freshness, a blessed resource. Pools and reservoirs were filled.

Everything could be washed. The power supply was secured.

For Hanck, the rainy season primarily meant irregular work schedules when he had to take the days as they came, an enforced freedom that his son might call 'laissez-faire', with a large dose of contempt. It was no doubt some sort of kitchen French for negligent behaviour.

His work consisted of repairing and selling machines. The humidity level indoors, inside his workshop, was often critical for a number of metals. They might look free of rust, but they seldom were. On this kind of day, when his antique hygrometer showed 99% relative humidity, he chose not to even open the door to his workshop. He didn't want to jeopardise the few machines he had left.

So he did what he usually did whenever there was nothing in particular to occupy his time: he walked round the flat and straightened up, putting his shoes in their proper place in the hall, hanging a coat on a hanger, making the beds.

He went into his son's room and picked up a few things here and there, cleaning up in a manner that he had developed over the years, meaning in a manner that wouldn't be discovered. He could continue in this way for quite a while before it would be noticed. The boy had a hard time keeping things tidy, except in the kitchen. He was a chef, and on the wall hung the diploma he had received after finishing culinary school. It hung between two old posters showing the cuts of meat on a steer, a pig and a sheep.

His son, Toby was his name, had undergone lengthy and thorough training without ever coming near a piece of meat. The posters on the wall portrayed something exciting, desirable and unobtainable. The sort of thing that all young men like to see on the wall.

The curtains in the room were usually kept closed. Toby worked far into the night, and during his hours off he mostly lay in bed and slept. Hanck stood in the dim light with a cushion in his hand, a soft cushion from his own childhood home that Toby had appropriated. The cushion used to have an embroidered pattern on it, but it had been rubbed off. The fabric was worn shiny. The cushion stank. It had seen better days, but he didn't dare throw it out.

He stood there, irresolute, almost dejected. He still hadn't got used to the idea that the boy was grown up. It had happened so fast. The kid could take care of himself now. He earned more money than his father did, and had a bright future ahead of him. Hanck should be happy, and he tried to persuade himself that he was, but it was a peculiar kind of happiness. It could make him feel paralysed, especially in here, inside the boy's old room.

This cramped, messy, foul-smelling cubbyhole was like some sort of end station. He found himself in the midst of a leave-taking. Later, when he would think back on this day, he pictured himself standing there with a filthy cushion in his hand, preparing himself for a different leave-taking, one that was more final. But that may have been an invention of hindsight, a way of interpreting the magic that had held him there.

It can appear at any moment, both in great tragedies and in the most everyday activities, in all human endeavours. It can happen suddenly, with a glance, a gesture, an intonation, without the phrase 'Once upon a time . . .' ever being uttered.

Even trivial stories that never start out by mentioning any remarkable events and that may disclose an inglorious end at the very beginning arouse anticipation, as well as trepidation regarding the inevitable end. No one wants to live in a world that has lost its lustre.

A person's prospects for settling into his life depend on

how he chooses to relate to this magic, whether he learns to regard it in the right way and is then capable of adapting accordingly.

Whoever chooses to deny its power may get far in the world but risks being remembered as a prodigy who never found his proper place.

Hanck had found his proper place, at least during the past twenty years, at least until now, when he seemed to haul himself up from a deep pit in order to drop that filthy cushion on the floor and get himself out of that room.

His son was supposed to come home that evening and take a few days off. Hanck was looking forward to it. He caught himself imagining all the things they would do together; things that, as soon as he became aware of them, made him feel ridiculous.

He knew in advance that nothing would ever come of it. He no longer had much to offer.

.

In the meantime, Hanck had a number of errands to take care of, as soon as the shops opened. Two machines, two of the last ones, stood ready for delivery in the hall. Both were going to a shop within walking distance. The machines were well packed in cellophane with little salt pouches inside their original cases, which in turn were protected by even more cellophane.

He put on his hat and a light raincoat, stepped out into the stairwell, fastened the three locks on the door and bolted the wrought-iron gate. Holding a machine in each hand, he started down the stairs.

By the time he reached the street, he had passed and partly climbed over six bodies in the stairwell. He had poked at two of them with his shoe to check that they were still alive. If not, he would be expected to take certain measures.

The pavement along his block was covered, and he made his way over to Vinterplatsen without getting his shoes wet. A tram clattered down the street, the overhead cables throwing off sparks that hissed in the damp air.

The market square was filled with rubbish that had been left behind after the latest clean-up. Street-cleaning was haphazard in this part of town. It looked like a battlefield after a conflict waged under the worst possible conditions, which actually suited the old warrior king whose statue stood in the middle of the square under a huge dome. The glass of the dome had been worn smooth by all the rain, creating a number of optical phenomena.

'The king is moving!' Toby used to say back then, every time they walked by. 'Is there going to be a war now?' The boy always looked terrified. Hanck had to reassure him, solemnly swearing that the king would never come out of his glass dome.

No one missed him. Yet sometime in the past this market-place had been named after him. Much later, people preferred to pay homage to one of the seasons, and then that too had become a thing of the past.

Hanck walked a couple of blocks along the main street and then turned into a side street, which was in an even worse state. In popular parlance this was called, with a certain amount of irony, the 'pleasure district'. The name signified an area of pubs and clubs frequented in the night only by the most desperate clientele. At the moment there were plenty of people who were desperate enough to fill these streets and establishments every night. In the mornings – weather permitting – those who were less desperate had to clean up the debris.

Hanck wound his way between piles of rubbish containing things that no one would want to examine. Occasionally he might be asked, as a corpse was pulled from such a heap, whether he could help with identification.

In the midst of these dubious haunts there were a number of serious-minded shopkeepers, including Hanck's retailer. The shop was just opening. A heavy roll-down metal shutter went up with a shrill screech.

The display window was crowded with objects made from extinct types of wood and metal that gleamed like gold. Instruments and tools from hundreds of years ago, machines from before the electronic era – collectors' items for an elite group of devotees, things that would be used by even fewer people.

There were telescopes, microscopes, navigational instruments, clocks and pendulums, scales, mechanical drawing sets, retorts and tongs, slide rules and a collection of machines and apparatuses which in the past had served human knowledge by specifying measurements and units in every conceivable context.

When the corrugated iron shutter reached the top, the shop's sign was also revealed. There it said in Swedish, in gold letters on a black background: 'Scientific instruments bought and sold.' The old-fashioned umlauts over the ö and ä bore witness to the fact that the shop had been at that site for several generations.

The owner came out with a broom to sweep off the pavement in front of the entrance. The clinking of broken glass could be heard from the gutter. He stopped this dreary housekeeping as soon as he caught sight of Hanck approaching. A smile lit up his face and he said, 'I love what I'm seeing . . .' Presumably that was true.

Hanck stepped inside the shop, where the only open floor space was limited to a narrow passageway between shelves and tables cluttered with objects of largely the same type as those displayed in the front window. The shop could instil a certain hesitation in customers, since most of the items were not marked with a price. The rule in the world of commerce is the lower the price the bigger the sign, and the higher the price the smaller the sign. Here not even the most minimal of price tags, such as those usually attached to valuable jewellery, were visible. The purpose of the goods for sale in this shop had once been to dispatch all relativism by providing precise readings in grams and degrees. Yet the price that they commanded today was highly relative; it was a subject open to discussion.

For new customers the owner himself instilled the same hesitation. He was soft-spoken and unobtrusive, but according to rumour he had shot two thieves in the back.

'The wizard is here!' he now whispered towards the back of the shop where he lived with his wife and daughter. The entrance was through a narrow passage between a binnacle from one of the last full-riggers – depicted in a painting that hung on the opposite wall – and a grandfather clock whose face was decorated with a gloomy *vanitas* motif consisting of a skull, a burnt-out candle and an empty hourglass. But there was life in the clockworks, and its chiming was merry. Right now the clock was striking ten.

'Coffee?'

Hanck nodded gratefully. He hadn't yet had any. He'd used up his rations at home.

'Coffee!' the owner whispered, or rather hissed, towards the back of the shop.

He looked at Hanck holding the two cases. His fingers fidgeted impatiently, almost greedily. 'People have been asking . . .' he said. 'What should I tell them? "He says that soon there won't be any more . . ." "The wizard works at his own pace . . ." Is that true? That soon there won't be any more?'

'I'm afraid so,' said Hanck.

'Fuck.'

'I still don't have any paper.'

'It's on the way.'

'How do you know that?'

Hanck didn't receive an answer, just a sly smile. They'd had this conversation many times before. It usually ended with the shopkeeper invoking some unnamed contact, saying,

'They've found a forest out there.' For someone who dealt in scientific instruments, he was quite slipshod with regard to documentation and proof. He never specified who 'they' were, or where 'out there' might be. He used them as collective terms for almost everything.

Now the itch in the shopkeeper's hands became unbearable. 'Let me have . . . Let me have . . .' He practically clawed at the air, reaching for Hanck's cases as if they were full of drugs.

As usual, there was nowhere to set them down. The shopkeeper picked up a wind-up gramophone, which he placed on top of a polished hardwood box containing a sextant. A corner of a felt-covered table was now clear.

Hanck carefully unwrapped the crackling cellophane from one of the cases, which he set on the table so he could open it. From the inside of the case rose the smell of sewing-machine oil. The shopkeeper studied the contents as if looking at the newly discovered relics of a saint.

'A Facit . . .' It sounded like a prayer in Latin.

'A 1962 model,' said Hanck. 'Mint condition.'

The shopkeeper stroked his fingertips over the keys. 'What a masterpiece . . .' He sighed and took a step back so as not to be too overwhelmed. He shook his head, as if confronting something incomprehensible. After he had looked his fill, he solemnly went over to a bureau, pulled out a drawer and took out a sheet of white paper. It was part of the procedure to sacrifice a sheet.

He put the paper in the machine, rolled it up on the platen and with an outstretched finger pressed down a key. With a solid clack a letter appeared on the paper. The shopkeeper rolled out the page and grabbed the loupe hanging from a chain round his neck. He aimed a lamp at the impression on the paper and examined – or rather, 'lorgnetted', as he said – the result. 'Perfect! As usual, it's perfect! World-class!'

After the other typewriter had undergone the same inspection, an examination that was more a matter of pleasure than scientific critique, and both machines were safely back in their cases, it was time for coffee.

Hanck followed the shopkeeper into his inner sanctum. 'I'm bringing the wizard in,' he hissed into the dark. The words were directed at his wife, a woman who preferred to remain secluded in the back with their red-haired daughter.

Against a backdrop of dark oak and oriental tapestries, his wife and daughter looked like two pale Renaissance women, garbed in clothing reminiscent of old folk-costumes – skirts of rough wool, white blouses made of linen and laced bodices of madonna-blue marocain.

'Hancken,' said the wife. 'How nice to see you.'

'Gerlinde,' said Hanck. He kissed her hand. The daughter, Saussyr, received the same proof of his affection.

After delivering his kisses, Hanck usually amused himself by speculating on how long it would take before he heard the trickling sound of running water from the next room where both women would be washing off the spot where he had pressed the back of their hands to his lips.

The shopkeeper pulled out a chair from the big oak table for his visitor. Sure enough, just as Hanck sat down and was asked the question 'How's it going with the chef?' he heard the sound of running water.

'He's coming home today,' said Hanck.

'Then you're bound to get some treats . . .'

Hanck nodded.

'Would the two of you like to come over some evening? Saussyr has been so filled with longing. Haven't you?'

His daughter came over to the table carrying a tray.

'Oh yes, I really have,' she said.

It smelled of coffee, real coffee.

'We'd like that,' said Hanck. 'As soon as he has a little rest.'

Saussyr and Toby were the same age. They had often played together when they were kids, and their fathers had of course envisioned the perfect marriage. But lately, whenever Hanck mentioned the shopkeeper and his family, Toby would roll his eyes and say something condescending. It usually had to do with how old-fashioned, passé and 'Iron-Age-like' they were, among other things.

Hanck might laugh at this, but it wasn't a heartfelt laugh because he feared that his son included him in the same context. He could get downright annoyed whenever the shopkeeper, a man who both lived off and lived for this inheritance from a distant past, took it for granted that Hanck was equally fascinated by, not to mention obsessed with, these inspired objects. 'Those of us who are obsolete . . .' he was in the habit of saying, referring to both himself and Hanck.

Since Hanck wished to preserve a good business relationship with the shopkeeper, he would let the matter pass. But it annoyed him. He'd ended up in this profession by accident, sheer coincidence. He was not in the least fascinated by or reverential about anything that happened to have a 'provenance'. That was an attitude based on the notion that everything was better in the past. As far as he knew, that was not something he had ever claimed. He would not even claim that he himself was better in the past. On the contrary.

He was actually quite incapable of that sense of reverence, or at least 'the proper reverence' as the shopkeeper liked to emphasise. Hanck could show respect for all sorts of different phenomena, both living and dead. But he felt no genuine respect for objects that were simply old and had survived the ravages of time, or for people who held some sort of position that in and of itself was intended to arouse respect.

He was actually more obstinate than obsolete. A fact that could make his son's insinuations all the more troubling.

It wasn't until Hanck reached a mature age that he came to an understanding about that issue. When he himself became a father it was no longer possible to avoid certain recollections and memories that arose, sometimes as totally conscious comparisons, sometimes as sheer repetitions that could occur with comical regularity. For instance, in the way he washed a casserole dish, or his manner when remarking on everyday trivialities.

Hanck grew up as the only child of a woman who worked with wigs and a man who called himself an entrepreneur. He felt that he'd had a good upbringing. Most of his childhood friends were gone now. Half had died in gang fights or other disputes; the other half had been wiped out by a virus that had swept over this part of the world like a wave. A man who was fifty years old, healthy, and the father of a talented son, couldn't complain.

Hanck's father hadn't even reached the age of fifty. His mother, who uttered her last words at sixty, blamed her husband's death on the injuries he suffered while working 'out there'.

'That's the way it goes,' was her remark, followed as always by a pause and the confusing reservation: 'But I don't really know.'

It was the usual story. Anyone who lived in the city but worked 'out there' remained 'out there'. A certain amount of time might pass in suspenseful waiting, and then a couple of men in lavender overalls would knock on the door to give the widow the news of her husband's death. If you were lucky, you might find the name of the missing person on the nearest monitor under the headline: 'Deaths in the Outlying Area.' That was an honour. The deceased was a hero who had made the ultimate sacrifice.

'Out there' referred to the entire world outside the city. The border was closed to ordinary citizens. With a certain amount of effort you could get out, but it was much harder to get in. Along the border lay a ring of quarantine areas where most people had to spend a long and vexing waiting period, only to be designated almost without exception as ill and then be turned away.

Hanck's father was part of a work team 'out there'. They would work for a month at a time, spend a week in quarantine to have specimens taken and undergo other procedures. After that they had a month off.

Hanck had never found out exactly what the work entailed. He later assumed that it had to do with transport lines that had to be secured, fires that had to be put out, or communities that had to be cleared.

His father had brushed aside all questions.

'What's it like out there, Pappa?'

'Pitch dark,' might be the reply.

'Is there a war going on?'

His father would smile, rather evasively, and pat his son on the head. On rare occasions he would say, 'It's like after a war . . .' That was all. Though of course supplemented by his mother's remarks: 'That's the way it goes . . . but I don't really know.'

The rest was left to the boy's imagination, firmly kept in check by the admonition: 'Don't worry about it.'

It had been easy for Hanck to obey, especially when it came to that type of admonition. He was dissuaded from developing fantasies that had to be reined in so as not to run riot and become troublesome. He was a very level-headed person, even as a child. But the world 'out there' was still a cherished topic of speculation, especially among young boys. There is no reason to repeat all the wild rumours here; they weren't particularly different from those of other eras or the notions of other peoples about the dark, unknown chaos that is always veiled behind warnings and prohibitions.

Yet one thing was clear: there was no joy to be found out there. Those who returned were marked by it; they were ill, injured, or else something in their souls had simply been broken. The money they had saved up was not worth the sacrifice.

During the months when his father was working 'out there', Hanck would accompany his mother to her job. She worked in a place that was also encumbered with a great many regulations. There were a number of dangerous tools and chemicals involved in wig-making, but of utmost concern was the humidity. The strands of hair had to be kept dry.

It was a popular industry. Healthy young citizens with long hair would come in to have their hair washed and cut. They would get it cropped short and receive good money for the locks they left behind. Then the wigs would be made, often on commission from the wealthy in the City Under the Roof. Some owned great quantities of wigs in various bright colours, long and straight or short and curly. For some reason the old ladies who were especially skinny and sickly preferred wigs that were pale blue in colour.

Much later, when Hanck wanted to describe his memories of this workplace to his son, it would have been natural for him to dwell on the peculiar atmosphere, the smell from the baths of dye, or the resonance in a room filled with hair. Or he might have tried to derive some useful life lesson from the transformation he witnessed when a young but impoverished girl was stripped of a beautiful head of hair, which would later adorn the skull of a rich, old woman. But he chose instead to emphasise the great craftsmanship of the wig-makers.

Focusing on the positive was an attitude which, strangely enough, he had inherited from his father's side of the family.

His father's departures and homecomings followed a specific pattern. During the days leading up to a departure he would be surly and irritable, cursing everything that had to do with 'out there'. He was so difficult that it was a relief when he finally left.

But it didn't take long before the boy began to miss him, counting the days and nagging to find out when he'd be back. That lasted a week until a certain routine was established, in which his father had no part.

And one day he was simply there again, sitting at the kitchen table with a bottle of vodka in front of him. Like a surprise. He might point at the bottle, at a spot just below the mid-point, and say: 'I'm not home yet. But that's when I'll be home . . .' And he was almost always right. The man was silent and unapproachable and not truly home until he'd downed at least half the bottle. Only then did he recover enough to start talking about a future without those trips 'out there'.

And that future did exist. After a few years 'out there', Hanck's father had saved up a small nest egg, but above all he had made contacts within the wholesale trade.

He started his own business and began buying and selling practically anything that could be bought and resold for a small profit, such as two hundred pairs of shoes, ten cases of vodka, or a large shipment of tinned goods.

How he had managed to obtain permission to operate this business was just as mysterious as everything else concerning the man. Presumably he didn't actually have permission. All business activities were regulated by the Administration, which in turn was controlled by the Clan. The Administration had reinstated old laws and ordinances that were impossibly complicated and in principle turned every task into a life's work for the civil servants in charge. For instance, it could take twenty-five years to reconstruct all the ordinances pertaining to the right to sing in public.

Consequently, no one paid any attention to the prevailing regulations. Yet everything flowed smoothly as long as the Clan didn't feel threatened. If a conflict should arise over an entrepreneur entering a particular market, the little upstart would be wise to withdraw quietly.

As a budding businessman, Hanck's father revealed sides of himself that he had previously kept hidden, such as a great self-confidence and an almost exaggerated sense of optimism. Apparently the world was turning in the right direction once again.

He owned the last car in the neighbourhood, a very worn black car that he nursed with the greatest tenderness. Every evening, after numerous trips to make deliveries to the fancy shops in the City Under the Roof, he would back the vehicle into the building's garage, which he had constructed himself inside an abandoned shop. When the car was behind lock and key, he would drape a covering over it, a big patchwork quilt made from old pairs of trousers.

Hanck quickly learned that the business was based on bribes. When the Christian Christmas holiday approached, he would accompany his father to the yearly palm-greasing. The first year, before Hanck made his debut, his father had carefully rehearsed at home what the boy should say and do.

He was supposed to go into the shop or the administrative office, tip his hat and say politely: 'Good day, is the manager in?' If that was the case, and he was introduced to the person, he was again supposed to tip his hat politely and hand over the Christmas gift he had brought, though it was proclaimed to be 'Just a small sample from Orn's wholesale business. Happy Christmas!'

It all went quite smoothly. Hanck had a knack for that sort of thing. His father would wait in the car while the young gentleman made his business calls, thereby developing a precocious worldly wisdom.

The gifts were always custom-designed for each individual manager. A woman might favour a particular eau de cologne that was, of course, impossible to find anywhere in the city, but Hanck's father had miraculously found some. Another manager might be especially fond of Highland Cream. And just by chance Hanck Sr happened to have a bottle inside a shiny bag.

That was why the German city of Cologne and the Scottish Highlands came to have a special meaning for Hanck. As bribes go, these types of Christmas gifts were quite modest. There was really no reason to feel ashamed, even though he did feel a sort of shame every time he tipped his hat and repeated the phrase, 'Good day, is the manager in?' But it wasn't shame over doing something immoral; rather, he was filled with an emotion that he didn't recognise, an uncomfortable feeling that he couldn't name and thus associated with something shameful.

Perhaps there was no name for that emotion, nothing other than 'Highlands' or 'Cologne'. At any rate, it became associated with the smell of whisky and eau de cologne, and the insidious, greedy grins on the faces of the recipients as they stretched out their hands for the gifts – grown-ups who were addressed as 'manager' and were regarded with respect and perhaps even fear by their subordinates.

Along with the onset of this emotion he developed skills that he would have preferred not to have acquired. Skills that upset the fragile balance of things. Hanck liked clarity and order but to keep a semblance of order in his own life, he was forced to develop a double vision that was extremely unsettling. Every time he saw through something, he had to overlook it. Seeing through and overlooking: that was the lesson.

His father tried to encourage the boy by saying: 'People are vile . . . and wonderful!' No matter what his intentions had been with these annual greasings-of-the-palm, they extracted a price that he could never have foreseen. It was as if, in the bottom of every gift bag, there was a small portion of respect that the son had learned to save up for the adults, the authorities, but that he gave away piece by piece. After a number of Christmases it was gone. The stock-pile was empty.

On the way home from these bribery missions, the boy would sit next to his father in the car, feeling empty and exhausted, worn out and disillusioned, at the young age of ten, but he retained a forgiving outlook worthy of a full-grown man.

His father would say, using one of his constant euphemisms: 'Look how easy that was. You're very clever!'

'At what?' asked Toby. 'At deceiving people?'

'Yes,' Hanck told his son. 'That was no doubt what my father meant.'

'Is that why you felt ashamed?'

He wanted to avoid discussing the other part, so he said, 'Yes.'

'It's important to tell the truth.'

'Yes,' said Hanck. 'That's preferable.'

Toby thought about this for a moment. As usual, Hanck worried that he might have said too much. Surely not every-thing had to be passed on to the next generation. But at least Toby had inherited some of the lighter side. He said, 'I'd like to ride in a car sometime too.'

'It's nothing special,' said Hanck.

The boy got up from the kitchen table and went into his room for a while. He rummaged around and then came back. 'Was it like this one?' He had an old toy car in his hand. Saussyr had given it to him as a birthday present. He had never really understood how to play with it. Now he rolled the car along the edge of the tablecloth.

'They made a noise too,' said Hanck. The boy asked how. Hanck tried to remember how the car had sounded and then mimicked the sound with his voice. Toby had no idea what the real sound might be and accepted his father's version without protest. Soon he could produce an exact imitation.

Unlike many of his peers, Hanck decided early on to learn to read and write. 'So typical for an obsolete!' the shop-keeper had exclaimed with great enthusiasm whenever the subject had come up. As usual, he had drawn a hasty conclusion by linking Hanck to obsoletes. Hanck's only intention in acquiring such skills was to find a job in the city and avoid ending up 'out there'.

With no merits other than his ability to read and write, he had won a position in an insurance company, a firm with a long and venerable past. It had survived numerous disasters.

But what had once been an entire industry with countless competing companies had withered to a more marginal enter-prise, catering to modest families who couldn't afford to pay for protection for their lives and possessions. The Clan was probably right in realising that it was better to prevent crimes and unfortunate events than to offer compensation to the victims after the fact. It was a simple principle that turned out to be quite difficult to implement.

Hanck, who was strong and tall for his age, was hired to be an investigator. His job was to find out whether the damage or crime for which an insured individual was claiming com-pensation had actually taken place. It was a job that in the past had been performed by the police, but it had ended up in the hands of the insurance companies for the simple reason that the power of the police had diminished.

A new-found calm had reigned, a peace that was still young, an entirely new era, and no one knew how long it would last. There were still people alive who could tell stories in a completely trustworthy fashion about other times, about chaos and lawlessness, even there in the heart of civilisation. All instruments for upholding order – registries, archives and libraries – had been emptied of flammable materials. Everything had to be burned. Not a victory fire or a celebratory fire or a sacrificial fire, but in order to provide heat, to keep the cold at bay, for the sake of the survivors. And with that, all official offices and all regulations had been burned up; the whole Administration with all its paper-shuffling, the whole bureaucracy had vanished in one thick cloud of smoke, never to return, or so some people thought. Like a peat bog of archives.

One of the few books that Hanck had read dealt with a bureaucratic process that occurred during the entire twentieth century. At that time the bureaucracy was presented as a living organism, with its own soul. The civil servants were interchangeable, and each cell in this organism was constantly reproducing itself.

The organism might have various purposes, but common to them all was administering decisions for which no one wanted to take personal responsibility. With its all-consuming and all-encompassing power, it was even above the church and the clergymen who were supposed to preach God's word. It had a soul but no heart. It was the perfect hybrid of the world of plants and the animal kingdom.

That was why all sorts of brutality could be administered without troubling those in charge. Each person was responsible for his own small, carefully defined area – something which demanded a strong work ethic and strict discipline. Maintaining this discipline could fill a civil servant with a great sense of satisfaction. His conscience was clear.

In the book that he read Hanck had recognised numerous observations. It was like some unusually complicated and long-winded report on the activities in one of the departments at the insurance company, but he sensed a negative tone in the author's voice that he didn't care for. Hanck appreciated law and order. He regarded this type of regulation as the only defence of the weak against raw power.

Over the years he had witnessed an enormous amount of misery. A large part of his job involved working in the field, among the victims. Although in his view he was acting on their behalf, he hadn't found it at all difficult to confront people who had fallen prey to misfortune with suspicion and insinuating questions. Fraud was rampant, and he had learned to see right through many intricate scams, some of which he would have actually enjoyed recounting to his son. But as time passed, he preferred to forget those years. He could dismiss them as summarily as his father had dealt with his time 'out there'.

It was during that epoch that the Clan had consolidated its position. Up until then its influence had been on a different level, as if in a higher department where its activities had a different substance, a greater dignity. For a while people had hoped that the paterfamilias, with his sense of style and integrity, would maintain the strategy. But he grew old and tired and didn't have the energy to withstand the new trends, the new ideas about an expanded involvement, an influence that was both deeper and more widespread.

Now it reached into the very heart of every citizen's life. Hanck had watched this happen during his years at the insurance company; it may have been the only lasting insight he had gained there, a troubling insight that was difficult to convey in amusing stories to his son.

Time after time he had seen the same pattern repeated –

how humble people who lived in straitened circumstances but who, year after year, scraped together the money to pay for the premium that would secure their lives and their modest possessions, would wake up in the middle of the night to see the walls ablaze in the hovel that was their home.

Sometimes the fires were carelessly set by henchmen who were even more lit up themselves. In those cases the flames could be put out before the whole building burned to the ground. But more often the fires were well set. And in those cases the ancient, desiccated structure would flare up like kindling. When the deliberately delayed fire brigade finally arrived on the scene, only a bare patch of ground remained, and the family was homeless.

Time after time Hanck had determined that the fires were arson, and the company had agreed. A new house would be erected on the old site, made from even worse materials than before, yet habitable for the distressed but grateful family, who faithfully continued to pay their premiums.

When the new house later caught fire in a similar fashion, there were only two paths to take: either intimate that the fires were part of a campaign to acquire customers for the Clan's protection operation, or intimate that the residents of the house were pyromaniacs. Over time the insurance company had been forced to take the latter path. And with that, the family would stop paying the premiums, choosing instead to join the Clan's circle of customers. No one could survive without protection.

It was in connection with one such process that Hanck had drifted into a new career. He had gone out to inspect a big charred pile on a windswept piece of land outside the city. An old warehouse which, before it burned down, had been filled with junk. The owner was an old man, a collector, who went round to the estates of the deceased and to rubbish heaps, gathering up whatever had once had or still had or someday might have value. There were plenty of characters like him; most lived an isolated existence as worn-out, filthy loners. This old man was no exception.

He ate and slept in a cabin that had escaped the flames, and when Hanck, wearing a mask and gloves, sat at a table with a greasy tablecloth in the kitchen, talking to the old fellow, he noticed that the whole place was filled with small cases. There were cases made of plastic and dried-up leather, along with some that tried to resemble plastic or leather, in all sorts of colours and designs, and yet they all had a certain similarity. They had been stored out there in the warehouse, and the old man had laboured all night to rescue the lot from destruction.

Their contents were unknown. Hanck never got around to asking. The old man wasn't much of a talker. 'Berserkers! Berserkers!' was all he could manage to say.

Later, when Hanck wrote up the report, he neglected to include those cases among the old man's total assets. It was one of his last reports. A few months later he was fired. And six months after that, the whole company went bankrupt. It was said that the company could no longer fight against the Clan.

It was not a nice world to describe to a son. Yet Hanck was forced to touch on the subject, especially when the boy entered his teenage years and started to think about the state of the world. Certain fundamental inferences regarding the city government were obvious to anyone who could think for himself.

The Clan ruled over everything, both big and small, and had done so for such a long time that it had become an accepted fact that might even be described as 'natural'. Schools and their teaching materials were precluded from presenting any alternatives to this system, since both the schools and their teaching materials were protected and financed by the Clan itself.

Sensitive individuals, especially young people, might perceive a claustrophobic lack of alternatives.

The very word 'claustrophobic', designating a specific emotion, had been given an official, authorised definition, which had led to a great spread in usage, turning it into a catchword. It could be found in popular texts distributed by young men on the street; it could be seen scribbled on the walls. The fact that it was now appearing in marketing ads probably meant that it was being co-opted, or at any rate was on its way to losing some of its critical punch, a politically explosive force that had been building for a generation.

The obstinate and anti-authoritarian streak in Hanck could sometimes cause him to doubt the good of the reigning order, but, as so often was the case, his inherited tendency to gloss over things usually took the upper hand.

'But it was thanks to that poor old man that you're even here!' he might say to his son.

By the time that story came out, the boy was nearly grown. Hanck was prepared; he'd had many years to think through the whole episode. The childish query: 'Who's my mamma?' or the more reproachful: 'Why don't I have a mother?' were easy to dismiss with palliative euphemisms.

Finally, one day a half-grown young man pressed his father to the wall and said: 'I have to know!'

Then Hanck was able to reply: 'That old man's misfortune turned out to be my good fortune, because that was where I met your mother.'

The old man's cabin stood at the very edge of the city, far beyond the old suburbs. If you continued on in the same direction, you would soon reach no-man's-land, which stretched all the way to the border. Hanck had never gone that far.

He stood in the yard between the old man's cabin and the burnt-down warehouse, looking across a boggy field. It was a day with weak sunlight; the rainy season was over. Out on the field scrawny sticks poked up from the ground. They were coppice shoots that would soon produce scanty leaves which would be almost instantly burnt away by the sunlight. After that the ground would become sun-scorched and the field would be filled with gaping cracks.

The land was unusable. A couple of centuries in the past it had been fertile soil, and the warehouse had been a barn filled with hay and grain.

On the other side of the field stood a cluster of ramshackle buildings or hovels. A column of smoke rose up from a chimney.

'Who lives over there?' asked Hanck.

'Etherists,' said the old man. He had calmed down and become more talkative after a while. 'Sneezers.'

'And they didn't see anything?'

The old man shook his head. 'They sleep in the evenings. Or they fornicate.'

After Hanck had said goodbye to the old man, he walked straight across the field to have a talk with the Sneezers. He had only vague notions about the group; he hadn't known such people even existed any more. It was one of the sects that had arisen after the Fourth Wave, the largest to date. It had been impossible to count the number of victims; entire communities had been wiped out. It had taken its place in history as a turning point, since that was when the borders were closed and the obligatory quarantine areas were instituted.

'The ones that your father lived in?' asked Toby.

'Yes,' said Hanck. 'When he was forced to stay there.'

'How many people died back then?'

The boy had a hard time with maths and abstract quantities. Hanck could have told him any number over ten and it wouldn't have made any difference.

'A billion billion?'

'Probably, yes,' said Hanck.

'But not you or Mamma?'

'We weren't even born back then.' That was another fact that the boy had a hard time comprehending.

It was even harder to explain who the Sneezers were. The pandemics had reawakened ancient phenomena such as groups of St Vitus's dancers, flagellants and others. Some became penitents, others caroused to the bitter end. People threw hurricane parties, even though there wasn't a breath of wind.

The last time Hanck was alone with his father, he heard about the Aronites, one of the many sects 'out there'. One of his father's workmates had run into them.

The man in question had got lost. The work team had been busy clearing up after a storm, securing a transport line. The man had gone astray, and after several days on foot, he had run into a group of people on a thoroughfare. Five women carrying some sort of tabernacle. It was just a simple panel made of boards with a handle, but in the middle of the sacred object was a figure that was supposed to represent 'St Aron of the New World'. The figure had oily black hair and was clad in a white suit with wide trouser legs, a high collar at his neck, stripes and gold buttons. His voice was said to cure the sick.

The workmate was well-treated by the women. They pitched camp and invited him to spend the night in their company. The figure, that strangely attired doll, was served wine and bread, and in some odd way everything worked out.

The women worshipped the saint and had dedicated their lives to serving him. They were on their way to a grand meeting where he would appear before the public.

The workmate was also offered wine to drink, and when his glass was empty, he was given more. The wine emboldened his tongue, and he asked whether the saint did everything that a man does with his wife. He was told that such was the case. The women took out a crude but lovingly polished forked branch and demonstrated.

He then asked whether the women wouldn't prefer a more blood-filled saint, one that ate and drank and spoke more clearly. They said that they would.

Late that night while the women slept, he took apart the stuffed doll, pulled on the outfit, and enjoyed himself all night long.

The next morning the subject was not broached with a single word. Fortified in their beliefs, the women continued on their way.

The workmate was found and ended up stuck in quarantine, where a short time later he died from an unknown infection.

Hanck had never told this story to his son. He had got it

into his head that the 'workmate' never actually existed, and that his father had wanted to make one last confession.

But of course Toby wanted to know who the Sneezers were.

'They were Christians,' said Hanck. 'Very devout Christians. The only thing they wanted was to commune with their God, the father of Jesus.' Toby nodded. He knew who Jesus was and that God was his father. 'They believed that when a person sneezed, he came close to God.'

'Sneezed?' said Toby. 'Like when you get a cold?'

'Yes, apparently.'

'I don't like sneezing.'

'Neither do I,' said Hanck. He noticed that the boy was thinking so hard that his cheeks turned red. 'You're thinking so loud I can hear it.' Toby nodded. 'What if you sneezed right now?'

'But I don't have a cold.'

'No,' said Hanck. 'But what if you sneezed anyway? What happens then, right at the moment when you sneeze?'

'It feels like . . . like I'm exploding.'

'And then . . . when it feels like you're exploding . . . What do you think at that moment?'

'Damn,' said Toby.

'No,' said Hanck. 'By then you're already done sneezing. I mean at the very instant that you sneeze.'

Toby again thought so hard that his cheeks flushed. Then he gave a big smile because he'd discovered the right answer. 'Nothing!'

'Exactly,' said Hanck. 'When you sneeze you're essentially dead. Something happens inside your body and . . . and you can't think or do anything. That's probably the whole point. There aren't any thoughts to disturb or annoy you. Your soul is empty, and then God can pay attention.'

Toby was by nature very gullible, but after thinking about this for a moment, he made up his mind.

'I don't believe that.'

'It's true,' said Hanck.

But his son shook his head. He had his doubts.

'Your mother was a Sneezer.'

Now Toby stopped shaking his head. He knew that his father would never joke about such a matter.

'Was she there?' he asked. 'Out there with that old man?'

Hanck nodded. He had walked across the sodden field, getting his feet wet. And from quite a distance away he had noticed that he was being observed by the people in the houses. There was movement behind the curtains. They didn't seem to care for uninvited guests.

When he arrived, the door was opened by a very ugly man. He had a big, filthy beard, and he wore a kind of tunic with a belt around his waist. He stepped out into the light and squinted his eyes.

Hanck nodded to the man and introduced himself in the way he always did when he was unwelcome. It made no impression. But the man did murmur, 'God's peace.'

Even though the Sneezers were reclusive, they were clearly curious as well. One by one they came out of the house. A woman, obviously mother to a number of half-grown children, and another, younger woman with toddlers who looked rather odd, and finally a woman that Hanck couldn't help looking at a bit closer. She had a marvellous smile.

Hanck paused in the storytelling so the boy could take everything in. The main character had just made her entrance.

When Toby started smiling in that happy way of his again, Hanck knew that he had realised that it was his own mother who had just stepped into the light.

'Was she nice?'

'Was she nice!' said Hanck. 'She was the nicest, most beautiful woman that I'd ever seen!' It sunk in easily, in spite of the fact that it was actually the only lie he had told so far. 'How else do you think you could have turned out to be so good-looking?'

Toby shrugged his shoulders, looking both embarrassed and sceptical, because he was still back there, he wanted to be there, on a boggy, tainted field far away, in that place where his mother once lived and where he himself was born under circumstances that had never been explained.

'I asked them politely whether they'd seen anything special in connection with the fire at their neighbour's warehouse. That was my job. I hoped that they would calm down and realise that I had no intention of troubling them . . .'

But they were clearly troubled, nevertheless. No one had seen anything. It had happened at night. 'And that's when we're in bed asleep,' the man had said, in a plaintive tone of voice. He was obviously the spokesman.

'What about Mamma?' said Toby. She was the only one he wanted to hear about. He didn't care about the old man or his old barn.

'I left my business card,' said Hanck, 'and thanked all of them.' He paused again.

Toby was disappointed. 'But . . .'

That was all that was needed. 'But a couple of days later, something happened . . .'

Toby's face brightened. An arrow was shot, a string trembled. He recognised the tone; it was a signal heralding something. He had no memory of his mother, had never even seen her, but he was going to see her soon, in someone else's memory, which he could then make his own.

It was afternoon. Hanck had come home from work earlier than usual because of a power outage. The Central Memory had its own backup electrical plant, and it had to be checked, so all the monitors in the whole block had been turned off. Hanck was happy to leave a little earlier. He had just moved into his flat and had plenty of things to put in order.

It was his very first flat of his own. For several years he'd taken rooms as a lodger in another part of the city, but he'd never been happy there. Big converted barracks filled with drunken Walloons. Constant antagonisms that made people simple-minded. Immigrants who wore wooden clogs and embraced their 'New Haarlem', using their clogs to pound the skulls of the native citizens, who persisted in sitting in the Old Flanders pub, drinking beer and bellowing. The barracks had been erected in one of the last parks in the city, a so-called green area. There was a ballad about that park, and the few old folks of the district would sit in the taverns roaring that song with a fervent sentimentality. As if they had once strolled around in the green park, even though that was utterly impossible. The site had been dead, barren ground for at least two generations. Not even the 'pond' mentioned in the ballad could have been a real memory. But they sang as if they'd bathed in the pond themselves.

Hanck had little sympathy for such patriotism, and he was glad to move away from there. The barracks where he had taken lodgings were also overcrowded. In the centre of the building lived a couple who had decided to populate the world with their offspring. The place was swarming with children of all ages, dirty laundry, pots and pans, and broken furniture. Hanck had lasted for three years in all that commotion without ever hearing the couple exchange a single kind word.

His own flat was located in one of the oldest neighbourhoods of the city, on the outskirts of the 'pleasure district'. It had three rooms. If his money ran short, he could always rent out one of them.

Like many other blocks of flats in the area, his was several centuries old, a solid structure with thick walls made of real bricks. There were chimneys and fireplaces, and the door was equipped with three locks and a wrought-iron gate. The cooker worked, and there was water in the taps.

But best of all was the silence. He'd lived so long in a crossfire of shrieks and quarrelling that the quiet was sheer luxury. It made absolutely no difference that the flat was worn and decrepit, that the floors sloped, or that a number of the windows were cracked. The silence compensated for any shortcomings.

Filled with enthusiasm he had brought his old mother over to show off his new living quarters. With pride he had opened the door for her. She had stepped inside, hung up her coat and indifferently sat down in a corner to stare at a TV she'd brought along. He had tried to spark her interest. 'Wouldn't you like to . . .' and 'Perhaps you'd like . . .' But it was pointless.

His mother, like so many people her age, had spent the past few years in front of TomBola. She was a gigantic woman who had been on TV for as long as Hanck could remember. The broadcast from her bed was filmed round the clock, and a large segment of the population slavishly followed her every move. They slept when she slept and ate when she ate – preferably the same food – and they took care of other needs in accordance with the same pattern.

With one exception. After devoting her day to cooking and reading stories – she provided an important forum for contemporary authors – every night, around midnight, she would go to bed with a different man. They were violent exhibitions. The men were often carried away from her bed unconscious, at times even lifeless. A man could end up with a rib puncturing his lung and blood spurting out of his mouth as he expired with a delighted smile on his face.

At the end of each month thirty men were chosen from an enormous group of prospects. The queues would wind around several blocks near the premises. Young, stylish men with 'upgraded bodies', tattooed from head to toe, were willing to put their lives at risk.

It was a process that engaged the entire viewing public. People would vote for their favourites and bet money on the men they thought would survive. The gambling increased whenever TomBola was pregnant, which happened with astonishing regularity. Then the betting and speculating about the father would go on for nine months. Well-known authors wrote lengthy CVs for the candidates of particular interest.

When the child finally came into the world, with the birth transmitted live to every single monitor, and the paternity was firmly established, new millionaires would crop up in the city.

Older viewers, like Hanck's mother, preferred to ignore that aspect of TomBola's life. Their attitude was a bit complicated: they adored her yet couldn't refrain from making derisive remarks. At least once a day Hanck's mother would say, 'What a bloody ugly wig! How can she?!'

On the day when Hanck had invited his mother to see his new living quarters, the gigantic woman was lying on the operating table to undergo liposuction. The fat that was going to be extracted from her was selling for unfathomable sums, as if it were some miraculous ambergris, an elixir that would bring happiness and promote fertility.

After the procedure was over, Hanck's mother went back home. She shuffled out to the hall, put on her coat, and said, 'Get yourself a TV.'

'I will,' he said.

'And a wife.'

'I will.'

But nothing had come of either promise.

Hanck had settled comfortably into the silence of the flat. When it occasionally felt as if something were missing, he could always listen to the organ and sink into a tone, to be filled with a sense of anticipation that was rarely satisfied.

Now the silence was broken by someone knocking on the door. A cautious knocking, shy and timid, if that could be said of a sound created by someone's knuckles tapping on an old wooden door.

She was one of the Sneezers. Her name was Rachel. He described her to his son: 'She was dressed in her best, wearing a hat and coat. She had big brown eyes just like yours. And she smiled, just like you do.'

That was true, and he received an immediate response. Toby smiled exactly like his mother, but the difference was that the boy's smiles always meant something. Hanck understood them. Rachel's smiles he had never understood, not entirely. In reality, at first they had made him hesitant; he wondered what they could mean. And when he couldn't find any clear explanation, they had made him feel uncertain, almost annoyed. This was part of his memory of her, the fact that he had tried to see something joyous in those smiles and had failed.

This was not something that he told his son. 'She was a Christian,' he said. 'But even though her family believed in a number of strange things, she was an honest person. She believed in some sort of justice. She knew exactly what had happened to that old man's barn, but her father had forbidden her to say anything. He was afraid that they would be punished if they gossiped.'

'Gossiped about what?'

'She'd gone out on that evening to use the privy. It was still light outside, and she could clearly see that two berserkers were lighting a fire right next to the wall of the building. She'd seen them before, and she could identify them if necessary.'

This much Hanck had found out. But he was never quite clear whether it was the only reason why the woman had come to see him – this sense of justice which could cause her much torment if it was infringed.

It was an unusual attitude. There was something almost Old Testament about it, something that might arouse suspicion.

Instead he told the boy that his mother had acted magnanimously, ready to sacrifice herself for an old man's rights in the face of strong and powerful forces and their formidable henchmen. Hanck had had time to think through everything, and since he'd never seen any clear and unambiguous truth in the matter, he could just as well choose the bright and hopeful version. The opposite was entirely conceivable and – her god forbid – possibly just as valid.

He actually hadn't recognised the person standing in the hallway. He saw a young woman who had tried to clean herself up as best she could before making this visit to the city, though she hadn't been completely successful. She had borrowed her big sister's coat and her mother's hat, or whatever it was she had actually been wearing. In reality, his first impression of her was that she must be a homeless person who had heard that he might have a room to rent, or someone who was intent on begging in an unusually bold manner.

But then came that smile. And when he recognised her, he had invited her in. She accepted a glass of lemonade and sat in silence with that inexplicable smile on her lips – something that he at first interpreted as a benevolent candour, a form of courtesy, a signal that she was prepared to offer trust.

She had been in his flat for quite a long time before the topic of the old man came up. When it did, Hanck had a feeling that the purpose of her visit, truth and justice, was merely a pretext. Judging by her smiles, she could very well have other reasons up her sleeve; excuses and evasions.

Hanck had been on his guard, well-trained in the art of reading people's intentions, looking for inconsistencies and faulty logic, minefields and deliberate falsifications, all meant to confuse an official from an insurance company.

But in her case, Hanck had failed. He didn't allow his son to hear any of these work-related ponderings when, ten years later, the story was retold; and by then it had accrued some of the glow of the past. Hanck preferred this gentler light. He harboured no romantic notions whatsoever, but he was a considerate and thoughtful father.

Actually it was Rachel herself who had sown doubt and voiced objections. She said, 'I know that I'm a worthless witness. I know what people think about us. Nobody would care what I may have seen.' And then that smile.

'I care,' said Hanck.

The smile that now came could mean that she didn't believe him. He decided that was exactly what it meant. So to convince her, he had set a monitor on the kitchen table and let her see with her own eyes how he typed up her statement.

'Take a look,' he said. 'You can see for yourself. I don't need to reveal my source, so I can protect you and your family.'

Rachel peered at the monitor. Hanck watched her eyes

move back and forth, up and down, and then start over at the top again. He assumed that she didn't know how to read.

When she said: 'You don't have to do that. God protects us,' her smile was totally different, filled with faith, almost a bit condescending since it was directed at a non-believer.

'If that were indeed the case,' said Hanck, 'then your father could have come forward as a witness.' That was at least one way to get her to stop smiling.

'He didn't want to get involved,' she said. 'He doesn't want anything to do with the *Adminsteration*.'

Hanck glanced at her, just a hasty, searching glance. The smile was back. Would it disappear again if he corrected her? Is that what he wanted? He could press her by asking whether it was actually called 'adminsteration', speaking in that tactful way that was nothing more than sheer arrogance.

No, he wanted to be cautious with this particular witness. He chose a different approach.

'I'm no authority,' he said.

'You know what I mean.'

'Of course,' said Hanck. 'I don't think any citizen really wants to have anything to do with the Administration.'

Again a quick glance. He thought that he had slid right over those 'istra' syllables almost undetectably. But he saw that she had noticed. She bit her lip, lowered her eyes. Maybe she was ashamed because she'd never gone to school. Maybe she was furious at feeling ashamed in front of someone who had learned a bunch of fancy words but nothing about the Word.

'It's the Clan's fault,' he said.

It was just a comment, so that she would understand where he stood. And she did understand, though it took a moment. She looked up again, studying him as if to say: 'Do you mean it?' As if it were an idea that surprised her.

For his part, he tried to look sincere and unwavering. That was truly what he thought. He didn't belong to any particular opposition group, or to those who had made the word 'claustrophobic' popular. But that didn't mean he had no opinions.

Presumably she saw a man who could think for himself, and then the smile reappeared. She trusted him. She reached out her hand to stroke his cheek. Just a light caress, but he didn't know what to do. He pretended to type a few more comments that appeared on the monitor, sincerely hoping that she really couldn't read, because he managed only some random remarks, repetitions, 'rhetorical redundancies' as his new boss called such things – a man who walked around with a sticky wooden cross hanging round his neck.

Hanck checked to see whether Rachel wore any sort of crucifix, but he didn't see one. She probably didn't need it. She noticed him looking at her. She raised a hand to her chest, swiftly, as if she had suddenly realised that she wasn't properly dressed, the way a God-fearing woman should be dressed, at least according to the image presented in historical illustrations.

She sat in silence on the other side of the kitchen table while Hanck pretended to be busy with important insurance matters. But there was nothing uncomfortable or embarrassed about her demeanour. She let her gaze roam over the kitchen, out towards the corridor leading to the living room. As if with those eyes and that smile she were trying to get a sense of what it might be like to live there and walk around as a different person from who she was at the moment, as someone that she might become.

To break the silence Hanck typed a full stop after a superfluous note and then said: 'I was thinking of having something to eat. Would you care for anything?'

'It's getting late,' she said.

'How did you get here?'

'I walked.'

'The whole way?'

She saw that he was trying to work out how long that might have taken. 'It took all day,' she said.

'You can't go back home now,' he said. 'It'll be dark before you're even halfway there.'

'I'm not afraid,' she said.

'You should be.'

He saw the smile again, the one that was slightly superior. 'Maybe you think that I'm completely naïve?'

He was more and more convinced that he actually didn't think so. He could easily imagine that she knew precisely what the world out there was like, and how she needed to move through the city at night, and which roads were passable without landing in the clutches of those who were evil and ruthless, and for whom she represented desirable raw material. Kidnapped and threatened, painted with make-up and drugged, she could be used for anything at all.

'What about the dogs?' he said. 'Did you see any?'

'That's nothing but talk,' she said. 'I've never seen a mad dog in all my life.'

'I saw them,' said Hanck. 'When I was a boy.'

They had appeared regularly, big herds of mad dogs that staged attacks on the city and bit to death anyone and anything they could find. It was a nightmare – to walk alone along a dark street and suddenly become aware of the sound of hundreds of claws clacking on the ground, and then turn around to see the horde attack. They didn't bark, they didn't howl, they crept along like a shaggy grey mass with claws and teeth as sharp as awls. No one knew where they came from, how the pack had formed, or why it was so bloodthirsty. The dogs never ate their prey. They just wanted to kill.

'I still think that you should stay here overnight,' said Hanck. 'A woman at work heard something about those dogs. And she's usually right.'

'If you believe her,' said Rachel, 'then maybe it's best if I stay.'

'You can take a bath,' he said, as if in passing. 'I mean, if that's something you like, taking baths . . .' The moment he brought up the subject of baths, he realised that she might take it as an insult, that he thought she was dirty.

And she did seem aware of that possibility, that she might feel or pretend to feel offended, but she chose another and perhaps more attractive option. 'I'd like that,' she said. 'I've never bathed in a tub.'

He would later notice that she left a grimy ring in the bathtub. He never mentioned that to his son. Nor did he mention what he felt when he later scrubbed the grime away.

Hanck heated up soup from a tin that he had in the flat while he listened to her splashing around in the bathroom. When the food was ready she stood in the hall, drying her hair with one of his towels. She was fully dressed. She had turned her jumper inside out.

'Do you need to call someone?' he asked. 'Your family?'

'Why?'

'They might be worried.'

'They're always worried,' she said and laughed. 'Is that vodka?'

Hanck had a glass in his hand. 'Would you like some?' She nodded. He gave her a glass, and they drank a toast to ancient luxuries like bathtubs.

He had set the kitchen table. She sat down in the place where he usually sat, but he didn't manage to say a word before she said, 'I'm ovulating and starving.'

'If I had a daughter,' said Hanck, 'I'd be – ' He stopped short, aware that she might find him boring.

'Yes?' she said. 'If you had a daughter . . .'

'I mean a little girl,' said Hanck. 'Then I'd be worried all the time too.'

'What about a boy?' said Rachel.

'Then I'd be even more worried.'

'Young men are their own worst enemies.'

Hanck set the pot of soup on the table. 'So you have brothers?' he said.

'They're tame,' she said. 'You don't need to be afraid of them.'

Hanck laughed. 'Why should I be afraid of them?'

'In case we have intercourse later on,' she said.

'I see,' said Hanck.

'Just so you know,' she said. 'You don't need to be afraid.'

'Why should I be afraid?'

'They might come here, kick in the door, demand retribution and cut your throat.'

'In that case,' said Hanck, 'I hope you're worth it.'

He didn't look at her but instead picked up her bowl and served the soup. This might indicate that he was familiar with the ways of the world, or unflinching in the face of death, or both. As if he were an experienced seducer, used to defying fate with more or less unknown women, the daughters and sisters of fathers and brothers who kept a number of outmoded ideas alive.

Unfortunately the vodka ran out while they were still at the kitchen table. Hanck realised that he would have needed more to forget about those threats. They were not repeated, not even in jest, but they were still there, hovering just below the surface, no matter what else they talked about.

He told her about his life, she told him about hers. They saw similarities that could unite them and bring them pleasure. The differences were, at the moment, less interesting.

But she had planted an idea that took root and grew and would soon blot out all other prospects. The idea that their connection might have long-term consequences. Hanck had touched on the very same matter, just in passing, with several colleagues at work. He seemed to understand that they viewed those risks as an incentive, like some sort of exciting spice. The risk of reprisals and other undesirable consequences seemed merely to have a stimulating effect. He had a hard time sharing their view, or taking the whole thing so casually. He was forced to acknowledge his fear, and he needed something to assuage it. Alcohol or pills. But the alcohol was gone, and the pills that he had were old; he was unsure what effect they would have, if they had any effect at all.

But the matter was solved; providence stepped in. After they had eaten and left their dishes in the kitchen and gone into the living room, he switched on the receiver. A mighty organ tone filled the whole room.

Rachel wasn't used to the organ. She'd heard it a couple of times before while visiting friends, but there was no receiver in her home. She was immediately gripped. Solemn, in a happy way.

They sat holding hands. And after they'd sat there for half an hour or so, something happened that neither of them had ever experienced before and would probably never experience in their lifetime again.

The organ changed tone. It had long remained on a G, but now it rose to an A, a major second. After a moment it rose to a B. Another major second. Stable. Breathtaking.

Although she was no expert, Rachel knew at once that she had been witness to something enormous, unprecedented. Hanck could see it on her face, although that may have been the only thing he saw on that occasion. She in turn only needed to glance at him to have it verified – he leapt up from the sofa, looking both dazed and radiant at the same time. Irresistible in his elation. And she was for him equally irresistible, as a participant in this major second.

No clearer portent was needed. They made love on the sofa, as if enveloped in the tone, which was still echoing from the major second of the organ.

Afterwards, in a tranquil moment, they were able to get up off the sofa and go to his bed. She whispered things in his ear in a language he didn't understand. He thought it sounded beautiful, as if she were speaking indecent things that she had never whispered in anyone's ear before. That made him even harder.

They fell asleep for a few hours and then made love again, in the dawn. He lay awake at her side for a while. A pale sun was on its way up. She was sound asleep when he was forced to leave her.

He washed himself, put on the best clothes that he owned, skipped breakfast, put on his hat and coat, and returned to the bedroom.

She was still asleep. He stood there a moment, looking at her. Even in her sleep, she was smiling. He decided that it was a satisfied smile.

He had refrained from asking very much about her faith, what it was like, what it might mean. At any rate, it didn't seem to stand in the way of much of anything.

He let her sleep and left without locking the door behind him. She was free to go. If she wanted to take something with her, she could do so. The pepper, he thought. She would probably steal his genuine pepper. It was worth it.

But more than anything, he wanted her to be there when he came home.

The report that Hanck wrote regarding the fire on the old man's property was the most unambiguous account he had ever produced. Citing witnesses, he concluded that the fire had been set by 'known berserkers'. But he didn't stop there. Since the event displayed such blatant similarities with others, he found it justified to call attention to a clear and obvious pattern of persecution of individual citizens and proprietors who had not yet voluntarily joined the Clan's protective operation. To emphasise the degree of persecution, he had used the old-fashioned term 'systematic terror'.

He had never before expressed himself so clearly. He knew that it might entail danger, at least for his future prospects with the company. There the most diplomatic of forces prevailed.

Such as his new boss, a matter-of-fact, unsentimental and almost heartless man. He was the one who, for some reason, wore a big wooden cross on a chain around his neck. Every time he sat down to eat in the employee cafeteria and leaned over the table to pull his chair forward, the cross would land in his plate. Then he would sit there wiping it off with a paper napkin as his food got cold.

One day when Hanck was in the process of finishing his report about the old man with the barn, the power went out just as they sat down at a table in the cafeteria.

'This is just like the Middle Ages!' his boss said.

Then someone at the table cautiously reminded him that there weren't any power outages in the Middle Ages since they didn't have electricity back then. The boss, not accustomed to being contradicted, had then triumphed by stating that electric current existed in all ages, people just hadn't understood how to use it. After saying that, he sat there in contented silence, wiping off his cross.

The talk then prompted someone else to ask what other discoveries or inventions each person at the table valued most. The suggestions that were offered were largely to be expected, except for one, which was proposed by an older woman from Hanck's department. She said quite firmly: 'The work day.'

Hanck found this extremely sensible. It wasn't really an invention, or even a discovery, but more a way of establishing an orderly life in which each person did his part; an absolute requirement so that a few select individuals could then make their inventions or discoveries. It was grey and lacklustre yet comforting for a young man who saw his whole life ahead of him confined to a labyrinth of archived reports.

Though Rachel would soon appear as the key witness to widespread nefarious acts. He had cited her without revealing her identity. He didn't even mention any neighbours, let alone any Sneezers or Etherists. He knew that she was right – they had a dubious reputation and were worthless as witnesses.

He had looked them up in New Memory, in which the whole phenomenon was described in the past tense, as an extinct '-ism', also found under the heading 'Etherism': 'One of the many crisis-related spiritual movements that arose between the First and Second Wave (cf Wave). Basically Christian in its creed, but linked to antiquity's idea of ether (cf Ether, Ether media, etc.), the noblest form of matter, further developed in Aristotle's idea of the fifth element, *quinta essentia*, the everlasting element that constitutes the heavenly spheres; among animists and spiritists regarded as a divine substance. Etherism added Christian ideas from medieval thinkers, primarily the mystics. The highest form of religious experience consisted of *unio mystica*, union with the divine in ecstasy. A prerequisite for this, according to the Etherists, was the extinguishing of desire and consciousness, a state in which an individual's sensitivity to his own body and surroundings ceased, and the soul became receptive to the divine; an experience preferably expressed in antithetical terms (a dark light, a roaring silence, a moment's eternity, etc). Etherism stressed that the path to this experience was not, as with its predecessors, through prayer, meditation or mortification. Etherism emphasised instead physical manifestations of the divine presence, primarily in the cavities in which the ether could penetrate the human body and arouse excitation. Etherism never became a widespread movement and soon split into two main branches following internal strife. The 'orthodox' group emphasised every perception of the divine as a spontaneous reaction to a natural blessing. In opposition to this 'passive' belief, the 'radical' movement stressed the importance of arousing this blessing. This consisted of an extensive use of stimuli such as essential oils, pepper, genuine pollen and so on. Of the two branches, the orthodox group became more widespread, partially due to the fact that access was limited to substances for arousing the desired excitation. Etherism's ideas are today regarded as antiquated, and no adherents are mentioned in the official registry of viable communities.'

Of course Hanck had rushed home from work on that day, the day after the major second, without being entirely conscious of doing so. Time had passed at an interminably slow pace. He had looked at the clock every other minute, something he usually never did.

He had stood in front of the water cooler, chugging down water. People had walked past and said: 'Hanck – you look radiant!'

And after that remark was delivered, someone else would say: 'You seem impatient.' And: 'Don't think that it's going to happen again tonight.'

On his way home he had run into a distant acquaintance who stopped him on a street corner simply to say: 'What's your hurry?' Only then did Hanck realise that he was more or less racing along.

But she wasn't there when he came home. The flat was silent and empty, almost desolate. The dirty dishes were still on the worktop. The bed was unmade. The light was on in the bathroom.

It was then that he saw the grimy ring in the tub. He stood there studying it for a long time before he decided to get rid of it. He got out the cleaner and a rag and started scrubbing, filled with a troubling, ambiguous feeling. No doubt it had been exhaustively described before, analysed and drained of all imaginable nuance. Under the heading 'Disappointment'.

There were no doubt a thousand paths to that experience, but the quickest way was probably via 'Anticipation'. That was the route he had taken, at any rate, a seductive, magical path that made the dreary reality of the destination bearable; yes, it was almost worth the price. He had never felt such anticipation before, not even when he was a boy.

When the bathtub was clean, he went out to the kitchen to see if the pepper was gone. But it stood right where it had always stood.

Disappointment turned to shame, because it had been stupid of him to suspect her of something like that.

She hadn't taken anything with her, he thought now. She had left information. She had left a ring of grime. She had given him an unforgettable memory.

He didn't know whether she would remember him. At least he had given her food and protection for the night. They had shared a major second. Maybe that was a fair trade.

It never crossed his mind that she, when she got home, was someone who had taken away much more than she had left behind.

That was pretty much all Hanck had to say about the woman who was Toby's mother, claiming that it was the truth. Of course there was more to say about her, but Hanck lacked access to that information. She'd had a big family, and she'd probably had friends and even one or two enemies. But Hanck had never had contact with any of them.

If he was ever forced to explain the circumstances surrounding the birth of his son in a trustworthy way, it would be a brief and concise report, exemplary in its clarity and easily comprehended, as his boss would say, but much too meagre for a son.

Before he became a father, Hanck had regarded himself as a level-headed person. There's good reason to assume that those around him perceived him in the same way. He wasn't troubled by an excess of imagination but possessed an excellent ability to see through others. That had been an asset when it came to interpreting the contradictory stories that victims of misfortune often devised.

It's commonly believed that someone whose job it is to gather information would be well-served by a sense of curiosity, an eagerness to learn and a thirst for knowledge, but that's a misconception. Those types of passions might possibly serve the practitioners of liberal professions, poets, and those who can handle facts, evidence and proof with less constraint.

As an author of reports, Hanck belonged to a strict school in which anything irrelevant was regarded as 'rhetorical redundancy' and eradicated. His first boss had been a more liberal type, one of the obsolete; an educated and cultivated gentleman who was prone to outpourings about the shabby use of language by the young. He spoke ardently about the literature of the past, and he recommended that everyone in the department should read at least one of the so-called classics each year.

Young and amenable as Hanck was, he had complied with this suggestion and started to read. Access to books was limited, but his boss had succeeded in procuring borrower status at the library, which could be used by his employees. That alone was considered a remarkable feat.

Hanck had read many books, though without understanding why. Of course he had latched onto a word here or an expression there, things that he could use in his daily work, but each time he finished reading a book, he ended up with a bad taste in his mouth. He felt somehow dirty, or sullied. Reluctantly he had to acknowledge that he'd been affected. The stories disturbed his otherwise peaceful slumber, and he might wake up several times in the night, fully convinced that his department boss was standing in his bedroom, rummaging through his dirty laundry and loudly commenting on every stain that he found.

There was an uncomfortable impertinence in the books, an intimacy that could seem downright offensive, as well as an indecent sentimentality that clung to the whole enterprise. Those old books were considered invaluable assets, true treasures that were tenderly safeguarded by a chosen few who themselves dripped with sentimentality whenever they talked about Literature. There had once been a golden age, of course, and that Age of Sagas lay encapsulated in a distant, shimmering glow. Whenever he read a book from that period, it turned out that the authors of that time all said approximately the same thing – in sentimental terms they eulogised the past.

Hanck remained unresponsive, unless he felt outright sullied. He couldn't come up with any better word for it. And that was undoubtedly the rub, as he and other critical readers had to admit: the fact that they got lost in emotion.

An international agreement had been reached long ago regarding the restoration of such aspects of the old culture as were deemed essential. In accordance with that agreement, the task of local commissions was to classify and define those emotions that were sufficiently essential to be preserved for the future.

Many emotions seemed simply to have become passé. At one time they had been experienced and described with such precision and depth that the description had become worthless, since their perfection was unattainable and incomprehensible to ordinary people. No one could fill those perfect works with any vital emotion. That particular emotion was hence found to be extinct. Psychobiologists had followed and recorded this ongoing depletion, pointing out a parallel with the biological forms of life that had disappeared. A number of species corresponded to a clearly specified emotional nuance.

In the meantime, new ones had emerged, and the task of the Affect Commission was also to determine which ones should be recognised and be given a common name.

The few contemporary stories that Hanck had become acquainted with had not alleviated the bad impression that he had. They were all permeated with sentimentality, self-pity and a false sense of ingratiation. Hovering over every page he saw the exhortation: 'Love me!' Or, in the best case, the somewhat more moderate: 'At least show me a little affection!' Few authors managed to conceal this entreaty. And to procure this favour, they resorted to low tricks that were hardly worthy of any decent human being. One commiserated over a birthmark, another mourned over a maternal grandfather who was dead. What remarkable things they were! And it was all swathed in an air of grandiose compassion for their fellow human beings, a blazing passion for what was right and true and beautiful.

Hanck had encountered just such a grandiose human being with a blazing passion for what was right and true and beautiful, meaning a real author. The man in question had come to the insurance company to deliver a damage report to one of Hanck's colleagues, along with an accompanying claim for compensation. A defect had occurred in his solarium, causing him to suffer burns that were of a moderate yet noticeable degree, something that was indisputably apparent in the attached photographs. They were definitely authentic.

The pictures showed a well-groomed author with a red face. The author, an expert on outmoded expressions, described the colour as 'lobster-red', referring to an extinct shellfish in a boiled state.

The unfortunate accident had occurred on the very day when the author had intended to make a well-paid appearance with TomBola, 'since today I'm considered to be the foremost . . .'

Hanck had spoken to the burnt author on the phone several times, and during the conversation the man had occasion to repeat the same things he had pointed out in his written report, including 'since today I'm considered to be the foremost . . .'

Based on the facts, Hanck had recommended rejecting the author's claim, and management had followed his recommendation. That led to the entire company being subjected to an extensive slander campaign, conducted by the author himself in all his bright-red glory. He was allowed to deliver a fiery but quite incoherent speech that was seen on every monitor in the whole city. The fact that he thereby discredited one of the few companies that at least occasionally spoke up for the little guy didn't seem to bother him at all. Instead, he emphasised that he was favoured by the friend of authors, the paterfamilias. He had sampled author's mead from the great man's treasure chamber.

Afterwards Hanck decided that he'd had enough of that sort, both living and dead. But he was still young, and he didn't know that authors can be their own worst enemies.

Without being aware of it, he was himself an author in the making. One day in the future his deep aversion to conceitedness and his distrust of grandiose claims would be an asset, yes, something even resembling a prerequisite for the writing process itself.

What was missing was a motive. But that was something fate would provide.

But Hanck had actually been writing ever since his son's birth. The information that had been revealed about Rachel may have been concrete, but it wasn't substantial enough to satisfy a son's curiosity. He bombarded his father with questions about her, about their time together.

When Hanck saw that his son was suffering from a lack of information, he felt compelled to make the meagre and paltry facts more detailed.

He made the boy's mother more beautiful than she was, her family bigger, her father uglier, and the house they lived in smaller and more decrepit. That was about as far as his imagination would go.

But his son said: 'Tell me more!' When Hanck confessed that there was no more to tell, the boy became furious. He sobbed and flailed his arms about, and Hanck saw no way out but to say: 'Hmm, well, that's right . . . I forgot about . . .' Then the boy would instantly calm down and start listening. Hanck was forced to come up with something. Out of necessity and compassion he invented a love story that never took place, though it might have taken place, and, in the eyes of a former insurance man, it even seemed plausible.

Hanck seized upon stories from everywhere, stories that he'd heard or had actually experienced himself with other women, but he made all of them refer to only one person. About how they had gone out celebrating when the whole city was filled with vodka; about dance palaces that no longer existed; about an old smuggler king who took a liking to her and gave her fabric for dresses, satins and silks, though god only knew where they'd come from; and about how cleverly she had managed to make their ration quota last each month.

Toby listened intently to all of this, and when the narrator occasionally hesitated or took a little too long to remember exactly how one thing or another had occurred, the boy would show great understanding or a type of indulgence – as if at heart he realised that it was all nothing but fiction.

Among his favourite stories was the one about Etherism and its adherents. They were called Etherists or, preferably, Sneezers. Hanck made them have permanently runny noses. They were born into snot, they lived their lives in snot and they died in snot. They were the happiest people with colds in the whole world. They regarded snot as holy. Their Church was a handkerchief, and snot was the sacrament. Each time they sneezed, god would send a spark through their soul. They did everything they could to sneeze as often and as much as possible.

They doused themselves with pollen, they stared at the sun and they tickled themselves under the nose with bird feathers sprinkled with finely ground pepper. They enticed forth such torrents of sneezing that the sound echoed all through the neighbourhood. They were blessed, filled with god at every audible 'Achoo!' Which was always followed by the congregation crying in unison: '*Gesundheit!*'

Every time they were mentioned, the boy would ask: 'Why don't they exist any more?' And Hanck had to explain how they had died out, how one by one they had passed away. Some had stared too long at the sun and got scorched. Others had plucked feathers from infected birds. The happiest of them had died in the midst of a torrent of sneezing that had split their brains apart. Finally not a single one was left.

By the time Toby turned ten and had heard these stories many times, he decided that he wanted to go there, to the place where he was born. 'I want to see if it looks like I've always pictured it.'

'There's nothing to see,' said Hanck. 'It's all gone.'

'I want to go, I want to, I want to.'

A week after the major second Hanck had gone out there to deliver his report to the old man. That might seem to show a rather exaggerated concern for a client, but Hanck had made it look like a momentous gesture on the part of the company, a question of policy, to look out for the interests of every client, no matter how insignificant the case might seem.

Then he had stood there, with his back to the client, facing the field with the hovels on the other side. He knew that his presence had been noticed; he had been seen by the people over there. And that constituted a danger, to be standing there – and bareheaded, no less. If any of them thought that he had done something inappropriate with Rachel, he was a ready target for any weapon they might have.

But nothing happened. Maybe they were letting the sun do the job. He hadn't given it any thought – the fact that he had appeared before the old man's ramshackle house with his hat in his hand. He had never allowed himself to do such a thing before, to stand in the strong sunlight with his head bare and his eyes stinging. It was not at all premeditated; it was an impulse that later surprised even him, when he finally came to his senses, maybe from a desire to sneeze, and went inside to see the old man. There he was called back to another reality that was filled with the old man's sour smells, the buzzing of newly awakened flies, and rags stained with coughed-up blood.

It later occurred to him that he had displayed a recklessness that flouted all regulations. He had stood out there in the glaring sunlight, bareheaded, and he had gone inside to see the old man without wearing gloves or any type of face mask.

The only explanation he could muster was that he was the one standing out there, for personal reasons and not as the official from an insurance company. He had been unaware of the real motive for his visit, or at least he had refused to admit it to himself – that it had less to do with notifying a client of a positive outcome and more to do with being seen and recognised by a woman on the other side of the field.

Hanck told the old man what he had written. The man stumbled around in bewilderment among all the small cases inside the house, and finally, when there was no more to be said and nothing had happened across the field, Hanck asked him what all the cases were for. He wanted to prolong the visit, give Rachel one last chance to put in an appearance.

But instead of hearing a few longed-for footsteps in the gravel of the front yard, or the discreet sound of her knocking, he listened to the old man's tedious account of a father and a grandfather and a great-grandfather who had all been collectors and junk dealers; a remarkable and noble family, as it turned out.

The treasures had been passed down through several generations. He opened a case and showed Hanck its contents: a typewriter. The old man had inherited some and collected others, and he now owned more than six hundred of the machines. Most of them were fully functioning.

For Hanck, that collection of typewriters was at the time merely a pile of scrap metal. His thoughts were elsewhere, his attention was directed outdoors, he was listening for sounds from across the field. But when he couldn't prolong the visit any longer, he thanked the old man and went outside to take up his position in front of the house.

He heard the old man coughing. Smoke was rising from the chimney of her house. A curtain fluttered. She didn't want to show herself.

At the risk of disappointing his son, Hanck had taken the boy out there, ten years later. It took several hours. They went through parts of town where Hanck had never set foot, and through others where he'd once had business, but the neighbourhoods had now changed beyond recognition.

But out there, after they left the city behind, everything was just the same. The old man's house was still there, as were the charred remains of his warehouse. Scattered all over the property were piles of empty glass jars.

They crossed the field. All that was left of Rachel's house was the foundation, an old granite foundation that must have been there for hundreds of years. A meagre relic. Hanck was worried about how his son would react.

But the boy walked around checking the place over, taking up position at various points and gazing in different directions, as if to take in the view, as if to see the world the way his mother had once seen it. It was quite a depressing view: the old man's hovel across a tainted field, and farther away, on the other side of a bare, rocky hill, the upper half of a big tenement building, grey and sooty; and even farther in the distance, a rusty minaret.

'This is where it was,' said Hanck, 'This is where her bedroom was.' He went over to stand on a corner of the foundation. He persuaded himself that it must have been a bedroom. 'This is where you were born.'

Toby went to stand next to his father; he seemed pleased by what he had heard. He poked at the ground and found a piece of brick, possibly from a chimney stack. He picked up the brick fragment, looked at it with satisfaction, and stuffed it in his pocket.

Many decisive events were to be played out in the vicinity of that ugly, inhospitable field. A steady wind blew out there, the wind of change. During the rainy season the wind could be harsh and brutal, whipping rain in the face of anyone who had business in that district. During the dry season the wind swept in hot gusts over the scorched ground, only aggravating the torturous heat. But it was always connected with change, new conditions, new circumstances.

The old man's insurance claim had its consequences. One day in the middle of the worst of the heat, Hanck was summoned to the office of his department boss. The air conditioning was going full blast, but it was still oppressively hot in the whole building. His boss was wearing shorts, he had his feet propped up on his desk, and he was scraping off bits of food from his wooden cross with a penknife. He was as blunt as usual. 'Sorry, Hancky,' he said, without taking his eyes off the cross. 'The coffee has gone cold.'

That was an in-house expression that meant you were getting the boot. It referred to the beginning of everything – how this company, like many others, had started out in a coffee shop. The founder had sat at his usual table in the harbour district, receiving skippers and supercargoes who bought insurance polices for valuable shipments, an enterprise that benefited from the invigorating effect of coffee.

Now Hanck's cup was ice-cold. It didn't come as any

surprise. The company had been showing poor profits, and other departments had already been shut down. Now it was Hanck's turn. Malicious rumours had even hinted that it was soft-hearted people like Hanck who had contributed to the flagging finances. Those who were allowed to stay were the more thick-skinned and hard-boiled types.

But it wasn't exactly a death blow. He was prepared. He received severance pay in accordance with the prevailing agreement, and he was sent home the very same day.

He stayed at home for a while, moving about behind drawn curtains to keep out the heat. But during those days it was still more than forty degrees Celsius in his flat. Now that he had no job to go to, he tried to change his daily routine, staying up at night and sleeping at the height of the heat. But it didn't really suit him.

He stuck to his routines, and when his lack of employment became too burdensome, he would listen to the organ. It carried him through a couple of dreary weeks until he had other things to occupy his mind.

His old mother fell ill. He had an inkling what was going on when he rang her to report that he had lost his job. She had listened attentively, commenting with what he thought was understanding and sympathy. She had even offered a few words of encouragement at the end, saying, 'I'm sure that you'll find . . . find another wife.'

'I was talking about my job,' he attempted to explain.

'All right,' she had said. 'Yes, well, that's the way it is . . .' Then she paused, and he had waited for the customary remark about how she didn't really know, but she didn't say it. He waited and waited, but the remark never came, and he realised that something serious had happened or was in the process of happening. By omitting that bewildering subordinate clause, she made him more uneasy than ever before.

She quickly grew worse, and it was obvious how things would end. When the cooling system broke down, which happened from time to time, everything went even faster. She lost her powers of perception. With some effort she could comprehend, but just barely, what was happening right in front of her eyes. If she turned even halfway round, she had no clue what was behind her or what she had just been looking at. The whole world became incomprehensible.

Hanck sat with her in the hospital. He had nothing else to occupy his days. He talked to her all the time. The staff claimed that his voice had a soothing and comforting effect, but he doubted it. Every time she came round, he had to re-introduce himself. And every time she realised who he was, she said, 'Yes, that's the way it is . . .' And each time he waited in vain to hear the rest. But the words stayed away.

As did the rest of the world. He heard the sound of TomBola out in the corridor and said, 'Maybe I should join the queue.'

'What queue?' his mother asked.

'For TomBola.'

'Who?'

'TomBola! The woman with the filthy wigs!'

'Wigs?'

Everything that had previously meant something to her was now irrelevant, unintelligible, wrapped in a veil. That included Hanck himself, but he sat with her until the end, through a long and unbearable dry spell.

He wanted to hear her last words. The course of her illness entailed a loss of all contact with her surroundings, and she entered an inaccessible state. There were other illnesses with similar symptoms, but this particular disease had a special stage that occurred towards the end, often preceded by a great stillness, as if the patient were mustering her forces, and then she would utter her last words, sometimes mysterious, sometimes crystal clear, but almost always memorable, regarded as a premonition, a unique moment of clairvoyance.

The last words spoken by Hanck's mother were: 'He's going to be a chef!' She said the words loud and clear, even though the meaning was not immediately understood.

She left behind a good deal of money that she herself had forgotten all about, money that she had presumably won from gambling.

The third time he went out there and knocked on the old man's door, he was more determined. He had been there once with a sense of restrained suspicion, a second time with undisguised anticipation, and now with a very clear purpose in mind.

A few days earlier he had spread his mother's ashes in a memorial park. The ground was grey between the walls, almost dusty. There hadn't been a drop of rain in more than three months. He had wandered around for half an hour, looking for a spot that hadn't been claimed and covered with someone else's ashes, but it was bone-dry, and the dust billowed up around his shoes wherever he went.

He saw a group that had joined forces in an attempt to clear away a patch with their tears.

Their grief made it easier for him to turn the urn upside down, feeling almost nonchalant about it, and empty the contents out onto the ground at a spot chosen at random.

An hour later he was sitting in a restaurant in the pleasure district having lunch. Tradition did not demand anything special, but he thought he would indulge himself by honouring his mother with a good lunch. He drank vodka and fell into conversation with a woman sitting at the next table.

They drank a toast and agreed that they were the freest individuals in the world, maybe even the freest individuals that had ever lived on this earth. She didn't have a job, he didn't either. She didn't have any family, he didn't either. She didn't have any diseases, he didn't either.

They exchanged phone numbers, and he left with an elated joie de vivre.

The narrow streets of the pleasure district offered shade that made it possible to be outdoors in the middle of the day. Hanck walked past a shop with scientific instruments. He'd never noticed the place before, probably because he was totally uninterested in such things.

But now he stopped and peered into the display window. There, amid all the outmoded instruments made of brass and hardwood, was a typewriter, sitting inside a case that was tipped forward. It looked very much like the ones he had seen at the old man's place near the field. And for a change there was an elegantly printed price tag stuck in the platen. The asking price was equal to a month's salary. A low salary, perhaps, but enough to get by on.

Hanck went inside the shop and greeted the owner. They talked a bit about the machine in the window. He learned that it had just come in and would most likely be there only a day, or possibly two. The machines were in high demand. Office workers were sick and tired of the constant power outages.

'Young people are crazy for those machines.'

'Young people?' said Hanck. 'Can they read and write?'

'It's become quite trendy.' The shopkeeper lowered his voice to a whisper, as if he were relaying dangerous information: 'There's a protest movement.'

'But what about paper?' said Hanck. 'There's never any paper.'

'It comes and goes,' said the shopkeeper. 'People hoard it.'

Hanck nodded, thinking about this. Something new, an entirely new phenomenon for him.

'The only problem,' said the shopkeeper, 'is that there aren't any more machines to be found. They're . . . obsolete.'

He said the word in a hushed tone, as if it were a password, a code intended to arouse some sort of response. Hanck gave him a totally blank look. He didn't want to reveal what he was thinking about.

A few days later he went back out to see the old man. He knocked on the door with one clear purpose in mind: to strike a deal. The old man had something that he wanted to acquire.

'The typewriters?' said the old man suspiciously, as if refusing to understand. 'You want to buy my machines?'

Hanck confirmed that this was true. The old man had perceived the matter correctly.

'What the hell do you want with them?'

Hanck said as politely as he could, 'That's my own affair.'

'You think there's a market for them?' The old man coughed and scratched his crotch. As if the very idea made him itch. 'Is that how things are over there?'

'I don't know,' said Hanck. 'It's a long shot. I got the sack because of what I wrote about your claim.'

'I don't owe you anything because of that,' said the old man.

'Correct,' said Hanck. 'That's why I want to make you a fair deal.'

'There aren't any fair deals,' said the old man. 'Someone always gets screwed.' He coughed again, much harder this time. He spat blood onto a rag.

'You're going to die out here,' said Hanck.

'Everyone dies out here,' said the old man.

'I've brought along two ingots. They're yours if I can have the machines.' The old man stared at him, looking him up

— 76 —

and down, as if those two 'trade ingots' might be sticking out of his pockets.

'Trade ingots?'

Hanck nodded.

'I've never seen one.'

Hanck took a gold ingot out of his inside pocket. 'With two of these you could eat and drink until – '

'Until I die,' said the old man. 'Undoubtedly. Undoubtedly.'

'Or move somewhere else.'

'Move . . .' said the old man scornfully. That would never come into consideration. But to be able to eat and drink himself to death . . . Now that would be something.

They shook hands on the deal, and a short time later Hanck returned with transport. He carried out the cases, two at a time, and loaded them onto the flatbed. Each machine weighed five kilos. They would add up to three tons in all.

He'd carried about half of them out when he saw Rachel come walking across the now sun-scorched field. She walked slowly, in a manner that he at first perceived as shy, rather tentative.

'Is he going to move?' she asked.

Hanck stopped, looked at her, tried to understand why she was smiling. 'No,' he said. 'We've made a deal.'

Rachel nodded. She probably had an ambiguous attitude towards typewriters. 'Your work,' she said, and pointed to the bulge of her belly.

Hanck paused, hot and sweaty and feeling strangely distracted. As if all the weight he was dealing with had somehow lifted a burden from his mind. It took him a moment to comprehend what she had just said. He stood still, holding a heavy case in each hand.

'My work?' Now he saw it: she was pregnant. Either she was pleased and happy about her condition, or else her smile meant that she was uncertain about how he would take the news.

And she had every reason to be wary. They hardly knew each other, after all.

'They say that it's going to be a boy,' she said. 'They can tell by looking at my belly.'

Hanck hadn't yet recovered enough to load the cases he was holding, much less set them down on the ground. He stood there with one in each hand and looked at this woman who said that she was expecting his child. A son.

'He . . . he . . .' stammered Hanck. 'He's going to be a chef . . .'

'I see,' said Rachel. Now she gave him a different kind of smile. Maybe she was relieved that he had accepted it so quickly and was already envisioning the future. 'Well, why not?'

'My mother . . .' said Hanck. 'She died. Recently. Those were her last words. "He's going to be a chef." I . . . I didn't understand. I've been thinking so much about . . . about . . .' He should have said 'you', but he didn't. He said, 'I've been thinking so much about it.'

'I see,' she said. 'Are you . . . ?'

'No,' said Hanck. 'Actually not. Actually not at all. I'm sure it's nothing but superstition, or . . .' He gave her a look that was tentative, almost entreating. He didn't want to put up any obstacles, but he would, no matter what he said.

'My maternal grandmother said: "Rosebud . . ." and we all thought that we were going to see a rose somewhere,' said Rachel. 'We went around looking for it. But then someone said that it was an old story. About an old man who died and said "Rosebud" and no one could understand why.'

'It was a sledge,' said Hanck.

Rachel gave him a look of incomprehension. Her smile was gone.

'Kids used to ride on them,' said Hanck, 'down hills.'

'I see,' she said. 'A cart.'

'No,' said Hanck. 'It didn't have wheels. They rode on the snow. Slid on it.' He had his hands full and had to gesture with his head to illustrate.

'Hmm . . .' she said, and Hanck assumed that she was unable to envision it very clearly. He'd had only a vague notion about the phenomenon himself until he was leafing through an old book with pictures of that substance called snow.

But Rachel nodded nevertheless, once again smiling and seeming to weigh what he had said, as if quite by surprise she had come into possession of valuable information. Or maybe it meant that it had once again been confirmed to her that occasionally life was incomprehensible. Not that God's work was incomprehensible, but rather His plans were. That which lay ahead, that which was called the future.

By all accounts their future was a son, and he already existed but had not yet shown his face. And because that fact was incomprehensible, it had made a man and a woman think about other incomprehensible things. As if, when faced with what was least comprehensible of all, they would turn to something else, something that could be touched, slid upon, shaped into balls and tossed at each other. Something that had once existed but had now disappeared, something that belonged to nature. Just like themselves.

Only now did Hanck realise that he was standing there holding two heavy cases in his hands. He heaved the load onto the flatbed truck. Rachel watched. She said, 'Well, well,' in a tone as if she were concluding or finishing something. 'So at least we know that much. He's going to be a chef.'

'Do you want – ?' He stopped himself but noticed that she

reacted at once, as if paying close attention, as if they both realised that they were not facing something that was over. On the contrary, they had touched on something that was extremely unfinished. 'Do you want . . . ?' he repeated but came to a halt once again. What had occurred to him may have seemed awkward, an intimation that might be perceived as presumptuous or simply as something generally askew in their world. 'Do you want me to . . . ? For us to – ?'

Hanck was interrupted by the old man coming out the door. He paid no attention to them. He took up position a few metres away and had a pee. Rachel watched.

She said, 'I saw you. Here. The first time. And the time before this.'

He said, 'I don't know what I was thinking.'

'You had your hat in your hand.'

'Yes,' he said, 'and I went into the old man's house without wearing gloves or a mask.'

In silence they pondered such recklessness. It should have meant something. She should have understood as much, if that was what she wanted.

'You knew nothing about me,' she said. 'Maybe you enjoy taking risks.'

'What about you?' he said. 'What did you know about me?'

'Enough,' she said. 'And they agreed . . .' She tipped her head towards the field, at the other side where her family was standing behind the curtains, staring. Watching and giving their blessing. Or perhaps they were completely indifferent, eyeing this encounter with the same interest that they would give to an empty cardboard box that the wind had blown across the field on a blustery day. It meant nothing at all, but with the proper attitude, it might offer a moment's diversion.

For Hanck, prey to a flood of emotions that were incomprehensible and maybe even undesirable, it was a relief to tackle the mechanisms of an old typewriter.

He turned one of the two rooms that faced the street into a workshop. Along the walls stood shelves, heavy-duty warehouse shelves, holding the machines in their cases, sorted and arranged into various categories, by series, manufacturer and quality.

Next to the window stood a solid workbench with tools neatly lined up, easily accessible. There were screwdrivers for every imaginable size of flathead screw, pliers, small wrenches, brushes for cleaning, various solvents, oils and everything else that was needed.

Hanck soon learned the basics of the mechanism, and by the time the rainy season set in he was making use of the skills that he had acquired as a child for keeping moisture out of his mother's wig workshop. By Christmas of that year, he had delivered four first-class machines to the shopkeeper. He'd become a valued supplier.

They had discovered one another. Hanck was reticent about his assets, always expressing himself rather vaguely, if not downright evasively, regarding the prospects for future deliveries. The shopkeeper accepted this uncertainty, deciding that Hanck was a wizard who was able to conjure up typewriters, which is what he told his customers. And that, in turn, had a favourable effect on the prices he charged.

Hanck thrived in his new life. He set his own schedule, delivering a machine now and then, taking in others that he inspected and then repaired if necessary, and earning good money. He was frugal with his rations, and had everything he needed. Considering what he knew about life, he couldn't complain.

One day he was sitting under the glow of the lamp with a machine that had to be adjusted to suit the wishes of a customer. The shopkeeper didn't like it when Hanck tampered with the typewriters, swapping out keys and modifying the keyboard so that it would satisfy a number of linguistic demands. But Hanck had no trouble with doing that. The machines were meant to be functional and put to use. It was of no consequence what he might think of how they were used.

He sat there filing off the dots and circles above the å, ä and ö – a change that in the eyes of the shopkeeper constituted a 'tremendous assault' or an 'utter violation'. Choose either one. Hanck considered it a reasonable measure, an acceptable alteration. He could easily return the machine to its original condition.

Hanck would end up remembering this incident well, in every detail, because he himself was facing a change that would put this momentary tampering with an old typewriter in its proper light. But the change he faced was irrevocable. His entire existence was about to be altered in a way that happens only a few times in a person's life.

'I sat there filing the capital Ö,' he might say later. 'The Ö that was once part of the Swedish word for eagle – *örn* – which was the name of my paternal great-grandfather. Like a proud bird. It had disappeared, taking the two dots with it.' It was the sort of thing that no longer concerned a single living soul, except obsoletes like the shopkeeper, who insisted on keeping the dots and the circles.

Hanck was sitting there filing away at those dots when someone knocked on the door. He put down his tool and went to open up, putting on the serious expression with which he preferred to greet his customers, an expression warning that whatever their problem might be, it was in principle unsolvable.

In the stairwell stood two men wearing lavender overalls. Communicators. It could mean several things – that he was about to receive the news that someone was dead, or that he was going to be asked to identify someone who had recently been found dead.

Naturally, Hanck was surprised, and he looked at the two men with an expression that they presumably saw every day – a look filled with terror, distaste, aversion. Their appearance was a good match, weighted down as they were with solemnity, worn out in the way that people get when they've gone beyond even cynicism and rough jargon to a dogged pleading.

'Hanck Orn?' said one of them. He was holding a clipboard with a well-thumbed, greasy, frayed piece of paper. They had to use every scrap until it was completely covered, erased clean and filled up again on both sides, until it was impossible to erase again.

'Yes?' said Hanck. 'What's this about?'

The man who had asked his name checked the paper. 'Your code?'

Hanck rattled off the numbers.

'You need to come with us.'

'Why?'

At first he received only a weary look in reply. Then the other man said, 'It's urgent.'

Hanck knew that he had to obey these men. It was the law, probably one of the few laws that no one had ever managed to break.

Outside the front entrance stood a delivery van painted the same lavender colour as the men's overalls. It was not an ambulance for emergency transports, but rather a hearse. It smelled of cadavers.

They drove north, making a wide arc around the City Under the Roof, heading out through the suburbs until the buildings grew sparser and the houses were of a different style. Characteristic of the northern slums there were huge complexes constructed of rusty steel and cracked cement. There were long, flat façades with fewer windows, old industrial areas that had been put to new use, first as temporary lodgings and later as permanent residences, where the ownership was unclear and the maintenance neglected. These were neighbourhoods where no one wanted to be seen outdoors, not even in daylight, not even the people who actually lived there. Outside every door stood a lavender delivery van, waiting.

Hanck would never forget that trip, even though he found it hard to describe. He didn't recall a single word that was exchanged. Perhaps that was simply because not a word was actually said. On the other hand, he distinctly remembered how he felt. He assumed that it had something to do with the concept of 'shock', a word without meaning, worn out and exhausted, a term that had been emptied of all value, plundered and stripped bare, just as these buildings once had been.

Eventually they arrived at the 'Asylum', an old car park, isolated from its surroundings by a zone of demolished structures with big open spaces of asphalt and more razed building sites that had been plundered of everything usable. The entire place was enclosed behind a high fence. The lavender van passed through a guarded gate, drove up to the main entrance and stopped.

'Go in and give them your name,' said the man with the clipboard. He slammed the door behind Hanck, and the vehicle turned and drove back out through the gate, on its way to the next victim.

The 'Asylum' had been used during an epidemic and after that had served mainly as a collection site for the dying and already deceased. When the Wave had ebbed away, a company within the healthcare sector had taken over the facilities. Its operating costs were financed by charities, private donations, minor subsidies from the Administration and large contributions from the Clan. The names of many prominent members were listed on a plaque posted in the lobby. It promoted goodwill.

Hanck entered a reception area with an asphalt floor and fluorescent lights on the ceiling. Sick people sat on benches or lay on the floor, waiting for help. Many were coughing. Some who were on their way out and regarded as cured were received by relatives beaming with joy. But they all spoke in low voices and without undue fuss. It was conspicuously quiet.

He gave his name at the reception desk. A woman dressed in blue sitting behind a window checked a monitor and gave him directions. He went up to a department on the third level, found another small window, and gave his name again, to another blue-clad woman. He was told to wait in a window-less room.

After a short wait a young person of indeterminate sex came over and asked for his name and ID number, then checked to see that this agreed with the information on a filthy piece of paper. Since it did, Hanck was asked to provide a blood sample. He didn't understand why, but he realised it would be pointless to object. He gave the sample, and the young person thanked him for his co-operation and left.

Half an hour later a woman wearing a blue coat over her blue garb came to the waiting room and asked for Hanck. He got up and shook hands. She introduced herself as a doctor and asked him to follow her into an office.

Hanck sat down on a visitor's chair with a worn seat cushion. The doctor sat down on the other side of a desk that was covered with computers, piles of loose, dirty papers and well-thumbed case-books.

She took a moment to check the monitor, looking at the results of his blood test. It was apparently sufficiently re-assuring for her to take off her face mask. She had a little sore on her lip that she had tried to conceal with some cream.

'Well . . .' she said. 'I suppose you're wondering why we've asked you to come here.'

I wouldn't exactly call it 'asked', thought Hanck. But he didn't want to make trouble with these people unnecessarily. He said, 'Yes, I did wonder.'

'So you have no idea?'

'No,' said Hanck. 'Should I?'

The doctor checked the monitor again, as if looking for some sort of final confirmation. She said, 'You have a child here with us. He's about three days old.'

That much Hanck could tell Toby without having to stop and think, to make sure he didn't say anything that might prove painful. He could also tell him, completely truthfully, how the child had ended up at the 'Asylum'. They said that the baby simply showed up there one morning, wrapped in swaddling clothes, dumped, or 'discarded', as they expressed it. A business card with Hanck's name and address was stuck in among the wrappings. Clumsily printed on the back were the words: 'Mother dead.'

But as for the rest, Hanck had to watch what he said. He felt ashamed about the fact that he had been unsympathetic and refused to acknowledge any sort of paternity, in spite of the proof. He hadn't been especially co-operative even when the evidence was presented to him.

But that wasn't all. The child was injured. An operation was required to save the child's life, an extensive and expensive procedure. Hanck had claimed that he didn't have the money to pay for the costs. The doctor had recommended that he take out a loan. Hanck had then implied that his application for credit would be rejected, since he was officially unemployed. He was a destitute has-been.

The doctor had listened to him, displaying a perfunctory composure and neutral expression. She had heard those excuses before.

'So,' she said, 'what are you getting at?'

Hanck said, 'I . . . I don't know.' That was the truth. He was confused.

'As for the financial matter,' said the doctor, 'that can always be solved. You're not alone. There's a boom going on. Presumably it has something to do with the organ music.' She gave Hanck an interested, almost searching look. Maybe she had her own memories from that night.

But he was in no mood for such things. 'I can't decide,' he said. 'How is he? What's going to happen to him?'

The doctor assured Hanck that with a little luck the boy would be restored to full health. She cited a diagnosis in Latin, said that the boy was fragile and exhausted, that 'he should have been dead'. But he wasn't. 'We've found infants that have lived for weeks in landslides after an earthquake.

With no water and hardly any oxygen. All the adults die, but the newborns survive. They want to live.'

Hanck said, 'And he does too?'

The doctor unconsciously poked at the little sore on her lip. 'You haven't seen him?'

'No,' said Hanck. With a candour that would later make him ashamed, and that he would prefer to keep secret, he said, 'I don't know if I want to.'

'Okay,' said the doctor. She pulled out a file drawer from her desk and took out a form, an old-fashioned bureaucratic questionnaire. That meant that the case was considered of high importance. 'We need to make sure the child receives the proper attention,' she said. 'You can relinquish all responsibility and leave here at once. There are plenty of people in this city who would be more than happy to take care of a child. They don't care about minor defects. They probably have much worse ones themselves.'

She placed the form on the desk and pushed it towards Hanck. It was simply designed, with information listed next to a couple of boxes that he was supposed to tick off and then sign his name underneath. No enquiries or investigations were required. Five X's and a tick in the corner, and Hanck could forget about the whole thing.

The fact that he sat there and even considered such a possibility was not something that he wanted to confess to his son, of course. The doctor was businesslike and dispassionate in her demeanour, making no attempt to influence him in either direction. She presented the facts, and if Hanck wanted to leave and continue on with his life as if nothing had happened, he was free to do so. No one would blame him.

'So how did she die?' he asked. 'Rachel.'

'The mother?' said the doctor. 'Was her name Rachel?' Hanck nodded. 'Do you have her last name?'

'No,' said Hanck. 'It was just a chance encounter.'

The doctor made note of this, still without displaying the least sign of involvement or any of her own personal views.

Maybe it was the thought of Rachel, the thought of what had happened at that remote field, that made him hesitate before the seductively simple design of the form.

He had left there on a scorchingly hot day, driving a transport filled with old typewriters. He had actually caught a glimpse of her in the rear-view mirror as she slowly plodded across the cracked ground, on her way home, pregnant, and by all accounts unconcerned about the fact that her child had a father, a real father. But clearly he wasn't needed any more. They undoubtedly had enough people to fill the position, men of the proper persuasion.

He and Rachel had shared a major second together. That was enough. That was his role. She and her people would take care of the rest. That was how he had perceived the situation.

Obviously something had happened. Otherwise they would never have let the child go.

'What if I . . . ?' said Hanck. 'What if I were to see him first?'

The doctor sat and waited, her expression blank. Not even blinking her eyes. Maybe that too was part of her routine, to sit there quietly and wait for things to happen. Her voice low, ordinary, the way people talk when it's a matter of life and death.

'What if I should . . . ? Would . . . ? What if I . . . ?' He couldn't say it. The thought was so overwhelming. 'What if I . . . ? Suppose that . . .'

Finally the doctor intervened. 'What if you wanted to take care of him?'

'Yes,' said Hanck, relieved. It was difficult to think about it, impossible to say. 'What would happen then?' he said.

For the first time the doctor smiled. She said, 'How the hell would I know? Presumably he would grow up big and strong.'

A bit of sarcasm. It lightened the mood. Hanck was not prepared to make the choice that had been presented to him; he was having a hard time thinking clearly. He was prepared to let someone else do it for him. Although he didn't know who that might be. One of these godlike doctors had already saved the child from death. They had already made that decision. Now they had left the rest up to him.

He hadn't yet seen him, the boy who would make the choice for him, the boy who would make the whole matter so simple that he would grow hot, sweaty and deeply troubled at the very thought that it had ever come into question. His only defence was to say to himself: 'I was actually a different person back them. I didn't really exist . . .'

The doctor had put on her mask; she handed Hanck a blue smock, cap and mask, and then led him down a corridor with an asphalt floor and strangely dry air.

Through a swinging door they entered the intensive care department. In a small room filled with apparatuses and machines that blinked on and off and emitted beeping sounds, amid a steady huffing and hissing, a row of incubators stood on tall legs.

The doctor pulled on a pair of latex gloves and handed Hanck a pair, showing him how to put them on. She stood close, almost indecently close, pulling the latex over his splayed fingers. He met her glance and realised that she was smiling behind the mask. As if she knew something about him, something that pleased her.

Then she turned round, stepped over to an incubator, and

nodded meaningfully at what was inside. 'This is your son,' she said. 'He's asleep.'

Hanck looked down into the incubator. It took a moment before he understood what he saw.

A little more than twenty years later the Affect Commission was ready with its seventh volume, which by all accounts would be the most comprehensive to date. The work had involved practically all the scholars that could be found, both those who were officially recognised and those who were self-proclaimed. Over the years the editorial staff had changed; people had died and been replaced, articles had been written by hundreds of co-workers, and the mood that enveloped the project was thought to have revived the spirit from the time of the great encyclopedias.

Attempts had been made to bridge the age-old antagonism between the natural sciences and the humanities. Engineers and skalds were to be brought together between the same covers. Even the idea of establishing a periodic table for emotions had been favourably received.

The number of emotions was estimated to be largely equal to the known elements, and their systematisation had been done in accordance with similar principles. While the properties of the elements were determined by atomic nuclei and the number of electrons, each emotion received its place in the system based on its innermost charge and its ability to combine with others. According to this approach you might perceive an emotion such as 'self-satisfaction', for example, as an appropriate entry in the column corresponding to copper, silver and gold. Consequently, 'desire', on the other hand, would be characterised by less stable isotopes and would exist only in compounds, or decay in toxic spirals.

A great deal of effort was invested in the experiments, and a certain optimism reigned until the system was applied in practice and tested against a number of examples. Then it was determined that almost every single emotion appeared in the wrong classification, and in the most unexpected contexts and combinations, so that its place in the periodic table was questioned, if not refuted. The system proved to be unreliable.

The primary word of the present volume from this period was 'Love', and for reasons that will later become apparent, Hanck felt called upon to contribute an article. When the attempts at a more conventional systematisation came to naught, a method had been devised in which every emotion was defined, based on a loose number of main categories, or 'families'. The emotion was described as clinically as possible, demarcated from other feelings, and presented in its purest possible form. Then it was illustrated with a number of examples, old as well as new. The confusion that subsequently arose was something that people simply had to accept.

And confusion did arise. Lengthy public debates raged over whether love could even appear in a pure state, or whether it existed only in combinations, in relation to one or more exponents, whether it presupposed a motive, regardless of whether this consisted of a subject or an object or a more comprehensive category.

Despite an entire epoch of devastation, a great deal of material was still available. Love had served as the basis for religious and political movements; it had provided, in particular, the incentive for a large share of historical art. It might appear as the motive for a cult. Preserved recordings and textual fragments from the period around the advent of the third millennium showed a widespread invocation of love as the only meaningful aspect of life. And examinations of political programmes indicated that love had been put into practice more or less successfully.

Other aspects characterised love as a source of energy, as a natural resource. Everyone agreed that love was strong and difficult to control, and that it most likely could influence anything and anyone. On the other hand, there was disagreement over whether it constituted an infinite resource or not.

When it came to the section of illustrations – examples of the expression of love – the public was invited to participate with personal contributions. These were reviewed by a special commission, and the ones that were deemed interesting were passed on; in many cases they ended up in the actual volume.

Hanck could attest that a grown man with an orderly life, a home and work, a man who absolutely did not belong to the 'seekers' and who, on the contrary, fended off any idea of big, drastic changes, could suddenly and quite unexpectedly be struck by love with such devastating force that all prevailing patterns and customs would cease to apply. That experience formed the basis of his expertise. He didn't need to offer any assessments, or determine whether this overwhelming event conveyed anything positive or negative. He could make do with stating that it had happened, that it was involuntary, and that it established a 'before' that was irretrievably lost, and an 'after' that was decisive and absolute. A demarcation which, in a number of respects, was a more distinct borderline than that between life and death.

Hanck's love had a very clearly defined object, even though, at first glance, it took him a long time to comprehend what he was actually facing.

★   ★   ★

It was a small room, not a hall by any means, in the department labelled 'Recovery'. The air inside was warm and dry. The floor consisted of stained asphalt. In the very spot where the incubator stood, cars had once been parked long ago. Motor oil and petrol had leaked grease into the foundation. Through a narrow window there was a view of a cemetery. Prostitutes who had attended to customers in the cars had looked at the same view, while for those who were beaten or murdered here, this floor and this view were the last things they would ever see in this world.

Hanck had looked at the contents of the incubator for a long time before he realised what it was: a three-day-old boy, weighing barely more than two kilos, with thick tubes and hoses sticking out of his body. His legs were as thin as sticks, his arms even skinnier. All subcutaneous fat had been consumed, tiny blood vessels branched out, making a delicate network that gave the boy's skin a bluish tinge, like old, cracked porcelain.

'Isn't he lovely?'

Hanck had a hard time saying anything. He heard the doctor explaining what sort of hoses were hooked up to the infant's body: providing a nutrient solution, measuring the oxygen supply, and ensuring various types of drainage. He didn't understand half of it. But he did understand this: 'You can put your hand inside and touch him.'

Hanck took this as an exhortation to conquer the respect or fear that couldn't have been greater if he'd been faced with a terrarium filled with poisonous snakes. In spite of all his objections, whether they were rooted in fear of the unknown or a feeling of being inadequate, he felt prompted to stick his hand through the hatch in the incubator to touch the child. First he stroked his index finger along the gaunt cheek, then he cupped his hand around the boy's head. His hand covered the head from ear to ear. The child's pulse filled his whole palm.

Then the boy opened his eyes. If Hanck, up until that moment, had been attempting to fend off any feelings of attachment, he was instantly forced into a position of involuntary capitulation. He looked into the boy's eyes and was transformed.

It was a look that seemed to force its way through all matter. It cut through the armour behind which Hanck had ensconced himself. An utterly new and yet ancient look that flinched at nothing but intended nothing. It simply allowed itself to be perceived. If those eyes represented innocence, something as yet unfinished and untested because they had seen nothing, they also represented an unfathomable freedom that emptied every concept of meaning and annihilated every attempt to describe it. It held no reproach, no demand and no entreaty, no exhortations, assertions, expectations or other views that might point forward, onward, intimating a movement in a specific direction for this new-born life, this new world.

Hanck felt it to be a great privilege to bask in that gaze. It invoked an unfamiliar sense of satisfaction, a solemn jubilation. It was as if he had suddenly been given back part of the respect that he had lost in his younger days.

The power was unmistakable. In the midst of that 'high-tech era', when every electronic apparatus was 'cutting edge', in this recovery room where patients who had recently undergone an operation would awake from an artificial sleep, something was also awakened in the visitor – a violent, irresistible force that raced through his body and took over his entire existence in a manner that was so persuasive and overwhelming that he was transformed.

He acquired a new type of internal order. It spread through

his body while all the phases of an intoxication appeared at once: the initial tipsiness followed by a sense of well-being as the whole world took on a golden shimmer, the euphoria, the peak that you want to maintain at all costs, and then the deep slumber, the restless sleep, and the awakening, that raw sensitivity, vulnerability, and regret at having revealed yourself and stood unprotected, as if wide open to the world.

And he accepted this, plain and simple. Because, in the midst of everything, it was so natural. It was as if he had gratefully received an answer to a question that he had been asking for a long time. He was caught unawares like a defence-less victim. Yet he wanted to emphasise the ease with which he underwent this transformation, so that almost after the fact he came to ask the questions for which he had already received answers. His whole previous life now appeared as something unformulated, a long, dubious waiting for something that was going to happen. The major second of a tiny human being.

In the case-book relating to this child there were also notes about the father. Hanck kept vigil at the incubator, filled with concern and occasionally suspicious about the appropriateness of the actions taken by the staff. He stayed there for several days straight, until he collapsed from exhaustion. He was given a camp bed in a waiting room, where he could get some rest.

They tried in a friendly manner to persuade the father that his presence was not necessary, that he could rely on the skill of the staff. When the father did not respond to that approach, they had to resort to stronger measures and prescribed a walk, a period of relaxation. When that didn't work either, they forbade him from visiting for a couple of days.

The message got through. Hanck left the hospital and

went home. His flat suddenly looked different, almost foreign, as if it were occupied by a bohemian, an irresponsible slacker. It was full of sharp tools, sharp edges, dangerous things, draughty windows, filthy corners.

He tried to work, but it was impossible. He couldn't concentrate on the dead machines. He cleaned up, moved the furniture around, cleared away dangers for small children. He brought home a child's cot and made long lists of things that he needed to get for the care of the infant.

That was how he managed to pass the time for a couple of days.

The first eighteen months he kept the boy inside the flat. He wanted to avoid contagion. And he succeeded. The lad put on weight, ate well, grew and sounded as he should.

Gerlinde, the shopkeeper's wife, occasionally stopped by to offer advice. She had given birth to a girl. The children were placed side by side and compared. The boy was slightly behind, a bit late in development, but over time the girl's advantage diminished.

He was given the name Toby. It was Gerlinde who came up with the name. '*Guten Morgen, Kleiner* Toby!' she would say as soon as the boy opened his eyes. Toby was the name of an old man painted on a vintage ceramic vessel, a beer stein that she brought out for important occasions. When Hanck saw that old stein with his own eyes, he had to admit that there was a definite resemblance with his son.

Toby was able to walk unassisted by the time they made their first foray outdoors. They walked under the roof over to Vinterplatsen and back. Afterwards the boy was so dazed by all the impressions that he slept for twenty-four hours straight.

After he got bigger and his resistance was greater, their walks became a daily event, and more prolonged when the weather improved. Step by step the world expanded for the little boy.

They would often drop by to visit the shopkeeper, who

had a look of panic in his eyes when the little boy came in the door. But his daughter enjoyed Toby's company, and that made up for anything else. And he never damaged anything in the shop. He was inquisitive and, like all boys, wanted to touch everything, but he showed 'the proper respect'.

Hanck and the shopkeeper might have different opinions about whether to keep the dots over the å, ä and ö, but they were in agreement about showing concern for the children.

The various ways in which love is expressed could undoubtedly fill an entire encyclopaedia; the one that manifested itself as 'concern' has a countless number of variations – and species – of its own. Saussyr was the apple of the shopkeeper's eye. He might light up as he fervently talked about some old instrument, but when the subject of his daughter came up, his face took on a whole new look.

Occasionally she would come into the shop, but usually she stayed in the inner rooms. She had red hair and pale skin and couldn't tolerate sunlight. The shop was located in a narrow, shady street, but during certain periods the sun would be low in the sky and reflect off the shiny surfaces of the old brass instruments. That was as much light as she could stand, in her father's opinion.

Those who were red-haired and pale belonged to a rare lineage. That was why she was particularly valuable. According to her father, the finest hygrometers relied on the capacity to utilise a strand of human hair to absorb moisture. An increase in length of a few percentage points in a strand of hair affected a sensitive mechanism connected to an indicator. The strands of hair best suited for this purpose came from a red-haired virgin. The shopkeeper, who happened to have at his disposal a large supply of this precious raw material, could strut about like a plantation-owner and meet any demand.

Something like this could never be expected of Toby. He was an unusually sensitive boy. On their way home from visiting the shopkeeper – a complete family with mamma, pappa and child – he might start nagging and begging for things that Hanck couldn't possibly afford. Toby might stand gaping at some expensive toy, and Hanck would grow tired of the boy and admit as much, resorting to harsh words to put an end to his nagging. In spite of his tender age, the boy would then realise that he had overstepped an invisible line and fall silent. Hanck would walk along the street with the boy, noticing his hand slip into his own, and feeling almost tearful with remorse after that sort of scene. In his heart he wished he could have given the boy everything he wanted. But that wasn't possible.

This type of sensitivity also showed up in the way Toby interacted with boys his own age. He preferred to stand last in a queue, he never made a fuss, and he had no need to draw attention to himself.

So it was with trepidation that Hanck took him to school. By the age of six Toby could count to ten and do a tolerable job of writing his name. There was nothing wrong with his intelligence, and he could express himself with a number of difficult words that were often used correctly. But he had a hard time with skills that were valued most highly in school. And he didn't want to go. He preferred to stay at home and create little countries, small kingdoms, orderly societies that could take weeks or even months to build, as he talked non-stop with his imaginary companions.

Hanck had grown accustomed to his chattering. He no longer really listened, hearing it mostly as a hum in the background as he worked on a machine at the workbench in his shop. Sometimes the chatter would stop and a long silence would follow, lasting for an alarming amount of time. Then

Hanck would get up to check on things. He would catch sight of the boy and suddenly encounter those old-man eyes, that ancient look that he had once seen in the incubator. And that look would scare him. It was familiar but at the same time alienating and inaccessible.

Toby's world was magic; everything was alive and able to speak. There were constant battles between good and evil, and there were Sneezers and Etherists who were often misunderstood. Toby had asked about his mother, and what he had learned over the years had, of course, affected his ideas about the world.

Hanck knew that he'd been a bit vague about certain points, but he thought he'd been quite firm with regard to the prospect that his mother might still be alive. She was dead. He didn't want to arouse any hopes in his son, or give him ideas that might grow into a conviction that she could be living someplace 'out there', and that his son should eventually go out and find her.

Toby had heard the story many times, about how he had been left in his swaddling clothes on the hospital steps with nothing but a dirty business card as the only link to Hanck.

One day he wanted to see that business card for himself. He didn't even know what it was. 'Everyone used to have them,' said Hanck, 'everyone who worked at the insurance company.'

It was kept in a drawer along with documents from the hospital. Toby was allowed to see it. With some effort he read what it said: Hanck's name and title and address. On the back were the words printed in a childish hand: 'Mother dead.'

'How do you know she was dead?' said Toby, of course.

'Because I was there,' said Hanck. He was forced to say it. 'Naturally I went out there and checked.'

★ ★ ★

Hanck had gone out to that field the day after he was sent home from the hospital while his son was still lying in the incubator.

It was February, it was raining hard, but nothing could have stopped him. He had felt so fulfilled, almost intoxicated by what had happened. He had stood there in the mud looking at what was left of Rachel's house – a few sooty timbers and broken roof tiles. It had been pillaged and burned, it was a ruin.

Only then and there did it occur to Hanck that she had fallen prey to berserkers, that it had been a question of retaliation, punishment resulting from her testimony, no matter how hidden and anonymous he had tried to present it in his report.

The old man's cabin still stood on the other side of the field. It was now his time to be a witness. Hanck went over and knocked on the door without getting an answer. He went in and found the old man lying on a sofa, drunk and sated. The stench was horrible. The old man had taken care of his needs right there on the floor or in the packaging that had previously held expensive foods.

He recognised Hanck, greeted him with a stupid grin. He realised what was up and made a slurred and incoherent attempt to explain something. They had been 'sent fleeing' and someone was 'out there' and 'the girl . . .'

'Yes?' said Hanck. 'What about her?'

The old man fell silent, closed his eyes, seemed to have dozed off with a worried expression. Hanck tried to rouse him, but the old man refused to wake up. He lifted the man up and dragged him out into the rain, letting the water gush over him.

He came back to life. Hanck screamed, 'What about the girl?!' And the old man had looked at him with eyes that expressed sorrow and anger and impotence.

They had 'stomped the kid out of her . . .' She had bled for a while out in the field.

'Who?!' shrieked Hanck. 'Who did it?'

The old man merely shook his head, muttered something, and got up. Soaked through, he shuffled back into the cabin. Hanck followed.

'Was it berserkers?'

The old man shook his head. No, it was somebody else. 'Religious . . .' he had said and then dragged himself over to the sofa, trampling through his own shit, and fumbling for a glass jar of vodka.

That was as much as Hanck managed to get out of him. That was what he had to cling to. Small comfort.

But it was not something that he wanted to pass on to his son. The boy would find out soon enough what sort of world it was out there. And besides, there were schoolmates who were willing to show him. To Hanck's surprise Toby was accepted by them; he even enjoyed a certain respect for his peculiarities, perhaps mostly for his independence, his genuine lack of interest in the lessons that the school had to offer.

Like most parents, Hanck became accustomed to living with his uneasiness, the constant anxiety that something would go wrong, that his son would be left out and then be lured into futile endeavours to win the recognition of the other kids.

He was put to the test, and he passed. During playtime a bunch of bullies had come over and asked him bluntly: 'A beating or a pile-on?' Toby hadn't done anything. He didn't know these boys, but he knew that he'd been singled out and would never get away. Filled with the agony of a condemned man faced with the choice between decapitation and hanging, he had chosen 'A pile-on.'

It was a common exercise. It consisted of selecting some poor boy to lie down on the ground and then as many as possible would throw themselves into a pyramidlike pile on top of him while the shouts rang out: 'Pile on! Pile on! Pile on!'

He found himself lying on the cold, wet playground with the shouts echoing as kids came running. Eager little devils from near and far. They came rushing out of doors, climbing out of windows, crawling under the fence, out of the chimneys, down the drainpipes, from all points of the compass and like moles from out of the ground. Everyone wanted at all costs to pile on top of him.

It really only hurt in the beginning. As if by gentleman's agreement, he was allowed to stretch out on his stomach, and at first he felt sharp knees and elbows in his back. But after a while the weight became distributed more evenly, and then it just felt very hot and sweaty and noisy since everyone was shouting 'Pile on!' at the top of their lungs.

As Toby lay at the bottom of a pile of fifty or so boys, he discovered that it could have been worse. A beating was worse. He had made a good choice.

And he had to make one more decision that was perhaps even more important. Release came in the form of a furious burst from a whistle. It was the playground attendant who had arrived and was starting to sort through the pile. The weight grew lighter, one after another, until the heap was finally so sparse that fresh air could seep in through a thick haze of sweat and dirt and bad breath.

'Who started this?' asked the attendant. It was the victim, as usual, the boy who lay at the very bottom, who would now be tormented even further. Sometimes the question was answered, sometimes it wasn't. It was the victim's choice whether to point out the guilty parties or not.

Toby didn't say a word. He had learned the rules of the game.

Hanck's concern gradually diminished. But when the boy got a cold he would put his son to bed and forbid him to get up until he was well for at least a whole day. He sat at the boy's bedside and fed him chicken broth, cup after cup.

'This has helped people survive war and epidemics down through history,' he said.

As soon as chicken broth was available somewhere in the city he would go out and buy as much as he could find. But his son ate the broth with an expression that was wary, if not dubious. He actually enjoyed having a cold. Whenever he sneezed, an air of contentment would come over him.

He knew only a few kids who had a mamma and a pappa and siblings. Most lived alone with their mother. Or their father. A few had no idea where they came from. There was nothing strange about that.

Yet he could lie in bed, sneezing long and loud, and while the echo of his sneeze was still resounding between the walls, he would think of his family as whole and complete. It was as if he were sneezing forth his mother's presence.

Maybe that was how he happened to find the sneezing powder up on a shelf in the kitchen. From that pepper mill it wasn't far to the cooker.

There's always a period in every child's life when he wants at all costs to help with the cooking. And then the parents' patience is put to the test. The one who has the energy for it sees something positive in the child's wish to help. The one who is tired and pressed for time, and perhaps even hungry, sees something else: nothing but trouble. It requires stretching a little further, twisting about at odd angles, and risking a slight case of lumbago.

Hanck was sceptical at first but soon realised the advantages of the boy's interest. The raw materials were often very simple: pickled root vegetables, dried beans and sprouts that Hanck had taught himself to handle in the traditional way to make them edible. Everything always tasted the same.

Toby soon learned the basics, and unconcerned with the demands of tradition, he might toss anything into the pot, and then entirely new flavours would arise. After many failures that nevertheless had to be eaten, Hanck realised that he had actually been demoted to helper. His son was in charge. Toby didn't have a head for reading, he had to struggle through the Bible and the Koran, and he plodded through the basic rules of arithmetic and the history of the Great Raw Material War with the same anguish that once struck those who had fought in it.

On the other hand, the raw materials that lay on the worktop aroused quite a different sense of desire. The boy was a born chef. The last words that Hanck's mother had uttered were finally coming to pass.

For a period during his teenage years Toby belonged to a gang. It was unavoidable; young men couldn't make it alone. But it was a decent gang that committed no crimes worse than the petty theft of edible goods. They devoted most of their time to various games. This often led to long, drawn-out parties when the boys spent the night someplace, playing without stopping. It was a closed world that was largely inaccessible to outsiders, in which the nature of the game, along with the rules, were constantly changing.

Strictly speaking, that was his only act of rebellion. He preferred staying with his gang, rather than going along to visit the shopkeeper when they were occasionally invited to dinner. Toby and Saussyr no longer spent time together. The teenagers would sit in separate corners, sulking, sighing and uttering strange sounds. The prospects for a future marriage were dim; in their fathers' opinion, they didn't know what was best for them. One day when they did realise what was best, it might be too late.

At first Hanck had a hard time getting used to Toby's absence, but there was nothing to be done about it; all parents had to deal with the same thing. He listened to the organ. Sometimes that helped, sometimes it didn't. He felt stupid and overprotective. He thought he had every right to be stupid and overprotective. It was difficult.

During one prolonged power outage the gang was holed

up someplace, engrossed in a game. But since the entire city was dark, all the parents began to worry. Hanck sat in the light of a burning lantern, and the hours passed without a word from Toby. He tried to distract himself with all sorts of things, tried to dispel his nervousness, to rein it in, but without success. Finally he grew so impatient that he went out. It would be pointless to try to find his son, but he could at least talk to someone, such as the mother of one of Toby's friends who lived in the same neighbourhood.

The power came back on just as he was knocking at her door. She asked who it was, and he replied by giving his name. She opened the door, and he stood there squinting at the light, explaining why he was there. He felt more idiotic than he'd ever felt before.

But she didn't think he should feel that way. She invited him to come in, now that he was there anyway. They had become acquainted during the boys' school days, meeting at various functions, but had never become good friends. They had exchanged experiences in the way that people do when they have children the same age. A smile might be enough, or a rolling of the eyes.

It turned out that she was single. Hanck assumed that his marital status was just as apparent. They were about the same age, more or less healthy, and conscientious. All the essential prerequisites for something that Hanck had never actually given a thought to until now, when he found himself seated on a prickly sofa in her home, and they both agreed, rather proudly, that 'Boys will be boys . . . They always manage to find electricity somewhere . . .'

They both felt a sense of relief. At any rate, their loving concern for the children ended up being pushed aside.

A different mood took over. It might be called the magic from a chain of events. The electrical light that suddenly lit up the whole flat was immediately turned off because the lit candles seemed more appealing, more suitable.

Hanck was offered vodka. He gladly accepted a glass, and she kept him company, already halfway through the bottle. Good vodka. Excellent brand. He asked her how she'd got it, giving her the opportunity to incriminate her son's father, who was involved with 'transports'.

The more darkness that was cast upon the man, the more light was left over for Hanck. He learned that he 'wasn't like that at all', that she 'had noticed that the very first time' and that she often 'thought of him' because he 'seemed so healthy'.

Embarrassed, Hanck had confessed that he felt quite healthy. She said, 'I am too. Word of honour.'

Then they made love on the sofa, slightly drunk, fumbling a bit, but eagerly, like two timid and lonely people. Hanck was unsure about her and came in a gush on the sofa. She lay on the cushions with her eyes closed as he wiped up after himself.

She changed position, turned onto her side. He crawled in behind her. They lay there, breathing together for a while. Then he reached over her hip and cupped his hand over her knee. It felt like a little skull.

That position, with his hand cupped around warm flesh, made him remember when he had stuck his hand inside the warm incubator and for the first time touched his new-born son. It was more than a memory, it was a reliving of the event. He heard the sounds from the apparatus, footsteps on the filthy asphalt; he noticed the scent, the warm sweetness of the infant.

Everything recurred as clearly as if it had happened quite recently, the encounter that ended with him losing himself in those eyes, the boy's gaze that had signalled a new direction, an arrow shot into an utterly new sky.

It was just as trivial and unfathomable as what was happening on this worn sofa. The woman who felt his hand cupped over her knee had noticed that he was far away, that his thoughts were elsewhere, that he was filled with the presence of someone else.

And naturally that could be misunderstood. If he had only said something about it, their affair might have ended in another way. His life might have changed, they could have joined forces, shared each other's burdens, taken care of their boys together. He had nothing against her, after all, and if only she had heard: 'Just imagine that . . .' or: 'This reminds me of . . .', she would have undoubtedly been willing to interpret it correctly and say: 'I knew that you weren't like all the others.'

But he didn't say anything. He lay there on the sofa, caught up in his thoughts. The sofa's upholstery prickled his skin, it started to itch. He sat up and scratched his shoulder.

The woman could interpret his silent absence in only one way. She said, 'So it's just thanks and goodbye?'

She wanted more, but he couldn't do it. She did everything possible to get him in the right mood. Ardently. Almost aggressively.

When that didn't work, she switched to a softer approach. 'I know!' she said and turned on a receiver. A retro-channel with music 'the way it used to sound'. A robust and rhythmic music. 'Now this is fucking music,' she said. All the lyrics were about love. She had evidently heard them many times before because she knew a lot of the words by heart and bellowed along with the refrains: 'Love, love, love . . .'

That didn't put Hanck in the right mood either. 'We should have lived back then,' she said. Hanck objected, saying that things actually might have been just the opposite; maybe they had sung and written so much about love out of sheer longing, because it had been such a loveless time.

But she didn't want to hear that. Her expression made it quite clear that she found such comments tiresome.

'Want to turn on TomBola?' It was approaching midnight, and the gigantic woman was bound to be involved in some lengthy foreplay.

Hanck shook his head. He had never felt turned on by her.

'I know!' she said, and shouted a string of words at the monitor. It started showing old, renovated movies from that past era of love. Brief stories about encounters between men and women who, seemingly without much ado, found themselves engaged in long, drawn-out acts of explicit copulation. 'This has got to get you going!' Hanck heard.

When this stimulation had no effect either, she gave up. 'I was born in the wrong century,' she said. 'Did you see the equipment they had back then?'

Hanck ventured, 'I'm not sure that everyone was so well endowed.' His remark was received as sullen jealousy, and so Hanck got dressed and left.

On his way home he heard the prophet of doom chanting on the corner, as usual.

Back then he had taken approximately the same route home through the pleasure district as he did now, as he walked home from the shopkeeper's premises on this rainy day that had started off so great and got even better.

And it was undoubtedly the same preacher on the street corner who, in apocalyptic terms, was proclaiming that the end was near. His words fell largely on deaf ears. The pleasure-seekers who took his words to heart most likely calculated that they might as well party and carry on for all they were worth.

Hanck was loaded with money. The shopkeeper always paid cash for the machines, straight into his pocket.

In a shop window he saw a red knitted jumper with a turtleneck, the kind that Toby liked. He went in and bought it and had it wrapped up in unusually fancy cellophane. The jumper was guaranteed to be a hit; he knew that Toby would like it because he'd received similar ones before. The first time the shopkeeper had seen him wearing that type of sweater he said, 'Oh, a turtleneck!' Toby had never seen a turtle in his life, so the shopkeeper had drawn one on a piece of paper, and Gerlinde had taken out a soup ladle. The bowl of the ladle was made from the shell of a small turtle, trimmed with silver. The handle was ebony, with a ball of ivory at the end. It was an orgy of extinct materials.

Hanck made it home in good time for lunch. He placed

the package with the jumper on Toby's unmade bed, went out to the kitchen and prepared a simple powdered soup. As he ate, he heard the bells in three different churches strike twelve, one after the other, in the proper order.

In all the years that he'd lived there, he'd never ceased to be surprised by that order. He took it for granted that each church wanted to be heard, since the bells in other places had been taken down because the bronze was needed for other purposes. So functioning bells were rare, and it was preferable that they be allowed to strike without being disturbed by others. Perhaps it was a phenomenon that had started sometime in the past, to the annoyance of many, and then was rectified when some genius came up with the idea of a less synchronous proclaiming of the hour. However the current prevailing order had been decided was beyond Hanck's comprehension, but he assumed that it had resulted from deep conflicts.

He cleaned up after himself in the kitchen, washed the dishes and meticulously wiped down the worktop. Sometime in the afternoon the chef would come home, hopefully in a good mood, go straight to the kitchen with his food satchel and pull out one delicacy after another, just as he usually did after working at some particularly elegant party.

Then it was important for Hanck to organise his kitchen. The counters had to be shiny, the cooker clean and preferably rubbed with baby oil. Hanck tried to follow all the rules that his son had instituted, and was often royally rewarded.

A brilliant career had been predicted for Toby. Chefs were compared to great magicians and performers. Other artists struggled with their situations, the lack of materials and distribution, but none enjoyed the same status as chefs. To maintain a consistently high level of food preparation was a struggle against the elements and a capricious market. The access to raw materials fluctuated, ranging from minimal to virtually nil. The long tradition that had previously supported the culinary arts had been broken; the gluttony of previous times now existed only among criminals; what had once stood on every man's table were now exclusive, coveted objects that were auctioned off in premises kept under heavily armed guard.

The father's constant worry had diminished over time; he was aware of it, both inside and out, like an old faded undershirt that he wore with reluctance, yet it continued to linger. He preferred a cautious pride, an emotion that only the next generation would see defined and described in the great book. But Hanck knew precisely how it felt. He had experienced it, pure and clear, when Toby passed his final exam with the highest marks. Each student had to prepare a dish of his choice that would be judged by a panel of well-known kitchen chefs.

Toby had chosen to make a Consommé à la Royale, a relatively simple and unsophisticated dish, an audacious choice. Hanck took it as a personal compliment from his son. He'd been given a sample portion at home, reverently partaking of twenty-three tablespoons of this heavenly soup, and with misty eyes he had stared at his son's certificate with its stamped wax seal, printed on real paper with a watermark.

The chef had found immediate employment and now worked for an innkeeper in the archipelago, in a restaurant that Hanck himself had never visited. Reservations had to be made several months in advance.

'It's not your style, old man,' Toby had said. 'It's very luxurious.' He had described the innkeeper as temperamental and something of a drunk. But he had nine daughters.

Hanck had to make do with the leftovers. Toby brought home food that ordinary people hadn't even heard of before.

Fillets from animals that you saw only in imaginary pictures, or read about in stories. Shellfish and fish from secret seas. Vegetables from underground fields. Once he sneaked out half a bottle of wine that they had drunk with particular ceremony.

That was what Hanck could look forward to now. This time Toby had gone to the outer archipelago a week earlier to prepare an 'especially brilliant menu', as he said. That often meant that the leftovers would be more elegant than the guests.

The chiming of the church bells at three o'clock would not happen on that afternoon. The mechanism that made the bells chime was driven by electric current, and the entire electrical net in the central part of the city would short-circuit due to a local overload. But that was still a couple of hours off.

Hanck devoted himself to cleaning up his workshop, dusting off the shelves that were starting to look alarmingly bare. He had only a few machines left to inspect and sell. The inventory had lasted a long time. The machines that he had once bought in one lump purchase had provided for him and Toby for many years. His son was now able to stand on his own two feet, and Hanck would have to get by on whatever servicing and repairs might bring in. It was not a brilliant future; the machines were much too good and durable for that. But he wasn't worried.

His life was becoming marked by stronger and more contradictory emotions. Relief because the responsibility that he had assumed for the upbringing of his son could now be considered over. And regret, for the exact same reason. Pride and relief on the one hand, regret and melancholy on the other.

Prey to such conflicting emotions, he might suddenly pause for a moment somewhere in the flat and then suddenly find himself holding a tool in his hand, or a dust-rag, or a piece of clothing that belonged to his son which he had meant to hang on a hook or put away in a wardrobe. Right now he had paused with a smelly old cushion in his hand.

One afternoon Hanck was sitting alone in Apoteket, having a drink at a window table, with a view of the street. He saw Toby come walking from Vinterplatsen, slowly, seemingly aimless. He had stopped right outside the restaurant, and Hanck had the only sensible impulse – to tap on the glass and catch Toby's attention.

But just as he raised his hand towards the window to knock, he stopped himself, only a centimetre away from the thick pane. His impulse reined in, everything spontaneous and natural faded away to a fumbling at the air, lacking all impetus.

There was something in the boy's expression that made him hold back, something he had never seen before, at least not as clearly or distinctly. A lost, awkward uncertainty; a young person's view of the world, a total lack of what might be called 'a convincing manner'.

Toby was at home in those neighbourhoods, he wasn't lost in that sense of the word. It had to do with something that Hanck had perceived, something that touched him so deeply that he found it impossible to complete the impulse that had seemed so natural.

Toby had stood out there on the pavement a long time, and Hanck realised that the situation would only get more difficult to interpret the longer it lasted, if the boy should later discover his father behind the window, with a full view of the pavement outside.

The only thing Hanck wanted to do was to break this event, to get up from the table and go out to give his son a big, wordless hug, just to show that he was still there. Hanck did manage to get to his feet, with a sudden feeling of warmth in his breast from some sort of 'empathy'.

But when he went outside, his son was gone. The sense of loss he had seen in his son's eyes was now his own.

And that was often how things were lately. The only thing that could remedy the situation was some sort of stronger input.

He listened to the organ.

There were pauses, service pauses written into the composition, but the manner of interpreting and conveying the music by the twelve organists on duty had become the norm for how long a pause could last without losing the music. The longest pause had lasted for seven months and, according to those in the know, had been precisely indicated in the score. The twelve organists had executed the pause in accordance with the same playing schedule as usual, sitting on the bench and counting out beats, keeping the pause alive with their own heartbeats.

Hanck remembered well when the long pause was broken as a mighty tone was struck that was heard through the open church doors and in the broadcast over the whole city, leading to popular rejoicing, as if at a great declaration of peace.

He was soon lost in his thoughts, sitting there calmly, listening for the mighty tone when the bells of the nearby churches would chime three, one by one and in the proper order.

But there was no chiming at three that day.

Because it was then that the power went out. The broadcast fell silent, and the flat went dark. The sky was a leaden grey above the city, and the only sound was the pattering of raindrops against the windowpane.

At first Hanck was annoyed and irritated, but when he realised that the outage was going to last for a while, he became furious.

He had been sitting on the sofa for a while, in the dark,

in the silence, when there was a knock on the door. It couldn't be Toby; it was too early, and he had a key. Annoyed, and with adrenaline already coursing through his body, Hanck went out to the dark hall and opened the door. He saw two dark silhouettes on the landing, and the beam of a pocket torch that had just lit up his nameplate and was now aimed at the floor. At the edge of the beam of light he saw the leg of a pair of trousers. Lavender fabric.

If he had still been wrapped in the organ's magic movement of increasing anticipation, he would have been more defenceless and would have been brutally yanked back to reality. But right now he was more wary, already prepared for conflict, unpleasantness.

'Hanck Orn?' It was a Communicator's voice, weary and dull.

When Hanck replied affirmatively to the question and gave his personal code, the next question came: 'Are you the guardian of Toby Orn?'

Hanck of course said, 'Yes.'

Without changing his tone of voice, the Communicator said, as if he were rambling off some sort of litany, a formula that had long ago become hackneyed and in which only the individual's name ever varied: 'It is my duty to inform you that Toby Orn is dead. I'm sorry. There is no further information. May I ask you for a signature?'

The Hurricane Party

The boat out to the archipelago left from a terminal that had once been used for ferry routes to the countries in the east. The traffic was safeguarded by strict security controls. Each passenger had to go through a harshly lit sluice with armed guards who were more intent on inspecting permits and passes than tickets.

The channel eastward was traversed only by regular routes between the city and the outer archipelago. People who lived out on the islands were allowed free passage and were known to the guards. They greeted each other in a familiar fashion, and they rarely had to show any documentation. Others, occasional travellers, had to bring permits that were stamped with the date and time of their departure.

Hanck Orn stood in the queue and watched well-dressed people chatting with the guards who fawned and grinned a bit more than usual. Wealthy individuals had lived out on the islands in the archipelago since time immemorial, at first as seasonal visitors, later as permanent residents, when conditions in the city grew worse. Now they lived in enclosed, guarded reserves, in huge villas with their own climate controls. Gases from the silted-up coves were horrible, and at times toxic to breathe.

But now, during the rainy period, it was better. The channel and the coves were mud-filled, and the growth of algae and grass had stopped for the season.

Hanck tried to offer a friendly smile to the guard who took his documents. The same guard had just laughed and pounded the back of a gentleman with a grey ponytail. Perhaps one of the more well-to-do set, with whom it would be wise to stay on good terms. The guard's grin changed to a stiff, arrogant expression as soon as he turned to Hanck, an unknown traveller with a permit that was much too fresh.

Two days earlier Hanck had visited the public office that processed permits. He had taken along a large banknote in one pocket and a firearm in the other. If any obstacles should arise, he would first try the banknote, but if the bribe didn't work, and his prospects of ever getting the permit seemed slim or non-existent (such news was sometimes handed out quite arbitrarily), then he was going to blow off the head of every single person in that public office. He had enough ammunition for the whole staff. No one would be exempt. He knew precisely how those sorts of civil servants reacted, how they thought, how they would seek shelter.

He'd been one of them himself, and just as unimaginative, an equally faithful protector of laws and ordinances. So he knew exactly how the woman with the blue wig, whose job description concerned the importance of maintaining the proper level of humidity in the ink pads and sponge cups, would react at the first shot. She would give a start, throw herself to the floor behind an old metal filing cabinet, and in this immediately life-threatening situation, she would be forced to stretch her imagination so far that she would take on the same colour and shape of that cabinet.

The thin-haired younger man next to her would also end up on the floor, but he would start to crawl and slither over to the corridor that led to the inner offices, a confusing labyrinth where he would be swallowed up and turn himself into a rejection slip.

The man at the counter window in front of Hanck would never need to denigrate himself in that way. He would simply – suddenly, like a receipt for his own misuse of power – feel an honourable old projectile, nine millimetres in diameter, tear through the convolutions of his brain and perhaps rip a hole in the back of his neck where – robbed of all force by that thick skull – it would slip out and settle into the sweaty crease between his neck and his shirt collar. Maybe that would be his last thought, the very last reflection of a soon-to-be-extinguished brain: 'I've got a tick on my neck, help, I've got a tick!'

But that was not a good plan. Hanck was a poor shot; he didn't know whether he could hit anything even at arm's length. Yet he still needed to be prepared that it might happen, at any time, at any place. That a connection might arise, a logical link, a clear and distinct pattern in which this gun and its use made up a very necessary consequence. It might happen anywhere at all, in any sort of context, and he would have to act accordingly, be prepared, have the gun to hand.

So he'd been carrying the weapon in his pocket for several days, even at home, inside his flat, behind three locks and a bolted wrought-iron gate. Not because he was expecting any sort of attack or assault. He didn't know if he even had any enemies; the fact that he was feeling hostile didn't mean that he had enemies. But he was on the alert. All of his perceptions were heightened. He thought he could hear conversations that were taking place at a great distance, could see what was going on behind his back, and could sense smells, waves of heat from living creatures in the most desolate of places.

Whoever looked at him had no idea about any of this. The man who processed his application saw a completely ordinary, grey citizen who had business in the outer archipelago. There was no reason to investigate the matter further. The application was approved and furnished with a valid stamp.

Where that stamp would lead him, Hanck had no idea. He was fumbling his way forward, at the mercy of instincts and whims, tormented and largely confused, but at times clear-headed and capable of thinking rationally.

At such a moment he had rung his son's boss, the innkeeper out in the archipelago, to straighten out what had to be a misunderstanding. Already annoyed by the power outage and the silenced organ, Hanck had done his duty as a citizen and signed the soiled piece of paper that the Communicator had held out, thereby confirming that he had received the news which must have been erroneous yet still required a receipt.

It had even occurred to him that he was actually unique in receiving an incorrect message from these grave-diggers.

The innkeeper had refused to pick up; the phone sometimes produced a busy signal, sometimes emitted long ringtones that went unanswered. Hanck waited, listening to it ring and ring. He kept trying for nearly an hour until a woman's voice from the outer archipelago finally answered.

Hanck explained what he wanted, calmly and matter-of-factly, saying that he was the father of Toby who worked out there as a chef. He wanted to speak to his son; the boy should have come home long ago, and Hanck was starting to get a bit worried since he hadn't heard from him; his son usually rang. He asked, calmly and politely, whether anyone out there knew what had happened.

'Just a minute . . .' said the woman's voice. Hanck heard a clattering sound, as if the phone had been placed on its side. In the background he heard voices, annoyed voices, harsh tones.

This went on for a quite a while, and then the receiver was evidently picked up by the innkeeper himself. 'Hello?' It was a rough voice. Hanck repeated what he had previously said, adding that he'd received a confusing visit from a couple of Communicators. He intimated, sounding strangely unconcerned, that the innkeeper might be able to straighten out this misunderstanding.

'Unfortunately . . .' he heard, 'it's correct.'

'What?' said Hanck. 'What's correct?'

'That he's dead,' said the innkeeper.

'Who?' said Hanck.

'Toby. Didn't you say that he was your son?'

'Yes, I did,' said Hanck. 'He is . . . he's my son.'

'He just dropped dead.'

'What do you mean?' said Hanck. 'Dropped dead?'

'Maybe it was his heart,' he heard. 'He worked hard.'

When Hanck didn't reply, the innkeeper had time to collect himself. He went on, unchallenged. 'He was a fine lad. Everyone applauded. The best chef I've had in years . . .'

Hanck apprehended these remarks the way he might receive news about some total stranger. 'What do you mean he dropped dead?' he said at last. 'He's twenty years old and perfectly healthy.'

'Unfortunately,' said the innkeeper, 'that's all I have to say. Once again, I'm very sorry.'

'I don't give a damn about that,' said Hanck. 'Where is he?'

The innkeeper removed the receiver from his ear, and Hanck heard him confer with someone else. 'He's no longer here. They usually . . .' He caught himself, perhaps so as not to say too much. 'They took him away.'

'Who?'

'The guests.' The innkeeper may have been drunk, because he said, 'We don't usually . . .' but was cut off, possibly because someone had kicked him in the shin. He said, 'Ow, what the hell . . . ?!'

Hanck said, 'What guests?'

'Unfortunately,' the innkeeper repeated, 'we can't give out that information.'

'Was it someone from the Clan?'

Now the innkeeper started coughing. Long, solid, racking coughs that came from deep inside. 'Sorry,' he managed to gasp. 'You'll have to excuse me.'

Hanck heard the man in the outer archipelago coughing, and he had time to think, to pull himself together, to try and understand something that he knew he never would.

The coughing into the receiver stopped. Hanck thought he could hear heavy panting. It was probably the innkeeper listening.

'I don't know what you're up to out there,' said Hanck. 'But I intend to find out.'

The innkeeper understood. He said, 'If I were you, I'd let it be.' In the midst of all the confusion, Hanck perceived something that resembled genuinely good intentions. 'Let it be.'

'Like hell I will.'

The innkeeper took a deep breath. He was forced to change his tone. 'You're a little shit. You're not going to get anywhere.'

'You know that, do you?'

'Believe me, I know.' The coughing had stopped. He sounded quite convincing.

'So someone from the Clan was out there?'

'No,' said the innkeeper. He was silent for a moment, considering what to say, and finally decided that an admission might make the tormented and confused father give in. 'No,' he repeated. 'It was the entire Clan.'

He was awakened, whether it was in the middle of the day or the middle of the night made no difference, by the sound of a key turning in the lock of the front door. It was a very distinct sound. He had waited for it so many times before, after he had gone to bed even though Toby hadn't yet come home. Sleeping uneasily, waking at the smallest sound and never falling asleep properly until he heard that sound of the key in the door, footsteps, the sound of wet outer garments being tossed in a heap.

He would lie there in a sort of torpor and hear that longed-for sound, and come a bit more awake and sit up on the edge of the bed. Still dazed with sleep, he would stagger out to the hall, convinced that the nightmare was about to be over – then he would come to his senses in front of a locked front door, standing alone in the hall, forced to acknowledge that he had only been dreaming.

Unable to sleep, he might go out in the middle of the night, aimlessly searching. He might meet a gang of boys on the street, and after they'd gone past, he'd suddenly think that Toby was among them.

He would stop, turn around, and shout, 'Toby?!' No one reacted, no one turned around. But boys were often ashamed of their fathers. He was forced to run after them, pass them, and then turn around to confront them once again to make sure.

This happened several times. Occasionally he might hear, 'Get the hell out of here, you fucking homo!'

After a few days he understood only one thing: shock.

It was as if the word had regained its original meaning. It had been worn out for so long, stripped away by much too frequent use in an epoch of alarms, shrieking horns and flashing lights that indicated an uninterrupted increase in destruction: deserts expanding, glaciers shrinking, forests dying, animals becoming extinct, clouds of gas piling up over entire continents, ozone holes making the sun deadly, multi-resistant bacteria and pandemics eradicating entire nations.

Then the alarms had finally fallen silent, the temperature and humidity had ceased to rise, reached a peak, stopped and stayed there.

The time of shocks was over. A cautious restoration began. The public was admonished: 'Don't rock the boat!'

No one was allowed to touch a button, every single lever was allowed to stay where it was. The world held its breath. The globe hibernated, its pulse was low, its respiration barely noticeable.

People stayed indoors when the sun shone, transport took place in the night, queues formed and became permanent, a way of life. At least they offered some sense of direction.

Industries in isolated locations, as if sleepwalking, ground out their products, vital goods according to a priority list that had taken an entire generation to negotiate and another to implement. The availability of anything beyond life-sustaining articles was erratic and unreliable. Suddenly supplies would be announced in some suburb, and the whole city would be on its feet to go out there and queue up. The City Under the Roof produced a surplus that was sold off in draughty hangars.

Those were muted days in a muted time. But the nights were different. The relentless sun was gone, the times seemed to have entered into a general state of emergency, a concept which from the start had meant that old laws and ordinances were cast aside, that the order of the day emanated from provisional agencies, crisis commands of military men and scientists, more or less haphazardly put together, regimes that in turn became corrupted and undermined and lost their power, just as their states of emergency and curfews did, and consequently the night became an exception unto itself, the darkness a part of an ungovernable eternity, as if untouched and unsullied in its pure blackness, an empty space that could be filled with anything at all, especially the desperation that always chose to persevere under its shroud.

It was the same as when the nights offered amnesty to the lawless and the lovers, as well as their slanderers, those doomsday prophets who stood on the street corners offering salvation from eternal damnation. They were always standing there. You could ask them to watch a child while you had a drink at the nearest brothel.

They never let up. When one of the old guys fell to the ground dead and a lavender delivery van transported him away, the spot would be vacant for only a brief time before it was occupied again. A new voice, younger and more powerful, would take up where the old one had left off. All the phases of hell would be described with new enthusiasm.

Hanck had seen and heard them all his life; their threats and promises were part of the daily roar of the city, but they had always been drowned out by others. He had perceived other signals that were stronger, had other things on his mind, just like most people. But now, cast into this darkness, he couldn't defend himself. He thought that they were speaking to him, directly to him.

Like the prostitutes, little Asian girls who pulled him into a doorway and said, 'Want some lucky, lucky mister?' He had to forcefully tear himself away, only to leap right into the arms of another type: an obese woman with giant udders under an angora jumper who drew him into a soft, moist embrace and said, 'That's right, come to mamma . . .'

Like the receivers of stolen goods who unabashedly lined up their wares on a bar counter – a few pieces of jewellery, a pile of gold teeth, tools, a container of paint – and then held a quick auction before a gathering of ordinary, decent citizens who were setting up house or courting someone in the old-fashioned way, exhibiting some form of decorum in broad daylight, with gear purchased in the lawless dark.

Like the smouldering fire-pits in the middle of the street where food was prepared from ingredients of unknown origin, that at times smelled familiar, at times foreign, that required strong chemicals to make them edible, noxious liquids that billowed out of the pit where only the tops of the heads were visible of the bowed, sweaty cooks who were so quick with their knives that no one managed to see what it was they were carving.

Like the begging women and children, filthy, deformed, who had deliberately maimed themselves in the hope of arousing some ancient residue of sympathy, an expression of a naïveté that denied everything that humanity had endured, almost touching in its hopefulness. Hanck would regard the children dispassionately, as if in this new life he had reclaimed something of his insurance-man distrust towards everything that was meant to arouse the emotions, as if his two decades as a father to his own child had been merely a parenthesis, yet another exception.

Like the chemical dealers, those barefoot pharmacists with substances for every possible purpose. In black briefcases with well-oiled locks that soundlessly opened with minutely practised manipulations and then revealed a whole world, divided into two parts, with rows of jars filled with pills in all the colours of the rainbow, pills for trips to all points of the compass, as well as those that would arise in the future, dimensions of existence that were constantly explored and discovered by smiling consumers, even if it was the last discovery they ever made. Hanck had supplied himself with enough substances for so many long trips that he never needed to worry about coming home again.

Because the denial phase was over. All that remained of it were fragments of a conversation that he muttered like a mantra, sometimes loudly and audibly into the air, directed at whoever happened to be in front of him.

A smugly grinning cook in a pit might hear: 'You're a little shit. You'll never get anywhere!'

A completely uncomprehending girl with her hand jammed into his crotch might hear: 'If I were you, I wouldn't do that!'

And a crook who, with astonishing dexterity, unrolled a piece of cloth with little pockets for stolen cutlery might be told: 'It was the entire Clan. The entire Clan!'

Hanck became a new figure in the nightly street scene. He had lived a conscientious life that had come to a brutal end and was plunged into a dense darkness. Day and night had become reversed. After days of artificially induced sleep, a sleep that was anything but restful and was brought on by chemicals, he would head out for the pleasure district, where he quickly won a reputation for being a confused and unpredictable person. He encountered the same scepticism that he showed towards others. He was aware that in the eyes of other people he belonged to the most desperate of the lot, those who had no sensible reason for being there, those who neither earned money nor spent any.

He devoted himself to a different type of bargaining. He had passed through the period of shock and denial. Moments of clarity and insight alternated with periods of great confusion. He tried to persuade himself that his son was away, but this was countered by an equally strong belief that it would be possible to win him back, to set up some sort of business connection, pay a price and regain the life that had been wasted. And what was needed for that was funding, a good deal of money, but above all a gun.

There were still a few machines on the shelves in his workshop. Hanck devoted several alert hours to servicing and inspecting them so that he ended up with two completely functioning machines. He could sell them and use the money to buy a weapon. In his mind he pictured a handgun, a pistol.

But he knew very little about the matter. Of course he could approach any thief or pimp or gang member. He saw them everywhere. But he didn't trust any of them.

The shopkeeper shared his grief. He was the one who uttered that very word: 'Grief.' Hanck didn't think of himself as grieving. A dignified, quiet grief was foreign to him, exotic, enticing, like some distant travel destination. He wasn't ready for that yet.

'My whole life has gone dark,' he said now as he sat in the shopkeeper's premises. The family had gathered around the table in the shop's inner sanctum – the owner, his wife and their red-haired daughter. They were all grieving, they even wore mourning bands, as one last obsolete tribute to the 'marvellous boy'.

'What can we do for you, Hanck?' When no answer came, they repeated the question over and over. 'What can we do for you, Hanck?'

He was inconsolable and difficult to reach. The only words he could muster were about his life going dark. He said it in the same tone of voice each time, almost bombastically and yet at the same time with astonishment. As if each time were the first.

It made the shopkeeper and his family think that his mind had also gone dark. So when he finally asked for one thing, a gun, a firearm, the shopkeeper was unwilling to offer his services. A gun should not be placed in the hands of a person with such a clouded mind. But when Hanck, suddenly clear and lucid and like his old self, threatened to leave with his machines and dispose of them elsewhere, the shopkeeper had to relent. He promised to see what he could do.

It took less than an hour to procure a firearm, 'a venerable old revolver' with the appropriate ammunition. The provenance of the gun was unknown, and Hanck was advised to test-fire it, regardless of what he planned to use it for.

'I don't know,' he said. 'I just want it. So I can mourn.' Even though this was an incomprehensible statement, no one in their world had any right to question it.

So he boarded the boat, which after a three-hour trip and a few dozen stops at docks along the route, would put in at the islet where the inn was located. He was prepared, revved up. He had test-fired the gun as the shopkeeper had advised him to do. The only place he was able to find that was sufficiently isolated for such an exercise was the remote, windblown field.

He went out there in the pouring rain and discovered that the old man's decrepit cabin was now abandoned as well. The old man must have finally passed away, having eaten or drunk himself to death. After the lavender-clad men had done their job, vandals, hooligans and berserkers had been there and emptied the shack. There was nothing left; the doors and windows were gone, the floor torn up. Even the empty vodka jars were gone.

Hanck loaded the revolver with two bullets. He held the gun with both hands and aimed at a reddish-brown spot on the wall. He was four paces away. He fired. The recoil was less forceful than he'd expected. He missed the target but was close enough. He fired another shot, this time using only one hand. He didn't hit the centre of the spot this time either, but he was satisfied. The gun worked. He was able to fire a shot, kill, injure, frighten. That was the only thing that mattered.

The boat ploughed through the muddy channel along the strip of land, past the bare cliffs, the rocky hills with crevices where stately old merchant villas had once stood, summer-time diversions for those who had been rich long ago. Glass verandas, towers, huge greenhouses in sun-scorched gardens. Many of the houses were still covered with decorations, jigsawed trim and borders, a style that was called ginger-bread. It merely looked like curlicues to the uninitiated, but those who were more knowledgeable recognised the shapes from artful patterns on rune stones from the Viking era. The old merchants had boasted of this heritage, a pre-Christian inheritance from the great saga age, those long-ago days when people offered sacrifices to the gods who granted ample harvests, fertility in marriage, good fortune in battle, and cures for disease. The occupants had sat in the shadows of their own trees, refreshing themselves with ice-cold punch and dreaming of a more carefree brutality.

At each dock someone got off; no one got on. There were fewer and fewer passengers on board. By the time the last bay was traversed, surrounded by low skerries polished shiny by the sea and naked like the gleaming backs of petrified prehistoric animals, Hanck was alone on board.

The inn stood on a windswept skerry in the outer archipelago, with a cluster of houses that had huddled in the wind since time immemorial, the haunts of fishermen, seamen and smugglers; later the meeting place for lusty pirates, who eventually, during the most brilliant of eras, came under the protection of the king.

Big black clouds passed, heading east. It started to rain as soon as Hanck stepped onto the dock. The boat turned round, stopping only as long as necessary. It would soon be dark, and lights were already burning in a number of hovels on the cliffs across from the dock.

He had seen her from far off, while they were still out in the bay — a woman standing at the very end of the dock, gazing out at the boat, as if she were waiting for someone. But Hanck was the only one left on board, aside from the captain and the deck-hand who put out the gangway.

Hanck stood on the foredeck as the boat approached the dock. He met the woman's eyes. She smiled at him, a radiant smile, as if he were expected, eagerly awaited.

As soon as he stepped off the gangway and the rain started falling, she came towards him, excited and impatient.

'It's you!' she said. 'You can't fool me!'

She was young, perhaps around twenty-five, dressed in a cape with a hood. Her bare legs were stuck inside a pair of rough boots as if she had flung on her clothes in great haste.

Her hair was covered with blood.

She threw her arms around him. Hanck pulled himself free, took a step back on the dock, and said, 'I'm sorry, but I think you've made a mistake.'

But the young woman opened her eyes wide and said to him, 'So what are you calling yourself today?'

Hanck didn't want to mention his name. He said, 'I'm just a guest.'

'I've hidden away all the fly-swatters for your sake. You've crept over me all those nights. You've licked at me.'

Hanck didn't know what to say. If he'd been expecting any kind of reception, it was something quite different from this. The young woman seemed under the influence of something, even more confused than he was, and he didn't want to tangle with her unnecessarily.

'You must think that I'm someone else,' he said.

'Stop it,' she said. All suspicion was gone; she was convinced that Hanck was the right person, the one she was waiting for. She moved close to him again, took his hand and slipped it inside her cape. 'Feel . . .' she said. 'I don't have anything on underneath. It's cold.'

— 139 —

Hanck pulled his hand out, drew back, making a wide arc around her, trying to head in another direction. 'I'm sorry,' he said. 'I'm just a guest here. You must be waiting for someone else.'

He took a few steps along the path up from the dock and promptly encountered two other women who had come from the village. They were a little older than the woman with the bloody hair, and more properly dressed.

'Don't think you can fool me!'

One of the other women stopped, turned to face Hanck, and said, 'Is she being difficult?'

Hanck shrugged his shoulders.

'She's a bit confused,' he was told.

'You fucking goat!' screamed the woman with the bloody hair. 'Cunt-fly!'

Hanck turned around just in time to see her receive a punch in the mouth. 'That's not something we say to strangers!'

'Can't you see?!' shrieked the confused woman. She refused to be hushed. 'Can't you see him?!'

The two other woman cast a quick glance at Hanck and managed to give him a conciliatory smile.

'Maybe we should throw you in,' said one of the woman. 'Is that what you want? Do you want us to throw you in?'

'I've had him in my crotch all week!'

'We're going to have to throw you in!'

One of the two level-headed women turned towards Hanck and, perhaps in a show of friendliness, tried to include him. 'Or what do you think?'

'About what?' said Hanck.

'See for yourself,' she said then and turned back to the confused woman. 'You think it's him? He would have done it himself; he would have thrown you off the dock and laughed.' She turned to face Hanck again. 'And who are you?'

'I'm just a guest,' said Hanck.

'Have you booked a room?'

Hanck shook his head. 'No,' he said. 'I was thinking of staying only one night.' He let his gaze sweep over the bay where the boat was heading for home. 'Maybe two.'

'There are rooms at the inn,' said the woman. 'Just keep following the path and you'll find it. We need to take care of our sister.'

Hanck nodded his thanks for the information. He assumed that the three women on the dock represented a third of the innkeeper's nine daughters. Toby hadn't said much about them, but the little he had mentioned made it sound as if they were quite wild.

Hanck headed up the rocks and ended up walking among the houses when the path turned into a lane. The inn was in the middle of the village; it was the biggest building on the island. It stood on an ancient site and had been rebuilt and expanded at various times and in various styles.

Behind the front desk in the lobby stood yet another sister. She wore a name badge: Kolga. Hanck greeted her and said, 'I was told by a woman down on the dock . . .'

This sister seemed to be of a different disposition, and she wasn't at all sure that they had an available room. She would have to look into the matter very carefully. With a worried expression she typed on a machine and double-checked in an analogue ledger.

Hanck had the impression that she was just play-acting, or that she wanted to demonstrate something. The lobby was quiet and deserted, he couldn't hear a sound from anywhere, there wasn't a single person in sight. He thought it possible that he was the only guest; it was an ordinary weekday in the middle of the rainy season.

Finally the woman was able to tell him that they actually

did have a room. With a view. She asked him how long he was planning to stay.

'Just one night,' he said. 'Maybe two.'

She asked him how he would like to pay. He said that he could pay cash, in advance. She gave him a pleased smile in reply, but it was only fleeting because she started asking him for personal information. Hanck lied about absolutely everything, and he wasn't particularly surprised when the machine accepted all the details. It should have reacted, realised that the information was false. But there were no objections. Hanck had the feeling that the machine wasn't even hooked up, and he thought he had seen through this Kolga. It gave him a refreshing advantage as her questions got more and more intrusive.

She asked him, in a cold and businesslike manner, about the state of his health.

Hanck replied, 'It's good, thanks.'

He received a doubtful look since he had answered so freely. The woman at the front desk clearly felt that he owed her an explanation. 'It's for our treatments,' she informed him.

'I'm not sure that I want any,' said Hanck.

'You don't?'

'I'm just here to rest.'

'A good treatment can be very restful.'

'I'm sure that's true,' said Hanck. 'But maybe we could just leave that question open for now.'

'By all means,' she said.

Hanck's relative lack of interest in such services was noted in the machine, and he immediately regretted his decision because it might seem odd and draw attention to himself. He said, 'But if it's included in the price . . .'

The woman named Kolga reacted to his remark just as he'd hoped. Her face lit up, instantly erasing all doubt.

He didn't care for her. On his way up to the room he decided that she was a liar and that he couldn't expect to get any worthwhile information from her.

The room was satisfactory. The carpet covered the whole floor, the bed was soft and wide and made up with sturdy sheets. The wardrobe had hangers, and Hanck hung up his clothes, the best that he owned. In the bathroom there were several towels and a big new bar of soap. He set down his toiletry case made of genuine animal leather which he'd once received as a Christmas present from the shopkeeper. It opened by means of an ingenious lock and had room for hygienic articles and pockets for a large assortment of pills.

The view was exceptional: twilight over a leaden grey bay, the silhouettes of black islets and skerries in the outer archipelago. And beyond that the sea began.

On the wall was a viewing screen that was voice-activated. Hanck said, 'TomBola.' The screen blinked on, and he saw the gigantic woman eating a stuffed baguette as she read the day's story. As bread crumbs and big scraps of something that looked like meat dribbled over her enormous bosom, she read with great feeling a newly written installment about Jesus. Hanck said 'off' and the screen went dark and silent again.

There was a brochure with pictures of various rooms at the inn: the bar, the restaurant, the breakfast room and other facilities for various kinds of recreation. There was a beautiful library. And room service. 'Our chefs are at your disposal around the clock.' There were examples of what they could provide. Toby was in the picture.

Hanck put down the brochure with shaking hands. He was overcome with rage. He clenched his jaw so tight that his teeth were about to crack. Blood vessels burst, everything went fuzzy before his eyes. He began to flail his arms blindly, lashing out at whatever he could find until his knuckles split open and he became aware of the pain.

He came to his senses and found himself kneeling in the middle of the room, his knuckles stinging and bleeding. He looked around. There was blood everywhere, but nothing was broken.

He held still for a moment to calm himself down, felt his breathing become more regular, listened for any sounds, whether anyone had heard anything. But it was quiet, dead quiet.

He got out an undershirt, soaked it in water, and wiped off the bloodstains on the walls and furniture. When all traces had been cleaned up he wrapped the wet shirt around his right fist and sat down on the edge of the bed, exhausted.

He wept. He just let the tears come, gushing out of him. He sobbed, bawled, blew his nose on the wet undershirt.

He stayed sitting there until the weeping stopped, leaving him with a tremendous, warm sense of calm.

He realised that he was lucky this had happened while he was alone in his room, that no one needed to see this man who was suddenly so beside himself with anger, a furious, unrestrained anger. Yet it had erupted there when he was all alone, maybe precisely because it was no longer unrestrained. Maybe he was in the process of learning to control it, releasing it only in seclusion. It was not intended for just anybody.

He felt quite calm, but he took a pill just to be sure. An 'Autobahn' that should keep him on an even keel for the next few hours.

A little while later he went down to the bar, having dressed for the evening, with his tender, swollen right hand stuck in the pocket where he had put the revolver.

The bar was empty. He climbed onto a high-legged stool, noticing the smell from an old drain or from rotting plants. He wasn't sure which.

'A drain,' he heard behind his back. 'In case you were wondering.'

Hanck turned round. Here was yet another sister, wearing a sealskin cap and a gown that glittered like fish scales.

'Bora, that's me!' Moving in an amusing, almost frantic manner, she took up position behind the bar. 'It's the same thing every year. You should smell me instead. Try it . . .' She leaned across the counter so that Hanck could take a sniff. He took a deep breath and brushed the tip of his nose against her cheek. She smelled good, spicy. Presumably some exclusive perfume.

'Nice,' he said.

'You think?' she said. 'Don't come and tell me that you recognise it.' That wasn't what he meant. 'Special delivery . . .'

'Does that go for the vodka too?' he asked.

'That depends on how much you want to pay.'

'That depends on what I get.'

'It's shit. All of it,' she said. 'It's the ice that's costly. Do you want the two-thousand, four-thousand, or six-thousand-year-old kind?'

'The two will be fine.'

'Coming right up.' With exaggerated care she poured him a glass of vodka. From one of the three cabinets glittering with gold she solemnly lifted out an ice cube, using a pair of tongs. A harsh chill billowed out from the cabinet. She was wrapped in a frosty vapour and struck a comical pose.

She served his drink, leaned over the counter, and said in a much lower and deeper voice, 'So you just happened to drop by . . . travelling over Yme's blood, the briny sea and the haunter of the gods . . .'

Hanck felt his face tighten. He heard someone laugh. It wasn't Bora, that peculiar person behind the bar. He glanced in the mirror behind the bottles. He saw himself. He was the one who was laughing.

'Oh, oh, oh . . .' She clapped her hand to her mouth and opened her eyes wide. 'I certainly think that, er . . . I'm afraid there's been a slight mistake.' She suddenly looked seriously worried. 'Did I open that cabinet over there?'

'No,' said Hanck. 'The one on the right.'

'Shit,' she said. 'That's the expensive one.'

At that moment resolute footsteps could be heard approaching across the stone floor in the next room. It was Kolga, the cold, hard woman from the front desk. 'What are you doing here?' She went around the counter to take her sister's place. 'You're not supposed to be here! You're supposed to be cleaning up!'

'I just . . .'

'Which kind of ice did you take out?'

'The kind he asked for.'

'So what kind did he order?'

Hanck made a quick decision. 'The cheap kind, on the left.'

Kolga gave him a malicious look. She hadn't asked him.

But she accepted his explanation. 'Get out of here,' she said to Bora. 'You have to clean up the staff quarters.'

The reprimanded woman in the sealskin cap gave Hanck a strained smile and said, 'That's life.' And then she left.

'I apologise,' said the cold woman. 'She's a bit . . .' She touched her temple with her index finger, moving a long, dark red fingernail in a circle. The nails were new. She had definitely not had them on before. Hanck hadn't seen such long, dark red fingernails in a very long time.

But he had no intention of admitting such a weakness to this particular woman, since he had decided not to like her. 'We would like to apologise,' she said, 'for what happened down at the dock.'

'That's okay,' said Hanck.

'She's also a bit . . .' A long, painted nail circled at her temple again.

'Are you related?' asked Hanck, feigning ignorance.

'Sisters,' said Kolga. 'Nine of us. But only two are . . .' She didn't know what to say. Hanck waited. She said, 'You understand . . .'

Hanck nodded. 'Broken hearts.'

She gave him a look as if he had touched on something sensitive, or something that was best kept under wraps. She said, 'Yes, something like that.' She pretended to take stock of the shelves, turning bottles so that the labels were visible, wiping off the counter which was already perfectly polished. 'Apropos that topic,' she said, 'have you decided . . . what you would like this evening?'

Hanck was expecting this. He calmly emptied his glass. 'Not yet,' he said. And then he added, just to provoke her, 'She has a nice perfume, your sister.'

Kolga heard him but chose to ignore the remark. She gave him a strained smile and asked if he'd like another drink.

He declined and said that he was going to take a walk before dinner.

She asked if he'd like to take a lantern along.

He said that he could see fine in the dark.

He went up to his room to get his hat and overcoat, feeling a bit deflated. He took another pill that was compatible with the previous one but this one would speed him up.

It was dark outside, very cold. He lost all desire to take a long walk and decided just to take a stroll around the property. He made it only halfway round because as he passed one long and narrow wing he saw Bora come out of a door. She was wearing overalls.

'What are you doing here?' she said.

Hanck was about to say something like 'taking a walk' or 'getting some fresh air' when he realised that she was just imitating her stern sister. So instead he ended up mustering a smile of sorts.

'Thanks. For what you said about the ice cubes,' she told him.

'It was nothing,' he said. 'She seems rather stern, your sister.'

'The worst of the lot,' she said. 'She thinks that she can order everybody around as she pleases just because father is on a binge.'

'I'm sorry to hear that,' said Hanck.

'Everything is going to hell.'

'What do you mean?' The wind was blowing hard, and he noticed that she was cold. Maybe she wanted to go back inside and continue with whatever she was doing. 'Where are the staff?' he said, to change the subject.

'They're off,' she said. 'Those who haven't quit, that is.'

'Quit for the season?'

'Quit for good,' she said. 'Isn't it all over town by now?'

'What?' asked Hanck. 'All I've heard is that this is supposed to be a luxurious place.'

'That was before,' she said. 'I'm freezing.'

She went back inside, and Hanck got the impression that she wanted him to follow.

'But the chefs are still here, aren't they?' he said.

'Nobody's still here,' she said. 'So we have to clean and cook and make the beds and put up with people that you wouldn't want to touch with a ten-foot pole.' She stopped herself and again said, 'Oh, oh, oh . . .' She had probably revealed too much; she began fluttering her eyelashes, put her hand to her forehead. 'But you don't need to worry. My sisters . . . They know how to cook. I can promise you that.'

'I'm sure they do,' he said. 'But why doesn't anyone want to work here?' He tried to sound suitably concerned.

'I thought the whole city would be talking about it,' she said. 'But obviously they've clamped a lid on the situation.'

'I haven't heard anything,' said Hanck. And that was largely the truth. He had heard so little that he had been forced to come out here to find out more. 'I'm sorry about that.'

'About what?' she said.

'What you said,' he replied. 'About putting up with people . . .'

'I don't want to put up with anything,' she said.

'So don't.'

'They say that I have to, and if I refuse, they get mad and yell at me. Did she tell you that I was crazy?'

'Something like that,' said Hanck.

'Did she really?'

'Yes,' he said.

'Don't believe her.'

'I don't,' he said. 'You don't seem the least bit crazy.'

But she peered at him with suspicion, shaking her head. 'You're just sweet-talking me because you want me.'

'Not at all,' he said.

'I can see it a mile away.'

'What do you mean?'

'I can see you checking.'

'Checking what?' he said. 'You?'

'All around,' she said. 'To see if there's anyone here. Because you don't know whether you dare . . .'

Hanck looked at her. She was quite serious. Maybe her sisters were right when it came to her state of mind. There was nothing wrong with her observations in and of themselves, but her conclusions were way off the mark.

'I'm sorry,' he said. 'I should go.'

'Just look around you!' she said. 'Nobody's here. Not a soul in the whole building. There's no one around to hear me scream.'

'Is that what you're going to do?' he said. 'Scream?'

'Maybe,' she said. 'Maybe not.'

The pill that Hanck had taken was having an effect. Things were happening fast now. Her misunderstanding offered an opportunity. 'So you have nothing against it if I . . .' and here he deliberately paused, '. . . have a look around?'

'You don't believe me?' she said. 'Go ahead, take a good look. I'll stay right here. I'm not going to budge an inch. I'm under your spell.'

Hanck walked down a corridor with doors along one wall. The doors were ajar, the rooms were small, simply furnished, all with the same furniture. Typical staff quarters. He peeked into six rooms, tidied up without any personal belongings whatsoever, before he opened a door and saw something lying on the floor.

There was a bed stripped of its covers and pillows, a small table, an armchair, a window facing the village and an empty wardrobe. In the middle of the floor lay a dustpan with a long handle. In the dustpan was dust, hair, a length of string and a piece of brick.

Hanck went into the room, leaned down, and picked up the piece of brick. He blew off the dust and hair and looked at it. It was Toby's piece of brick. A chunk from an old chimney stack that was once part of the ruins of that house, near a windswept, toxic field in no-man's-land.

He was positive. He didn't have the slightest doubt. He recognised the shape, the weight, an almost human presence in the oily, glistening sheen it had acquired. He didn't know how many times he had fished that piece of brick out of the boy's trouser pocket when his clothes needed washing. He would put it on his son's nightstand in the evening, and in the morning Toby would stuff it in his pocket again. The boy had carried it around like a lucky charm.

Hanck clasped the piece of brick in his hand, as if to feel some sort of closeness. But it merely felt like a confirmation that Toby really was gone.

He stood there in that shabby room for a good long time before he heard Bora's footsteps out in the corridor. He stuffed the piece of brick in his pocket, turned round, and met her in the doorway.

'Are you thinking of molesting me on that bed without sheets?'

'No,' he said. 'I'm not thinking of doing that.' His voice was gruff, almost hoarse.

'What is it?' she said. 'Are you crying?'

'No,' he said.

'You're sad . . .' He admitted as much, nodding, unable to say a word. 'We all are. This is Fimafeng's room.'

'Who?'

'Our best chef. That's what we called him. I don't know his real name.' Hanck nodded in silence, swallowed a big lump in his throat, turned his back to her, and looked out the window. 'I liked him,' she said. 'He was nice, and kind.' Hanck was afraid of having another attack. Anything might happen. 'I think I must have put on several pounds while he was here. This dress is about to burst its seams.'

'Where . . . ?' said Hanck. 'Where did he go?'

Bora came into the room, looked in the same direction as Hanck, out the window. Lights were shining in the small houses down in the village. A navigational light was gleaming down by the dock. 'He's no longer alive.'

'Was he old?'

'He . . .' said Bora. 'He was younger than me.'

'So how did he die?' Only someone who was tone deaf could avoid hearing the emotion in his voice.

'There was a party,' she said. 'The annual party. He was killed.'

'Why?'

'I don't know,' she said. 'It was so stupid.'

'Stupid?'

'I wasn't there,' she said. 'I wasn't there when it happened.'

'Where was that?'

'In the gold hall. It's a protected place. They're the only ones who are allowed inside.'

'Who do you mean by "they"?'

'The Clan. Father invites them to a bribe party once a year. They're allowed to drink and behave like pigs.'

'And then they killed . . . the best chef?'

'Yes,' she said. 'Because he sneezed.'

'Because he sneezed?'

'At least that's what they said. That he just sneezed, right into the air. Without apologising. A chef really shouldn't sneeze. If he does, he ought to apologise.'

'But he didn't do that?'

'Apparently not,' said Bora. She smiled sadly. 'He just grinned and looked incredibly happy. So typical for him. I can picture him smiling. It's impossible to describe. You've never seen a smile like that.'

Hanck thought: at least Toby saw his mother. That was some small consolation. 'No,' he said. 'I probably haven't.'

'It was Loki.'

'Loki?'

'Who killed him.'

The door to the annex stood open, creating a draught that swept a few leaves into the house, across the entrance floor and into the corridor. Big brown leaves that were withered and dry. Hanck looked at them in surprise. He hadn't seen a single tree outside. Bora looked at them with the eyes of a cleaning woman, as something disruptive, an extra bother. But when the leaves came rustling across the floor with erratic little lurches, she looked at them almost with love.

'Father has been looking after that tree for all these years,' she said. 'But now it will just have to fend for itself. He has given up. Everything has degenerated.'

'What do you mean?'

'It turned into a hurricane party. That probably wasn't intended. It just happened that way.'

'What hurricane?' said Hanck. He hadn't heard of any for a long time.

'It will come when it comes.'

'I'd like . . .' He stopped himself. Thoughts were racing through his mind, and he realised that he shouldn't explain what he would like. He was certainly prepared to make use of any possible means to find out what he needed to know. Violent or not. But he had to avoid honesty, until it was needed as a last resort.

She had apparently been forbidden to talk, and had already said far too much. But there was more, and he didn't know how he was going to get it out of her. Everything he had learned about interrogation techniques, the roundabout routes a conversation could take before it approached the central issues, the diversionary sidetracks that might seem irrelevant but would later turn out to provide a shortcut – all of that was gone. He felt lost and clumsy, like a beginner.

She could see it in his face. For a moment he had felt or imagined feeling some sort of desire, as if he were standing before a woman who was just about to say: 'Once upon a time . . .' and start something, create something, a chain of events which, once it had started, would be difficult to stop.

But she never said that, not there, not then. 'Well?' she said instead. 'What is it you would like?'

He felt completely disarmed by her words. He said, 'That chef's smile that you mentioned . . . You said it was impossible to describe . . .'

'Yes?' she said. 'What about it?'

'Do you know when I saw it for the very first time? No, you wouldn't know. It was twenty years ago, on a sunny day in May. The first smile. A person never forgets it. He was my son. His name was Toby.'

For some reason he didn't regret telling her. He had made an about-turn, put his cards on the table. Maybe he was tired of all this pretending, tired of denying the one truth that meant something. Maybe he simply couldn't stand there in his dead son's staff room and pretend to be somebody else.

Bora said, 'I can see it.'

'Unfortunately,' said Hanck. 'He got that smile from his mother.'

'So you didn't come here looking for love? Like all the others?'

'I just wanted to know.'

'And seek revenge?'

'Maybe,' he said. 'Maybe not.'

'Forget about that.'

'It's impossible to forget,' he said.

'If we could have sought revenge, we would have done it ourselves. But Loki belongs to a different world. They can't be touched. You'll never get near them.'

'At least I now know a name,' said Hanck.

'The name of an absolute shit,' she said. 'He's distorted my sister's sight. She even thought that you were him down there on the dock when you arrived.'

'The sister with the bloody hair?'

'He appears to her in all sorts of guises, as every fly that buzzes past. We're not allowed to kill a single insect. If she hears a fly swatter she threatens to take her own life. The whole house is crawling with cockroaches. Her scalp is swarming with lice, she scratches at open sores, and if she sees a flea she loses all control. Every bite is proof of his love. It makes no difference what anyone tells her, that he has a wife and children, that he's deceitful and unreliable, that he's homosexual or anything else.'

'An outstanding representative of the Clan,' said Hanck.

'Even they have grown tired of him. He knows that, so he's gone underground. You don't have a chance; just so you know.'

'I got myself here,' said Hanck.

'You won't get any further.'

'Why not?'

'Their world is closed. Inaccessible to ordinary mortals.'

'I want to try.'

'It's pointless. Besides, everything will be over soon.'

'I want to see my son.'

'He's dead.'

'I want to see remorse.'

'Give up.'

'Never. If I could stand here on the dock one day . . . With Loki's head in a box . . .'

'. . . then my sister could live in a perfect marriage with that box for the rest of her life. Unfortunately, there's no chance of that.'

'You don't know me.'

'I know enough.'

He didn't believe her.

She gave him a cold, appraising look. 'Describe a spring day.'

'What do you mean?' he said. 'Why?'

'Describe a spring day.'

'I . . . I can't,' he admitted.

'Try a summer day, then.'

'Er . . .' he said. 'It's hot . . . and sunny . . . and the flowers . . .'

'What kind of flowers?' Hanck was at a loss. She knew it. He didn't understand what she was getting at. 'What about autumn?'

'That's when the leaves fall from the trees . . .'

'And?'

Hanck hesitated.

'How about winter?'

'Snow.' His voice sounded dejected.

Bora shook her head. 'You've never experienced the four seasons. Heard the sound of birds singing and brooks murmuring in the spring, trembled at the thunder on a summer day, tramped through frost-bitten leaves in the autumn, been snowed-in and freezing in winter.'

'No. So what?'

'That's their world,' she said. 'Blood in the brooks, blood in the dew, blood in the frost and blood in the snow.'

'I've seen blood,' he said. 'Plenty of it.'

'But you've never seen them.'

'No,' he acknowledged. 'I've never seen any of them.'

'Their style. You may have seen a black limousine with tinted windows rush past one evening.'

'That's happened.'

'But you've never sat inside. Slid around in a new suit on a leather-covered seat . . .'

'Where are you going with all this?'

'You're the one who wants to go somewhere. You need to know something about your enemy. How he moves, where he moves.'

'I know what he did,' said Hanck. 'That's enough.'

'You don't even know what he looks like. If you ever did run into Loki, he'd make you forget all your hatred and all your despair in two seconds flat. He'd turn your whole world upside down, and then you'd sit there drinking and offering toasts like old brothers.'

'I don't believe you.'

'You know nothing about him. Or his style.'

Hanck paused to think for a moment. Touched the piece of brick in his pocket. 'Okay,' he said. 'I give in. I can't . . . I can't think very clearly in here.'

'Of course not,' she said. 'Ask for a treatment.'

'Why?'

'I can come to you as anyone you please. Just tell me the kind that you like.'

'Stop it.'

'I haven't had a customer in years. My sisters would stop complaining about me. It's a fair offer.'

Hanck couldn't understand her reasoning. He could see a connection, in the same way you might see a train come clattering in the distance – you may know where it's coming from and where it's going, but other than that, it has nothing to do with you.

'Okay,' he said, in spite of everything. He had to make some small attempt. 'Then come as you are.'

'Reserve the library,' she said. 'For midnight.'

'The library?' he said. 'Books have no shame.'

'That's exactly the reason.'

On his way to the dining room, he stopped in the lobby to make the reservation. Kolga was standing behind the front desk. Hanck said, 'Regarding this evening, I've made up my mind . . .'

'Oh, yes?' said Kolga. She smiled suggestively.

'I'd like Bora to show me the library.'

The cold woman's expression turned pensive. 'The library . . . with Bora. That's quite . . . advanced.' She let her glance travel up and down, as if to inspect what she could see of him, again with that suggestive smile. It was as if he'd just ordered the most shameless thing that the house had to offer. 'Yes, well . . .' It almost sounded like a sigh.

'Is there a problem?'

'Not at all. As long as you're up to it. It's not something that we recommend on the first visit.' She gave him a broad but ice-cold smile.

'Do I have a table in the dining room?'

'You can sit wherever you like.'

He was alone in the dining room. There were items on the menu that he'd never heard of before, along with others that he hadn't tasted in years. He ordered a full dinner, served to him in a most cordial and accommodating way by sisters in various guises but all with the same style.

He drank vodka and beer and took another 'Autobahn', just to be on the safe side. He needed it, because he had to keep a poker face. He was deep in enemy territory. Anything at all might happen, the whole set-up could open up and then snap shut like a huge trap, and that would be it for him.

He ordered coffee and more drinks. It was Kolga who served him this time. She paused for a moment at his table to chat. Without the fingernails. She had switched to a different, less formal tone. She asked about his job, where he lived, whether he was married and had children.

Hanck answered as best he could without revealing too much. He had the impression that she already knew everything, that she just wanted to put his feeble imagination to the test and see how he handled the situation.

She had the professional service person's way of touching on certain matters that were private and even intimate with an ease that could make the guest feel insecure. Hanck could have said with complete honesty that he was sitting there with a loaded revolver in his pocket, prepared at any moment to blow the head off anyone who happened to fit the vague image he had of a mortal enemy. And she would have merely smiled at him, tilting her head to one side, and said: 'Is that right?' and 'Well, of course.'

But there was also another possibility, which became more and more plausible the more he drank: that the cold woman he had encountered before was her professional side, while this one was more personal. If she knew how everything stood and still showed him such friendliness, it might be because she and her sisters basically wished him well, that they shared his disgust. The kindness and concern that he thought he was seeing might be because they saw him as a benefactor, a man who defied all the nasty slander, someone who didn't follow the mainstream, someone who went his own way.

He had the same impression of the innkeeper. Late that

evening the inkeeper made his own grand tour through the room. He needed no introduction; only a legendary old innkeeper could move through an empty and desolate salon and make it look as if he had to weave his way through a swarm of waiters, servers, buffet attendants and busboys, not to mention all the prominent guests he saw crowded around the tables, greeting them with a discreet nod, a small, secretive smile, perhaps also a glance of approval if the guest were there with a new female companion – all of them guests who had died long ago, who had first lent splendour to the place and later enjoyed it themselves; people who never paid, who obtained everything on credit, who behaved badly, quarrelling and flailing about, until finally, in the best of cases, they fired a shot into their temple, leaving unpaid bills behind. But now they were sitting there again, still, in the inner mind of the innkeeper, forcing him to don an expression of goodwill on his swollen, ruddy visage, a grimace which, as soon as it faded, looked like a scream of the utmost horror.

The library more than matched Hanck's expectations. It was housed in a salon with panelled walls. Heavy drapes hung in front of the leaded windows, and on the floor was a dark green carpet that was the same colour as the glass shades of the brass lamps. It was a complete branch of the Old Memory, filled with collected knowledge from various fields. There were even stuffed small animals and fish, pairs of mounted antlers and dried insects and butterflies affixed to boards on the walls.

On the shelves were books with pale leather bindings, but the light was dim at midnight, and Hanck couldn't read the titles. In the middle of the room, in front of the fireplace, stood a dark red leather sofa and a couple of armchairs, as well as an oval table with a marble top. On the table was a tray with vodka and two glasses.

Hanck sat down in one of the armchairs, poured himself a drink from the bottle, and took a sip. By the time he set down the empty glass, Bora came in, promptly locking the door behind her. She had on a grey suit, her hair was pulled back into a knot at the nape of her neck and she wore glasses. Hanck assumed that she was supposed to represent a 'horny conveyor of knowledge', a category that he'd seen described somewhere.

'High as a kite?'

'More or less.'

'Okey-dokey.'

Before sitting down on the sofa, she went over to the fire-place, checked the burning wood and stirred the embers with a poker, in a confident and accustomed manner, the way that you do only with a fire that you've made yourself and regard as your own.

Bora sat down on the sofa facing Hanck, crossed her legs and pulled her skirt down over her knees. She poured herself a glass of vodka, and then sat holding the glass as she stared into the fire. Hanck looked at her, silently, with a newly aroused feeling of anticipation. He turned in his chair, and then he too stared at the fire.

A long time passed in that manner. As if she were waiting for something to appear or for something that might disappear with the smoke up the chimney. Finally she spoke. Her voice sounded different, slightly deeper, less resonant, impersonal.

'Everyone was there, that's the sort of evening it was, the big night of the year, in Egir's hall, glittering with gold. A gala evening for such prominent and legendary guests that no words of praise are worthy of them. They are unapproachable, beyond all description. If you've ever stood before them and watched them arrive, and then later you're asked to recount to someone what you saw, you will immediately doubt your own ability, question the means at your disposal . . .'

She described this glittering retinue, reflected in the gleam from gold and precious gems in tiaras, from earrings, teeth, rings and plunging décolletages. Njord and Skadi were 'seldom seen near each other', their Frej and Freja arrived with Gerd and Od, respectively; the one-handed 'Tyr the Adventurer'; the 'well-read' Bragi with his 'eternally young Idun'; Vidar the Silent and Heimdall the fair-haired; Gefion the maiden, and Sif, on her own since her spouse, as usual, was away on business; and there came Loki, 'as always clad in something new'. The entourage included a large contingent of attendants with chauffeurs and underlings who stood with their legs astride, watching every move. Last of all, wearing a blue paletot and a black patch over one eye, came Odin with his wolves and ravens, Our Lord, paterfamilias, accompanied by his wife Frigg, tested and wise.

It started out so well. Everyone kissed each other on the cheek, said friendly things to each other, praised one person's jewellery and another person's boat. Everyone behaved themselves. 'But they all knew of the prevailing bad mood. They had accumulated so much shit. The situation was downright explosive. Anything at all might happen, and if anyone lost his temper they might tear the whole place apart . . .'

The Old Man could be angry and cross for reasons that he kept to himself. He could sit in a corner and sulk over a glass of white wine and turn any evening into a torment. But on this night he was in good spirits. He sampled both the drink and the food, like a regular fellow.

The tables were set. The staff bustled about. The Old Man expressed his satisfaction with all the arrangements, graciously but also a bit sharply. He knew that the innkeeper had disapproved of the whole event from the very start, but that he felt under pressure from the Clan to hold this celebration year after year. And he had been rewarded for it.

Everyone sat down at the tables, and the staff bustled about even more. When the platters were empty more were brought in, appearing as if of their own volition. Glasses and plates seemed to sail through the air, no one needed to ask for anything, new dishes were suddenly there in the middle of the table, glasses were filled and set in the hands of those who were thirsty.

The tense atmosphere grew lighter. Hands began groping freely here and there under the tablecloth, and feet, which only the dogs could see, slipped off their shoes and crept up other people's legs, landing in crotches, coaxing with their toes, shooed away with a hand belonging to someone with a blustering face, grinning foolishly, high above.

What one of the ravens overheard in the Ladies' matched what the other learned in the Gents'. Everything ended up in the ears of the Old Man.

'Freja wants to sleep with her brother.'

'Frej wants to sleep with his sister.'

'Skadi says no to the coast.'

'Njord says no to the forest.'

'Sif has slept with Loki.'

'Loki isn't feeling well.'

Disturbing news perhaps, but nothing new. The Old Man didn't let all the information trouble him, not yet. He wouldn't intervene; they all deserved a celebration. It had been a good season, the warehouses were full, the supplies were bountiful, the money flowed. So it was a matter of maintaining the concord and peace.

He raised his glass for a toast, to the host of the inn and his nine daughters, to the excellent staff, especially the chefs. Everyone joined in. They drank toasts, applauded, emptied their glasses and flung them away. Those goblets that were caught before they struck the ground were refilled, set on the table, spilled, toppled, emptied onto the trousers of one person or into the plunging neckline of another. People laughed and screamed. They were intent on drinking and fornicating all night long.

'Exactly as usual, year in and year out. Always the same thing, the same commotion. Repetitions and reiterations. A magic that was not to be broken even though everyone knew that someday it would have to come to an end.'

She wanted to emphasise that her father had tried to get

out of it. They had demanded fresh beer in honour of the day, and he had said that he didn't have the resources to brew beer in such quantities. Which happened to be true, but they refused to let that stop them.

'That was at the beginning of time,' as she said. Tyr the One-Handed knew where a vat could be found that was big enough for the task. His mother had one in her home, 'out there', far away in hostile territory.

Would she voluntarily let it go?

No, but with a bit of cunning they would be able to wrest it away from her.

So they went out there in Thor's wagon. It moved quite slowly; one of the goats was lame. They stopped to rest at a farm and left the wagon there to let the goat recover.

They could just as easily continue on foot. They were out in the wild. Endless forests soon spread out in all directions, dark refuges for dark forces, a menacing chaos beyond all honour and integrity.

But that was of no concern if you were young and the sun was glittering on an unspoiled lake, and the forest was fragrant with mushrooms, buzzing with life and animals that rushed about bringing in supplies.

You stand on a rocky hill where the canopy of pines and spruce trees opens to the blue sky, and you see a flock of birds up there slowing down, dispersing, regrouping into the shape of a sharply carved arrow heading south.

In the shiny centre of a bog stands a pair of cranes, peering at the surrounding strip of land, the pines and birches, lavender heather and golden cloudberries.

Then cones crackle in the sun, ants cross a stretch of ground, a slug pauses motionless in the moss on a rock.

A woodpecker taps on a tree trunk, an eagle shrieks loudly above everything else, a desolate sound.

They wandered through all that wilderness until the days grew shorter, the sun paler, and the leaves on the trees lost their fresh green colour and faded, turning yellow, red, brown.

'You have to see all of this,' she said, 'in order to understand the rest.'

'I see it,' said Hanck. 'I see it.'

They arrived at the place where Tyr's mother lived, a blonde, strong and stately woman. She in turn kept her own mother in the house, an old crone with nine hundred heads, terrifying to look at and even worse to hear.

No wonder that the master of the house – Hymer was his name – was surly and cross, with a mother-in-law like that so close at hand. Whenever her ears were cold he had to ransack a whole forest for game. Nine hundred caps had to be sewn from the pelts of bears and beavers, mink and ermine, foxes and squirrels. When she was hungry there were nine hundred mouths to feed. If she still wasn't satisfied, and it must be assumed that she never was, he had to face the criticism of an entire league.

Whether the daughter was worth all this trouble only Hymer could say. Generally speaking he was savage and violent, flinging about objects and curses. According to hearsay, he was capable of crushing anything at all with a mere glance. But there was a woman even for someone like Hymer.

Tyr's mother was of course glad to see her son. She immediately took out what there was in the larder, making an extra effort because he'd brought along such a fine and famous comrade: Thor, the protector of humans, the slayer of beasts; not a great conversationalist, but a man of action.

After the youths had eaten they found themselves barricaded behind an array of household utensils, jars, buckets, pans and wash tubs. No one knew how Hymer might react to a surprise visit. What he would think of Thor could be surmised in advance. It was best to proceed cautiously.

Then the fierce-tempered Hymer came home from the forest with icicles in his beard and a terrifying countenance. He far exceeded his reputation.

No doubt all he wanted was to come inside where it was warm, to eat and drink, to have a go at his wife, and then fall asleep until spring, or until his mother-in-law started kicking up a row again.

His wife fussed and fawned over him as much as she could, chirping a stifled ballad about her son Tyr and his comrade Thor, hinting that they might be . . . in fact they already had . . . and so on. The picture emerged, little by little, even for a worn-out and exhausted giant.

He got up on top of the bin and looked all around, glaring, sniffing, putting two and two together. Finally he caught sight of a pillar behind which the guests were huddled. The stone burst apart under the giant's gaze. Out of the fragments and junk crept the youths; they brushed off the dust and dirt, bowed and uttered a greeting, standing there empty-handed.

No matter what sort of gifts they might have brought for Hymer, he would have been just as ill-tempered. Right now, to top it all off, he was hungry.

Three bulls were slaughtered, and Thor ate two of them all by himself. The host found him gluttonous and decided that from now on the guests would have to survive on whatever they caught themselves.

The next day they went out in the boat with the gear they would need to go fishing. Thor had brought along his own bait. He had been out in the woods, wrung the neck of a bull and secretly dragged the carcass aboard.

The boat heaved and the giant complained. The crew were bunglers. They didn't know how to row.

Hymer himself pulled up two whales with a single yank on the line. That should have outdone almost anybody.

But Thor sat in the stern and surreptitiously baited his line, a bait suitable for the most monstrous of beasts. And it worked. The very Midgard serpent took the hook, the beast that wrapped around the whole known world, where all was ordered and organised, allotted and arranged, deployed for the sake of man and beast. And the whole world shook, it trembled and tumbled in an incomparable duel until the Evil One was clubbed and sank lifeless into the deep. The world grew still once more, resuming its proper course.

But Hymer was not particularly impressed by this. Maybe it should be explained that he was a simple man with simple pleasures. He could sit in front of a fire with his feet on a footstool and drink beer from an old tankard, completely content. That sort of thing goes a long way for a simple man.

But he was annoyed. Later, he wanted to put that mother-in-law of his in her place. He picked up his old tankard, it was certifiably solid and strong, in reality unbreakable. He proclaimed a contest to see who could smash it to pieces.

Thor accepted the challenge, picked up the tankard and threw it with all his might against a rough stone pillar that stood in the hall. The pillar was crushed to bits, but the tankard remained whole. Hymer was pleased.

Hymer's beloved wife then took Thor aside and in a whisper advised him to strike the tankard against her husband's skull. Thor was quick to comply. With all the strength he could muster he slammed the tankard against the forehead of the unsuspecting giant. The crash could be heard far and wide. His forehead held, but the tankard was destroyed.

Contrary to all expectations, a cherished old possession had been lost. The giant was aggrieved, bitter, angry, and in the end enraged. He wanted revenge and came up with a new challenge; not a living soul stood a chance.

That was when the brew vat was brought out – the biggest, heaviest and bulkiest item on the whole farm. Hymer challenged Thor to lift it. He himself demonstrated, putting all his strength into the effort. The vat didn't budge from the spot.

Then Thor stepped forward, spat on his palms, grabbed hold of the vat and lifted. It rose up from the ground and hovered there; he was carrying it! Across creaking floorboards he carried the vat out through the door and kept on going, heading straight for the woods.

That was not part of the wager. Behind him was a ravaged farm and soon a band of hostile giants. When they caught up with Thor, he set the vat down and knocked them out, one by one.

He reached home in good time, and the celebration was saved.

'So that was how the cursed vat ended up with us. And the story has to be told year after year, word for word, and it arouses the same strained sort of merriment each time. People laugh, slap their knees, pound each other on the back. Your son had never heard the story before.'

'Did he laugh?'

'Yes, I think he did.'

Loki was the only one who didn't laugh. He wasn't in the mood. He had remained mostly silent the whole time, standing off by himself, not really taking part, barely noticed, drinking toasts and looking generally tense.

'Your son was standing right behind him. That was when he sneezed. Loki may have been the only one who heard it . . .'

The young chef, the procurer who had won so much

acclaim, sneezed, right out into the air, without holding his hand over his face. He even had the impudence to look pleased and delighted.

Loki looked at him. Offering an apology was clearly not even a possibility. The young man just stood there, beaming.

No doubt that was all that was necessary for Loki, the airborne, the volatile, the unreliable. Without saying a word, he tossed his glass aside and launched himself at the chef, punching him so hard that any of the blows could have been lethal.

Maybe the young man was already lost by the time his head struck the floor, hitting the edge of a stone step, sharp enough to extinguish a life.

At first most of them didn't notice a thing. It happened so fast, as if off in a corner. But one of the nine sisters had seen it all. She ran over to the lifeless chef, thinking that he could be revived. She slapped his cheeks hard, then saw the blood running out of the wound at the back of his neck; she examined him more closely, found no pulse. He wasn't breathing.

A shout, a sudden hush, a silence that spread along the tables. Something had happened. Several rushed over, examined the sprawled body, made clumsy attempts to revive him, gave up. The one they called Fimafeng was dead.

Loki stood nearby, again with a glass in his hand, drinking. More had now seen what happened, that he was the one who had struck the blow, that he was the one who took the young man's life. The silence was so complete in the hall that they could hear the murderer swallow.

'Even he looked surprised. He stood there rubbing the knuckles of one hand, peering at the dead man, and looking surprised. As if he were asking the same question himself and trying to find an answer.'

He said he was disgusted by all the fawning of the others and their pointless flattery, their empty praise of people that they detested.

Hmm. And? That wasn't enough.

Because . . . because that devil had stood there and sneezed.

Sneezed?

Yes, sneezed, right out into the air, without apologising.

Hmm. And?

That was all. Finito.

People exchanged glances. Conversations started up again. They shook their heads, frowned; all the expressions and gestures of incomprehension were displayed by one person after another.

Loki seemed more inscrutable than ever.

Someone claimed to be tired of him.

Another had always been tired of him.

Someone wondered why he was there at all.

Another asked if he had actually been formally invited.

Everyone's eyes turned to the Old Man. He hadn't yet said a word. He could have answered a number of questions, explained a number of connections, but such old truths meant nothing at the moment, with a murder victim lying on the floor.

No one could see it as anything other than an act of insanity, a completely meaningless death. Not even Odin, the Old Man.

He told the perpetrator to go, to get out of his sight.

'I had just come back in when I heard him say that. And he said it with pain, with obvious distress that might seem, well, surprising.'

'Why?'

'Because this sort of thing happens all the time. Shit happens. Especially with Loki. The Old Man has always cleaned up after him. Thrown him out and then taken him back into favour. But there was something different about this time. It was just as meaningless as usual. He saw no point to what had happened, but maybe he saw consequences.'

'And my son?'

'Was put on ice.' That was no consolation, but at any rate it was a mark of distinction: 'I included a few pieces of the expensive kind . . .'

'And then what? Was that all?'

'No, I'm afraid not. That was just the beginning.'

Everyone probably would have preferred to see it end, to have the celebration be over after that. But that wasn't what happened. A death among the rank and file didn't mean much. It was a commonplace event. No, if in hindsight they would have preferred to see the celebration come to an end after that, it was because of other things. Not because of what had already occurred but rather because of what was ahead.

'Loki was thrown out and he set off for the islet. It was dark outside, and my sister, the one with the bloody hair, ran after him with a lantern. She wanted to make him calm down and come back home with her. She's the sort who likes unreliable men. No one understands her better than I do. I've heard them talk. He's different then. He's . . . different.'

'Is it even possible to talk with her?'

'No, not any more. I don't know what happened out there. She was gone for a long time, and he was gone even longer. She was nervous and upset when she set out after him, but she was completely crazy by the time she came back. She's been just as crazy ever since. Nobody knows what he did to her. Maybe nothing.'

He returned several hours later, calmed by the cold and frightened into submission by the wind – or so one might think. But not him, no. He stepped right up to the door and started bandying words with Eldir, who was actually part of the kitchen staff but who now stood guard.

Eldir was tense, prepared to block the way and deter that madman. But Loki told him not to worry. He just wanted to know what they were talking about, all those fine guests.

About the old days, of course. Memories. A lost world. When fellows spat on their palms and people knew their place. The usual topics.

And what about Loki? What were they saying about him?

No one, not one, had said a kind word about him.

He insisted, 'Let me in. I have to sow discord. Provoke wrath. Mix harm into the mead.'

Eldir realised how unwise this would be and tried to warn him. 'No matter what you may get into your head, or how much scorn and derision you may spew, they're just going to throw it back on you. You don't have a chance in there.'

Loki had wrangled with stubborn doorkeepers before. 'Listen, no matter what you think – just forget it. Shut your trap and open the door.'

Eldir had no desire to lose his job as a chef. He had to relent. Loki went inside.

The fine guests were not so far gone that they didn't see what was happening immediately. Loki was back.

A hush fell over the hall once again.

When everyone suddenly falls silent at a celebration like that, the silence seems enormous. Loki controlled himself, showed no rancour. He was unobtrusive, almost tactful, but received everyone's attention even so.

'I've been outside for a long time . . . I'm thirsty. All I want is a drink.'

A modest request. In the eyes of a drunk it might even seem like a sign of remorse or humility.

But the room was still silent.

The practice of silence has had its interpreters, observers who long afterwards have seen both a short-term tactic and a more long-term strategy in this art. There were masters who had grown up with it, sensing it long before they understood the words that occasionally broke through. Someone who was expert at keeping silent was a shaman who could summon any sort of phantom, a sorcerer who could banish or inflict pain, a king who could control an entire people with the enervation of absence, of neglect, of being passed over.

Sitting there, in Egil's golden hall, were just such masters of the art of keeping silent, both men and women. One demonstrated the silence of yearning, another that of reproach; one knew the silence of the insulted, another showed a sample of satisfaction; one mastered the silence of surprise, another that of satiety; one knew the silence of accusation, another that of envy.

Loki had been subjected to this before, but that made it no less troubling. 'Why are you all so silent? Haven't you got tongues in your heads? Just give me somewhere to sit, or else you can throw me out for good.'

Finally, in any case, someone was forced to speak. Bragi was drunk but considered a good speaker when something had to be said. He shared the Old Man's affection for the skaldic art.

Now, in hindsight, anyone can see that he ought to have chosen to keep quiet like all the rest. But he spoke out, loudly and clearly, saying that they wanted nothing more to do with Loki.

It was not great oratory, but the intent was plain and no one objected. It seemed to be an expression of the general opinion.

But Loki did not deign to offer any defence. He turned at once to the Old Man, stepped forward, and said: 'We are blood brothers, you and I. You said that you would never accept a beer unless one was offered to both of us . . .'

The Old Man could not deny this. It was an insidious truth. Everyone knew what it meant. And even though he would have preferred something else, he had to stand behind it and take the consequences. He asked his son Vidar to stand up and make room for Loki. A conciliatory measure, to lighten the mood. For the good of everyone.

The silent man got up from the table, offered his seat to Loki, and poured him a drink. Loki, in turn, had a chance to enhance his subdued behaviour, to drink, keep quiet, behave himself, and see how things went.

If he had done that – complied, accepted this offer of peace and reconciliation – everything would have turned out differently. A different story would have been told, carried forward to a different end.

Loki was thirsty so he drank. The conversation around the table resumed. He was allowed to sit there. If the Old Man had ordained it, then so it must be. It was actually a golden opportunity. He had the chance to do simply nothing, silently exceed his own limitations, break with his habits, defy all expectations.

But Loki was true to himself and followed his own destructive nature. At all costs he had to offer a toast. '*Skål*, all you highborn and holy.' He managed in his inimitable way to make it sound like he was saying 'you fucking highborn and holy hypocrites'. '*Skål*,' he said, 'all you highborn and holy. Except for Sideburn . . .'

A new stone in the air, a new torch lit. Even so, Bragi, with his side-whiskers, raised his glass. He had seen the looks cast in his direction, heard the hushed rebukes. He had understood them; he was supposed to be conciliatory, like the Old Man.

'Here,' Bragi said. It was a ring, a big, greasy ring that he wriggled off his finger. 'This is for you. Take it. I have a number of weapons that you haven't seen. You would like them. I'll give them to you. Take whatever you like, just don't cause any trouble.'

Loki picked up the ring, looked it over and tossed it aside. 'Fucking bling-bling. You're such a chicken-shit!'

'If we weren't sitting here . . .' Bragi was surly, offended. 'If we weren't . . .'

'Yes? If we weren't what?'

'If we weren't sitting here . . .' Bragi was having a hard time switching gears, going back to the hostile scenario. He had started out there but had been forced to retreat. Now he wanted to return there, but it was taking time. He was drunk. Drink makes some people fickle and volatile, others sluggish and fixated. He belonged to the latter. The drastic threats, the malicious phrases that could so easily provoke laughter, seemed to be at the other end of the table. He couldn't reach them. 'If we weren't sitting here I'd be out there with your skull in my hands . . .'

Loki whistled. 'Oy.' Scornfully he ran his hand across his throat. 'If only . . . oh, yes. If only. Just sit here and do your boasting. How brave you are sitting in a chair, Sideburn. A fucking chicken-shit. A brave person doesn't sit and think.'

Perhaps Idun could have persuaded Loki, as she'd done before. If only she had turned to him, given him a look that promised something, a pledge, or the false support that the wife of a humiliated man might express. But she turned instead to her husband. 'Stop it. Be still. Think of the children!'

Loki no doubt took that as an insult, a form of disrespect, that she considered it pointless to speak to him directly. He was furious. 'Be still?! You man-crazy cow! Think of the children?! How can you say that?'

But he didn't succeed in rattling her composure. Now she turned to him and said quite calmly: 'I have no intention of quarrelling with you tonight. Just so you know that. So back off.' She knew what was going to happen: her husband was drunk, it could lead to a fight and still more bloodletting.

A reasonable assumption. Loki looked at her for a long time. She stared back without hesitating or wavering. His contempt was unmistakable, it radiated from him, giving off a strong and unpleasant glow. She stood there in the light, not saying a word, sipping her drink, shrugging her shoulders, shaking her head in a knowing way.

Yet another effective form of silence.

They stood there looking at each other, and he muttered, 'Forever young . . .' in a way that was not only sarcastic but also contained a sorrow and a melancholy that at least those who didn't know him might regard as genuine and honest.

There was a good deal of information available about her. Idun grew apples. She had many different kinds, but one was particularly valued: a big golden apple. If you ate it you would stay young.

Anyone who has ever eaten a sweet, juicy apple knows that time stops, or in any case you sense its passing in a different way. You can devote a good amount of time to eating that one piece of fruit, taking a bite now and then, prolonging the pleasure, closing your eyes and surrendering to the tricks that your senses can play. You may feel yourself transported to another time, another life, maybe to the other side of a great sea, to another country. You may steal an apple from someone else's garden, crouch down behind a bush and eat it in secret, hidden from the rest of the world – stolen fruit, stolen time.

But you can't draw out the experience too long. After the peel is pierced, an irrevocable process begins; the surface where you take a bite soon turns brown, it oxidises, becoming ugly and unappetising. You have to learn to observe the pace of consumption, always one step ahead of decay. This is an elementary lesson added to many others gained from an apple

– memories, knowledge, dreams, everything that has such a vitalising effect on the ability to feel sorrow and melancholy: two hints of brown from the place where the fortunate one has taken a bite.

Idun was there in her garden, in an ordered part of the world, an esteemed cultivator, precious to her friends and . . . desired by those who had never tasted her fruit, those who were not authorised.

Odin and Loki, the blood brothers, were once out wandering at the beginning of time, far from home, out in the wilderness. On mountains and plateaux above the tree line, as close to the sky as it was possible to get, in tracts swept bare by the wind and harsh cold, punctuated with glaciers and blocks of ice, an inhospitable region. They were cold and hungry, they longed for home but clung to these rugged realms, enduring severe hardships in their will to conquer something. Not land or riches, not gold or honour, it was something more lasting than that, a dearly-bought experience, an insight into the human condition.

Sorely tested, they gradually approached more hospitable regions. They descended to milder valleys, saw a herd of oxen, felled one of the animals, dug a pit and began to roast the meat. They were hungry, they were ravenous.

After several hours of impatient waiting, they assumed the meat was ready to eat. They tasted it, but it still wasn't done. They had to wait. And wait. Finally, after many hours of roasting, they tasted it again. But the meat was raw.

They began to argue. The one who had gathered the firewood must have gathered bad logs. The one who had cut up the meat must have cut it up wrong. In the midst of this hungry and agitated argument a voice was heard from above. It was coming from a tree, and in the tree sat an eagle. A big, magnificent eagle. The eagle said he would see to it that the meat was roasted properly if they gave him part of the ox.

Of course they were prepared to accept the offer. By now they were prepared to go along with anything at all; they were hallucinating from hunger. So the eagle twisted off both the thighs and the shoulders from the ox. Loki flew into a rage and began flailing at the insolent bird with a long pole.

The end of the pole got stuck on the eagle's back, and Loki refused to let go. He was dragged off, over hill and dale, and was nearly pounded to a pulp before the bird rose up into the air. They were suddenly high up among the clouds.

Loki begged and pleaded to be released. The eagle said that he would let him go under one condition – that he handed over Idun, with the apples.

Loki was scared out of his wits and could do nothing but promise to meet this demand. A deal was struck. He landed unharmed and was finally allowed to eat.

Deals must be kept among gods and gangsters. Loki was forced to fulfil his part of the bargain. He went to Idun and showed her new sides of himself. He was suddenly very interested in her gardening arts, displayed a number of his own skills in the area, knew the names of rare varieties, expressed opinions on various kinds of bees, and was even able to comment on her style of pruning.

It made an impression; Idun was flattered. Her husband, who was a bookish type, seldom showed any interest. He was impractical, by his own admission. Lazy, according to her. Thought he was too good to dig in the earth, didn't want to get dirt under his nails. It was so easy to get spots on his books. But he did want the fruit.

Loki was more pragmatic. He opened a book the same way he opened a box of tools. Something needed to be done, and for that purpose he needed a tool; whether wielding a sledgehammer or agreeing to a pact, it made no difference. At least that was why he had read up on apples. The little knowledge he had acquired was enough to fool Idun.

When he claimed to have seen in an inaccessible place a rare and hardy tree with dazzling fruit, she was curious. He described it so well that she wanted to see it. He suggested an expedition. And she could take along some of her own apples to compare.

Loki and Idun set off without informing Sideburn; he would just be suspicious. They walked through desolate, frightening tracts. She had never been out there before.

All of a sudden Loki pretended to be unsure of the way, began vacillating back and forth. That was the signal. Then came the eagle rushing in, digging his claws into the one who was both desired and betrayed.

Idun found herself in the clutches of Tjatse, locked up in a remote farm. There the giant would have her all to himself, to enjoy the pleasure of her fruits and stay forever young.

The Clan back home was faced with a crisis. Everyone was shaken, indignant. Idun's absence was immediately noticed; they felt old, they saw signs of age everywhere, acquired wrinkles, turned grey, felt stiff and tired.

A desperate council meeting was held. A number of sightings had been made, someone had caught a glimpse of Idun on the day she disappeared, accompanied by Loki, on her way somewhere. One thing was added to another, mere suspicions, no proof. But it was enough to arouse anger, a wrath that was nurtured by their fear of ageing prematurely. That sort of anger had to be taken seriously.

Without acknowledging anything at all, Loki hinted that he too had his suspicions. Pretending to be generous and self-sacrificing, he offered to go out and scout around.

His suggestion met with approval. Loki was sent out. He knew where he had to go; he headed straight to the remote farm where Tjatse lived.

He was in luck. Idun was alone. The giant was out at sea, far beyond the horizon. He wouldn't be back for a long time.

How did she react – a frightened woman who had been abducted and locked up – when she suddenly heard the rush of feathers in the air, a pair of flapping wings, and she turned around to see a handsome man, an inscrutable figure, as satisfied and enthusiastic no matter what he attempted, who straightened out the mess he had made with equal ardour and delight?

What constituted a man like that? Could he play the part of a rescuer – he who had so recently betrayed her?

And what did he see, with his insights about submission and degradation? Could he see what was stirring in her heart, make use of it, exploit it to his advantage? Or was he merely a man who saw a woman who didn't know whether she should laugh or cry, a woman who may have accepted her fate and had learned to mollify a rough and brutal giant? A woman who had learned the art of survival and had set all honour and virtue aside, accepting what was called a 'woman's lot'?

Perhaps he persuaded her to understand it in this way: that it was she who needed to rescue him, that he was the one who needed her.

And they were all alone in the world, in that place, at that moment. They were totally free, able to play whatever role they pleased.

As they were now, standing there looking at each other in the banquet hall, on that fateful evening in the outer archipelago. No one knew what they thought of each other these days.

Idun had turned up again, order had been restored,

and all the circumstances had been explained until only one question mark remained: Loki.

He got away without punishment, but they put the giant to death. The killing became known far and wide. The giant left behind a daughter who was later admitted as a member of the Clan. She was there at the party, standing right there in the room, thinking: someday this has to come to an end.

'Loki is out of the picture. Everyone despises him . . .' That was Gefion, the unmarried maiden with the clear eyes.

'Shut up! I know all about your innocence. And what it cost. Just a few trinkets and you'd lie there spread-eagled.'

The scandal was a fact, the evening had degenerated long ago, but perhaps it was still possible to ward off a total disaster. The Old Man had to intervene.

'Loki, you're ill, you're out of your mind. You know what she can . . .'

'No doubt much better than you, in any case. You've lost your grip, ceded victory to those who are inferior. Who wins at your roulette wheels? Not me, at any rate.'

'No?' said the Old Man. 'At least you don't have to stand underground milking cows . . .'

'You yourself have wandered about as a woman, casting spells like a seeress.'

Under other circumstances that would have been enough to incite a brawl. But here, in this protected hall, they had to bide their time. Something was irrevocably over, something was irretrievably lost. Just two men, sorrow-stricken perhaps, indignant and offended. Men who had once had their arms full, but now could no longer remember what they held.

Fate had brought them together, a couple of young survivors constantly searching for food for the day, in a time of chaos, a time without standards.

Everything had been subordinated to survival.

Only the ones who made it were able to demean and be demeaned, affirm and deny with no differentiation, feign complete agreement with a stone-dead god, be a man among men and a woman among women, and occasionally vice versa, without prejudice, acquiring knowledge that the cowardly scorned.

Some lost everything to this misappropriation, others acquired more and more. That was how their power was established, in godlike forbearance and through access to the riches of the poor.

And all was well and good.

Until someone discovered a vein that came to light somewhere, a forgotten deposit containing a substance that was valued and refined and mixed into an alloy of substances that had never been combined before. It was given the name of honour.

A rust-free gauge. Honour was weighed, measured and named. Honour was acquired, defended, and when it was occasionally lost, it could be restored with blood and tears. It had its own magic, it couldn't be seen or heard, it had no scent, but it was as strong as the elements – lethal, idolised, a blessing for one person, a curse for another.

And wherever honour went in, freedom went out. Everything was soon weighed, measured and named. The world was elucidated. A minutely described prison.

This approximate state made people mad. No one wanted to distinguish one person from another, no one was cast in one piece, cut and dried. Everyone lacked contours. The skin was merely a membrane; surrounding each individual was an aura of secretions that made the person indistinct, diffuse, a wandering dust cloud without purpose, without meaning. And so they began to weigh, measure and name this freedom too, and they found it boundless. Someone might regard this truth as unbearable and think that a return was called for, back to the sources, the original definitions.

And that was how things continued. Those who could explain the world could also obscure it.

But now honour was gone. It had been used up and restored so many times that it was simply worn out.

No one knew what lay ahead.

That was the reason for this sorrowful, lost feeling. Loki had flung about his accusations with a strange mixture of surprise, delight and loathing. Like a child who has found a knife and discovers how it's supposed to be used, but then grows weary when everything around him ends up destroyed.

But it was not 'whore' or 'queer' or 'cuckold' that was the sharp and effective weapon. The words caused no harm on their own. They served only as reminders, and that was the irksome part. They pointed out a hollow where once a fully operational organ had existed, serving a function that seemed more and more expendable until its usefulness finally ceased altogether, which caused the organ itself to atrophy, shrinking into a rudimentary speck of unknown origin.

'You're two of a kind, you two. What you did in the past is nothing to crow about.' The Old Man's wife Frigg was a tested woman, wise and unafraid. 'Or go settle it in private, whatever good that will do.'

'I can understand that you think so. If I had slept with my brother-in-law, I would keep my mouth shut too.'

A slight quiver from an exhausted heart. 'Balder,' she said, 'if only I had Balder here . . .'

'And what then? What if you did have Balder here?'

'Then he would put an end to you.'

'No doubt,' said Loki. 'But you don't have him here.'

'No. Because of you.'

'That's right. I take the blame for that too. Is there anything else? I'll take the blame for anything. Balder. Okay. He's on my account.'

Balder, the good guy, loved by everyone. Beautiful, wise and kind. Spreading light, infusing hope.

But for a time he was haunted by evil and menacing dreams.

He told this to his friends, who considered the matter sufficiently serious that they decided to act. He had to be protected, be made invulnerable.

Frigg, his mother, demanded a promise from everything in the whole world that nothing would harm her son: fire and water, iron and all types of ore, stones, earth, trees, diseases, four-footed animals, birds, venom and snakes.

Everything and everyone swore to spare Balder.

He himself was delighted by this invulnerability and challenged his friends to test it. They shot arrows at him, threw things at him, any loose object they could find. But nothing did any harm.

This provoked a general sense of satisfaction, except in Loki. He had a different view of the arrangement. No one really knew why. Perhaps it was just that he had to be different, at all costs. He differed so much that the very act of differing became his trademark. As soon as a line was drawn and then breached, you knew that Loki had been there.

Disguised as a woman, he now went to the home of Frigg to obtain information. This required trust. To achieve this, he was forced to reveal some secret of his own, a secret that he had been strictly forbidden to tell, though it could be about anything at all. Then he would be given a secret in exchange. It would be a sort of factual inconsistency, which is something that characterises many human interactions and tends to be the sole province of women. Men prefer solid facts and solid truths, and thus become more irrational, clumsy and ineffective when they are faced with the more nebulous concepts and emotions of women. But Loki, with his godlike ambivalence, could play the whole field.

In this way he found out that everything on earth had sworn an oath to spare Balder, everything except for one lowly plant. A mistletoe, so small and humble that Frigg hadn't bothered to approach it.

Loki promptly went to the nearest mistletoe, cut off a branch, and shaped it into an arrow. Then he went to the site where the boorish men were still plying the invulnerable Balder with crude weapons. Balder stood there untouched, grinning his sunniest grin.

At the very edge of the group stood Höder, Balder's blind brother.

Loki asked him why he wasn't taking part in the game. Höder said that he would just miss and might end up hurting someone else, an ordinary mortal.

Loki offered to remedy that. He took out a bow and the arrow made from mistletoe and helped the blind man take aim.

'He himself had a brother who was blind. I once heard him talk about him. That was the kind of thing my sister fell for – who wouldn't fall for something like that? They had gone out into the world, two little boys. Loki had described everything to him, all that was beautiful, dangerous, good to eat or poisonous. He had given a name to everything they came across, both living and dead, so precisely and properly that the blind brother thought he understood the very nature of each thing and knew how it looked. Loki had even made the blind man bring down a bird in flight.'

Now he helped Höder aim the bow and shoot his arrow. It hit the mark and passed right through Balder. He dropped to the ground dead.

It was a great sorrow. The greatest to ever occur, according to some.

'Do I need to describe the despair?'

'No.'

'Do I need to explain that they wanted the dead man back, that they were prepared to bargain with Hel in the realm of the dead?'

'No.'

Hermod rode down, northwards all the way down into the realm of the dead. There he found Hel with Balder sitting in the high seat. Hermod presented his case. Hel listened and understood. She was prepared to release Balder and allow him to live under one condition: that everything, both alive and dead, would weep for him. Absolutely everything. If even one refused to shed a tear, he would have to stay where he was.

Word was sent out around the world that tears would bring Balder back from the realm of the dead. Everything wept – the trees, the stones, the grass. Every living thing wept.

Except for one, an ugly old giant woman sitting in a cave. Her name was Tökk. Her eyes were dry.

She too was another of Loki's guises.

Balder was lost.

And so Loki assumed responsibility, admitting it to the very face of the dead man's mother. She herself was weighed down with guilt, since she had neglected one small, lowly plant, barely big enough to carve into a stick.

An explanation was demanded of Loki, of course. He was pressed against the wall, but he merely shrugged his shoulders, perhaps at a loss what to say, perhaps being secretive, like an inscrutable idiot.

Wise and benevolent people – those who didn't flinch from difficult or troublesome cases – had asked: Do you begrudge love a face?

He merely shrugged – maybe so.

Others asked: Do you believe, in all your stupidity, that the love Balder enjoyed would remain without an object and then end up bestowed on others?

Once again he shrugged – maybe so.

Their patience wore thin, and the benevolence of those who were wise gave out. Loki was let be. His value was debated. Only the Old Man insisted that Loki actually had some worth. As if it were much too vexing for an ordinary mortal to appreciate.

Freja, ever prone to tears, who knew what loss was, stepped forward to defend Frigg. 'You're out of your mind! No one wants to hear about it, don't you realise that? She knows exactly how things stand. But maybe she doesn't feel like talking about it right now.'

'Because she's smarter than you are.'

'And who was it who stood right here a short time ago, complaining that no one was talking? And now, when people have plenty to say, and quite clearly, then you go crazy and scream at everyone to shut up!'

'He's never satisfied,' someone said.

Loki turned to find out who had said that; he saw nothing but cold, hostile eyes directed at him. He looked around, from one person to the other, and started laughing and sneering with scorn.

'There's not a single devil in here that you haven't slept with. Every one of them has screwed you.'

'So what? At least I don't tell lies.'

'What am I lying about?'

Freja hesitated, tried to look as scornful as he did.

'Tell me one thing that I'm lying about,' said Loki.

'You're a phoney,' she said 'A horrible phoney.'

That was everyone's opinion. Perhaps even his own. But if it had ever bothered him, he could no longer remember when. That was simply the way he was. Everything straightforward and unambiguous was foreign to him; he preferred to be true to himself, and for some reason he chose to be true to himself more than ever before, right now, in the middle of all this shamelessness.

'Shut up, you witch. You're so full of shit. Go ahead and sleep with anyone you want, even your brother.'

The latter was sitting there on a bench, fidgeting. His wife sat next to him, staring angrily at the table, her cheeks red; she was breathing with difficulty.

Others turned to the Old Man, wanting him to act. He had to do something now, pound the table with his fist, put at end to all this. But not even he was capable of stopping the course of events.

'I was there at that moment. Looking at him. Everyone was looking at him. I think he realised that it was over, right there, right then. It had turned into a hurricane party . . .'

Loki went over to Freja, and stood very close, much too close. She took a step back, he followed. She knew that she couldn't escape. He had walked all over her, explored every inch of her, as a fly, as a flea.

No matter how much she scrubbed herself afterwards, the feeling had remained on her skin, the fact that he had been all over her, in every nook, pushing his way inside her, taking his pleasure, and no doubt boasting about it later on. He had undertaken a long journey in those parts, through the wild thicket of her hair, down the heights and hollows of her face; he had stood on the tip of her nose, tumbled over her chin and throat, out onto her bosom, down into the groves of her armpits, along her hips and up onto the desolate plain of her belly; he had sought shelter and rested for a moment in the pit of her navel, then continued down the mound of her abdomen and into the dense, almost impenetrable forest of twining lianas, climbing and falling, crawling and wriggling forward, making his way through that dark forest, enticed by the scent from the furrow way down inside a deep ravine, a water course from a sacred spring into which he had finally thrown himself from a warm, flat cliff, down into the exquisite must . . .

In the past she had once belonged to the Old Man and lived under his protection. He hadn't been able to resist her beauty. That was long ago, but whoever looked at her now could fully understand it. She had preserved her assets well. The sorrow prompted by the decay that strikes a beauty over time was of more concern to the Old Man than to her. He was the one who would fight against it with furious wrath and be forced to give up and grow bitter. Not her. Freja had aged with dignity.

She was still irresistible. As soon as Loki realised this, when he stood so close and was about to be drawn into another, overpowering chain of events, he was forced to back away. He couldn't yield now, couldn't turn weak. He had to go on.

He now stood an arm's length away, stretching out his hand towards her, towards her bosom where the necklace hung. That famous piece of jewellery. He took it in his hand. She stood motionless and didn't stop him.

Everyone knew what base desire had once raged around that necklace. The desire to covet and possess, the urge to conquer.

It was an extraordinary piece of jewellery. Four dwarves had forged it underground. She had wanted it. The dwarves wanted her. A deal was struck.

She slept one night with the first of them, one night with the second, one night with the third and one night with the fourth. Everyone was satisfied.

Then she went home and didn't say a word about the

matter. When she looked in the mirror, she saw only the necklace. And an exquisite necklace it was.

In a roundabout way Loki heard talk of the acquisition and mentioned it to the Old Man, repeating the gossip. The Old Man didn't feel threatened by four dwarves, but he had his honour to consider. Some sort of punishment was in order.

His blood brother was assigned the task of stealing the necklace. Loki was given a free hand, could employ whatever means necessary. Which would undoubtedly be required, since Freja lived in her own house, securely locked and guarded. She never let in uninvited guests, she kept herself and her possessions well protected.

On a cold night he flitted around the place. Every door was locked, every shutter was closed. He couldn't find a single gap, but he was stubborn and disguised as a fly. It was cold, and flies grow drowsy in the cold. He warmed himself next to the chimney and continued his search. Finally he found an opening and crept inside the house. The warmth revived him.

All were asleep in their rooms. Quietly he flew over to Freja's bed. She was lying there with the necklace on. The clasp was at the back of her neck. He buzzed around a few times, a big, fat, shiny fly. Too big for such a delicate task. And unable to bite.

So he attacked her as a flea. He bit her on the cheek. She gave a start and turned over, changed position so that he had access to what he sought, a clasp, a locking mechanism, a seal that he could prise open, calmly and cautiously.

She slept like a child, he might say. Noticed nothing. He was a skilful burglar.

No one could deny it. Least of all her, because no matter what she had lost, he had left her honour there on the pillow, whatever his motive might have been. Perhaps he preferred to be known as a master of thieves, rather than a seducer.

Sleep was as good a mantle as any other, a disguise, practical and comfortable. She had pulled it up over her, resting in its irresponsible warmth. She had recognised him, the henchman of the mighty man, and made herself comfortable, allowing him to do what he liked in the belief that she was asleep. In an unspoken agreement she had given Loki the illusion that he had the upper hand, if only because he was wide awake.

Then a moment of complete equilibrium arose, a perfect balance, when their relative strengths met on an absolutely level playing field; a position so sensitive that the least little breath would disturb the equilibrium. A state that was pondered for all eternity, alternately trivialised and blessed, leaving traces in the bark of the trees, in words and pictures on cave walls, school desks and draughty privies, extolled in ballads and chants, projected on screens as big as arenas, collected in documents and archives for thousands of years, and still it preserved its mystery.

In the morning both the man and the necklace were gone. But she had slept well.

And now she wore that necklace around her neck again, standing there and waiting for Loki to let it go. She still had the sympathy of the others. They saw nothing of the shamefulness that had been hammered into the smallest detail, every little section of chasing, every little ornament. They saw only the splendour, the lustre of a masterpiece.

Then he let go of the necklace and heard Njord say, 'Brilliant. Brilliant . . .'

Loki turned round and cast a glance at the Outsider. 'Brilliant?'

'That women fall for men, real men, their own men or others' men, all of them shit. It's brilliant.'

'Hmm,' said Loki. 'Well, that's one opinion.'

'But it's less brilliant when men do the same.'

'Oh, really?'

'Like you, you faggot.' He took a quick look around. Saw grins. Agreement. 'Didn't he get pregnant too?' He turned to the others, noticing one person here, another there, enough to feel supported and encouraged. 'How the hell did that happen?'

In that jumble of vying wills, impulses and malicious gossip there arose an image, like the remains of a shattered memory: a prison underground, a little boy, horns of bulls, assaults, rapes. An image of illicit rutting, a degradation that causes men to give birth: phantoms, demons, monsters.

'Do we have to open that sewer again? Didn't they use your trap for a shithouse over there in the east? You were held hostage by some bigshot over there, some bloody oligarch with lots of daughters who filled your mouth with piss.'

'Yes,' said Njord. 'And you know personally how it tastes.'

'Absolutely.'

'But do you know what I thought?'

'No,' said Loki. 'I have no idea.'

'I'm aware of that. I'm aware that you don't know. I could endure all that shit because I thought to myself: at least I have a son back home, a boy that everyone loves. And that's more than you have.'

'Absolutely,' said Loki. 'I don't have a son with my sister. Those kinds of kids usually turn out simple-minded.'

The Outsider glared at everyone, dumbfounded. He had revealed too much by talking, standing there wrangling with an impossible opponent. He moved away and sat down.

Tyr the One-Handed stepped forward in his defence. 'Not a bad word about Frej. Is there anyone who has anything bad to say about him?' There was none, neither man nor woman.

'Don't get involved in this. You can't keep apart a couple that's quarrelling. For that you'd need two hands,' said Loki.

'I may have lost a hand, but you lost a son. And he's going to suffer torment until the world comes to an end. If you happen to care.'

'I do care.'

'I can't tell.'

'Because I'm the only one who does.'

That merely provoked laughter, derision and ridicule. The fact that he, the upstart, would care – he who had trod on corpses to make his way forward, or back.

He had moved unhindered between the chaos out there and the order in here. He'd had free passage, knew the codes on both sides of the border.

Out there they took him for one of their own, so giant-like he was, so unscrupulous and raw. A raging, rational folly. A man fit for a life of lawlessness.

Loki had a whole life behind him out there. With a woman who belonged in that place. Together they'd had three children that only a mother could love. Three offspring who had become famous, notorious, feared.

The children took turns being worse than the others. They were wild, ill-bred, impossible to discipline, more at home among the forces of nature than in any furnished room.

It was apparent early on, for anyone who cared to listen or took the time to see: minor disparities, in the way one of them walked, the way another spoke, in the third child's tendency to bite.

And it got worse with each year that passed. The kids fought and clawed, scratched and bit, lashing out at everyone and everything; they were kept apart, on a leash, so as not to injure each other. They were beasts – they ate like beasts, slept like beasts, were easily roused, became quickly agitated, sniffed the night air for dangers; they never bathed, preferring the rough swipe of the tongue, or they rolled in the sand.

Over time their father gave up. He was in despair; life out there was hopeless. He wanted to see grander vistas; he fled from that home, changed sides, crossed the border and became blood brothers with the Old Man. In the world of order all his connections proved to be a significant asset. Rational folly could be easily masked as irrational reason. Dressed in new clothes he looked like anyone else in there.

But there was one requirement. Subordinates were not

tolerated if they had children out there. Children were unreliable; they could become future avengers. A deceitful father could never feel secure.

It was decided that the kids would be taken in hand and removed from their mother, since she was unable to manage them anyway.

The daughter was found to be so ugly that no living soul would even look at her. She was put in charge of death. A sad but secure occupation.

One of the sons was so ungovernable and wriggly that he was tossed into the sea to cool off. He never resurfaced. Yet no one believed that he had drowned; he was still out there, making the sea more threatening than ever.

The other son they tried to control. He was difficult and unruly, yet still only a whelp. He grew and grew and finally, after many frustrating attempts to train him, they gave up. He was a hopeless case. They called him the Wolf. He had powerful jaws.

It was foretold that he would bring misfortune with those jaws. The simplest thing would have been to kill him, but no one wanted to sully the earth with such evil blood. They decided to tie him up with a chain. A very strong chain.

The Wolf gave a yank of his neck, and the chain was shattered.

A new, thicker cable was made, twice as strong as the first. The Wolf, who had no desire to remain tied up, was persuaded to put it on because he would win renown if he then managed to get free.

The prospect was tempting. After a great howling and rooting about, the new chain was broken as well. Pieces were flung about like projectiles. The wise men scratched their heads.

They decided to consult the dwarves. They presented the

problem; the purpose of the chain was described, and the dwarves accepted the challenge. They had to mobilise all their professional skills in the art of forging. They produced an alloy from six ingredients: the yowls of a cat and the beard of a woman, the roots of a mountain and the sinews of a bear, the breath of a fish and the spittle of a bird. The chain was as sleek and soft as a silk ribbon.

The Wolf was lured to a remote islet. It was a summer evening. The sun was on its way down, mosquitoes and gnats were buzzing and biting at everyone's skin. Gulls shrieked from the nearby archipelago. The rock slabs on the islet were warm from the sun and rough with lichen that tore at the soles of everyone's feet. Dried kelp and drifts of seashells gave off a stench as they lay on the shore.

All the men cast long shadows across the Archaean rock, across the crevices filled with sedge, bird's-foot trefoil and bulrushes. They felt like leaping and jumping over deep clefts, from rock to rock, chasing each other like children, like boys again.

They grew hot and sweaty, swam in a warm cove, lay on their backs and floated in the water with the North Star between their toes.

The Wolf stood on the rock, shaking off the water. Like one of them. The men had brought along a ribbon, a soft, thin ribbon, and they amused themselves by pulling on it, trying to snap it in two. But it held. Not even the strongest of them could break it. Did he want to try?

The Wolf was not at all disconcerted. He argued that if the ribbon was as pitiful as it looked, he would hardly win renown if he snapped it in two.

But then he was told that if he couldn't break it, no one would be afraid of him any longer and he could go free.

The Wolf took this to mean that his courage was being

questioned. And he wasn't pleased. But fair's fair, so one of the men would have to place his hand in the Wolf's mouth as a pledge that no duplicity was involved.

What an idea. They could understand his reasoning, but no one had any desire to volunteer. After much hesitation, Tyr stepped forward.

The ribbon was placed around the Wolf's neck, and he began to tug and pull for all he was worth. The ribbon held. It just got stronger and tougher the more he strained.

The dwarves had done a good job, and everyone was pleased. Except for Tyr. He lost his hand.

The Wolf struggled until he was almost dead. When they left him on that distant islet, the Wolf was shackled to the ribbon, beneath huge boulders, badly wounded, with blood gushing from his jaws.

His howls could be heard far and wide.

That was the price Loki had to pay to be included in the group; he had to denounce a burdensome past, break former ties, purify himself through fire and blood.

Demonise old love.

Turn a deaf ear to the cries of his abandoned children.

Start over, find a new woman and set up house, see the old light fall across new floors, acquire household goods, set a new table for new acquaintances, all the bastards that came along with the bargain; unpack utensils and pretend to be unaccustomed to such things, line up glasses to find matching pairs, polish silverware that had never been stabbed through warm and bloody meat, uncork and sniff and gargle and nod and look ridiculously pleased, talk shit, make up lies about a suitable background, drink sweet liqueurs with dessert, watch how the smiles begin to go askew, the lipstick smears, hands begin to grope; watch how the elegant façades crack like masks from their calves all the way up to the crotch; shuffle about to dreary music with some superior's old woman, arrange for rides home, stand in the chill of the night and look at the stars and hear more shit and then straighten up the mess, wash the dishes, stand there wearing an apron and kiss the new woman good-night and repeat a joke as if he'd never heard it before.

And all the matching pairs in the cabinet back home. Plates and glasses fly around in the night, night after night, until only the odd leftovers remain. A collection of singles.

They are better suited to the table that he, the upstart, wants to set: for the irregulars, the misfits.

He fulfils his duties, ravages, abuses and flattens all opposition. He is a berserker when obliged to be one, a cavalier when that is required.

But it's only when he falls that he recognises himself. When everything collapses and goes to pieces, when glasses are shattered; when hearts, confidences, relationships, agreements and deals, hopes, teeth, furniture, nasal bones, strings, kneecaps — when they all break, fall off, fall apart, fall to pieces.

In the midst of the whole mess he might stand there sweating, with battered knuckles and torn clothing and feel utterly cleansed. Somehow liberated. On a private battlefield, a disaster area, unknown to the general public. Everything has been levelled to the ground, not a stone rests on top of another. Every purpose is gone; every idea, concept, vision about life has been swept away.

A desolate, empty and tragic site for the foolish. But not for him. Everything is there, standing where it has always stood; whatever is supposed to shine is shining; life continues as it has always done, but in a greater, larger, more intense manner now that sorrow, pain and loss have struck, leaving an enormous, wide-open crater right in the middle of the heart of the orderly world, an entire district, the antithesis of the 'pleasure district', entirely devoted to the mystery of the meaningless.

He knows this, is fully aware of it, now that he has made himself the object of the others' disdain. He has asked for it, dragging it out of each one of them. He has succeeded.

'I took your wife,' he said. 'With her I had a son.' The one-handed man faltered, reeled back a step. 'And what did you get out of it?' No answer. 'You didn't get shit, not a damn thing!'

'If you don't shut up right now, you're going to end up

out there yourself one day. Like the Wolf . . .' That was the Outsider's boy who spoke now. Tyr had staggered back to his chair, silenced. 'Shackled. Until the end of time.'

'You worthless nonentity. What would you fight with then? You who lay down your weapons to get a woman.'

'Nothing is free. Or is it?'

'No . . .'

For a moment there was silence. One person was thirsty and took a drink. Another went out to relieve himself. No one said a word; the only sound was from the swinging doors moving back and forth, until they too fell silent.

'I hadn't moved from the spot for an hour. No one had asked for anything, everything seemed to have come to a standstill, in the middle of it all. And I didn't want to miss a thing. I didn't want take part in it, but I didn't want to miss a word . . . For a moment I thought: good, it's over, he's done, the wind has gone out of his sails. He had realised long ago that it was all over, that he had burned his bridges. He would never be able to make amends. And now he just seemed tired, as if all the fury had run out of him. He said, "No, precisely. Nothing is free . . ." And it sounded exactly like: "That's it. Thank you very much." But there was an idiot who had been included at the last minute. He'd been downing glass after glass all evening, and by now he was drunk. Pappa had warned him, but he was part of Frej's staff and could do what he liked.'

This insignificant individual, who rarely had a voice in anything, now stepped forward to avail himself of the opportunity: 'If I were my boss . . . with his re . . . re . . . sources . . . I'd pulverise such a bloody . . . bloody liar!'

Loki, who had looked tired, almost resigned, ready to put down his weapons because there wasn't much more to do, now peered at the person standing before him, a tottering little underling.

'And who the hell are you supposed to be?'

'My name . . . my name is Byggvir.'

It looked as if Loki were considering this. Then, to everyone's regret, he found renewed strength. 'Are you asking for a beating?'

'I . . . I'm known to be hot-tempered. Everyone says so.'

'Am I supposed to take that as a threat?'

'He's mine,' said Frej. 'Pay him no mind.'

'So that's the one you creep and grovel for?' Loki said to Byggvir.

'It's a matter of honour,' said the drunk. 'A matter of honour that these fine . . . people . . . should enjoy . . . enjoy this quite ex . . . excellent beer . . .'

'Now he's going to kill him too,' someone said.

'Stop it now! Loki, you're drunk!' That was Heimdall the fair-haired speaking. 'Calm down now.'

Those who were paying attention could see how Loki's right hand kept clenching into a fist, then he would relax it and straighten his fingers, clenching and unclenching. But whoever was paying attention and also had experience of Loki knew that he wouldn't strike. He had begun to think, to deliberate. By then it was too late. 'It's just a bunch of drunken blather . . . Pay it no mind.'

'A matter of honour,' said Loki. 'A matter of honour . . . You poor slob.' You might think it was the pitiful, drunken underling he meant, but he had turned to face Heimdall the fair-haired. 'You poor slob, doing your shitty job, for all these years. As guard for all of them . . .' He let his gaze survey the entire assembly again. 'Keeping watch over this lot . . . who can't even look out for themselves. Who run around behind each other's backs. Is that anything to be keeping an eye on? To give your life for?'

Heimdall had no immediate reply. He was probably prepared for something else. He was still standing there, ready to intervene and prevent yet another assault. But that wasn't necessary. So he didn't say a word. Perhaps he silently had to admit to himself that Loki was partially correct, that there was actually something to what he had said, that he, Heimdall, had put his life at risk to protect a group of individuals who were unworthy.

His silence might be taken as assent. He should have said something, objected, at least out of duty; claimed that Loki was mistaken, as he was about everything else, taken up the issue of 'duty', 'honour' and 'reputation'. But he didn't do that. He chose not to speak. He sat down, took a drink. 'What the hell . . .'

There were only a few people left who had managed to keep out of the fray. Loki stood at the head of the long table. The tipsy waiter had made himself scarce, seized his chance as soon as everyone's attention was directed elsewhere.

Skadi had still not said a word. She had remained calm all evening, drinking a good deal, and listening to how her husband, the Outsider, was harangued, demeaned, almost annihilated, without showing any great interest. It was just a rehash of the same old stuff for her. She had been fooled before and survived it.

It's impossible to tell whether a silence is as weighty as it was just a moment before, when it is invoked by masters of the art, those who force the victim to interpret it, to fill the void with meaning. Someone skilled at keeping silent can make his victim interpret an enormous, telling genius in the silence that can seem particularly deadly since it takes all its power from the victim himself. This was the quality of Skadi's silence.

Now she stood up, slowly walked along the table, rounded the corner and came out onto the floor, to a free space in the middle of the room.

Skadi was magnificent. She came from out there. She too had paid a high price for being allowed to enjoy the privileges of the Clan. She had been thoroughly duped but had endured it with style and grace. No one saw any bitterness in her.

She was tall. She wore a tight, slinky gown with bare shoulders, long gloves, her make-up skilfully applied, her lips red. She pulled off her gloves, one finger at a time, placed the gloves on a table, neatly folded. She had long, red fingernails.

Loki knew what those nails could do. He had felt them on his back. He had seen those blazing red nails stroke his cock, sharp and hard like little knives, which only increased his desire, as if the thought of what they could accomplish, the damage they could do, merely increased the pleasure.

'I wouldn't . . .' she said. 'I wouldn't be so . . . arrogant if I were you.' She had a deep voice, a low voice. People craned their necks to hear better. They didn't want to miss anything, and even those who were so drunk that they couldn't comprehend a word, no matter how much they craned to hear, realised that something was going on even before Loki drew himself up. For once even he wanted to hear what she had to say.

'I would be careful, if I were you. I would take it damned easy, if I were you.'

Loki fired off a smile, still in that superior mode.

She went on. 'You may not be allowed to roam freely much longer. Swinging your . . .' She ran her long, red nails over his crotch. '. . . tail.'

Those who were paying close attention could see that the

superior smile changed. The basic outline remained, but something was added now, something less certain.

'Shit happens,' he said.

'Shit happens,' she said. 'I've seen things . . . Felt things. In here . . .' She touched, or rather caressed her body, from her groin, up along her belly, all the way up to her breasts. 'Gut feelings . . .'

'Something you ate?' he ventured. The superior smile was starting to look more strained.

'Deep inside . . .' said Skadi. 'Way deep inside. In the intestines.'

'You should talk to the restaurant owner.'

'It's easier to split someone open, rip out his intestines . . .'

With her clawlike fingers Skadi pulled out her intestines with a motion that was not to be misunderstood. She turned her back on Loki, took a few steps away.

'It's possible to split open anyone, a child . . .'

If everyone had been paying close attention before, they were now utterly gripped.

'You're a strange woman.' His voice sounded different, less strained and rancorous. As if he had sobered up. 'They're listening.'

She had noticed it herself, the fact that they were listening. She was no spokesperson, and no one had levelled any sort of threat at Loki before now, other than by insinuation, but she was respected. She had been tested by enduring great suffering.

'You're a strange woman . . . I was there when we killed your father.'

'I know that.'

'But I made you laugh.'

'Undeniably.'

'But honestly,' he said. 'Shall we be quite honest?'

'Isn't that the theme of the evening?'

'Okay, if we're going to be honest . . .' Loki was disconcerted; he tried to hide his confusion, but it was still noticeable. He wasn't getting a handle on this. 'If we're going to be honest . . .'

She fixed her eyes on him, frowned as if perplexed, but said in an ice-cold voice, 'Not again, sweetheart.'

'That's it,' said Loki, 'that's it right there!' He pointed at her. 'That attitude . . .'

'Attitude?' she said. 'Attitude?!'

'Yes,' said Loki. 'Attitude.'

'What about it?'

'I don't like it.'

Skadi frowned again, glanced away for a moment, as if to consider whether she had understood the situation correctly. 'You mean that you have a problem with my attitude?' she said.

There was a sudden shift. People realised the absurdity of the moment and started to laugh. As the mood lightened, those who were most drunk woke up and saw that it was all right to laugh, so they availed themselves of the opportunity, laughing a bit too much, too loudly and too long.

Then Loki screamed, as furious as before: 'You sounded fucking different before, when you said you were so horny that you could hardly stand up!'

The jeer fell on empty air. No one wanted to share his outrage.

Skadi looked at him with something almost resembling sympathy. As if she already knew. As if she had already seen what was going to happen. He, the irrational man, was invoking some sort of consistency from a rational woman.

People laughed until they cried. Even the Old Man was forced to laugh, although it would be the last time he did so with this group of people. He had seen that woman fight, humiliate herself, be demeaned, grovel in the dust, and then get up, start over, slowly but steadily reclaim her reputation, day by day. Now she could stand there in the middle of the room and with her head held high meet the eyes of anyone present. A person like that had to be respected. But to look for consistency was simply ridiculous.

Once upon a time he had been involved in a feud with another clan, equal in strength. Long, bitter battles were fought. It took a toll on their forces, on both sides. Many valuable soldiers were squandered. Everyone grew weary; peace was declared, and prisoners were exchanged, one commander and one advisor from each side.

The Old Man had an advisor who had acquired a reputation as one of the wisest ever. He possessed a fount of wisdom, a well, an unfathomable abyss. The person who was able to observe the world from this abyss could see and comprehend more than anyone else. A skill that no powerful man can do without. He had made a sacrifice, gouged out his own eye and lowered it into the dark abyss of the well. It was something he never regretted.

The wise advisor was sent along with a commander to the former foes. It was a bad move. The commander seemed hesitant in manner, almost timid. The former foes grew suspicious, conferred with each other, and came to the conclusion that the consultant was not nearly as wise as was claimed. They chopped off his head and sent it back. The Old Man received the head, smeared it with herbs, and got it to speak to him. With the same wisdom as before.

He, in turn, had received Njord from the enemy. The Outsider was pleasant and soon learned their customs and became well-liked, taking part in battles against foes with whom they could never establish any sort of lasting peace – demons, witches, giants and trolls.

One of the most relentless was the giant who had taken Idun. After she was returned, her kidnapper was killed, slaughtered in an ambush.

He'd had a daughter, Skadi, who was inconsolable with grief, which aroused a certain amount of surprise. It was thought that she didn't know what was best for her. But to live in the shadow of a great, brutal and domineering father might nurture a number of peculiar notions about light. You can accept your fate and avail yourself of the benefits of the dark. Or rebel and dream of a place in the sun.

When the shadow is gone, at any rate, things aren't at all the way you imagined. Strangely enough, you may feel less free than before. You're forced the whole time to 'take advantage', 'make use of the opportunity' and 'seize the day' – possibilities that didn't exist before and that force lengthy and time-consuming choices, a freedom from which you were previously spared.

Skadi felt anything but free. She was unhappy and wanted revenge. She organised a vendetta.

A daughter raging with grief is a mighty enemy. The Old Man asked Mimer's head for advice. Skadi was offered a compromise. She would be allowed to choose a husband from among those who were free. Anyone at all, but with one condition – she would be permitted to see only their feet.

Skadi accepted the condition and added another – that they would have to make her laugh. If they didn't, it would be open warfare again.

The men were lined up with only their bare feet visible. There were many single men who might be suitable, though Balder was the most enticing. Skadi pointed to a pair of feet that were unusually beautiful and well-tended. There was nothing unlovely about them.

But the feet belonged to Njord.

Skadi accepted her lot and kept her side of the bargain. All that remained was to make her laugh. Her husband-to-be tried, in his fumbling outsider manner, but without success, and when the marriage was about to take place, the matter was still unresolved.

Then Loki brought out a goat and placed it in front of the bridal couple's high seat. He tied the goat to a long piece of rope. Then he took off his clothes and tied the other end of the rope to his own testicles. A tug of war was about to ensue. And that was exactly what happened. The goat pulled in one direction. Loki pulled with his testicles in the other.

Both shrieked equally loudly, and the battle ended without a winner.

When Loki finally fell at the bride's feet, she couldn't help but laugh.

The marriage, however, did not succeed. Njord wanted to live near the sea. Skadi in the forest.

Both had their way.

One by one they had been singled out, accused and dragged into a chain of events that could not be controlled. One had offered counter-arguments, another had attempted to defend himself, a third had appealed to common sense, exhorting restraint. But all of it was futile.

There was now only one who had gone free: Sif, who had listened and observed without interceding, who had watched and managed to escape, until now.

If her husband had been there, the evening would have turned out differently. Thor was a man of action. When it was apparent which way things were headed, he would have long ago done the only right thing – smote Loki down and silenced him before it was too late.

But he wasn't there; he was on his way, but he had been delayed. For reasons known only to the Old Man, Thor had been sent to negotiate with a people in the east, ponderous, powerful forces. The fact that the Enforcer had been sent there might be considered ominous. Former enemies could become foes again if Thor were sent after them. Anyone who was paying attention and following events might interpret this as a major diplomatic error, see it as a sign that the Old Man was completely losing his grip, that he was lacking in judgement or had bad advisors. Someone might see it as a clear warning.

But this was a private party in a private room. There

wasn't a single window, no means to look out. It was a bunker, adorned with gold. With supreme contempt for the rest of the world, here they could devote themselves exclusively to one another.

In any case, Sif felt safe. She picked up a full glass, stepped forward and said, 'All right then . . . *skål*. Perhaps I'll be the one to emerge unscathed.'

Loki took the glass, drank a toast with her. 'You might have at that. If you had acted properly. But you haven't.'

She was certain that she had behaved as properly as she could. She hadn't laughed or screamed at him.

But he was referring to something more.

'Your Enforcer is just as big a cuckold as all the others here.'

That seemed way off the mark. She had never expected this. 'And you know that?'

'Yes, I do.'

She had been confident that he would never go that far. Anyone could see that only a madman would do so, a person who wanted to die and was trying to ensure that someone would kill him.

Sighs and groans were heard as the extent of this truth became apparent to all. It was reminiscent of a board meeting when serious deficits have occurred in one company after another, facts that are alarming enough in and of themselves, and yet not fatal as long as the core, the bank itself, remains solid. But in this situation the bank was threatened. If it plunged into bankruptcy everyone would be dragged down with it.

The abyss opened up. With a gust of wind from the wrong direction everything would topple over the edge, in free fall.

'Why else would she go around wearing that ridiculous wig?' he said. 'It's expensive. Pure gold.' He went over to her, ran his fingers through her gleaming hair. 'Was it worth it? How the hell would I know? Maybe. Maybe not. Who knows?'

Sif stared at him, totally uncomprehending. She didn't seem particularly angry or upset; instead she looked puzzled, or remorseful at how badly she had miscalculated. This was an act of public suicide, yet he seemed utterly indifferent.

'What . . . ? What is it you want?'

'Want? I don't know what you mean by want,' Loki said. 'I don't want anything else.'

'That's not true.'

'True? Want?' He took a few steps away from her. Perhaps that was necessary. 'You've always wanted a great deal, haven't you? Once you wanted everything . . . and nothing at all. Am I right?' He got no reaction, no reply. 'The Enforcer was off somewhere, as usual. You said, "I can't do this . . . can't do this to him. I'll end up denying it to my dying day." Do you remember that?' Again Loki got no reply, but everyone could see that she did remember. 'At that point what did it matter what I wanted? We had already started . . . And no will in the world can stop that sort of thing. Not even the will to live.'

'Did he say that?' Hanck asked.

'Yes, word for word,' said Bora. 'I remember the words exactly. I was still there, I couldn't move from the spot. I was on the verge of tears, all I wanted was to get out of there, I wanted to run as far away as I could. But I was stuck there, couldn't move a muscle. No one else could, either. It was as if everyone had finally realised what was about to happen.'

Loki spoke quite calmly, gesturing with his hands: 'I picked up a pair of scissors and said, "It will cost you a lock of your hair for every thrust I make." You knew I was serious, that I would toss in your face every snipped-off lock of hair so that you would see what it had cost, so you would tell me to stop. Or at least that's what I thought! And you agreed. Why would I joke about such a matter? Why shouldn't it cost you something? So I thrust and cut and paused and said: "Should I stop?" But there was no question of stopping. You wanted more and more and more. I thrust and cut until the whole bed was covered with hair. And you lay there, bald, with your cheeks flushed. Guilty and blissful.'

'What is it you want?' Sif couldn't object or accuse him of lying. That must have been what really happened, in spite of any fanciful reconstruction after the fact. 'Do you want to die?'

'Death in truth, life in lies. All of it is shit.'

'You have a wife and children back home. Don't you care about them?'

'I've heard, I've understood. I've already taken precautions.'

'You understand the consequences?'

'Consequence is my middle name.'

A swinging door squeaked. There stood Thor, the Enforcer. He'd been there for a while, listening; the situation had already been made clear to him. On his way up from the dock he'd come upon a couple of underlings having a pee. 'By devil, don't go inside!' they told him. 'It's Loki . . . No one knows what he's taken, but he's gone completely mental, he's been attacking everyone. He doesn't want to be part of the group any more.'

But nothing had ever made the Enforcer back down. And now there he stood, having been served up a full confession, realising that his wife and an old friend had betrayed him while he was out on missions, long, perilous journeys, exerting himself in order to maintain some sort of peace and quiet.

He had arrived in good spirits, terribly late of course, and yet counting on making another of his jubilant entrances, his pockets filled with 'the very last jars' of caviar.

And this was what awaited him instead. Thor, the upright and unequivocal, the always reliable, was a cuckold. Perhaps this wasn't even news to the others, perhaps he was the last to find out. None of them seemed especially surprised, at any rate. They were more surprised at seeing him standing there. He was more used to being eagerly awaited, coming as a liberator, someone who would mete out a righteous punishment.

Instead he felt embarrassed faces glancing his way, alternately filled with anguished sympathy and the contempt that people gladly bestow on someone who has been betrayed. Things had deteriorated so much that it would make no difference what he did.

He wasn't good at intrigues, he liked things to be black and white, in straight lines. He could listen for a while in a crisis situation, and if what he heard aroused his anger, he would usually start delivering blows until things calmed down. That was his method. It had taken him far. Good, old-fashioned violence; of benefit to them all.

He saw no reason now to try anything different. He came into the hall, went right over to Loki and said, 'I'm going to kill you.' That usually worked when he said it to people who had encroached into their realm and had done things they shouldn't have done. Especially when he put force behind his words and knocked someone down first. He didn't take them aside, drag them out to an alley, or even into the next room. He knocked people down on the spot, right where they were standing, so the blood sprayed all around, across tables and chairs, onto gowns and suits.

But this place was protected, and Loki could calmly reply: 'You have people out there, I know that.'

'You have to leave here. For good.'

'Where am I supposed to go? Out east? Get a pain in my arse?'

'One more word and I'll kill you.'

Loki moved closer to the Enforcer, stepped within reach. 'I don't believe you,' he said. 'You'll let the others outside do the job. Not that I mind. Somebody has to do it. Am I right?'

A question. Thor tried to work out what it meant.

'Maybe you want to, but you can't. Am I right?' said Loki.

Another question.

'I'm going to bash . . .'

Loki turned to the others again. They sat there without moving, wooden, no matter how much they'd had to drink. 'You should see him as a woman. So ladylike. They're wild about him out there.'

The Enforcer was breathing hard as he stood utterly motionless, as if preparing to lunge, launch an attack. But he was thinking, trying to think so hard and with such intensity that his body felt heavy, almost intractable.

'We've taken a lot of shit, you and I. Wept and laughed. You can kill me, send me wherever you like. But it no longer makes any difference.'

'I'm going to kill you.'

'You are?'

'I'm going to kill you.'

'So do it! Do it!'

Loki waited a moment, with his hands hanging limply at his sides, as if ready to be killed on the spot. But he waited in vain. He turned his back to Thor, giving him time to pull himself together.

No blows were delivered. Loki let his gaze sweep over the whole party, every single guest, the entire Clan. He knew that he was seeing them for the last time in this life. On his way out he stopped and said, 'I just said whatever I felt like saying.'

At the door stood the innkeeper. He too was sweaty, drunk and upset. The prospect of finally getting rid of Loki didn't seem to make him particularly relieved.

Loki cast a glance at him, gave him an icy smile. 'You can close this place down. It's going to burn. And you'll have fire up your arse.'

He left. If his intent was to 'sow discord, provoke wrath, mix harm into the mead', then he had succeeded. Nothing would ever be the same again.

Maybe his intent wasn't clear in the beginning, other than as an obscure, unformulated discontent, an unpleasant feeling that something was going on that no one dared see, except for him.

It didn't become clear until the young chef stood at his side and sneezed, right out into the air. Contradictory as it may seem, that had caused everything to look sharp and distinct.

A little, insignificant sneeze had stirred up the air, setting a whirlwind in motion; the swinging doors had fanned in more oxygen, giving it nourishment, making it bigger and stronger, feeding it with all the sins, all the betrayals and all the guilt that hovered in the air in there until it grew into a storm that would soon reach hurricane force.

Five Fathoms of Guilt

The Colonial Club was located in the area around the old Central Station, wedged between a shop selling protective clothing and a bicycle repair shop. It was in a large, red-brick building that took up a whole block, the bricks laid in Gothic formation with columns and arches around the windows and doors. It looked like an old factory.

The entrance was on the reclaimed ground underneath a steel railway bridge. The train heading for the outskirts of town clattered past, causing a draught that made the dry dust under the bridge swirl up into the air and then settle back onto the ground. Everything was covered with dust, soot and a fine-grained sand. The rain never reached this area. The water spilled down like thick curtains on either side of the bridge. A bunch of homeless people stood coughing around a fire they'd made in an oil drum.

It was just after five in the morning, and the Colonial Club was packed. The lighting was as dim inside as it was out on the truncated stretch of road under the bridge. Bare bulbs cast a faint glow over the tables so that the guests sitting there appeared as a murmuring grey mass in which only small, defined parts could be distinguished: a hand with broken nails wrapped around a beer glass, a heavily powdered cheek, a shiny forehead with a deep gash, an ear sporting a dozen little rings.

Hanck had never been there before. He stepped inside the

doorway, coughing from the dust out on the street. The clientele was not his sort – they were bohemians, artists and intellectuals, along with those who tried to look and behave like them, plus a few ragged souls asleep on the floor, leaning against a cast-iron pillar.

He went over to the bar. It was presided over by two men who looked like twins, both bald, with big, drooping moustaches. A beer appeared on the counter before he even asked for it.

'Shot?'

He nodded, and received a glass of vodka. He swallowed it in one gulp and washed it down with the cold beer. Neither the vodka nor the beer was any worse than others he'd had. Maybe even a little better.

He looked around the room. His eyes were now used to the dim light. He saw a woman with pink hair singing softly as she took up position in front of a man who looked as if he were asleep except that now and then a big smile would light up his whole face. Maybe it was a bawdy tune about what he had to look forward to if he decided to go home with her.

At one table sat four young men involved in a heated discussion, or rather an animated conversation, since they seemed more in agreement than agitated. Hanck caught a few words in the mumble of voices. 'An illusion about restoration . . .' and 'A democratic deficit . . .' A number of comments prompted loud laughter, the kind of scornful laughter that young men emit to indicate that they've seen through something and find it contemptible.

They had brought papers with them, sheets of paper printed with words, brief texts that they occasionally picked up and passed round or read aloud to each other. Maybe they were the ones who bought his old typewriters, young radicals who wrote poetry about 'claustrophobia'.

There were also a number of older men and women; most of them seemed to be alone, and they neither received nor heard any promises about imminent pleasures or freedoms. They'd probably been drinking all night and would soon head home before it got light. It made no difference whether it was raining or not. They had their routines.

Hanck surveyed the room, and whoever happened to observe him in turn could see that he was looking for someone or something. Though no one was observing him that closely. He looked most of all like one of those chance guests who might turn up late at night to have a drink on his way home without mixing with the regular customers. It was a peaceful place with a peaceful clientele. They might be dangerous to the system, critical and questioning, but not dangerous to him. He felt certain that he was the only person in the place who was armed.

From his position at the bar he could see through a doorway into a back room, slightly smaller than the room facing the street, with an arched window looking out on the back courtyard, wainscoting of dark wood, and walls yellow with nicotine. Hanging on the walls were glass display cases holding newspaper placards that no living soul ever read. There were booths with tables and benches. Smoke from pipes rose up towards the ceiling, swirling into the dark globes of the lamps.

Hanck got another vodka and beer and went into the back room. A few men were asleep, leaning over the tables with their heads resting on their arms. Others sat quietly with their smoking paraphernalia. A young couple was snogging.

The newspaper readers had once sat there – men of industry, financiers, entrepreneurs – with cups of coffee on the table. And in the light from the window they had read the stock exchange quotations, the raw-material futures; they had followed the market and stock prices, read accounts of military operations in the colonies where the latest mineral deposits had been found. They may have sat there since the very first cup of coffee was ever made and served at that latitude, coffee that was just as exclusive and desirable as it was now, subversive in its fortifying and invigorating effect.

It was a room for quiet reading, discreet calculations, hushed conversations. The rustling of the newspapers, the clacking of a spoon chopping up a sugar cube in the bottom of a steaming cup, the scrape of a safety match against a striking surface, sputtering as it was lit, the crackle of tobacco starting to burn in a pipe.

Smoke from pipes, cigars and cigarettes had swirled up towards the cornices and mirrors in the stucco of the ceiling as from a factory smokestack, colouring the surface first a golden yellow, then a mahogany brown, and finally a tar-like black.

It was as if all that exploiting, extracting and refining had left traces in the room, on the ceiling and the walls, like smoke and steam from the combustion that has been the end and the purpose of everything. A consumption which in turn aroused visions of new markets, new speculation. The discreet sound of a spoon against a saucer in the same key as the ringing of a steel beam being unloaded at the railway station off in the distance and, even farther away, the rattling of a sabre.

But that was back then, in a bygone and lost world. Now the place had been taken over by a different clientele with a different mindset. The rustling of newspapers was gone, the reports from the outside world were monotonous and stripped of illusion, prompting no visions of raw materials other than sand and salt.

There was an empty booth in the room. Hanck sat down

with the glasses of beer and vodka in front of him. He tried to collect his thoughts and stopped looking around. He assumed it might bother people, attract unnecessary attention. He was restless and upset, tired and worn out, emotion raging through his body; he had tried to counter them with alcohol and various pills, but could find no balance. Violent attacks of sobbing gave way to long, lethargic spells of depression which in turn could be replaced by brief, intense periods of feverish activity that immediately afterwards seemed inexplicably meaningless. And the thoughts that tried to keep pace might take shape as evil, destructive plans that he was able to perceive and comprehend for only brief moments. The next second they would become vague, as if lost, contradicted by another emotion, a new impulse.

His visit to the archipelago had hardly made his intentions any clearer. He had woken up, or rather come to, as soon as dawn arrived. He was freezing, sitting on an uncomfortable Windsor chair in a cold room. A table and a chair on a bare floor. No curtains, no other furnishings.

His body felt stiff, as if he'd been sitting there a long time. When he stood up, his legs protested – they had fallen asleep and could hardly hold him up. He had to lean against the table to stand upright.

He had no idea how he had ended up there, how long he had sat in that chair, or how the evening had ended. This place was nothing like the snug library where he had sat with Bora; there were no bookshelves, no wonderful armchairs, no fireplace. Only a table and a chair.

He felt his pockets to see if anything was missing. But everything was still there: pills, money, the piece of brick and the revolver.

As soon as he felt more or less steady, he went over to the only door in the room and tried the handle. Then, only then, with his hand holding onto the door handle, did he notice that he had blood on his fingers, along the cuticles. He sniffed, noticed the faint smell of iron. Using a fingernail he scraped off a little; it was brittle and crumbly, exactly like dried blood.

He saw no other traces anywhere, not on his hands or his clothes. His hands were otherwise clean, as if he had washed them carefully but missed a strip along three fingernails on his right hand.

The door led to a narrow corridor. At the other end he found another door. That too he was able to open. It led to the lobby. A night-light glowed from the front desk. It was quiet and still; no staff members in sight. The breakfast service hadn't yet started.

He went up one flight of stairs to his room. It looked exactly as he had left it the night before. His overcoat was flung across the bed, along with the brochure with the picture of Toby.

He was too restless to stay there. He washed himself, studying his naked body in the bathroom mirror to see if there were any traces from the night. Then he put on clean clothes and a pair of shoes with heavy soles, and his coat and hat.

He went out. After only a couple of minutes on foot he had left the buildings behind. Daylight was appearing in earnest, the contours of the island emerged, looking clear and distinct against the sea and the sky. A rocky hill formed both the centre and the highest point of the landscape. The sea hadn't reached that high in thousands of years. But big storms and torrential rains had filled the hollows and crevices farther down, creating stagnant pools that stank. Farther down towards the sea the rocks were flat, forming smooth slabs that were shiny and slippery.

The wind was moderate and the waves calm. Hanck made his way diagonally across the island, from the harbour in the north-west to the outermost cliff in the south-east, as far away from the inn as he could get.

He stood there, looking out at the sea. On the horizon, far away to the east, lights were visible on a platform that once upon a time had been used to guard a gas line running along the sea floor. A serpent circling the visible world, a dangerous creature not to be disturbed by anyone who was not authorised. It had to be guarded round the clock, as if it were still filled with energy. But no one believed that any more.

So this was where he had stood, the murderer, gazing out into the darkness, looking at the little lights on the distant horizon and taking the opportunity to think, to ponder his life, if he were even capable of doing such a thing. He had struck down a young and innocent person. Maybe his knuckles still hurt.

A barren rock near the sea, beneath the stars. A place for regret, for drastic decisions about penance and for making amends, a humble capitulation before all this grandeur.

But he hadn't shown any regret or acknowledged any guilt. He never went back to appeal for understanding, to beg forgiveness, nor had he come up with some explanation so he would be restored to favour, like so often before. If only to allow the world to continue on its way, to maintain the fragile balance.

No, no matter how it had come about, he had found something else out there; he saw that there was no going back, that all the boats and bridges had been burned. All he could do was go forward, keep going, proceed along the path already marked out.

He could have walked straight out into the sea, a few steps

forward on the rocky beach until the bottom sloped steeply down towards the deep, until he was surrounded by water and drowned, gone, vanished, until his remains turned up somewhere, a pale, leached corpse that no one could identify.

But he had remained standing there. Maybe he heard the voice of a beloved woman calling his name into the wind. He refused to answer and heard her sob in despair, in the belief that he really had walked out into the sea, in the belief that she knew who he was and ascribed feelings to him that he reasonably ought to possess.

Which was a serious mistake. Loki could not be understood in that way. Even the consistency he would show that evening was inconsistent – he had never shown it before.

No one would ever know what his thoughts were out there on the rocks, whether he made a conscious choice or was merely struck by a whim of the moment, whether he regarded himself as an individual responsible for his actions or merely as a small piece in a larger puzzle. It was a foregone conclusion, and he would emerge as the one who had hastened the downfall.

That was how Hanck had heard it described. He had been given the facts, the circumstances surrounding his son's death. But it was still just as meaningless, the result of an inexplicable assault, committed by an equally inexplicable assailant.

It was unacceptable. He could soberly and clearly talk about the possibility that his son was dead, but that this death should be so meaningless, that was what he couldn't bear. It created a void in a chain of events, a cause and effect, that he couldn't abide. There had to be some meaning.

Maybe it was this feeling that was largely responsible for the fact that the shock of widespread killing by human hands, and the even more widespread death by anonymous plagues, had not made him more amenable to such a fate. With his inclination towards objectivity, and his extensive experience of human tragedies, perhaps he ought to have been capable of accepting what had happened.

But that was impossible. He couldn't even imagine that shadowy figure of the past, that coldly observant functionary at the insurance company. He couldn't understand him. Just as he couldn't understand the person he was now. This convulsive notion about seeing some sort of meaning. Was it another example of his lack of imagination? The fixed idea of an obstinate person who had been robbed of the only thing he had ever loved?

In the midst of all these confused and desperate questions a coherence emerged that he had never seen or even suspected before. Clear, irrefutable. At times inconceivable. Alternately ruthless and beautiful.

As if there might be a meaning in allowing the death to be displayed against a backdrop of inexpressible beauty.

'Happy and satisfied?'

That was Kolga, the cold one, who stood there writing out a receipt behind the front desk in the lobby. She was professional again. Hanck thought he caught an insinuating smile, as if she doubted her sister's ability to make a guest happy and satisfied. 'With the evening, I mean . . .'

Hanck should have said: I'm sure you know better than I. Or: What the hell do you think? I've been around the block a few times. But he said: 'Very, thank you.'

She was wearing the long fingernails again. No matter how fake they might be, they still could have kept him there another day.

'I'm glad to hear it,' she said.

'I'll tell all my friends.'

Kolga gave a start, raised her eyes from the desk and looked at him with more suspicion than ever. As if she actually knew that he didn't have any friends to speak of, much less any to tell about this place. No matter how she acted, she had an ability to make him feel worthless. That sort of ability and those sort of red nails could have convinced him to stay out there for all eternity.

But he had decided to go home. After he had paid and obtained his receipt, he thanked her and went down to the dock in plenty of time for the boat's departure.

He was allowed to stand there in peace until the boat was

visible across the bay. Then Bora came down. She was wearing her sealskin cap. She was pale and without make-up, as if unprepared, as if she hadn't planned to say goodbye to him but had changed her mind at the last minute when she saw the boat approaching in the distance.

'Thank you for yesterday,' he said.

'My pleasure,' she said.

'I conveyed – '

'I know,' she interrupted him. 'What are you planning to do?'

He looked out across the bay, at the grey water with wide strips of red and brown algae. 'I don't know,' he said. Honestly. 'I'm feeling a little dazed.' He ran his thumb over the three fingers that had had traces of blood in the morning. He was thinking of asking her about that.

But she seemed a bit embarrassed. She kicked her boot at a stone lying on the dock. It flew over the side and landed in the water.

'I did the best I could,' she said.

'It was more than enough,' he said. 'I hope she realised that. Your sister . . .'

'To hell with her.'

'It was for your sake.'

'To hell with me too. If only you . . . if only you understood something.'

'Not all of it,' he said. 'But I'm sure it will become clear. I want . . . I want to see my son.'

'Good luck.'

'Thanks.'

'If you happen to come ashore here one day with Loki's head in your hands . . .'

'Yes?' said Hanck. 'What would happen then?'

'Then I'd marry you.'

'Is that a promise?'

'Not much chance,' she said. There was another stone lying on the dock. It flew in the same direction as the first one. The boat was getting closer. They could hear the hiss of the bow wave.

'That depends,' said Hanck. 'Maybe that's what he wants himself.'

'He's gone underground,' she said. 'Try the Colonial. That's where he used to meet my sister.'

'The Colonial?' It meant nothing to him.

'The Colonial Club. He usually ends his evenings there. At least he used to, when he collected the cash from casinos. It's a dreary joint.'

'Unbeknownst to me,' he said.

Bora smiled, a bit sadly, and repeated, 'Unbeknownst to me . . .'

He could hear how stiff and formal that sounded.

'That's not how you sounded yesterday . . .'

'No, well.' He had no idea how he had sounded.

The boat arrived and put into dock. The gangway was set out. Two locals stepped ashore. Hanck was the only passenger who was going back to the city.

He gave her his hand. Bora did the same, but she didn't let go of his. She pulled him towards her and gave him a kiss, in the middle of the forehead.

The skipper was watching them and sounded the horn. She laughed. He had undoubtedly watched her grow up.

New squalls of rain had drifted in from the west and met the ferry halfway to the city. Hanck had seen nothing out of the window because of the lowering clouds and the vapour on the inside. It was like travelling in an old submarine. He had washed down an 'Autobahn' with a couple of beers at the bar to keep himself calm.

The flat was cold and damp when he got home. As soon as he stepped inside, he stood still in the hall while water poured off his clothes, and he listened for the sound of the person who should have been home, waiting for him. It was as if the rain had flushed straight through his consciousness and washed away the most urgent, insistent of thoughts. Even though it was dim and cold and silent in there, he stood and listened for sounds, a little boy's quiet chatter with an imaginary figure, the melody of a tune with incomprehensible lyrics, or a clattering from the kitchen.

But everything was absolutely quiet.

Hanck hung up his soaked outer garments, carried his suitcase into the bedroom, quickly unpacked, and hung up some of the clothes, while he piled up others to be washed.

He went out to the kitchen and poured himself a glass of vodka.

He opened wide the door to his workshop, in spite of the humidity. There were only a few machines left on the shelves.

That no longer mattered. They were part of a life that had come to an end.

He set his glass on the workbench, placed the revolver and the piece of brick next to each other, and sat down on the high stool.

An hour passed. Maybe two.

Then he shuffled out to the kitchen to open another bottle of vodka. He took it with him into the living room and sat there for a while until he turned on the receiver and listened to the broadcast from the Cathedral. The organ boomed through the flat for a while. He wept, tried to surrender, to give in to the event, but he couldn't do it. Something held him back, kept him in his own world.

His coat was still damp when he put it on and went out. With the piece of brick in his hand and the revolver in the inside pocket of his coat, a piece of precision-made steel that was heavy and affected his balance, his whole posture. It gave him no feeling of security whatsoever, no illusion of safety. On the contrary. The possibilities that opened before him with a firearm in his hand were so numerous that he felt even more confused. In a matter of seconds he could change the lives of a great number of people, set in motion a reaction with unfathomable consequences. An explosion inside a little steel tube aimed at the most vulnerable point of a living organism, a lead bullet which, after a short path through the air, would penetrate a vital part, tear through tissues, blood vessels, a muscle or a nerve centre, and disrupt its function, causing the entire organism to collapse. Behind the seemingly insignificant movement of his index finger on the trigger there should be a chain of logical deductions from which this movement emerged as the only crystal-clear consequence.

His motive was clear, but the target was vague. A moving

object, evasive, changeable. Someone who was easy to confuse with someone else, described in the most variable of terms, sometimes gentle and humorous, sometimes harsh and ruthless, sometimes greedy and selfish, sometimes cowardly and compliant. A generous family man and a charming seducer.

Who would he be shooting if he fired at such a person? Did he have enough ammunition to fell all of these creatures?

He had a vague notion of wanting to see remorse in the eyes of the guilty party, that he would see real and genuine remorse, and that he could then decide. If he didn't see it, that might make things easier.

But he would wait until then, until he could see more clearly, get a more definite picture; or, on the contrary, become even more confused, go completely mad. Like the woman with the bloody hair. She was prepared to throw herself into the arms of anyone at all, willing to accept her beloved in any guise that he chose to assume.

Hanck had felt that great madness swirling when his loss sank its claws into him, leaning over a filthy certificate from the lavender-clad men on which Toby's name and personal information had been entered. It passed like a shooting pain through his body, a wave of something cold and stinging. The outside world was blocked out, a dead silence descended, he was breathing but felt no air in his lungs, smelled nothing, tasted nothing. He could slam his hand against the wall without feeling any pain.

Many times he had sat with the barrel of the revolver in his mouth, and with utter indifference he had tensed his index finger and pressed the trigger partway into the mechanism, sitting there until he finally felt a cramp in his other hand, which was clasped around the piece of brick.

That was what he had left of his son: a cramp, a painful contraction.

He never fired the gun. He stopped himself, because first he wanted to see his son, see him with his own eyes.

He had no right to make such a demand, there were no rules or rediscovered laws to invoke, only the crude practices that had been worked out by the lavender-clad forces. They cleaned away sad remains, informed the next of kin, and occasionally granted citizens who were worth remembering an announcement on the monitors. After that the ashes had to be claimed, to be dumped in areas designated for that purpose. If you wanted anything else, all you could do was ask for some sort of dispensation, special privileges.

There were institutions whose purpose it was to arouse and maintain an ancient sense of justice in the citizens, especially when it came to their obligations, and occasionally they would set an example through publicly administered punishments. But these entities were seriously understaffed, and every action took an endless amount of time. The entire apparatus had become the object of justified suspicion. Hanck knew all about it.

But he had a right to make an appeal. He could do so just about anywhere; there were queues all over.

Hanck wanted to present his case to the Old Man.

The Old Man's residence was a nineteenth-century address, located in one of the finer districts of the City Under the Roof. The lower two floors were walled up with concrete, like a sarcophagus, forming the foundation for the skyscraper that towered over the neighbourhood.

The queue was at least a thousand metres long. There were old people and young people, men and women of all types. Some were mute, almost listless, while others chatted, laughed, sang or ate. Many seemed filled with something indefinable, neither sorrow nor joy. They muttered their litanies quietly to themselves, or spoke the words out loud into the air, without embarrassment. As if the queue itself were a forum and the wait was so long and drawn-out that it had to be filled with something. As if they were forced to talk about themselves in order to remember who they really were.

Hanck walked along the queue from the entrance and around the whole block to its end. He had the impression that it hadn't moved a metre since he last walked past. He recognised a number of faces, perhaps the most noteworthy, the most confused and desperate. There were a number of weepers who emitted loud bellows with a credibility worthy of great actors.

Nothing had happened, not one person had taken a single step closer to the entrance. Some had even perished from old age or disease and been carted away, and the gap was then instantly filled by the next person in line.

There were mobile kitchens that moved back and forth along the queue; deals were struck, and all sorts of trades took place. When someone died, an auction was held for whatever they had left behind. The remaining funds were then managed by a council responsible for general security and keeping things clean.

Sometimes a woman would let loose a heart-rending scream, a commotion would ensue in the queue all around her, people would form a wall. The woman would give birth under open sky. The child would grow up and perhaps live his whole life in that queue. If it ever happened to shrink, and that child passed through the doors and was granted an audience, a peculiar situation might arise, since the case to be presented was a matter concerning relatives who were long since deceased. Perhaps it might even be completely forgotten, and the person granted an audience had no purpose at all, other than perhaps to see if there really existed someone to whom he might appeal.

Though this was a truth never doubted in the queue. If someone occasionally grew weary and expressed scepticism, the person was immediately driven off, frozen out and excluded. It was even said that someone who had been zealously critical was actually killed. It was considered unforgivable to express any doubts in public.

Hanck of course went to the end of the queue, giving as friendly a nod as he could to those standing in front of him. He was inspected, from head to toe. An old woman who sat on a stool knitting something that looked like a long scarf gave him a particularly long look of appraisal. She sold knitted goods and probably assumed that he would soon start to feel cold.

'And?' said a man wearing fingerless mitts and a thermal vest. He looked expectant, as if the new arrival would have something interesting to add. But Hanck didn't.

'A personal matter,' he said curtly.

That was the wrong answer. The man drew himself up, exchanged meaningful glances with several others.

'I see . . .' he said. 'A personal matter.' There were a few laughs, several grunts. 'That's what she said too.' He nodded at a young woman who stood leaning against the wall of the building with her eyes closed. She seemed to be asleep. 'After a couple of months the whole queue knew what she'd been involved in.'

The man with the fingerless mitts seemed convinced of his own pleasant and even winning manner; he turned to face Hanck and said calmly, his voice carefully modulated: 'We're one big family here, you see. It's a matter of give and take. You can't just take without giving something back. It's a way of life.'

That sounded like a threat. At least Hanck took it to be a threat, veiled as pleasant and well-intentioned information.

And he was genuinely frightened. The man in the fingerless mitts raised one hand and placed it on his shoulder. 'Easy, easy . . . It'll all work out. You don't have to share with me right now. We can go into that later.'

It was a misunderstanding, one in a series of misunderstandings that Hanck would encounter. As soon as he realised this he knew at once that it would never be worked out. He was absolutely unwilling to discuss his case with this crowd, and he wasn't afraid to disappoint the expectations that were clearly aimed at a newcomer. On the other hand, he was afraid of himself. He was aware of the man's pretentious and self-satisfied manner, and he felt an impulse to pull out the revolver and shoot the man in the head.

A crazy reaction. But the impulse was so strong that it took enormous willpower to resist. He would never be able to explain it in a sensible manner, and he felt compelled to leave, to disappear before something fatal took place.

So he backed away, holding his hands up in front of him. The man gave him a surly look, the woman stopped knitting. Hanck turned on his heel. He heard someone say: 'It's not over with that one . . .'

No doubt they knew what they were talking about. He wasn't finished with it. He'd done nothing but spread a bad mood all around him, started questioning one thing after another. A hateful person. A dissident.

So eventually he ended up at the Colonial Club. It was the only lead he had. A false lead, by all accounts. When his glasses were empty, he went over to the bar to buy another round. A number of people had crowded up to the bar at that moment. When he went back to his booth, a woman was sitting on the other side of the table.

'Was this place taken?'

'Be my guest,' he said.

She had a blue drink in a big whisky tumbler with a straw. She pursed her lips and sucked up a few drops without taking her eyes off him. She was quite large and voluptuous, with a wig of straight black hair and harsh make-up. He was grateful to see that she had short fingernails bitten down to the quick.

'Subversive?' she said.

Hanck wondered if he'd heard correctly. 'Pardon?'

'I'm sorry,' she said. 'I was just wondering whether you're like all the others in here.'

'That's possible,' he said. 'Although I can't say I know what they're like.'

'Me neither,' she admitted. 'Not exactly. But I think that they're those subversive types.'

'And what does that mean?'

'Critical elements . . .' Her long, straight hair shook as she made a show of quoting what seemed to be the general consensus: 'Critical of society.'

'I see,' he said. 'Claustrophobics.'

'Sort of,' she said. 'But I'm not one of them. I think we're living in the best of all possible worlds.'

She wanted to drink a toast to that. He clinked glasses with her, albeit reluctantly. If he had objected or argued, he would have been immediately drawn into something; she seemed to be that type, someone who 'liked to talk', someone who could talk about anything.

But it was too late, he already was mixed up in something.

'You're sad,' she said.

'Am I?' he said.

She tilted her head, squinted her eyes. 'I know men.'

'I suspected as much,' he said.

She opened her eyes wide, pretended to be surprised, even slightly offended. 'Now how am I supposed to interpret that?'

Hanck laughed, or smiled at least. He could feel it on his face.

'All right,' she said. 'That looks much better. You could sell teeth.'

'No doubt,' he said.

'Are they real?'

'Believe so.'

'Hmm,' she said. 'You're a believer.'

'I believe in my teeth.'

'That's all?'

'That's all.'

'A person with such beautiful teeth should be happy,' she said. 'But then you have to believe.'

'I tried,' said Hanck. 'Yesterday.' He regretted his words at once. He didn't want to get involved in a longer conversation.

'Okay,' she said.

'Forget it,' he said. As soon as he said that, he again regretted his words. The woman on the other side of the table seemed totally deflated, annihilated. As if she had found herself engaged in a more or less sensible conversation with a perfectly respectable man who suddenly, in the blink of an eye, had changed tone and wanted to get rid of her because she was embarrassing, coarse, a worn-out old hooker. She hunched her shoulders, her face fell. For some idiotic reason she made him feel ashamed. 'Okay,' he said. 'I was standing in a queue.'

Nothing more was needed for her to regain her sparkle.

'A queue for what?' she said. 'TomBola or the Old Man or . . . ?

'Take a guess,' he said.

'Hard to tell,' she said.

'You're the one who knows men.'

'As far as colleagues go, I've never doubted TomBola,' she said. 'So it was the Old Man.'

Hanck nodded. 'That queue hasn't moved a metre in two weeks.'

'It hasn't moved a metre in two years.'

'And how are we supposed to interpret that?'

'Maybe it means that he's very busy.'

'But with what? Keeping tabs on his decadent family?'

'Aha,' she said. 'A critical tone.'

'Fuck it,' he said. 'In any case, I couldn't bear it.'

'The queue?'

'The mood.'

She nodded a bit pensively, sipped her drink, and took out a case of hand-rolled cigarettes. She lit one, and like everyone else she blew the smoke up towards the globe of the lamp, then plucked off a scrap of tobacco that had stuck to her lipstick.

'And what was your purpose for being there?' Apparently she then realised that Hanck had no desire to discuss it. 'Forgive me,' she said. 'Of course it's none of my business.'

'No,' he said, 'it's not.'

Suddenly she held out her hand across the table. 'I'm Lucy.'

'Hanck,' he said. She had a big but very soft hand, warm and dry.

'If only I weren't so tired . . .' she said. 'But I'm dreadfully tired . . .'

Hanck didn't bite; he declined to ask her why. He sat there in silence for a moment, looking around the room in a way that he thought was discreet. But he was mistaken.

'Are you waiting for someone?'

'What do you mean?'

'You look like some sort of lousy detective.'

'I may be lousy,' he said. 'But I'm not a detective.'

'So what do you do when you're not sitting here at five in the morning?'

He seized on the least plausible explanation: 'I'm a writer.'

Lucy gave a big yawn, holding her hand in front of her mouth and lightly fluttering her fingers, as if in apology. 'I see,' she said. 'A skald or an author?'

'Either,' he said.

She paused to think, as if it were a reply that required a certain amount of contemplation. 'Difficult profession.'

'Definitely,' he said.

'But . . . but then you're like all the others here.' Her face lit up, she seemed almost relieved. 'There are both skalds and poets here, but between you and me, most of them are really lousy.'

'Unbeknownst to me,' he said.

'How pedantic you are.'

'That's my style.'

'They're just . . .' She leaned across the table so as to speak more softly, more intimately. 'They're just drunken pieces of shit, if you get what I mean . . .'

Hanck nodded. He understood. 'The world isn't fair.'

'If you'll forgive me, I assume that's why you wanted to see the Old Man.' She smiled, sure that she was right. He saw no reason to correct her. 'To get a little head start . . . Okay, he's the right person for that. Absolutely.'

She sat there nodding for a moment. The matter was clear. It was time for Hanck to return her friendly interest. He said obligingly, 'What about you? What do you do otherwise?'

She gave him a big smile, showing yellow teeth, a gap in her upper jaw. 'Isn't it obvious?'

'Even the obvious can have different names,' he said.

'Difficult profession too.'

'No doubt,' he said. 'Rather similar.'

He stood up, excused himself politely, and headed in the direction of the arrows on the signs for the toilet. They led out to a long corridor with shiny, yellowing paint on the walls, through a door and out to the yard where at last he found two metal swinging doors labelled 'Ladies' and 'Gents'.

On the men's side there was a long, stinking urinal along one wall and several stalls with doors. The drain from the urinal was clogged up, so he opened the door to the first stall. It was occupied. In the fraction of a second before he closed the door again, he glimpsed a number of details that only later could be put together into a coherent scene: a black clergyman's cassock, a white collar, a bright red face, a leather belt, the nape of another person's neck, a well-shaved leg, a large-size woman's shoe, a filthy floor.

He relieved himself in another stall and left. Lucy was still sitting at the table when he came back. He sat down, sipped his drink. The beer was starting to get warm and stale.

'What is it?'

'What do you mean?'

'You look so . . . Hmm, I don't know.'

'The beer has gone stale.'

'That's not it.' She turned her head, gave him a sidelong glance. As if that would make him easier to read.

'A clergyman is dying out in the toilet,' he said.

'Dying?' she said. 'What do you mean?'

He described what he had seen, in great detail, interpreting the fragments that he'd glimpsed in the brief moment when the stall door had stood open: a clergyman who was pressed into a corner with a belt around his neck, with the end tied to a water pipe up near the ceiling, orally penetrating a woman who would soon see him blessedly deceased and plunder him of anything of value he had in his possession.

Lucy stared at him, first wide-eyed, then giving him that sidelong glance again.

'Typical author,' she said.

'What do you mean?'

'Nothing but prejudices.'

'I saw what I saw,' he said.

'There's nothing to indicate that the man is a clergyman even though he's wearing a clergyman's cassock. And there's nothing to indicate that the other person was a woman just because a high-heeled shoe was on the floor.'

'Okay,' said Hanck. 'I'm sure death doesn't give a shit.'

'How shocking.'

'I'll never do it again.'

She smiled, perhaps thinking that he meant to be funny. 'I mean how squalid.'

'A nice way to go.'

'To think that no one has ever asked me for that.'

Well, at least the matter of her profession was now cleared up. 'Don't look at me,' Hanck said. 'I have no intention of asking you.'

'There's no order in here,' she said. 'It's just like out there. I'll be damned if there's any difference any more.'

'Have you been out there?'

'You can bloody-well believe it,' she said. 'I've given head to giants. Sucked-off the great ones.' She raised her hands to ward off any questions. 'No names. Nobody is going to come here and say that I tell tales.'

But he had no intention of asking her any questions. He said, 'I've never been out there.'

'It's hell for a woman alone. A matter of survival. Staying on your feet. But I was lucky. One day, after many years of waiting, I was found worthy to move here, to be allowed in. I came here believing that things would be better. Some semblance of law and order. Like in the past. But there's sodding little of that. Pretty soon it's going to be as bad in here as it is out there. They've lost control. What's needed is . . .'

She fell silent, stopped herself. Hanck wondered just how far she would go. He recognised this type of talk, he'd heard it in other places. Perhaps the exact same opinions were being vented at the other tables, among the young radicals who lacked personal experience about how things were in the past but had a clear notion that times had been better, that laws and regulations had guaranteed the safety of citizens, that people had elected a government for the common good. It was impossible to say whether they were reactionary or revolutionary, or perhaps one presupposed the other.

'Yes?' he said. 'What is it that's needed?'

'Oh, I don't know,' she said, taking out a cigarette and lighting it. She took a drag, calm and controlled. 'So what are you unhappy about?'

'Did I say I was unhappy?'

'I can tell. There's something blocking your way.'

'Isn't there always something blocking the way?'

Lucy shrugged her shoulders. 'I'm who I want to be,' she said. 'Do you get to be who you want to be?'

'I did once,' he said. 'Not any more.'

'Thrown out?' she said. 'Not allowed to be with the one you want to be with?'

'You could look at it like that,' he said.

'But you're a writer,' she said. 'Don't let anything stop you.'

That was a truth he had never even considered. Of course he couldn't admit as much to her, and he wondered what he should say in order to seem as familiar, in a professional sense, with this truth as he ought to be. But he didn't have to come up with anything. Lucy gave a big yawn, spread out her arms on the tabletop, leaned her head on her arms and fell asleep. She must have had a long and strenuous night behind her.

A short time later Lucy woke up.

'Good morning,' said Hanck.

She stretched, composed her features, blinked her eyes, patted her cheeks lightly with her fingertips. She was soon herself again. 'What time is it?'

Hanck looked at his old wristwatch. 'Five-thirty.'

'It'll be daylight soon,' she said. 'Do your teeth get even bigger then?'

'No,' said Hanck. 'I promise you.'

'There!' she said. 'Look!' She signalled with a tilt of her head. 'There you have your clergyman!'

Hanck looked. He saw a man wearing a black clergyman's cassock coming from the yellow corridor. It was him. The man had survived. Hanck felt relieved.

'How nice you are,' said Lucy. 'You care.'

He didn't exactly see it that way, but he let her believe whatever she liked. 'A life is a life.'

'Or else you're just drunk.'

'I'm not drunk,' he said.

A conciliatory smile, very tactful and carefully weighed, appeared on her face. She was good at that, she'd undoubtedly had the same discussion on a daily basis, with other men who claimed to be more or less stone-cold sober. Only a foolish or at least an inexperienced woman would have insisted otherwise.

In hindsight he had to admit that he'd been both a miserable and a drunken detective. If Lucy had made an indecent proposal then, he would have jumped at the chance. He had a rather vague concept of what qualities he valued in women; he regarded himself as broadminded, but in this situation he was quite sure that the woman in question had just the opposite characteristics of the few he liked.

But no invitation was forthcoming. On the other hand, she took a piece of paper and a pen out of her handbag and started writing. 'Wait,' was all she said. She wanted him to wait and allow her to write in peace. And she actually knew how to write. The pen raced over the paper, shaping the words, as far as he could see in the dim light, in an elegant and restrained hand.

Hanck didn't understand what she was up to, so he focused his attention on considering whether to toss back another round or whether he'd had enough. The night had already been squandered and ruined. None of his hopes had been met. The one he sought hadn't shown up; he would be forced to come here again, on another night, maybe several. He should go home, get some sleep, rest up so he'd have the strength to come back.

Lucy covered two full pages, took out an envelope, slipped the papers inside and licked the flap closed. She inscribed a name on the front and held the envelope in her hand for a moment before handing it to Hanck. 'Here,' she said. 'Take this to the VIP entrance.'

Hanck took the envelope and looked at the addressee. It said: 'O'Dean aux mains.' He looked puzzled.

'The VIP entrance,' she repeated. 'It'll take five minutes, tops, before he's standing there with his trousers down.'

'Thanks,' said Hanck, 'but that wasn't exactly what I had in mind.'

Lucy placed one of her big warm hands on his arm. 'Metaphorically speaking. Excuse me a minute . . .' She got up from the table, picked up her handbag, and disappeared in the direction of the ladies'.

She never came back. Hanck sat there for a while, he didn't know how long, holding the envelope in his hand and waiting. But the woman was gone.

He stuck the envelope in his coat pocket and left. On his way home he passed a smoking dustbin. He decided to throw the envelope away.

Then the night came to an end, a wasted night, or so it might seem.

It was daylight by the time he got home, and he fell asleep at once. When he awoke late in the afternoon, he couldn't remember exactly how the night had ended, but he was absolutely positive that somewhere he had stood leaning over a smoking dustbin with that envelope in his hand and then watched it glowing amid the remnants of all sorts of rubbish.

He hauled himself out of bed, feeling terrible, and went out to the hall where his coat lay tossed on the floor, wrinkled and wet. In the inside pocket were both the revolver and the envelope. It smelled of smoke. Part of the addressee's name had dissolved in the rain, but he could still see that it said: 'O'Dean aux mains.'

He stood there holding the envelope and felt himself reeling. There was a knock on the door. He didn't want to see anyone, didn't want to talk to anyone. He held his breath, standing as still as he could manage.

Another knock, a bit harder, a bit louder.

Hanck stood there, without moving, waiting for who-ever was out in the stairwell to give up and go away. It was probably a customer. They usually gave up after a few minutes.

But this was clearly someone who possessed both will and patience. Another knock. 'Hancken?' he heard from the stair-well. 'Hancken . . . are you at home?' It was the shopkeeper.

His eyes opened wide when Hanck finally opened the door. 'Hancken . . . what's happened?'

He hadn't looked at himself in the mirror for a couple of days, and judging by the shopkeeper's expression, an unpleasant sight awaited him.

'We've been over here looking for you,' said the shopkeeper. 'Several times.'

'I've been away,' said Hanck. His voice was hoarse, his eyes were running. He wiped the moisture from the corner of his eyes with a cloth that smelled of machine oil.

'We were getting worried,' said the shopkeeper.

'About what?' said Hanck.

'You know.'

'That I might shoot someone and then the gun would be traced back to you?'

The shopkeeper hadn't thought of that possibility. He looked offended. Genuinely offended. 'Don't be stupid, Hanck. It was you . . . We were thinking about you.'

Hanck was tired and dull-witted, but he still noticed that 'we'. He would never be able to express himself that way again. We were thinking about you. We're on our way. We're going there. We're about to eat.

'We've made a big casserole, the big kind that you like. You have to eat, Hancken.'

'I do eat.'

'No, you're being eaten alive,' said the shopkeeper. 'Look at you – gaunt and hollow-eyed! Why don't you come with me?'

Hanck gave him a long, entreating look. 'I can't.'

'Why not?'

'Not like this.'

'Then tidy yourself up,' said the shopkeeper. 'I'll wait.'

The shopkeeper refused to budge. No doubt he'd been given strict instructions by his wife to be firm and resolute.

Now he was planning to stay there and wait until Hanck got tidied up. And Hanck was too weak and fragile to fend him off. He coaxed the shopkeeper into the living room and then went out to the kitchen where he downed what was left of the vodka.

A while later he had washed and changed clothes. There was no question of shaving. He would have cut off his ear if he had even tried.

They walked through the rain to Vinterplatsen, then over to the pleasure district. It was early evening, and the nightlife hadn't yet got going.

The shop was closed, but the shopkeeper's wife stood at the door and unlocked it. 'There he is,' she said. As if Hanck were the only thing they'd been talking about. 'We've been so worried!'

The pot simmering out in the kitchen filled the whole shop with its aroma. They'd had it boiling for several days, throwing in everything they could find. Tough old roosters and salty bacon rinds.

Saussyr looked more miserable than usual. She came over and wordlessly gave him a hug. Hanck was hungover and sensitive to the slightest vibration. He had a feeling that she had put on that expression for his sake, to show respect and sympathy. He had a feeling it had required a good deal of effort.

He felt encouraged, not because of her genuine or exaggerated sympathy, but because he thought he could see through it. He'd been aware of and receptive to sensory impressions and moods before, but finally he'd become so worn out from the strain that he'd shut down the whole machinery so as not to be shattered or torn apart. Those dead, numb periods had become more lasting, a sort of restful indifference, unpleasant but perhaps necessary.

Now he was fragile and vulnerable and, in this snug flat behind the shop, with a drink in his hand, he was clearly able to notice the subtle changes in the young woman – the fact that out of consideration for him she looked sombre and dejected, but behind the mask she was filled with a sparkling joy, some sort of news, a secret.

The more he studied her, as she placed a cloth on the table, set out the fine East Indian porcelain, the silverware and crystal glasses, the more convinced he became that his observations were correct. She was really having to make an effort to hide her feelings.

And a little later, when the meal was fully under way and he had pleased his hosts by eating a good portion, accepting a second helping and showering them with praise, he finally had his suspicions confirmed.

'Hancken . . .' said the shopkeeper. 'We have some news to tell you. We have . . .' He hesitated, searching for the proper tone. Hanck could see that he too was having a hard time restraining his joy. 'The thing is . . . we've been given a space . . . in the City Under the Roof. Our request has been granted!'

They had been worried about how he would take the news, whether he might feel deserted. But without reservation he could say, straight from his heart, 'Congratulations! This calls for a toast!'

The shopkeeper looked at his daughter, beaming radiantly, as if he were now releasing her from her obligation to grieve. Saussyr's face lit up like a sun, like the sun that she couldn't tolerate and would now be able to evade in the City Under the Roof.

'She can go outside whenever she likes,' said the shop-keeper. 'She can visit friends and spend all day outdoors.'

He didn't mean to puncture the happy mood, on the

contrary, but Hanck then said: 'That was what Toby always used to say – poor Saussyr, who can never go outside.'

He hadn't mentioned his son's name before, but now, when he did so on such a joyous occasion, they asked him questions. They wanted to know.

Hanck said that he'd received reliable information about the circumstances surrounding his death.

He said that he hadn't yet been allowed to see his son's remains.

He described the queue at the Clan's headquarters, said that he'd tried to present his case, but without success.

Perhaps under the influence of all the alcohol he'd been drinking, he now pulled the crumpled envelope out of his coat pocket and showed it to them. 'I got this from a woman,' he said. 'A letter of reference.'

The envelope was passed around, everyone read the name of the addressee, silently and pensively.

'What sort of woman?' asked the shopkeeper.

'One of those wanton types,' said Hanck.

'Do it!' said the shopkeeper at once.

'Do what?' said Hanck.

'Go there! You should always trust a whore.'

Gerlinde, his wife, rarely engaged in arguments in Hanck's presence. But now she turned in her chair and said, '*Liebling*, what would you know about that?'

A new mood arose at the table. The ticking of various watches, pendulums and grandfather clocks could be heard from all directions, and the combined ticking sounded as if a different type of counting had started up – a sort of marital calculator that would be better off out of commission.

The shopkeeper's spontaneous advice turned out to be costly. The certainty and conviction with which he had offered this advice aroused the attention of his wife and daughter, questions were raised and voiced, very bluntly, at times in quite coarse and sweeping terms. Every little trip the shopkeeper had ever made, as far back as they could remember, now had to be supported with receipts and documents.

Hanck suddenly found himself involved in a row that for a time looked as if it might jeopardise their move to the City Under the Roof. Later, when he thanked them for dinner and made his escape, emotions were still running high. A business trip to the other end of the city had proved difficult to explain in any sensible manner.

For some reason he wasn't at all worried. The shopkeeper was above suspicion. He might be slippery in his business dealings, and he might defend his property with brutal violence if necessary, but he was a loyal and considerate father, and a sterling spouse. The ardour that his wife had displayed was almost touching, almost hopeful, in the midst of this shabby and sinful district.

The argument made Hanck feel guilty about following the shopkeeper's advice. Maybe he should refrain, as a symbolic gesture, albeit a hollow one. He had practically destroyed a marriage just by waving a letter with a well-known addressee, presented as almighty, from an unknown sender, presented as a 'whore'.

The queue encircling the Old Man's residence produced great quantities of both tangible and intangible wares: rubbish, handiwork, poems, latrines, music, icons, dreams and illusions. But perhaps most of all: rumours. They seeped out around the clock, all year long, each rumour wilder than the rest. Most of them had to do with the Old Man himself, his health, his past, his manner of exercising power. In a number of anecdotes he resembled the head of a corporation with iron claws; in others he was a gentle old patron of the arts, or a wizard, a ladies' man, a he-man.

But what might start out as a stray word at the front of the queue, a mere whisper, might then be overheard by a someone who immediately passed it on, possibly in a slightly distorted form or embellished with supplementary information. Soon it would take on the shape of a real rumour that spread from mouth to mouth all the way to the very last person. And of course the information gradually grew even more distorted each time it was passed on. A statement that began as: 'Loki has gone underground' would soon become: 'Loki has committed suicide', and by the time the story had reached the end of the queue and turned around, it would come back to the first person in an entirely new form: 'Loki no longer lives in the North.'

But most often all the talk had to do with the Old Man himself. His figure was cloaked in a wild flora of half-truths and pure lies, idle fantasies in which his powers were portrayed as almost inconceivable. Especially when it came to exploits in the past, during the dark, chaotic times before the borders were established, when the interaction with neighbouring peoples and states was closer and the conflicts ran much deeper.

The disputes with rival clans were countless, bloody and intense, particularly when they concerned the dwindling supply of raw materials. No treaties applied, everything was permitted, and personal honour was a rare phenomenon, as desirable as an untouched forest.

The Old Man was no stranger to employing means which in a more stable era would have been subjected to harsh punishments. A mighty oligarch in the east had committed a blatant error of judgement in a business deal; he had drawn the shortest straw but later denied any irregularities and refused to respond to the Old Man's demand for compensation.

Heads rolled on both sides, time passed, the matter grew cold and weapons were laid down or were aimed in other directions, towards new foes. The oligarch probably thought that the Old Man had decided to let the matter drop, that the whole thing was history.

But the Old Man had forgotten nothing. On the contrary. He was furious and brooded over revenge. And he was determined to exact it, ruthlessly and in a spectacular fashion.

The oligarch had a daughter. She was beautiful, at least in her father's opinion, a real jewel, destined to marry someone of high standing, perhaps some leftover from a tattered royal family.

For that reason she was constantly guarded, day and night, by her own bodyguards. If she ever went anywhere, a minor military operation was set in motion to secure the road.

Naturally her father saw envious and malevolent eyes

everywhere, and even worse: avaricious, covetous looks. He instituted his own laws, making it illegal even to look in the young woman's direction. And naturally he saw these laws broken; disobedience was rampant.

If he thought that someone unauthorised had so much as cast a sidelong glance in his daughter's direction, the eyeballs of the perpetrator were soon tossed into a big glass jar filled with a saline solution, a vessel that was shown as a test pattern on the local TV station. Once a month it would fill to the brim. The part of the country where the oligarch ruled soon became populated only by blind people.

When the daughter became aware of this insane jealousy, this incomparable cruelty, she developed a disease of the nerves. She tried to appeal to her father, but without success. In fact, he countered her sensitivity with even greater resolve.

The woman was suffering from melancholia. It became chronic. Finally she went stark raving mad and tried to take her own life, but she failed and became the object of intensive medical care. Powerful medicines were prescribed, and she was kept under observation round the clock. Specialists from the whole world were consulted, but her condition did not improve. She was a jewel, enclosed in tiles and chemicals.

And this precious gem was what the Old Man intended to steal and violate. Somehow he managed to ingratiate himself with the staff caring for the oligarch's daughter. There was a steady turnover of personnel. The father might decide that someone was unsuitable or unworthy, and then she'd be out.

The incident supposedly took place during the night shift. The Old Man, who was young at the time, had gained access to the keys and ended up on a shift. A vacancy had occurred, and he had written his pseudonym on a dirty whiteboard in a hospital manager's office. A woman's name. During the graveyard shift he was going to achieve his goal and take his revenge.

Finally it was time, after long and protracted preparations. It was just the two of them. He entered the room of the drugged, defenceless woman, and tied her arms and legs to the bedposts. And then he cast off his female disguise. He raped her, in a thorough and businesslike way.

This was described as a great feat, even by women standing in the queue. It was seen as an act of heroic courage, such was their fear of the people in the east.

When the oligarch's daughter later realised that she was pregnant, a truly dark time descended upon that part of the world. An entire hospital, an entire section of the city, was levelled to the ground. Any man who entered the area was found carved into a blood eagle, wearing a Colombian necktie, or (if time forbade such elaborate executions) was bludgeoned in half without ceremony.

The wealth of human inventiveness when it comes to torture is limitless, but no known methods in the world succeeded in forcing or pressing or squeezing or burning or hacking or pulling or cauterising or ripping or cutting or dragging a confession out of anyone.

It should be remembered that the oligarch belonged to a church. He was a devout believer, and this faith had also forced his daughter into submission. She would keep the child. The oligarch would have to accept the fate of being the grandfather of a bastard.

It was unprecedented; the utmost ignominy.

The bastard child turned out to be a son, big and well-formed.

No one in the known world dared offer congratulations, except for one – the Old Man. He sent a greeting. With acidic and elegant irony he offered congratulations on the birth, an occurrence which he had been looking forward to with particular joy, given that he was the father of the child. For practical reasons he did not intend to make any claims whatsoever regarding custody of the boy.

It was the final death blow. It made the daughter and the oligarch exchange roles. Motherhood had cured the woman; she had fully recovered her health. Her father, for his part, entered a great depression. He stepped down from the throne, stopped meting out punishments left and right, and instead devoted himself to an assiduous penance. He walked naked through the biting cold, he stopped eating and drinking, he whipped himself bloody. He chopped off his frozen, emaciated limbs with a machete and left them behind on his way to the salvation that ought to await someone who showed such repentance.

It was one of the Old Man's greatest triumphs. It always aroused the same response among the public. To recount it with all the details and complicated facts could take a week for someone who was eloquent. Someone who was hesitant, or who presented any doubts as to the credibility of the events, might keep the magic alive for a month.

Other stories presented more peaceful and more appealing aspects of the Old Man. Such as his wit, his popularity with the ladies, and his preference for the art of poetry, to which he had made significant contributions. Many could attest to his benevolence and encouraging manner.

Some even went so far as to proclaim the Old Man the father of the art of poetry, saying that it was the almighty father who had once provided the means and established the conditions that poetry required for its very existence.

In popular parlance, poetry was called 'the dwarves' vessel'. Many understandably took this to mean that it was an aid for little people in a world that wasn't set up in accordance with their needs. A world in which you feel uncomfortable, and everything that you desire is far beyond your reach.

Many authors, as Hanck in particular had noted, were basically little people, spiritually shrivelled, atrophied and care-worn personalities. Petty. Vulnerable and frightened. They needed help in their daily lives in order to seem bigger, or at least like everyone else. They sought compensation in poetry, resorted to words because words seemed harmless and free of prejudice; they didn't bite, they didn't provoke, they didn't infect. And besides, they didn't cost a thing. They were a suitable material to use for revenge-seeking cretins.

No matter how apt such a premise might appear, it was wrong. The fact that poetry was called 'the dwarves' vessel' had to do with the Old Man and the hardships he had endured to find the raw material of poetry and bring it to safety.

It existed in the form of a drink, an intoxicating drink, a cider pressed from the fruits of wisdom, the fruits of love and the bounties of peace.

The drink filled a kettle and two tubs; it was created by a couple of dwarves, clever blenders who knew how to extract the best effect from their raw materials. Whoever drank it would grow wise and become a skald.

A drink like that is not kept out in plain sight. It's kept under lock and key.

For reasons that won't be further elucidated, the two dwarves happened to kill a giant and his wife. Their son, Suttung, was filled with wrath and a desire for revenge. He managed to seize the dwarves, and as punishment he placed them on a rock that stuck up above the surface of the water only at ebb tide. When the tide rose, they would drown. The tide came in, the water rose, and the dwarves were filled with great anguish. They began to bargain with the orphaned son. They offered him the marvellous drink. He accepted and gave the dwarves a lifeboat in exchange. In this vessel they made their way to shore and out of the story.

The drink now had a new owner. The kettle and the two tubs – Odrärer, Sön and Bodn, as they were called – were kept deep inside a mountain cave. Suttung put his daughter Gunnlöd in charge of guarding them. She was considered intractable, utterly unrelenting.

Living with a relative in the area was a boy who called himself Bölverk. He did the work of nine and was cheap to feed. When it came to wages, the only thing he asked for was a glass of the famous drink; it had to be somewhere in the neighbourhood. His request was denied. But he did find out where the drink was stored.

Bölverk picked up a drill and bored his way into the mountain, wriggling his way through the hole like a snake until he entered the cave where the obstinate Gunnlöd kept watch.

She didn't see many people inside that cellar, of course. Yet suddenly here was a man in the prime of his life, saying that she certainly could tolerate the light of day. One thing led to another. After the first night, a desire awakened that was found to be pleasant and right and proper. After the second night, they became even more aroused.

Only after three long nights was their desire assuaged. Bölverk was thirsty. He asked to be allowed to take three gulps from the famous drink. Gunnlöd was sated and compliant. He could do whatever the hell he liked.

With the first gulp he emptied Odrärer, with the second gulp Bodn and with the third Sön.

Only the Old Man, at the height of his powers, could possibly hold so much. Wise but drunk, he flew home as an eagle. Suttung, the rightful owner, was hot on his heels. The Old Man managed to get all the way home, although he shat a good deal onto the ground.

The shit was allowed to pass for second-rate goods, the allotment for lousy skalds, what any mediocre poet could lap up.

The real goods were well protected, a mighty vomit that was poured into fine, new casks. It would turn many chosen individuals into wise and great skalds. Perhaps their appearance might give a hint as to how the drink tasted. Those that Hanck had seen perform had a number of features in common. They might seem different in both appearance and style, but they nearly always had a stern, solemn, almost tormented look on their faces, perhaps an appropriate look for men and women who were burdened by serious thoughts and who cultivated this expression so that it might evoke the desired credence. But once you found out what they had tasted, their expression took on a whole different meaning. Hanck refused to draw the conclusion that all knowledge was meant to awaken disgust, no matter how tempting that concept might be.

He took a roundabout way this time, avoiding the open square in front of the palace and approaching the queue from a different direction, heading straight for the main entrance. There stood a couple of stolid-looking guards in uniform to keep order and receive testimonials and letters of recommendation of various types that people submitted. With an indifferent expression a young giant accepted Hanck's crumpled letter. He cast an eye at the addressee, as if he were able to read, but kept to himself whatever he might be thinking about the matter. The letter was sent on into the building.

Hanck moved a short distance away, turning his back to the queue. He didn't want to meet the gaze of any of the desperate people who had stood there waiting for so long. It was clear what they thought about someone who tried to get in through the VIP entrance, people with contacts, a type of *nomenklatura* that were always given precedence.

Actually, Hanck had never heard of anyone who had gained admission in this way. No doubt there were other avenues for very important people. Perhaps that door was just an illusory possibility, the gap that had to exist in every closed system so that it wouldn't seem totally hopeless and inhumane.

And yet, if it did work, if against all reasonable expectations it happened, then he ought to know what he was going to say. Like all the others in the queue he ought to rehearse his requests so that he could present them in a convincing manner: explain that his son had been killed by a member of the Clan and that he therefore considered it his right to see his son one last time.

Next to the queue stood a bunch of black singers who were singing a tune that Hanck recognised. The refrain went like this: 'I'd rather live in his world than live without him in mine . . .'

If only he could convey even an ounce of that feeling he'd be able to convince anyone, even the most hard-hearted, that his request was a reasonable one.

'You over there!' he heard behind his back. 'You over there!'

He turned round. The young giant was pointing at him. At Hanck. He'd been waiting only five or ten minutes. 'You're wanted inside! Hurry up!'

Silence fell over the crowd; even the soul singers broke off. The woman who was serving up porridge in the mobile food cart stopped abruptly with the ladle hovering over a bowl. Hanck had been singled out, specially chosen.

The tall doors opened onto a narrow shaft with walls that were twenty metres high and made of sheer concrete. At the end of this shaft was a long stairway. Hanck was subjected to a thorough search, first done manually, then by X-rays in an enclosed chute. Having passed, he was then taken over to the stairs and told to hurry up.

It was a long climb. He had to stop and rest several times. The stairs ended at the roof level of the original buildings, the old façades that served as a template for the massive foundation. There a huge vista stretched out before him, an open hall with marble floors and tall pillars.

An intense amount of activity was going on. Hundreds, perhaps thousands of people were busy at long desks with telephones and monitors where they were working with codes made up of numbers and abbreviations, exchanging them with others, from desk to desk, or with people who stood at a podium beneath a big monitor with other charts, numbers and codes. White-clad functionaries ran back and forth along the rows, their heels clacking on the floor; machines roared and telephones rang. The noise was deafening. Someone screamed out a code in panic; another shouted out a different code in triumph. One person was overjoyed and received slaps on the back. Another collapsed in despair.

It was business as usual, and had nothing to do with Hanck. His arrival was expected. Guards stood in a long row and seemed to be competing in the art of looking officious and concerned. They ushered him into a lift.

The lift went straight up to the top floor, to the director's residence. Here an entirely different atmosphere prevailed – unobtrusive, confidential, discreet, almost intimate. Two wolf-like dogs were waiting in the hall outside the lift. They inspected him, nodded approval, and then led the way across a burgundy, wall-to-wall carpet, through velvet drapes, doors of subdued woods with brass fittings, art on the walls in elegant gilt frames. Nineteenth-century masterpieces of the national romantic period depicting the Æsir gods, kings, ancient Nordic sacrifices, landings on faraway shores.

The dogs left Hanck in a room with low sofas, trays holding bottles, a glass table covered with newspapers and magazines with shiny covers, with more naked, rosy flesh painted in oils on the walls.

He went over to a row of windows and looked out over the city. Far below he could glimpse the swarm of people in the queue, the open square where sporadic and unpredictable commerce was conducted. Over there stretched the City Under the Roof, in a labyrinth of folds, nooks and crannies. Farther south was his part of the city; the three church towers rose up from a shapeless muddle, a frayed silhouette in the grey mist.

With a hissing, scraping sound a set of double doors opened. Hanck turned round and looked into an adjacent room that seemed completely dark until his eyes became accustomed to the dim light. From behind a heavy curtain a figure appeared, seated in a chair with a high back. A thin, grey-haired man with a patch over one eye, wearing a dark-blue silk robe, with a pair of skinny legs in transparent stockings and his feet stuck into a pair of dapper shoes with tassels. Two ravens, black-clad and moiré-glossy informants, perched on the armrests on either side of him.

It was a tableau, a scene intended to evoke respect, perhaps. But it didn't look at all the way Hanck had imagined; the man bore very little resemblance to the one who had been described to him. He looked more like a modest government official, a relic from an old department that had been established by a king no one could remember, embedded somewhere in the Archaean rock, with duties that only those with a good memory could explain.

But that was just a first impression. After a moment the man's face emerged more clearly, the image became more contradictory. The lean, furrowed face was covered with spots, marks, and strangely shaped patches. It was weather-beaten in a way that only someone who had seen it with his own eyes would believe: realising that this man had sought knowledge in places where no one either dared go or was even capable of going. He had sat outside, in the open, under the hanged corpses and drawn in the essence of death in a quiet rain of rancid fat and maggots, letting slow vermin dig passages of light where the sun was shaded, like an endless, painful tattooing with blurred, secretive signs, duelling scars from the other side.

The Old Man was used to provoking surprise. He allowed

himself to be studied, and out of routine and courtesy he chose to start with the arrangements surrounding him. 'Security . . .' he said lightly, as if dismissing it all.

Hanck could only nod mutely, a movement that with a moderate amount of exaggeration might seem like a courtly bow.

'Please have a seat.' The voice was powerful. It was a command. Hanck sat down in one of the deep sofas.

He now noticed that the Old Man was holding his letter of recommendation in one hand and tapping it with the other, pensively, or perhaps with a certain curiosity and animation. As if it contained a welcome surprise.

And he got straight to the point. 'Where did you meet?'

Hanck said, 'I beg your pardon?' He heard the question but didn't understand it.

'Whereabouts did you meet?'

'Meet who?' said Hanck.

'Loki.'

'I'm sorry,' he said, 'but I've never met this Loki. I've merely requested an audience so that – '

The Old Man interrupted him without needing to raise his voice. 'This letter . . .' He waved the sheets of paper in his hand. 'It's about you, isn't it? You're a . . . a poet . . . it says here. And you were the one who submitted this letter. Didn't you?' He held up the two sheets covered with writing. Hanck recognised the elegant handwriting that he'd seen Lucy produce in the dim light of the Colonial Club.

'Yes,' he admitted. 'It was a woman who wanted to put in a good word for me. But it was a – '

'A "woman" . . .' It wasn't said sceptically but rather with scorn. 'If you'd said a whore . . .'

'I . . . I don't usually judge,' said Hanck.

'Judging and writing are often the same thing.'

'I'm sorry,' said Hanck, 'but that's not exactly – '

This time all the Old Man had to do was raise his hand. Hanck broke off.

'This woman, whore or shithead . . .' said the Old Man. 'Call him what you like, but he's made himself unavailable. It's most unfortunate. Dangerous for all of us. I want to contact him. So I want to know where you met.'

'We're going to cut off his cock!' said one of the moiré-glossy ravens.

'We'll have to see about that,' said the Old Man.

He had the feeling that this whole thing was based on a misunderstanding. He felt dizzy.

The Old Man noticed. 'Have a drink.'

Hanck did. He poured himself a healthy portion and downed as much as he could.

The Old Man waited in silence, allowing his guest to pull himself together. In hindsight Hanck would think that the man waited too long; a surprising breach of routine. The Old Man wanted something. Hanck was allowed to drink, reflect, and realise that he was in possession of some interesting information, and that he could make use of it. That he, the grey and anonymous person, had something of value.

'What's your name?'

'Hanck Orn. Hanck with "ck" and Orn without the umlaut over the O.'

The Old Man cast a glance at one of the ravens. That was enough. The black moiré figure slipped soundlessly out of the room.

'Have I read something about you?'

'No,' said Hanck, 'that's impossible, because I'm – '

'Wait!' said the Old Man. 'Hanck Orn . . . Hanck Orn . . . I recognise that name . . . Wait! I know it'll come to me . . .'

He muttered Hanck's name to himself for a moment without

getting anywhere. 'Oh well, it'll come . . . So . . . where did the two of you meet?'

'You mean the person who wrote that letter was Loki?' said Hanck.

The Old Man nodded. 'Correct.'

'What if I had my doubts about that?'

'That's your problem. Where did you meet?'

One mistake after another, thought Hanck. The man shouldn't have told him the truth, and he shouldn't have offered him a drink. He reached for the bottle. 'May I?'

The Old Man nodded in a friendly manner. 'Help yourself.'

Hanck poured himself another good-sized drink and sank back against the sofa, aware that it might look lacking in respect.

The Old Man's expression didn't change. He had asked a question and knew that he would get an answer. He was prepared to go further. He held up the letter and read aloud, "'O Allfucker . . . I bring to you a bungler that I rescued from an abyss. He wants to write literature. He's totally ingenuous, completely naïve and utterly self-absorbed. That's the way you want them, isn't that right?'" The Old Man's good eye was visible peering over the top edge of the paper. Perhaps he was waiting to see indignation, or at least the flush of shame. Hanck displayed neither.

The Old Man continued reading: "'I've also saved a cassock-wearing clergyman from death in a pool of piss and shit, where so many nowadays find salvation. But it was accidental (I happened to tickle him back to his senses). Who wouldn't want to be the first fly on such a cadaver? Hence a total of two souls. And the day has just begun. What else can I do to appease you? Yours, Loki.'"

The Old Man lowered the piece of paper to his lap and

looked at his guest, who at the moment was having a hard time meeting his glance. The guest was faced with a re-evaluation that would upset anyone's equilibrium, no matter what sort of trump card he might be holding.

Hanck was allowed to gather his thoughts in peace and quiet, subjecting the testimony of his own senses to a merciless critique, realising that he had been blind, and that he might be blind still.

At any rate he didn't notice when one of the ravens returned to the Old Man's throne and delivered his report, informing his master of almost everything concerning this guest.

So when Hanck tried to handle the situation by laying his cards on the table, and saying, 'I'd like to explain why I'm here . . . and correct a misunderstanding . . .' he saw an entirely new expression on the Old Man's face. He looked so utterly unlike the man who had just been contemplating him that it was almost as if he were a different person.

He was still old, but now he was also a gentle, sympathetic and infinitely sorrowful person. Someone who had seen and heard everything, someone who had seen and heard too much.

'That won't be necessary.' Even his voice sounded different. 'I know who you are, who you were and who you're going to be.'

Hanck was dumbfounded. It felt as if certain words at that moment could fill his lungs with the air they were lacking, fill his heart with warmth and his soul with peace. Perhaps it was simply fatigue, an almost paralysing fatigue that sooner or later strikes someone who has spent day and night in conflict with the world, who awakes, is active all day long, and finally falls asleep in his armour. His whole being screams to be allowed to rest for a while, to dare to believe and trust in someone, to surrender, at least to sleep.

'I'm sorry for your loss.'

'I can't grieve,' said Hanck, 'until I'm allowed to see my son.'

'Whose life we once saved,' said the Old Man. 'Have you forgotten that?'

'No,' said Hanck. 'But that doesn't give you the right to take him away from me.'

'Let's not talk about right,' said the Old Man. 'Was that why you stopped writing your critical reports?'

'I was fired. The company was doing poorly.'

'Exactly,' said the Old Man. 'That company was one of ours too.'

Hanck wasn't surprised. 'Of course,' he said.

'But your reports were well-written. They were read with great respect.'

'I was just following regulations,' said Hanck.

'Others did that too. But with less brilliance. I thought I recognised your name. It was linked to problems, even back then.'

'Am I supposed to feel flattered?'

'That was back when we started to lose our grip,' said the Old Man. 'Our people out in the field were getting unruly. The ones you called "berserkers" were starting to operate on their own. Everything got out of hand. And that's where we now stand. But you know that yourself . . .'

'No,' said Hanck. 'What do I know?'

'You've talked to the girls out in the archipelago.'

Hanck admitted as much. 'I had to.'

'Under the guise of a false identity,' said the Old Man. 'A night spent in the library with Miss Bora.' Hanck nodded. 'So you must have had that unfortunate celebration described to you.'

'The hurricane party?' said Hanck.

'That's one thing to call it,' said the Old Man. 'What are your own thoughts?'

'Nothing,' said Hanck. 'Nothing at the moment.'

The Old Man looked down at the floor with his one good eye. 'Do you see that head over there?' and he cocked his head to the side.

In a dim corner stood a pedestal with a glass dome over a round object that was shaped like a skull.

'Yes, I see it.'

'It talks to me occasionally. It once sat on the wisest person I've ever met. I'm not perfect. I've always surrounded myself with advisors, some of them good, some of them not so good. He was the best.'

Hanck thought he could make out a pair of eye-sockets in the dark brown skull, a jaw, a few tufts of hair on the back.

'Do you listen to the organ?'

'Sometimes,' said Hanck.

'I don't know how many times I've asked that skull to tell me whether it's a toccata or a fugue. He's explained hundreds of times, and each time I think I understand, but then it's gone. Can you explain it?'

'Unfortunately, no,' said Hanck. 'It's not my forte.'

'I have respect for that,' said the Old Man. 'If they send out messages that I don't understand, having seen things that I don't see. The exposition took fifty years, then came the pause. Perhaps it's time for a cadence . . . Or is that just a fool's cadence that presages a false ending?'

'I suppose one can only hope,' said Hanck.

'Is that what people believe down there, where you live?'

'Presumably.'

'But there are doomsday prophets on every street corner!'

'They've been standing there for ever.'

'And no one cares?'

'No,' said Hanck, 'no one cares.'

'No one believes in the sagas any more. It was so long ago that anyone succeeded in reciting one.' He paused, looked at Hanck intently, sternly. 'For some reason I think that you could do it.'

'Me?' said Hanck. 'Why do you think that?'

'You know what love is.'

'I have no imagination.'

'You don't need any. You've experienced twenty years of love. That's more than most people get. Write about that, about looking after a child, raising a son, instilling in him the desire to live, the joy of existing and working in this world . . . Write a saga for him.'

'I can't. I can't see any of that any more.'

'Because you're full of shit. But it'll recede, I promise you. It'll fall away.'

Hanck looked at the Old Man sceptically. He didn't understand where all of this was heading.

'Since you once loved a child . . . Since you once made yourself vulnerable, exposed yourself to the world, you can't ever hide again, block things out, grow cold.'

'I don't believe that,' said Hanck. 'I'm incapable of it.'

'Just listen to you!' said the Old Man. '"I'm incapable of it." Your dry, official language is perfect for the task of describing the nature of love. Someday someone will have to succeed.'

'Why?' said Hanck. 'Can't we just let it be?'

'The end of the world,' said the Old Man. 'Anyone can describe that. All a person has to do is go out on the street or look at himself in the mirror. It has no meaning any more. But rebirth in love? That's something altogether different.'

'But what purpose would it serve?'

'Can you turn love into something sensible, rational and even logical? If you can, then you would also be capable of forgiving.'

'Is that the goal?'

'That would be the miracle that would bring about the downfall. Human beings can pull it off if they know how love works.'

'Why should I participate in that?'

'You have the ability. It's your duty. You've suffered a loss.'

'Surely that applies to most people.'

'But they never get this far.' The Old Man smiled; whether it was a nasty smile or a kind one, it was impossible to say. 'And you've been drinking.'

'They have too.'

'But not that.' He nodded at the tray with the bottles.

'Is that . . . ?'

The Old Man nodded. 'You're full of capability.'

'I don't feel anything.'

'It'll come,' said the Old Man. 'It'll come.'

Hanck tried to object to the very last. 'I'm no friend of big words.'

'It's not the words that matter here. Especially not big words. Any idiot can look them up in a book. It's being able to see that counts. Seeing. Do you think I use this to see?' He pointed a gaunt finger at his good eye and shook his head. 'It may sound surprising . . . But you have to understand that I see with this.' He pointed now at his other eye, the empty socket.

'I still want to see my son,' said Hanck.

'You will see your son.'

'And what about the one responsible?'

'What about him?' said the Old Man. 'If he's allowed to roam free much longer, it won't make any difference what we sit here wishing for the future.'

'Is that right?'

The Old Man nodded. 'So . . .' He rose from his seat and leaned forward. 'Where did you meet?'

'At the Colonial Club,' said Hanck.

With clear but disjointed impressions from a lengthy transport, he at last landed in the realm of the dead. A long ride
down in a lift inside a chilly garage, a dark moiré shimmer
over soft leather seats in a long limousine, a cabinet for drinks,
a monitor with the Old Man droning on about the destination of the journey, like an electronic brochure from a travel
agency; well-tended conduits with warm, dry air; naked
fluorescent lights on the ceiling, swinging doors made of
stainless steel, a hall filled with trolleys, gusts of ice-cold air
from a cold-storage room, sombre-looking people wearing
vinyl-coated aprons and clogs with perforated leather tops;
the clatter of metal instruments in stainless steel bowls,
acrid odours, organ tones from a loudspeaker built into a
nightstand on wheels.

Details without any context from which to form a whole
picture, cut out of a flow from which he had taken small
snippets, with a limited ability to make note of more than
mere fragments; like during a long trip in a warm train
compartment when you doze off in one town, awake in
another and imagine you noticed a third.

His sense of loss had created a void that could be filled
with anything at all, a vacuum, an inner vortex that could
suck in anything, big or small. All his impressions were of equal
value, and every detail was so rich that it could be pondered
for any length of time without having its hidden qualities

extracted. The materials seemed to communicate to him, describing their origins, a lineage that would ordinarily be ignored in favour of their function.

In accordance with this new way of seeing – whether it was the result of an act of will or disturbance – the concrete of the walls, which otherwise were like a mute grey statement, might stand there harping about gravel pits, enormous plateaux of abandoned open-pit mines, ulcerated precipices, entire ridges from the ice age that had been worked, excavated away, mixed with limestone from other mines, as well as water and loose aggregates, in an arrangement of the Earth's crust that was altered and combined and cast in a new form.

The wood of the floor whispered of branches that pointed in another direction, trunks that had stood in a different part of the world, in forests that had stood in another era, with rings that spread out, year after year, to all points of the compass, a growth process that was cut short. Now the forests were felled, dried, sawed, planed and trampled by perforated clogs.

The hinges on the doors creaked about mining, about ore and iron and steel and forging, entire regions that were under-mined and collapsed and turned into lakes where sludge and swamp and algae and primitive organisms now slowly claimed all the flooded bedrooms with tulle curtains that billowed like kelp in a feeble current.

He saw the Old Man intoning on the monitor, with a faint gleam in his one good eye, a barely visible flush on his hollowed cheek. 'You arrive as a miraculous accident, a random accumulation, a collision between coercion and freedom. You lick forth your own face. No one wants to look anything meaningless right in the eye. Everyone wants to see order, consistency, logic; the facial features of ancestors are licked forth and licked away until only an anonymous skull remains. A face is a dense fog that slowly accumulates and is then dispersed around a white headland . . .'

But the love he had spoken of would clearly embrace the whole world, every living creature: 'All this will pass away, paintings, songs, cathedrals . . . All will collapse, rot, burn, wash away and fade . . . Only to be born again, an entire world will be licked forth out of nothing, everything will happen once more, yet again. A warm muzzle, a rough and strong muscle will eagerly lick forth a new progeny; that is our fate, to lick forth people to rejoice at this meaningless glory. Even Bach will be licked forth out of the silence, note by note . . .'

Finally he found himself released out into the open, someplace 'out there', on his way down, northward.

A colourless sky above a desolate land. Neither light nor dark, an eternal hour of the wolf without wolves, a pale moon, pale stars.

The two ravens lead the way, black against black, with the rustling of crinkled moiré; they are reluctant, of course, but display a forced politeness. 'This way . . .', and then silence for a while, and then again from far off: 'Over here, this way . . .'

A huge territory with the primeval rock exposed where expanses of forests, meadows and bogs had previously existed for millions of years, waiting to be used, waiting for the proper conditions, the perfect mechanics in the instantaneous destruction from a hydraulic flow.

Bones blasted by shifting sand.

Uprooted trees impregnated with rain-borne heavy metals.

The undercarriage of a freight car rusted fast to the rails.

'This way . . .' As indifferent as an usher.

Across endless expanses of motionless, lifeless waste products, unbearable in their monotony until the ground begins to slope, the dark grows more intense. Methane gases. The reek of sulphur.

'As far as we go,' he hears. 'We'll wait at the exit.'

He continues alone. There is only one way to go, only one direction, downward, northward. The vapours make tears well up in his eyes, he feels the air seep out of his lungs. He begins to have doubts, wants to turn round, but knows it's not possible. The sand is loose under his feet, he can't crawl back up, he has to continue downward, onward, into an even deeper darkness that soon envelops him completely. He can no longer tell whether he's outside or inside, but he starts to hear voices, living voices. Shouting. Weeping. Moaning. All the sounds of human suffering.

Hanck had never been out this far. All his kinsmen who had died had bid farewell much closer to life. It was only the most desperate who went out this far, those who refused to accept the reliably conveyed news of a death, who could not ignore the missing link between a beloved person and a bag of ashes.

You had to be prepared to stay out there, to feel so tired, so worn-out and tested, that you would never have the strength to take the long road back. Hanck was prepared for this eventuality, accepting it without the least hesitation.

So there were no actual visiting routines. Everything looked like desolate rubbish that nature had tossed about in its aimless fashion. Perhaps at one time in the past certain measures had been taken, some sort of portal erected, an entrance, a number of rocks placed in a row to mark the path.

Hanck thought he could make out an entrance and headed that way, but as soon as he turned round, what he had just perceived as a straight and distinct path was merely a huge heap, without the slightest discernible shape.

Only a great yearning for someone who was beloved could make little, inconsequential things look like signs to follow – two sticks on the ground that the wind had blown across each other could form an arrow pointing the right way. Three stones that, viewed from a certain angle, lay in a row were another confirmation.

That was enough to revive his courage. But not enough to instil in him faith and trust; it was sheer willpower that drove him on, the search for meaning.

Hel, who was in charge of this realm of death, had seen him coming, perhaps even heard him from far away. She had turned her head, listening with first one ear, showing her pale, lifeless side; then with the other, revealing the half of her face that was red, purple and black with rotting flesh.

She was the killer's daughter, an entrepreneur, serious and sympathetic, with a kind of dignified confidence and a natural aura of authority. Hanck could respect that, and he showed his respect by looking at her openly, without lowering his eyes. She was supposed to instil fear and terror, and she knew how to make use of her resources, and her frightful appearance which had once exiled her to this region. But she wasn't repellent to him. He stated his name and business without a quaver in his voice, prepared to accept any status whatsoever: temporary guest or permanent resident.

Hel had broken away from this inherited disposition. She was now friendly and forthcoming, not at all unreceptive to the sense of loss that can plague those left behind.

She said that he was welcome.

She said that she knew what the case concerned.

She said that she would help him and make the best of the situation. Although of course there was no question of giving his son back.

There was a cloakroom, with a coat hook and a shelf for hats. A wastebasket filled with blue plastic coverings to put on over dirty shoes. It felt almost natural to pull on a pair of these protective coverings and then walk into a dead and sterile area where the acrid, pungent odour might be perceived as something good, the odour of life.

He entered a waiting room with a sofa, a table covered with weekly magazines. On the front covers the latest winner of the TomBola lottery exclaimed: 'Now I'm just going to live life!'

Handkerchiefs were everywhere, neatly folded and pressed into dispensers made of stainless steel.

And he wept. He needed only to see a glimpse of Toby's fate for his vision to become clouded, his throat tight. Sobs welled up from inside him, wrapping the place in a thick fog.

He heard a scream that seemed to come out of the walls, out of the concrete, out of the ice age.

Every time someone pulled out a handkerchief, a flap rattled shut, attached by a spring mechanism. Hanck dried his tears, blew his nose, dried his tears again. The little flaps made a metallic clattering sound. His soft, shapeless sobbing, a cloud of despair and impotence, was captured by these artificially constructed, highly absorbent fibres made for undesirable secretions, preserved in stainless steel.

'Don't cry, Pappa.' That was the first thing he heard. 'Pappa, don't cry.' That only made him cry harder, his sobs even more overwhelming. How he had longed to hear that voice! He had missed it so much that he had walked around back home conjuring it up, forcing it out of all the mute objects that his son had left behind – a jacket, a pair of shoes, a piece of brick.

'There, there . . .' The metallic clanging of the flaps on the dispensers sounded clearer the more handkerchiefs were pulled out. Hanck emptied an entire storeroom, leaving a pile of crumpled wads.

He had never wept like that before and never would do so again.

And he had wept his son out of the haze. Hanck saw him, as clearly and distinctly as ever before – the infant with the inscrutable eyes lying in an incubator, the boy with the soft hair and the straight shoulders, a grown young man with his mother's smile.

'Is it okay?'

Hanck nodded. He was utterly shaken, he coughed but was able to breathe again. 'I miss you terribly.'

'I miss you too.'

'Are you in pain?'

'Er . . .' He didn't want to make a big deal out of the whole thing. He had a deep red patch on one cheek, a wound on his forehead, a tooth that had been knocked out, and a big gash on the back of his head. 'I can hardly feel it. It happened so fast.'

'Someone told me about it.'

'Probably made it sound worse.'

'Damn it . . .'

'When I was a kid . . .' His son paused, waited for his father to blow his nose.

'Yes, what about it?'

'I prayed to god to let me die before you did. I didn't think I'd ever be able to stand the grief.'

'I thought the same way,' said Hanck.

'But my prayer was answered.'

'Because you prayed to an idiot.'

The son looked at his father for a moment. He shook his

head, as if displeased by what he saw. 'You need to pull yourself together.'

'I know.'

'When did you last shave?'

'No idea.'

'Pull yourself together.'

'We'll see.'

'What do you mean by "we'll see"?'

'I'm stuck.'

'Stuck how?'

'I can't grieve. I want revenge. I want to see that devil suffer.'

'That's pointless. You don't have a chance.'

'That's what she said too. Bora. But . . .'

'Bora? Did you talk to her?'

'Yes,' said Hanck. 'I was there. I've been to your room.'

'You're out of your mind.'

'That's possible. But I had to. I had to find out what happened.'

'Bora . . .' repeated Toby. 'Bora . . .'

'She had a crush on you.'

'Those sisters are deadly dangerous.'

'She told me everything. Said that you had sneezed. I found this . . .' Hanck took out the piece of brick, held it out towards Toby. But he didn't want it.

'Keep it.'

'Is that true? That you sneezed?'

Toby smiled, almost laughed. 'Yes,' he said. 'I couldn't help it. It was wonderful.'

'But that sneeze brought you here.'

'I couldn't know that would happen.'

'That wasn't what I meant.'

'What did you mean?'

'I don't know.' Hanck fell silent for a moment. 'I thought that I had so much to say. But now I can't remember a thing.'

'You don't need to say much. You've already said all that's necessary.'

'It doesn't feel like it.'

'Maybe not to you, but to me it does.'

'But it was all just . . . beginning.'

'I have to be content. There are plenty of young people here who have seen nothing but shit. Not even a lot of shit. A little shit, because they never had time to see more. At least I got some applause.'

'I know,' said Hanck. 'I'm proud of you.'

'Me too. I have to be content.'

'Content?' It sounded like the viewpoint of someone who was old and worn-out, or a desperate attempt to convince himself of this, when the spirit was still bubbling in a body that was spent. He had to say it: 'You're just saying that to comfort me.'

'Absolutely not,' said Toby. 'I mean it. I don't give a shit about you.'

'You don't?'

'Not unless you get hold of yourself.'

'I promise I will. I've never had anyone else to care about.'

'I know.'

'I didn't know what love was.'

'I realised that. But I was so furious at you for a while.'

'Why?'

'I met Mamma.'

'What did she say?' Hanck glanced around, nervously, almost guiltily, as if he feared seeing her somewhere close by.

'She wasn't the person I thought she was.'

'No,' said Hanck. 'Of course not.'

'Why did you make it all up?'

'What was I supposed to do? You were so young. You wanted to know. I had so little to tell you. It wasn't enough.'

'You could have told me the truth.'

'The truth?'

'The simple truth.'

'It was too awful.'

'It's still too awful. She looks terrible. She thought that I knew. I felt so stupid, and then I got mad at you.'

'I'm sorry.'

'Nothing matched.'

'Maybe you can get to know each other now.'

'I don't know if I want to. Or if she does.'

'Should I talk to her?'

'You don't love her enough.'

'What can I do?'

'*Nada. Rien.* I'm over it. I'm not mad at you any more.'

'You're sure?'

'I think I understand.'

'What?'

'Why you made up everything.'

Hanck looked at his son, saw that he knew, that he understood. All he could do was give him a mute hug, hold him, stroke his head.

Would he ever find words for this? There were words for practically everything, every object and phenomenon. In the known world. In the ordered world. But this was chaos.

'The Old Man,' said Hanck, 'is demanding that I write a report.'

'The Old Man? Have you met him?'

'Yes, that's the way it goes.' And then, quite naturally, he added, 'But I don't know.'

It sounded as if that were the right thing to say.

'Did you have to stand in the queue?'

'I had to stoop to that, yes.'

Toby nodded.

'Otherwise I would have never been able to come here.'

'So what kind of report?'

'About you,' said Hanck. 'And me. About us.'

'Then at least you have a reason for going back home.'

'I don't think I can.'

'What? Go back or write the report?'

'Write,' said Hanck. 'I don't know whether I want to.'

'If he demands it, then you have to do it.'

'I don't know.'

'You will. I can tell you will. Was that why you came here?'

'What do you mean?'

'To ask my permission?'

'Not at all.'

'Go home, Pappa. There's something you have to do.'

'I don't want to.'

'I'm here. I'll be waiting.'

'I can't.'

'You can. If you don't go, then I will. There is a death after death . . .'

'No, wait.'

'I'm going.'

'No,' said Hanck. 'I'll go. Stay here. I'll be back soon. My dear, beloved boy, stay here . . .'

'Okay,' said Toby. 'But then I want to watch you leave.'

Hanck stood up. His legs could hardly hold him up. He needed help to stay on his feet until his strength returned.

'I want to watch you leave.'

'You will.'

'Don't look back.'

'I love you. I'll keep talking about you until we meet again.'

'As long as I don't have to listen. Don't forget your hat. And take those ridiculous coverings off your shoes . . .'

Eventually he was once again outdoors, under an open sky, in another region, another climate; he stood near a drab exit with automatic doors under a sign with a red X and the words 'Exit/Way Out' and he had the sun in his eyes, dazzled but with no fear of harm; he saw a park with benches and litter bins, signs forbidding the walking of dogs, and well-tended flower beds along raked paths. He saw roses growing along paths that he had never taken.

Every path led out into the wild. There were trees, wild trees beneath a clear sky, a whole forest, needle-covered paths with roots that had cropped up and were polished shiny by those who had gone astray before him, who had seen moss and lichen on the rocks in the shadows like he did, heard insects buzzing and animals rustling in the thickets with the same surprise.

Blue-tinged mountains in the distance.

In the world that had been described to him as an intolerable chaos, ravaged by disease and lawlessness, a wasteland, devastated, perilous and poisoned, there was also this.

He began walking, slowly and cautiously, unaccustomed to the ground beneath him. He should have felt afraid and lost when faced with this almost impenetrable wilderness. He lacked faith and felt no trust, he understood nothing of what he saw, these forms in nature, what they were supposed to be called, how they fitted together. But he took it all in with an open heart. Wanting to see. Daring to see.

Black moiré shimmer in the shadow of a pine tree.

'Time flies . . .'

They had waited for him. He should have felt flattered.

'Leave me alone.'

'He's recovering . . .'

'So it seems.'

'Where are you going?'

'To scatter my son's ashes.'

'Where?'

'I don't know.'

'You're walking with such firm steps.'

'I'm following a path.'

'There are other paths.'

'This happens to be the one.'

'You have to go home. You made a promise.'

'We'll see.'

'A lot has been going on . . .'

'. . . that ought to interest you.'

'Like what?'

'He's been caught.'

Hanck stopped, with one leg resting against a toppled tree trunk.

'He?'

'The inscrutable one.'

'The murderer.'

'The airborne one.'

'The outlaw.'

'The seducer.'

'The family man.'

'The queer.'

'The marvellous one.'

'The Old Man thought you ought to know.'

'It was in your waters, so to speak, that the net was cast.'

'And the punishment?'

'Already carried out.'

'Is he dead?'

'No. Too easy.'

'You're not the only one who wanted to see good, old-fashioned remorse.'

'Has he expressed remorse?'

'Most likely.'

'How?' said Hanck. 'I want to know how.'

'Difficult to describe.'

'Worth seeing . . .'

'This way . . .' And soon, farther off: 'This way.'

Soon it was looming in front of him, a mighty granite plinth, and at the base of this formation was the entrance to a cave. The ground in front of the opening was trampled flat, as if by many feet; it was foul and dead. Nothing could grow there.

Hanck hesitated, as if before a bloody turnstile.

'It's free.'

'Free admission . . .'

Inside awaited a scene that was of particularly cunning cruelty.

Loki was bound, lying next to several boulders in a cold and damp pit. He was unrecognisable.

Above his head, on a ledge in the rock, coiled a long snake that now and then spat venom on the naked captive.

His wife Sigyn was there. She held a bowl under the jaws of the snake to catch the corrosive acid. When the bowl was full, it had to be emptied onto the ground outside the cave. Each time this happened, a few drops landed on the defence-less Loki. He roared and yanked on his shackles, making the ground shake. So great was his pain.

A picture of the gods' punishment and a wife's compassion, perhaps.

'Ponder carefully what you see.' It was cold and matter-of-fact advice.

Hanck forced himself to study every detail as intently as he could. It was revolting, but worth the effort.

The mechanism was rather simple, almost self-perpetuating. The requirements were access to venom, gravity and the patience of a wife.

Something in the woman's expression indicated that this could go on for all eternity as far as she was concerned. Her patience was as reliable as the gravitational pull of the earth. To put it quite simply, she radiated a surprising resolve. The torment had been going on for a while now, and she had become accustomed to it, or at least was making the best of things. Other than that, there were also traces of desperation, tears and cries of anguish and horror – outbursts that had raged, fallen silent and hardened into a darkness in her eyes.

But that was not all.

Now and then, in between harrowing shouts of pain and despair, in moments of calm – of the kind that can arise around a hopeless, chronic invalid – the man could be heard whispering or snarling: 'Go . . . get out of here . . .', and even more touching: 'Please . . .', and when he wasn't obeyed: 'Begone, old woman!'

It sounded almost like a grandiose exhortation; the concern of a man who was lost for the one who had a chance of saving herself.

She was still young, she had her whole life left to live. She was beautiful, she could find another husband, start over. She didn't have to sacrifice herself, spend the rest of her life in this hopeless pit.

Her refusal to obey such loving advice could, in turn, seem just as grandiose. She said, calmly and firmly, 'I'll never abandon you.'

'How touching,' Hanck heard. Cold, without an ounce of compassion.

Because there was something that he'd missed. 'Look at the shackles.'

They didn't look especially remarkable. There were no straps of tanned leather, no ropes of tarred hawsers, no cables of tempered steel. They looked mostly like thin, soft ribbons, supple and pliable.

'They were still warm when they were tied.'

The ravens explained. Loki had gone to ground, with his wife and their two sons, heading for the mountains to hide. It would have worked out fine if he had stayed there, if he'd had a stronger character. But he just couldn't do it. His passions or inclinations, call them what you will, drew him away from there, down to the city, the taverns, all the temptations. And while there he was discovered, of course, recognised and shadowed, followed all the way home to his secret hiding place. A troop had surrounded the area, plucking up first one son, then the other, forcing one brother to stab a knife into the other, to slit open his belly, rip out his guts and, before he lost his senses, wind them into a handy ball. Eight metres of intestines, a paltry twine, one might think, but the husband and father who is tied with that bond will never be able to get loose.

What could release five fathoms of such guilt?

Perhaps behind the prisoner's entreaty was concern for his wife, but also a simple, selfish calculation – if she stopped protecting him from the snake's venom, he could open his mouth, swallow drop after drop, and finally be allowed to die.

Behind her apparent sacrifice, there was also a less compassionate calculation. The man she loved and to whom she had sworn to be faithful had betrayed her year in and year out. If she hadn't had those two sons to care for, she might have given up long ago. Now they too had been involved, dragged into their father's world of deceit and inconceivable cruelty.

A man like that should not be granted the mercy of death. Her patience would sharpen the torment, prolong the torture. She didn't want to start over somewhere else. She wanted to be right here.

Hanck saw what it was that seemed strange about her face. Behind the haggard expression of horror there was also an element of bitter triumph, or the solace that can be found in the words 'What did I tell you?!'

'Have you looked your fill?' said one raven.

'Are you satisfied?' said the other.

Hanck was done. He didn't need to see more. Whether he was satisfied or not remained unsaid.

They left the cave. The ground where Sigyn emptied the bowl of venom was poisoned. A dead space.

Hanck stood there for a moment, looking at the sterile, barren ground. That was where he would scatter his son's ashes. That was where they would do some good.

If only for a blade of grass.

The rain poured down. A thick stream from a leaking roof gutter that had rusted through drummed onto the window ledge. It had been going on for months now, the whole city had been flushed clean, thoroughly soaked. Reservoirs and pools were full to the brim. Stairwells and vestibules had begun to smell foul, rank and sour from mildew and mould that had crept up along the floors. Drains were overflowing, entire sections of the city were starting to smell like an open sewer.

But it would soon be over, at least for this time around. One day the rain would stop. It wouldn't taper off, turn to drizzle or to scattered showers that came and went. It would just stop, abruptly, like a sudden power outage.

That was what he had to look forward to. Everything else was uncertain.

He could sit at his workbench in his workshop from morning to night, with a bottle of vodka and a glass, a revolver, a piece of brick and an old typewriter that still didn't show any signs of rust. It was fully functional.

As was the revolver. He knew that he would never use it, at least not to threaten anyone or to coerce anything, such as remorse or answers to certain questions. He had seen what he wanted to see, heard what he needed to hear.

Not that he had gained any definitive clarity. Questions still remained. His need to have them answered in a satisfactory manner had only made their number increase, prompting new questions, pointing out connections and associations that made the uncertainties even greater and more numerous.

He would have to live with them, these anomalies, these meaningless speculations that follow a life cut short.

That too was a certainty.

But he didn't know whether he'd be able to bear it. He had to make his way forward, breath by breath, day by day.

Many people throw themselves into their grief and fumble about in the dark, fall down, end up bloody. They emerge as soon as they can, badly lacerated, with a sort of hate-filled hunger and their spirit darkened for all time.

But it's possible to enter your grief with no intention of coming out, with no intentions at all because there is nothing else to do. You fumble about in the dark, like the others, fall over and hurt yourself, just like the others. But cuts and bruises will heal and fade, while you remain in there until your eyes get used to the dark and begin to see how even blackness has its nuances.

It takes time to get used to it. A situation that gradually becomes clear.

But everything was rained away, washed clean. Perhaps even the emptiness would be leached out, become colourless and transparent.

Perhaps one day he would have only one question left, utterly forgotten by the future, like a sprig preserved between the pages of an old book that he had never opened.

Could he ever forgive?

He would never be able to understand. But forgive? What would it mean for him to forgive? That his love for the one he had lost could be set free and used for anything whatever, even for the most absurd: to embrace even death?

Would it then be just as strong and powerful? And above all, was it genuine or fabricated?

The revolver could never force any answers.

But perhaps the typewriter could. He was bound to it by a promise: to bear witness, to tell a story, to deliver a report about love, as he had experienced it.

At the same time he had been presented with an odd predicament: that the world would continue to exist until love was explained.

The destroyer of the world would lie bound in his cave as long as love remained a mystery. Or at least until someone with an open heart felt capable of forgiving him, with sincere and genuine love.

That would dissolve his guilt, set him free. Not changed in the least; rather, he would be hardened in his determination to destroy the world. He would join with the powers in Muspelheim and launch the last, devastating battle.

Then it was said that the sun would turn black, the earth would sink into the sea, the gleaming stars would fall from the heavens; flames would lick at the bulwark of life, the heat would blaze towards the sky.

There was no sophistry about it, it was a simple observation: that deep, acknowledged love can take on any sort of appearance, embrace anyone and anything, grow, develop and change, until in the end it resembles its own opposite. But it could never be shaped into a tool, an instrument in the service of any one person.

Every description of love had to be highly provisional, a suggestion, a temporary compromise to rally round for the moment. Soon all the conditions may have changed, and the presentation of circumstances would have to be redone, using new words.

Love refused to be defined, because it was impossible to

explain, because perfect love destroys and any attempt to define it presented the perfect balance of terror, for an eternity of eternities.

Hanck wondered whether he was prepared to dedicate his life to such an arduous and risky endeavour. He had promised to do so. It was a matter of honour. He had made a few binding promises in his day, and had always considered it his duty to keep them.

But this was different, associated with a risk that was actually negligible, and yet it did exist. A troublesome dilemma, even for a person with modest expectations.

He was no friend of big words, he shied away from lofty pretensions, and he might even hesitate at the most ordinary of expressions, finding them awkward, heavy and cumbersome. He felt sweaty, filthy and sullied whenever he had to deal with them. And besides, they were unreliable.

Should he jeopardise his dignified grief and the memory of his dead son with words and statements that anyone might misunderstand, and out of sheer malice distort, misuse and drag through the mud?

He had seen the most pure-hearted of people be insulted; he had even contributed himself with his ingrained distrust. What was there to indicate that he would succeed? Nothing. Absolutely nothing.

Time passed. In an uncertain, fruitless waiting for something unknown.

An invitation came from the Affect Commission to participate in one of their open forums. An unnamed source had
recommended him as an expert with experience that might
be of value to the current project. He was said to have
experience that ought to be utilised.

Hanck assumed that the unnamed person was the shopkeeper. The man harboured great respect for all so-called
scientific activity, and he had probably recommended Hanck
out of sheer benevolence. He may have thought that Hanck
needed to get out a bit, see people, meet some like-minded
individuals, other experts who were dedicated to the very
same matters.

The shopkeeper was extremely busy with his move to the
City Under the Roof, but he still made time to come and say
hello every once in a while. One day he stood there in Hanck's
workshop, looked at the workbench with the bottle of vodka,
the revolver, the piece of brick and the typewriter holding
a blank piece of paper.

'Not one word?' he said.

'Not one word.'

'In other words, you're going to need a lot of paper.'

Later he returned with several reams of paper that he'd
found when they were cleaning up. He wanted to offer as
much encouragement as he could. Writing and science had a
great deal in common. 'And you're a true obsolete, Hancken.'

They no longer had any business dealings with each other, and Hanck could have told him to go to hell without paying a price for his rudeness. But he didn't. He let things remain as they were. Perhaps the old fellow was right. He'd been right before.

And Hanck had nothing to lose by accepting the invitation.

He was prepared to subject himself to anything at all, he feared absolutely nothing. He'd been to the bottom, and had crawled his way out of the abyss, inch by inch, day by day. Whoever met him on the street might take him for anyone at all, a short, grey fellow-citizen who might be approached for directions. Nothing in his appearance gave any inkling of the demons that he'd dealt with, the furies and maledictions that had plagued and tormented him, keeping him awake for weeks at a time, lucid and bewildered, dangerous to the public.

Sometimes he wished that he was back there again, back in that state of demented recklessness and self-glorifying despair, the feeling of standing at the centre of the world, in the eye of the storm. That was gone; it was a passage, a lost world. Sometimes he missed it now when his courage deserted him, when he sat down in front of the typewriter and that blank piece of white paper. He felt powerless and incompetent, an amateur, a bungler, obliterated out of respect for his subject matter. Perhaps it was a form of humility, which also belonged to love.

That was his state of mind when he was awakened one morning by a familiar silence.

It had stopped raining. Abruptly and brutally, as expected.

He got out of bed, opened the window facing the street, and peered into the pale morning light, at the streets that were starting to dry out. No more rain coming down steadily day and night. Only tranquillity and quiet.

He had to show up for that meeting. He needed clothes, clean clothes, dry clothes. He had neglected that aspect of his life, wearing his old, worn-out clothes for the entire rainy season. They smelled of mould.

He had no real idea how the other participants would be dressed, but he didn't want to stand out or draw attention.

Finally he went into Toby's room. It had been closed up for months. He hadn't had the strength to go inside, out of some sort of deference, perhaps mostly to himself.

It was still messy and in need of cleaning. The filthy old cushion was still lying on the floor where he had once left it. The bed was unmade. But in the middle of the bed lay a package, a present, a turtleneck sweater, wrapped in cellophane.

With a vague pang of guilt he picked up the package, opened it, and pulled out the unworn sweater that still smelled new. It might be a little warm for this time of year, but he'd just have to put up with that.

Wearing this new garment he showed up at the meeting of the Affect Commission. They held their meetings on the first Wednesday of each month, in premises that had been put at their disposal by the Administration, since their work had once been deemed to be of public interest.

The origin of these premises was disputed; perhaps they had housed some sort of former secretariat with a number of offices and a large, elaborately decorated hall. The address was centrally located, in the City Under the Roof. On weekends the premises were used for a casino.

The waves had reached high levels inside. During one era it had been considered of great importance to reach out, to engage the man on the street, to popularise the whole thing. They had made use of consultants to facilitate these contacts, and prominent members had ended up on the sofa – or, as was then the case, on the rack – on TomBola's show and become known to the public, 'out there in the heart-land', as the saying goes. It had been a huge success.

Especially when they reached the section that would be exclusively devoted to 'Happiness'. It prompted a national uproar. The golden hall was packed with representatives of the public who believed that they possessed valuable information on the subject and felt called to testify. Occasionally the meetings were stormed by berserkers, who, with a great hullabaloo, demonstrated that it was a valid expression of happiness to wreck the premises and scare the shit out of those who were present.

Even this sort of happiness deserved recognition. But it had become difficult to heed, especially since the antagonisms within the commission were so great. Widely differing approaches came to light, expressed in words and actions that could make sporadically-appearing saboteurs look like virtuous noblemen.

The 'Happiness' section became a watershed. Members lied, slandered one another, carried on campaigns behind each other's back, all for the purpose of promoting their own points of view. Some people left, citing health reasons and blaming the pressure from the public, or they simply refused to show up. Some people died under mysterious circumstances.

After several decades of strife, a volume was finally produced that satisfactorily fulfilled the demand for scientific integrity, but it was written in a spirit that had very little to do with the actual topic itself.

Subsequently a number of corrections to policy were made, new forces were summoned. So when the part dealing with topics ranging from 'Hatred' to 'Ill will' was to be compiled, the entire commission seemed to be inspired by the 'Harmony' of the previous part. A much longed-for peace and quiet was established for their work, and the project proceeded calmly and serenely, without conflicts, as if they had finally found themselves on firm ground.

This sense of peace had lasted all the way to 'Love'. They were on the threshold of a new era, under yet another of these headings that seemed to have such a strong attraction for troublemakers, quarrelsome, self-appointed experts who could turn the simplest statement into an insoluble topic of contention.

Hanck was lucky enough to appear on a Wednesday that looked to be calm and quiet. Other activities were taking place in the city: a big shipment of vodka was due to be sold in a barn, and there were rumours of a marketplace in the suburbs that was filled with new monitors.

Not even everyone on the commission seemed to be present. Hanck had previously held a vague notion that they were scrawny, dried-up old fogeys, but now as they one by one took their seats on a podium, he saw that this was only partially correct. They were rather young, at most middle-aged. Grey and diffident, a bit suspicious-looking. There was no display of feelings other than apprehension.

After a number of introductory remarks from the chair-person, the members and attendees were welcomed. The floor was then yielded to a member who was supposed to explain some of the basic principles for the research.

She was a short woman with prematurely greying hair; she wore chequered trousers with what looked like egg stains on her beige jumper.

Hanck didn't need to feel apologetic for his attire. His sweater was in better shape than hers. But it was already starting to feel hot.

She was a professional, a specialist, a scholar, and that was how she talked. Hanck heard terms such as 'dubious postulate' and 'ontological structures', words that very quickly made him feel unsure of himself. He listened as attentively as he could, but the harder he tried, the less he understood.

And his sweater was much too hot.

But the people in the audience seemed spellbound, nodding in agreement at one thing or another. They were engrossed, they took notes, and sometimes they looked as if they wanted to interrupt the speaker to make comments.

The presentation seemed to be about the fact that the basics were still fluid, that the topic hadn't yet been clearly defined and laid bare, that it had a tendency to join forces with others and could get mixed up with entirely alien phenomena, that this had been found to be so insidious that in some circles people were questioning the fundamental premise itself, as if it were a topic that could be extracted, delimited and demonstrated in a pure form.

This took an entire morning to explain. The involvement of the audience sank at the same pace as the oxygen was used up in the hall. Some of the members on the podium had even arranged their bodies in reclining positions and were listening with their eyes closed.

By the time they approached the lunch break, Hanck was completely soaked with sweat. He couldn't take off the sweater because he had nothing on underneath. Perhaps he would have understood things better if he weren't suffering from the heat of that sweater. Toby's sweater. A fine, warm sweater of the highest quality, purchased one day long ago, a good day, when life could still sing. Hanck had walked along the street with his pockets full of money, looking forward to a delicious dinner prepared by a young master of the kitchen. A day full of love, up until three o'clock.

Now, long afterwards, he sat here listening to this monotonous droning, incomprehensible wording that could crack anyone, turning even the most impassioned amateur into a listless wreck.

But Hanck didn't take it that way. By lunchtime he had already left, with a light step, feeling fortified and encouraged. He had heard precisely what he needed to hear. It was as if Toby had spoken to him through the sweater, roaring straight at him: 'Don't listen! This is not for you! You don't have to worry, calm down, there's no risk at all. No one will ever be able to explain anything. Love is unfathomable! The world will go on! If it should be obliterated – so what? Should that risk stop anyone from thinking about love? Whoever doesn't dare take that risk, whoever isn't willing to jeopardise the whole world, will never be able to love. No way, José. Whoever can explain the world can also obscure it. That's their job. They don't want to change anything. They're working for the status quo!'

Hanck felt strong and uplifted in the most unexpected way. On his way home he passed the shopkeeper's premises. A bookmaking agency had taken over the place. It already looked well-established.

It was in an entirely new frame of mind that he sat down at his workbench, shoved the revolver aside, poked a little at the piece of brick, refrained from tasting the vodka, and, with a typical lack of imagination, wrote: 'Once upon a time . . .'

And something happened.

It was indescribable. He felt it in his whole body. Like some strange new substance. Like a drug.

Hanck was so agitated that he had to stand up and take a few turns around the flat before he could return to the paper and read those four words ten more times. Then, after that was done, he added: 'Once upon a time a boy . . .'

It was reminiscent of that time when the whole city had gone dark during a major power failure. When the electricity came back on, life returned and everything started up from where it had left off. Time had passed in darkness and silence, time that now would soon be forgotten, drowned out by the highly charged present.

He was back, the boy. Hanck could see him, talk to him as if he were still alive, again follow the life that he loved. He was there, and no one could take him away.

Hanck read those six words ten times, a hundred times. Then he realised that he was hungry. He hadn't eaten in a long time.

There was no food in the flat. He was forced to go out to

find something to cook. It was a specific task, to find a place that was open and had something to sell, to carry home his purchases and make something he could eat.

As he tied his shoes out in the hall he could imagine that soon he would be standing in the kitchen at the cooker and thinking: now how did he used to do that?

In the past it had prevented him from making any attempts on his own. But things were different now. Nothing had happened.

He could prove it. He would resort to the power of example, steer clear of theories and claims of applicability. He would describe love so strongly and intensely and matter-of-factly that it would comprise a proof in itself; it would free itself from any context and emerge as its own *materia*, its own myth, as tangible as a piece of brick.

He would linger over the introduction, deciding where and how he should begin. He couldn't start with his son's birth; there were circumstances that preceded it that had to be clarified. Nor could he start with his own birth, since that too had been preceded by events of significance.

He would have to go further and further back in time to find an appropriate beginning. Perhaps he was facing a task that would keep him occupied for the rest of his life. One day when the heat came, the window facing the street would be open. A black raven would be sitting on the window ledge.

He had never seen a raven there before. After a while another raven would be sitting there. Both of them would regard him in silence from their black moiré shimmer.

He would have difficulty concentrating. 'Shoo! You're bothering me!'

The birds would glance away, as if they were thinking about something; then once again they would fix their eyes on him.

He would understand. He would say: 'Yes, send my greet-ings! Tell him that I'm full up!'

Both of the birds take off. He follows them with his eyes as they soar over the street, rise up into the air and caw above the whole neighbourhood, above the whole city: '*Sona-torekk* . . . *Sona-torekk* . . .' A son is lost.

A little feather remains on the windowsill. It flutters in the breeze. He picks up the feather, sits there for a moment, holding it.

Then he will run it under his nose and make himself sneeze.

LAS RIMAS DE BÉCQUER: SU MODERNIDAD

APRIL 1990

MARIO A. BLANC
Washington University in St. Louis

LAS RIMAS DE BECQUER: SU MODERNIDAD

EDITORIAL PLIEGOS
MADRID

I.S.B.N.: 84-86214-34-3
Depósito Legal: 13.618-1988

Colección Pliegos de Ensayo
Diseño: Fabo
EDITORIAL PLIEGOS
Gobernador, 29 - 4.º A - 28014 Madrid
Apartado 50.358

Printed in Spain
Impreso en España
por PRUDENCIO IBÁÑEZ CAMPOS
Cerro del Viso, 16
Torrejón de Ardoz (Madrid)

«ansia perpetua de algo mejor
eso soy yo»

Para Miriam

ÍNDICE

ÍNDICE

ACCÉSIT

La importancia de la obra de Gustavo Adolfo Bécquer para la poesía española de nuestro siglo es innegable, y se ha destacado más con el paso de los años: la hondura, la precisión verbal, y el equilibrio de las Rimas becquerianas trascienden la altisonancia de mucha poesía anterior, y nos encaminan hacia la época de la modernidad. Hasta ahora, sin embargo, no se había estudiado detenidamente cómo las características de la obra becqueriana apuntaban a las formas, al estilo, a las imágenes y al efecto de los grandes libros de poesía de nuestro siglo. El presente estudio de Mario Blanc logra plenamente tal propósito, ofreciendo intuiciones indispensables para los críticos de la poesía española moderna.

Dotado de gran erudición por una parte y de una sobresaliente capacidad para el análisis de textos por otra, el profesor Blanc ha logrado iluminar una gran variedad de rasgos y aspectos de las Rimas que las relacionan con obras y autores posteriores. Sus comentarios se basan en la tradición de la crítica estilística, lo que les da rigor y precisión; pero se extienden también más allá, haciendo uso de conceptos semióticos por un lado, y de elementos de la teoría de la recepción por otro. Su mérito reside, precisamente, en aplicar estos diversos enfoques con originalidad y con gran intuición, desarrollando explicaciones importantes y novedosas sin caer en abstracciones innecesarias.

Mediante perspicaces estudios de poemas becquerianos, Blanc ubica las Rimas dentro de la tradición romántica, a la vez que las deslinda de muchos aspectos de esta tradición. Luego examina con gran originalidad sus correspondencias con la poesía modernista finisecular, pasando después a ofrecernos perspectivas novedosas acerca de los paralelos entre las obras de Bécquer, de Juan Ramón y de Antonio Machado.

Acto seguido comenta poemas becquerianos con relación a los de los grandes autores de la Generación del 27. Su estudio no sólo demuestra relaciones muy estrechas entre el estilo y los efectos de las Rimas *y de la poesía del 27, pero también sugiere la necesidad de modificar y reordenar ciertas nociones de la historia de la poesía moderna. Se nos ofrece, en suma, una obra crítica de gran importancia y originalidad, tanto por sus comentarios detallados como por la visión más amplia que implica.*

ANDREW P. DEBICKI

PRÓLOGO

En 1986 nos separan ya ciento cincuenta años del nacimiento de Gustavo Adolfo Bécquer (17 de febrero de 1836). Con su breve volumen de las *Rimas* consigue elaborar la poesía de más alta calidad del siglo XIX español. Pero la gloria y el reconocimiento llegarán más tarde; no le tocó en vida disfrutarlos. A la temprana edad de 34 años, el 22 de diciembre de 1870, una enfermedad que venía minando su organismo por más de una década pone punto final a su existencia.

A finales del año 1868 Bécquer recompone sus poemas y los reúne en un volumen, pero será su amigo Campillo quien se encargará posteriormente, en 1871, de darle la organización final, tal como lo conocemos hoy día. En la década de los años setenta las *Rimas* logran cierto impacto, pero no alcanzan un éxito absoluto. La poesía oficialista del rimbombante Campoamor y la del elocuente Núñez de Arce atenúan los efectos del canto acompasado y tenue que fluye de las composiciones becquerianas. En las dos décadas siguientes el foco de atención en la producción poética del mundo hispánico cambiará de sitio. Rubén Darío y los modernistas de Latinoamérica, en los años ochenta y noventa, desviarán la atención de los lectores hacia el Nuevo Mundo.

Recién a comienzos del siglo XX es cuando las *Rimas* se empiezan a leer más extensamente. Además, en este siglo nuestro es cuando se llevan a cabo análisis de los poemas becquerianos con más detenimiento para descubrir ese canto renovador y a la vez antecesor de técnicas y estilos de nuestro tiempo.

La poesía que nos trae Gustavo Adolfo Bécquer anuncia cambios fundamentales en la lírica española del siglo XIX. Aunque encontramos al poeta, cronológicamente hablando,

dentro del siglo XIX, su producción rompe ciertas barreras
generacionales. A pesar que se le suele encasillar como el gran
poeta español de fines del siglo y de la escuela romántica, su
creación poética niega aseveración tan absoluta.

En las *Rimas* germinan aspectos que vinculan a Bécquer
fuertemente con la poesía española del siglo XX. Su técnica
nos presenta en embrión las características de poetas posteriores. Si se observan en detalle sus rimas es posible comprobar
que en ellas anidan elementos modernos. Es verdad que contienen también un bagaje romántico que sería erróneo e infruc-
tuoso tratar de ocultar o negar. Pero lo que hay de romántico
en Bécquer está modificado con recursos poéticos que hasta
ese momento ningún poeta español se aventuró a emplear con
la eficacia con que lo hizo Bécquer. Es ahí justamente donde
radica su importancia.

Sus poesías imponen un freno al desbordante romanticismo, muestran un horizonte nuevo para la poética de España
y nos conducen hacia un camino intransitado hasta entonces.
Las rimas de Bécquer abren las puertas a concepciones renovadoras de la lírica y cumplen la función principal de ser pre-
cursoras de la forma diferente en que se escribirá poesía en
nuestro siglo. Si analizamos su obra detenidamente, ella nos
revela que Bécquer es la base fundamental donde se cimenta
la poesía del siglo XX.

Los críticos literarios, últimamente, van aceptando y enfatizando estos factores. Poco a poco se ha ido rompiendo con
la actitud simplista de ubicar a Bécquer como posromántico,
se han ido borrando y desdibujando estos preconceptos que le
restan importancia como poeta que se adelanta a su época.
Hoy día, las antologías y los análisis críticos de la obra del
poeta sevillano lo conectan más y más con los de este siglo.
En nuestros días, se ve a Bécquer más como precursor moderno que como romántico y se lee su poesía conectándola
con los poetas posteriores. Esta es una postura acertada que
concuerda con la orientación que seguiremos en el presente
trabajo.

Como ejemplos de esta reciente transición de la crítica en
las tendencias expuestas se puede citar la opinión sucinta de

Ángel del Río en *Antología general de la literatura española*, 1960:

> Es Bécquer el último de los grandes románticos, pero por su sensibilidad y el sentido íntimo de su lirismo es el precursor más caracterizado del espíritu poético del Siglo XX. (247)

Más tarde, en *Resumen de historia de las literaturas hispánicas*, 1965, José García López declara en forma concisa: «Los críticos ven hoy en su forma desnuda y alada y en el hondo subjetivismo de su lírica el comienzo de una línea que lleva a la poesía contemporánea» (228). Richard E. Chandler y Kessel Schwartz en *A New History of Spanish Literature*, 1967, ubican a Bécquer como premodernista: «Juan Ramón Jiménez, Rubén Darío and others truly appreciated him, and modern critics agree that he is the principal precursor of Modernism» (355). Ángel Valbuena Prat en *Historia de la literatura española*, 1968, propone escuetamente: «En el modernismo, el valor Bécquer queda como un enlace y un emotivo maestro» (244). Más tarde agrega: «La interrumpida 'Generación del 27' coincide en el culto a Bécquer» (245).

Además de estas sentencias reveladoras sobre la manera de mirar la poesía de Bécquer en antologías de estos días, tenemos la contribución de análisis críticos que incursionan en esta misma dirección. Jorge Guillén, un representante de la generación del 27, ya en 1943, en *La poética de Bécquer* observa en forma perspicaz:

> Bécquer define en general e intenta en su obra la poesía del amor inefable: algo que, en su principio, fue sentimiento se convierte en recuerdo, después en sueño, y por último en verso, en palabra de sugestión. Partiendo del romanticismo, henos ya en la atmósfera que anuncia el simbolismo. Si Bécquer parece a primera vista un rezagado, ahora se nos revela un precursor del movimiento moderno. (18)

En su análisis, Guillén menciona a Dámaso Alonso. Este último ve en Bécquer un quebrar con lo anterior, una gestación de algo no existente en la tradición poética de hasta ese entonces:

> Lo esencial en las palabras de Bécquer es la distinción entre la

poesía pomposa, adornada, desarrollada, y la poesía breve, desnuda, desembarazada en una forma libre... Toda nuestra poesía
—no popular— anterior a Bécquer, lo mismo la clásica que la
romántica, pertenecía al primer tipo, y el gran hallazgo, el gran
regalo del autor de las *Rimas* a la poesía española, consiste en
el descubrimiento de esta nueva manera... (17)

José Pedro Díaz, crítico importante del poeta sevillano,
dice en *Bécquer*, 1968: «La obra de Bécquer tiene una significación singular en el conjunto de la creación lírica española
del siglo XIX. Las *Rimas* son una obra de excepcional calidad,
que ha influido fuertemente sobre los poetas de las generaciones siguientes...» (7).

En 1970, con motivo del centenario de la muerte del célebre poeta, aparecen trabajos críticos que sostienen esta postura y reúnen opiniones de poetas que apoyan la tendencia.
Estas declaraciones de críticos afamados expresan ideas aceptadas por muchos y cumplen la importante función de revelar
las actitudes compartidas por el lector en general. Luis Jiménez Martos en *Rimas, leyendas y cartas*, 1970, lo relaciona con
los poetas del siglo XX:

> La importancia de esta vinculación es fundamental... Para
> Juan Ramón, lo becqueriano tuvo, pues, carácter fundante, y así
> lo sostuvo siempre, por ejemplo, entre las ocasiones, cuando dijo
> a José Luis Cano que con Bécquer habría de comenzar toda an-
> tología de poesía contemporánea española. (41)

Luego, en forma breve, Jiménez Martos observa que es Bécquer la base para la producción poética de Antonio Machado,
Jorge Guillén, Gerardo Diego, Rafael Alberti, Luis Cernuda y
Vicente Aleixandre entre otros. En el mismo año 1970, José
María Guelbenzu en *Gustavo Adolfo Bécquer: poética, narrativa, papeles personales* nos afirma: «Bécquer... sí, se encuentra en el umbral de la gran literatura moderna: eso crea y
aporta a toda la literatura española hasta nuestros días. He
aquí por qué Bécquer es el primer escritor español contemporáneo» (17).

La crítica de Bécquer en nuestros días resalta su modernidad. José Luis Cano en *Rimas*, 1976, su trabajo más reciente, resume la actitud del lector actual:

> El gran acierto, pues, de Bécquer, su trascendente aportación a la lírica española —con él comienza, en efecto, nuestra poesía contemparánea— es, de un lado, el haber llevado su intimidad, en carne viva, a sus versos, de modo que el lector que toque esos versos está tocando el dolor y la tragedia de un hombre; y de otro, el haber sabido expresar ese dolor, esa historia íntima de amor y sufrimiento, en una forma original, desnuda de artificio, y de sobria y directa belleza, que nada tenía que ver ya con la retórica romántica a la que el lector estaba acostumbrado, pero de la que empezaba a cansarse, al comprobar sus tópicos. (27)

Cano, al igual que otros críticos que hemos mencionado, no analiza las rimas. Estos estudiosos comparten una postura en común con el lector de nuestra época, pero que carece de un análisis detenido que vaya justificándola. Es verdad que se ha dado un paso muy importante en la renovación crítica de las *Rimas* al coincidir en ver a Bécquer como un precursor. Pero como críticos no podemos quedarnos en el simple hecho de enunciar tal postura. Se hace necesario analizar sus poesías en detalle para descubrir en ellas esos aspectos modernos.

El aporte principal de este estudio consistirá en analizar las *Rimas* bien de cerca para detectar los elementos modernos. A través del análisis se buscará identificar qué características y técnicas modernas se hallan en ellas, y cómo operan dentro de su propio contexto. Como primer paso en el análisis detenido de las poesías de Bécquer abordaremos sus técnicas y aspectos que las separan del estilo romántico anterior. Luego, como otra parte de este estudio, destacaremos en los poemas becquerianos rasgos e indicios del parnasianismo, simbolismo y modernismo, movimientos que se desarrollarán tanto contemporáneamente como con posterioridad a la producción del poeta de Sevilla. Hacia el final de nuestro trabajo de investigación y análisis de las *Rimas*, escudriñaremos elementos esenciales de la poética de Bécquer que lo ligan tanto a Juan Ramón y Antonio Machado como a los miembros de la Generación del 27.

Hemos comprobado hasta este punto que partimos del hecho de pisar un terreno en común con la crítica última so-

bre Bécquer. De aquí en adelante se realizará el esfuerzo de
precisar los aspectos modernos y se analizarán específicamente
poesías que apoyen y evidencien tales características. Todo esto
no se ha hecho todavía en la forma extensa que el caso requie-
re; por lo tanto, el presente estudio propone emprender este
proyecto tan necesario como urgente.

LA CONTEMPORANEIDAD DE BÉCQUER

Bécquer se basa en los fundamentos del movimiento romántico, pero no se ata a él. Su poesía nos trae un lenguaje mesurado, en contraposición a la exageración retórica en que el romanticismo se había desvirtuado. Bécquer se apoya en los sentimientos y las emociones sutiles sin caer en el sentimentalismo, en el desborde emocional casi cursi en que el romanticismo había caído. La poesía de Bécquer es controlada por un lenguaje más depurado, contenido, y las emociones se someten también a este control lingüístico. Podemos afirmar, sin temor a equivocarnos, que Bécquer, en esto, más que posromántico, es sobre todo un nexo, un puente hacia la producción poética del siglo XX. Es un poeta que se adelanta a su tiempo, desprendiéndose del romanticismo trillado todavía en boga en sus días. Bécquer comienza a experimentar, abre brecha, da base y sirve como precursor para las generaciones modernas.

Para esta introducción escogeremos tres poesías de las *Rimas* donde se señalarán aspectos que unen al destacado poeta sevillano del siglo XIX con la producción poética posterior. El control de las emociones por medio de las formas y el lenguaje separa a Bécquer de la tradición romántica. Una característica que conecta a Bécquer con los poetas posteriores es el empleo de un lenguaje donde se combinan hábilmente lo poético y lo cotidiano para producir una experiencia exclusiva. Los términos y expresiones modernistas en sus poemas constituyen recursos que también lo adelantan a su época. En resumen, el control de las emociones, el lenguaje coloquial mezclado con el poético y los toques modernistas en el estilo de las *Rimas* hacen de Bécquer un poeta renovador. Estos aspectos se destacarán con el análisis de las rimas I, III y

LIII. Estas tres poesías están entre las más famosas del volumen por constituir el eje conductor de la producción becqueriana. A continuación transcribimos la primera[1]:

I

(1)   Yo sé un himno gigante y extraño
        que anuncia en la noche del alma una aurora,
        y estas páginas son de ese himno,
        cadencias que el aire dilata en las sombras.

(2)   Yo quisiera escribirle, del hombre
        domando el rebelde, mezquino idioma,
        con palabras que fuesen a un tiempo
        suspiros y risas, colores y notas.

(3)   Pero en vano es luchar, que no hay cifra
        capaz de encerrarlo, y apenas, ¡oh hermosa!,
        si, teniendo en mis manos las tuyas,
        pudiera, al oído, cantártelo a solas. (401)

En el primer verso el hablante llama la atención sobre su producción denominándola solemnemente: «himno». En las primeras rimas, Bécquer introduce las reglas de juego; constituyen, artísticamente hablando, su poética. Antes de darlas a conocer, en *La soledad* de Augusto Ferrán[2], resume sus ambiciones creadoras. Allí establece diferencias y contrastes entre lo hecho en materia poética hasta entonces y lo que él se propone alcanzar. Oigamos a Bécquer:

> Hay una poesía magnífica y sonora; una poesía hija de la meditación y el arte, que se engalana con todas las pompas de la lengua, que se mueve con una cadenciosa majestad, habla a la imaginación, completa sus cuadros y la conduce a su antojo por un sendero desconocido, seduciéndola con su armonía y su hermosura.

---

[1] GUSTAVO ADOLFO BÉCQUER, *Obras completas*, 13.ª ed. (Madrid: Aguilar, S. A. de Ediciones, 1969), p. 401. Este volumen reúne la totalidad de los trabajos de Bécquer, tanto en prosa como en poesía. En lo sucesivo, las citas que hagamos de Bécquer provendrán de esta edición, fuente esencial y primordial de nuestra investigación. Los números de páginas de las citas estarán indicados entre paréntesis en el texto.

[2] En el volumen identificado en nuestra primera nota se incluye el prólogo que G. A. BÉCQUER escribió para *La Soledad*, colección de cantares por Augusto Ferrán y Fornies, pp. 1.184-95.

Hay otra natural, breve, seca, que brota del alma como una chispa eléctrica, que hiere el sentimiento con una palabra y huye, desnuda de artificio, desembarazada dentro de una forma libre, despierta, con una que las toca, las mil ideas que duermen en el océano sin fondo de la fantasía.

La primera tiene un valor dado: es la poesía de todo el mundo.

La segunda carece de medida absoluta, adquiere las proporciones de la imaginación que impresiona; puede llamarse la poesía de los poetas. (1186)

La primera estrofa de la rima I concentra en poesía lo que ha explicado en prosa sobre el segundo tipo de poemas:

(1)   Yo sé un himno gigante y extraño
que anuncia en la noche del alma una aurora,
y estas páginas son de ese himno,
cadencia que el aire dilata en las sombras.

Su canto apunta a lo inefable. Desde el principio lo tangible y lo efímero están en tensión. Compara la aurora con las características del himno que se entonará. Entramos en una zona donde lo impreciso e incierto dominan. Luego, suma una visión impresionista en la que el efecto de la luz sobre las sombras crea el ambiente evasivo predominante de su poesía. Este efecto de dispersión logrado por una imagen que impresiona nuestros sentidos por su cualidad evanescente es algo que manejan muy bien Bécquer y los poetas posteriores a su época. Los simbolistas buscarán en esos próximos años una poesía que sugiera, donde la impresión de las imágenes quede vibrando en la mente del lector.

La primera estrofa empieza siendo muy afirmativa: «Yo sé un himno...» Las pretensiones del hablante disminuyen en la segunda estrofa comenzando con: «Yo quisiera escribirle...» Escribirle incluye a una posible destinataria y receptora de estos versos, pero no sabemos quién es, ni se especifica, ni se desarrolla. Se mantiene el anonimato. Esta segunda estrofa es una situación transitoria:

(2)   Yo quisiera escribirle, del hombre
domando el rebelde, mezquino idioma,
con palabras que fuesen a un tiempo
suspiros y risas, colores y notas.

En esta estrofa el poeta apunta al esfuerzo tenaz, a la lucha
constante por conciliar extremos en el proceso artístico. Bécquer nos brinda una enumeración del contenido principal de
sus rimas; los sentimientos y las emociones en «suspiros y
risas» se unen a los efectos artísticos que invocan cierto dominio en «colores y notas». Estos elementos visuales y audi-
tivos que se someten al dictado del artista se mezclan con
aquellas expresiones de sentimientos que escapan de su control. Este concepto, que queda enunciado en forma concen-
tradísima en dicha rima, se amplía en la rima III, como veremos más adelante.

En la estrofa final de la rima I el poeta trae al plano cotidiano y real todo aquello que podría haber quedado en el
plano abstracto y teórico:

(3)   Pero en vano es luchar; que no hay cifra
           capaz de encerrarlo, y apenas, ¡oh hermosa!,
           si, teniendo en mis manos las tuyas,
           pudiera, al oído, cantártelo a solas.

Es aquí, ya en la tercera estrofa, que el hablante toma cuerpo
físico y hay una amante, una receptora concreta de estas
emociones y elementos artísticos: «... en mis manos las tuyas,
/ pudiera, al oído...» Lo general del comienzo se hace específico al final, la posible presencia de un hablante con el «yo»
en la primera y segunda estrofa no se concreta hasta la tercera. Es en la tercera estrofa, y no antes, donde las manos
de los amantes se unen. De un ambiente amplio y sin límites
en las dos estrofas anteriores, nuestra atención pasa a con-
centrarse en un ámbito íntimo y personal en esta última:
«...cantártelo a solas». Aquello tan efímero y sutil del tono
poético de las dos primeras estrofas, se transporta a lo coloquial y conversacional de la última cuando el poeta susurra
al oído de su amada.

Sin llegar a lo puramente anecdótico, que rebajaría su
valor poético, Bécquer nos lleva a ese mundo artístico de sus
rimas que no está totalmente desprendido del terrenal. Tampoco comete el error de someterlo demasiado a lo cotidiano
y que su trascendencia artística quede así limitada o dañada.

Esta es una interesante y balanceada combinación que se mantiene en su poética y que merece verse de más cerca con otra rima que analizaremos más adelante, la LIII.

El empleo de lo sentimental controlado artísticamente es un aspecto implicado en la rima I. Otro elemento presente son ciertas imágenes impresionistas que afloran combinando lo visual (colores) y lo auditivo (notas). La pintura y la música son disciplinas artísticas que se conjugan con la palabra escrita, el arte literario, conformando el mundo moderno de los poemas. Los parnasianos, en los próximos años, buscarían en su poética la imbricación de disciplinas artísticas separadas hasta entonces, especialmente la pintura y la música con la literatura. El tercer aspecto que vimos es el uso de lo vago y efímero combinados, más que contrapuestos, a lo concreto, específico y real de sus rimas.

La frase autorreferencial en: «...estas páginas son de ese himno...» nos pone en alerta indicando que esta primera rima sirve de introducción a las demás. También propone un formato y guía de cómo se leerán las siguientes. Por lo tanto, nos parece importante haber tomado los aspectos presentes en esta rima introductoria para ampliarlos, hacerlos resaltar y observarlos minuciosamente en otras dos rimas.

Tal como sucede en el caso de la rima I, las primeras poesías en el volumen sirven para delinear la forma de su poética; y también se revelan en ellas ciertas técnicas y recursos estilísticos que se emplean en los otros poemas del volumen. La tercera rima entra dentro de este primer grupo de poesías claves:

III

(1)   Sacudimiento extraño
que agita las ideas,
como huracán que empuja
las olas en tropel;

(2)   murmullo que en el alma
se eleva y va creciendo,
como volcán que sordo
anuncia que va a arder;

(3)   deformes siluetas
            de seres imposibles;
            paisajes que aparecen
            como a través de un tul;

(4)   colores que fundiéndose
            remedan en el aire
            los átomos del iris,
            que nadan en la luz;

(5)   ideas sin palabras,
            palabras sin sentido;
            cadencias que no tienen
            ni ritmo ni compás;

(6)   memorias y deseos
            de cosas que no existen;
            accesos de alegría,
            impulsos de llorar;

(7)   actividad nerviosa
            que no halla en qué emplearse;
            sin rienda que le guíe,
            caballo volador;

(8)   locura que el espíritu
            exalta y enardece;
            embriaguez divina
            del genio creador...

            ¡Tal es la inspiración!

(1)   Gigante voz que el caos
            ordena en el cerebro,
            y entre las sombras hace
            la luz aparecer;

(2)   brillante rienda de oro
            que poderosa enfrena
            de la exaltada mente
            el volador corcel;

(3)   hilo de luz que en haces
            los pensamientos ata;
            sol que las nubes rompe
            y toca en el cenit;

(4)   inteligente mano
            que en un collar de perlas
            consigue las indóciles
            palabras reunir;

(5)   armonioso ritmo
que con cadencia y número
las fugitivas notas
encierra en el compás;

(6)   cincel que el bloque muerde
la estatua modelando,
y la belleza plástica
añade a la ideal;

(7)   atmósfera en que giran
con orden las ideas,
cual átomos que agrupa
recóndita atracción;

(8)   raudal en cuyas ondas
su sed la fiebre apaga;
oasis que al espíritu
devuelve su vigor...

¡Tal es nuestra razón!

Con ambas siempre en lucha
y de ambas vencedor,
tan solo el genio puede
a un yugo atar las dos. (402-05)

Con esta rima Bécquer extiende, expande y elabora las concentradas formulaciones que teníamos en la rima I.

En esta rima, al igual que en la anterior, hay una tensión entre lo concreto y lo intangible. En las primeras dos estrofas del poema se repite el mismo esquema. Los dos primeros versos parten de algo abstracto para luego adquirir cuerpo y consistencia comparándose por medio de símiles a los elementos concretos del huracán y el volcán:

(1)   Sacudimiento extraño
que agita las ideas,
como *huracán* que empuja
las olas en tropel;

(2)   murmullo que en el alma
se eleva y van creciendo,
como *volcán* que sordo
anuncia que va a arder;

En estas dos estrofas iniciales se percibe un paralelismo organizador en los sonidos acentuados de las dos palabras se-

ñaladas, y el efecto que evocan ambas es de caos, violencia y
destrucción. Llama la atención la manera ordenada de expo-
nerlo, contrapuesta al caos que se describe. Lo abstracto y lo
tangible interactúan; el orden y el desorden habitan en pugna,
sin predominar ninguno.

En la tercera estrofa notamos que lo efímero se va imponiendo sobre lo concreto:

> (3)   deformes siluetas
> de seres imposibles;
> paisajes que aparecen
> como a través de un tul;

A partir de la cuarta estrofa, ya estamos claramente en el
terreno de la inspiración, fuera de la lógica; es el predominio
de las emociones sobre la razón. Pero esto es lo que se dice
y no lo que se hace. Obsérvese con cuidado que aunque la
inspiración es el asunto que se desarrolla, se hace imponién-
dose cierto dominio y control. Por ejemplo: «ideas sin palabras, / palabras sin sentido» resulta un juego ingenioso de
palabras, casi barroco y conceptual.

Otro ejemplo de esta situación contradictoria son los per-
fectos paralelismos de: «accesos de alegría, / impulsos de
llorar» que aunque aluden directamente a las emociones des-
bordadas de sus límites, van refrenadas con comas. La puntuación hasta ese entonces en el poema ha venido sirviendo
como pequeños diques que demoran el fluir de los versos.
Cuando parece que se alcanzará un desenfreno, la puntuación
se sobrecarga para contrabalancear el efecto. Esto muestra el
control emotivo, no sólo por medio del lenguaje y las imágenes que se emplean, sino también por medio de la forma contenida de sus versos. De esta manera sentimos la presencia
del genio creador que sujeta con hilos casi imperceptibles las
fuerzas en dispersión. El genio impone sutil control a aquello
que parece desbocarse a cada momento. Si se releen las primeras seis estrofas poniendo atención a la puntuación se verá
dicho efecto.

Otro ejemplo donde se dice algo y se hace lo contrario
son los versos de la quinta estrofa: «cadencias que no tienen

/ ni ritmo ni compás». Sí que estas estrofas tienen ritmo, sí que reinan en ellas la cadencia y el compás. Esta es una contradicción que queda latente en el aire, sin resolución. En el momento que le proporcionáramos una explicación le estaríamos robando lo artístico que ellas poseen. Esta es una paradoja que queda aleteando en su vuelo incierto pero magistral.

Otro ejemplo de la tensión en estas primeras seis estrofas es el hecho de que se va describiendo la arrebatada inspiración, pero se hace a través de una secuencia metonímica llamativamente ordenada. Casi hasta metódicamente se van enumerando elementos que conforman ese mundo huidizo y vagoroso de la inspiración.

Ya en la parte de la inspiración podemos empezar a vislumbrar que Bécquer combina soberbiamente lo instintivo y lo racional, lo intuitivo y lo lógico. No hay que llegar al final del poema para intuir las reglas del juego; sugiero que éstas están enunciadas desde el comienzo. Este posible caos del huracán y el volcán, que vuelve más tarde a lo concreto con la metáfora de «caballo volador sin rienda», va dominado paradójicamente por la creación poética del lenguaje y las formas mesuradas en manos del genio que se menciona al final de la sección.

Hemos hecho una minuciosa disección de esta primera parte de la rima III. Ella contiene ecos de la rima I, resulta ser una ampliación, como si viéramos a través de una lupa. La imagen «...del hombre / domando el rebelde, mezquino idioma» de la rima I, encuentra fuerte conexión con la metáfora de «caballo volador sin riendas» de la rima III; sólo que en este poema los efectos han ido en aumento por los símiles, descripciones y metáforas que proliferan.

Algo más que es importante puntualizar en esta primera sección de la rima III es lo llamativo de observar que las comparaciones se hacen a base de símiles: «*como* huracán que empuja / las olas en tropel» o «*como* volcán que sordo / anuncia que va a arder». Así, las asociaciones tienen mayor fluidez, el aspecto intuitivo de nuestro cerebro es el que opera y los

elementos comparados se asocian de manera natural, sin mayor esfuerzo. Este proceso de lectura corresponde perfectamente al campo predominante en que se describe la inspiración.

La rima III recoge y reelabora el tema y las imágenes ya
vistas en la rima I. Volviendo a la rima I, quiero subrayar «con
palabras que fuesen a un tiempo». Esta sentencia enuncia que
aunque predomine un elemento como la inspiración primero,
y luego la razón, como sucede en la rima III, se produce realmente una superposición de ambas. Hemos visto ya que esta
sensación de simultaneidad está presente en la sección de la
inspiración de la rima III.

En la enumeración ya mencionada antes en la rima I,
«suspiros y risas», refiere a las emociones y la inspiración
que se desarrolla en la primera parte de la rima III. El otro
grupo de la rima I, «colores y notas», apunta a algo más or-
ganizado, como un pintor que da forma a su obra artística en
el empleo acertado y calculado de los colores y el músico con
las notas. De esta forma, la razón queda sutilmente enunciada
y es el elemento que ampliaremos ahora, como Bécquer lo
hizo, pasando de la rima I a la segunda parte de la rima III.

El comienzo de esta sección nos sorprende porque existe
en ella un cambio significativo. Hasta ahora se había presen-
tado una serie de símiles, pero a continuación el hablante nos
detiene, frena el proceso de nuestra lectura con una serie de
metáforas. Esta comparación metafórica de la segunda parte
no es tan fluida como la serie de símiles en la primera; el
proceso de lectura y asociación se lentifica. Tanto el símil
como la metáfora tienen en común que ambas son comparaciones. Pero el símil muestra una equivalencia mayor entre
los elementos comparados que se ligan con una preposición.
En cambio, la metáfora compara elementos sin emplear términos que funcionen como conexión. La metáfora resulta ser
una comparación más indirecta, deja más espacio y demanda
más atención dado que es uno como lector quien tiene que
formular y extender los hilos que conectan posiblemente los
objetos comparados. Las metáforas de esta segunda sección

nos imponen un proceso de lectura más racional por lo complejo, más cerebral, como alude el hablante desde un principio en: «Gigante voz que el caos / ordena en el cerebro».

Recordando el aspecto expuesto de preponderancias en cada sector, pero teniendo también en mente la superposición de la inspiración y la razón, vemos que el poeta recoge la metáfora «caballo volador» como lenguaje indomable en la primera parte de la rima III. Esta imagen arrastra ecos y tiene sus orígenes en: «domando el rebelde, mezquino idioma» de la rima I. Por cierto, la modifica y amplía, pero en base a lo ya hecho antes, apoyándose en la idea e imagen que venía gestándose. En forma similar, también vuelve a referir en la parte de la razón a las riendas: «brillante rienda de oro / que poderosa enfrena», ya citadas en la sección de la inspiración. Estas imágenes que reaparecen y se reelaboran dentro de un contexto diferente producen el efecto de imbricación que hemos señalado anteriormente.

Aunque físicamente, en el poema, se observa la parte de la inspiración primero, luego un descanso y más tarde la parte sobre la razón, la separación, en realidad, no es tan absoluta. La inspiración y la razón se yuxtaponen.

Los románticos hacían prevalecer las emociones. Por otro lado, en la poesía de Bécquer la razón tiene casi tanta relevancia como la inspiración y lo emotivo. Es digno de destacarse que en este poema hay exactamente igual cantidad de versos dedicados a la inspiración como a la razón.

En la primera estrofa de la segunda parte se menciona «cerebro», en la segunda estrofa «mente», en la tercera «pensamientos» y en la cuarta «inteligente»:

(1)   Gigante voz que el caos
ordena en el *cerebro,*
y entre las sombras hace
la luz aparecer;

(2)   brillante rienda de oro
que poderosa enfrena
de la exaltada *mente*
el volador corcel;

(3)   hilo de luz que en haces
               los *pensamientos* ata;
               sol que las nubes rompe
               y toca en el cenit;

(4)   *inteligente* mano
               ....

Así, el hablante nos introduce en el mundo de la razón, pero
siempre en base a lo hecho con la inspiración. Para remarcar
este aspecto veamos que refiere a la mente, pero dice «la
exaltada mente» que contiene fuertes ecos de la faz anterior
que concluía en la octava estrofa con «locura... embriaguez
divina». De esta manera se percibe que se ha hecho un cambio de terreno sin abandonar definitivamente el anterior. Las
estrofas cuatro y cinco repiten pisadas sobre las huellas de-
jadas por la estrofa cinco de la primera parte. También reco-
gen la idea ya expuesta sobre «notas» de la rima I, como principio organizador de la razón, tal como haría un músico en
el proceso de ir componiendo su creación. Obsérvese que la
idea se expone en una línea en la rima I, casi concentrada en
una sola palabra, «notas»; luego, se extiende a una estrofa
en la parte de la inspiración en la rima III; y más tarde, el
mismo concepto se expande a dos estrofas en la sección de la
razón. Este asunto que recogemos de la rima I: «suspiros y
risas, colores y *notas*», se expande en la rima III de esta
forma; en la estrofa cinco de la primera parte:

(5)   ideas sin palabras,
               palabras sin sentido;
               cadencias que no tienen
               ni ritmo ni compás;

Y luego, en las estrofas cuatro y cinco de la segunda:

(4)   inteligente mano
               que en un collar de perlas
               consigue las indóciles
               palabras reunir;

(5)   armonioso ritmo
               que con cadencia y número
               las fugitivas notas
               encierra en el compás;

En la estrofa seis la labor del poeta creador es paralela a la función artística del escultor. Este paralelismo de diferentes disciplinas artísticas lo harán muchas veces los parnasianos y modernistas:

(6)   cincel que el bloque muerde
             la estatua modelando,
             y la belleza plástica
             añade a la ideal;

Luego, la estrofa siete se combina, más que contrastarse, con la cuatro de la primera parte en lo que sucede con los átomos. Ambas estrofas completan la idea de los «colores» originada en la rima I, como concepto organizador por efecto de la razón, tal como haría un pintor:

(4)   colores que fundiéndose
             remedan en el aire
             los átomos del iris,
             que nadan en la luz;

(7)   atmósfera en que giran
             con orden las ideas,
             cual átomos que agrupa
             recóndita atracción;

Pero es interesante observar aquí que la idea de organización de los colores no es aludida directamente en la séptima estrofa en el área de la razón. Para completar el concepto se hace necesario volver a invadir la zona de la inspiración donde los colores aparecen mencionados en su cuarta estrofa.

Lo que se comprueba a través de lo observado es que más allá de un contraste superficial y obvio en el formato de las partes de este poema, existe una interdependencia entre la inspiración y la razón. Este aspecto quedó enunciado en la rima I, y se ha deasrrollado en la rima III.

Ya vamos confluyendo así a esa unidad totalizadora que observamos en Bécquer, vamos viendo unirse polos que habían estado hasta entonces separados. Tal reconciliación se contrapone al desequilibrio emocional que asociamos con un romanticismo convencional y vacío. Al final de ambas sec-

ciones de la rima III convergemos en la última estrofa del
poema invocándose al genio creador de Bécquer que logra in-
corporar e integrar en sus poemas los elementos dispares:

> Con ambas siempre en lucha
> y de ambas vencedor,
> tan solo el genio puede
> a un yugo atar las dos.

El genio creador une y ciñe al final ambas facetas artísticas.
Logra armonizar elementos que veíamos en conflicto al principio. Las pretensiones indicadas en la rima I se han logrado
y cristalizado en la rima III.

Bécquer se desprende así de lo puramente romántico. En
sus rimas se percibe una equilibrada conjugación de las emociones que van moderadas estilísticamente por medio del lenguaje y formas finamente ordenadas. Este equilibrio puede
apreciarse a lo largo de la lectura de sus rimas. Este procedimiento resulta ser un avance significativo que lo desliga del
movimiento romántico donde gravitó. Bécquer se desprende
de este movimiento y forja un nexo, una unión muy fuerte a
lo que se produciría en materia poética en el siglo xx, iniciado
con el movimiento modernista.

Bécquer controla lo sentimental por medio del lenguaje y
las formas sin prescindir de las emociones. Con ocho estrofas
tanto para la razón como para la inspiración y emoción, en la
rima III, se produce un balance extraordinario. Este equilibrio
había quedado enunciado en la rima I: «con palabras que fuesen a un tiempo / suspiros y risas, colores y notas.»

En la rima LIII se destaca el empleo del lenguaje poético
y el conversacional asociados diestramente para producir una
experiencia exclusiva, particular y única, imprimiéndole intimidad al poema. Este otro aspecto de la poesía de Bécquer se
había insinuado en la rima I como puntualizamos antes, donde
de un himno difuso al principio, se pasaba al ambiente recluido
e íntimo de los amantes, al final del poema. Este pasaje del
lenguaje artístico que llega a combinarse con el coloquial, y el

cambio de un escenario amplio y sin límites a uno íntimo se desarrollan más en esta otra rima:

LIII

(1) Volverán las oscuras golondrinas
en tu balcón sus nidos a colgar,
y otra vez a la tarde, aún más hermosas,
  jugando llamarán;
(2) pero aquellas que el vuelo refrenaban,
tu hermosura y mi dicha al contemplar;
aquellas que aprendieron nuestros nombres
  esas... ¡no volverán!

(3) Volverán las tupidas madreselvas
de tu jardín las tapias a escalar,
y otra vez a la tarde, aún más hermosas,
  sus flores se abrirán;
(4) pero aquellas cuajadas de rocío,
cuyas gotas mirábamos temblar
y caer, como lágrimas del día...
  esas... ¡no volverán!

(5) Volverán del amor en tus oídos
las palabras ardientes a sonar;
tu corazón, de su profundo sueño
  tal vez despertará;
(6) pero mudo y absorto y de rodillas,
como se adora a Dios ante su altar,
como yo te he querido..., desengáñate:
  ¡así no te querrán! (436-37)

Bécquer mezcla finamente el lenguaje poético, pero sencillo, con otro coloquial, produciendo así una experiencia paradójicamente universal y particular, única y exclusiva en su fundamento artístico de la expresión íntima.

En la rima LIII, hay una clara oposición entre las estrofas 1 y 2, y entre 3 y 4, que se señala con los «pero» al comienzo de la 2 y la 4 como se indica a continuación:

(1) *Volverán* las oscuras golondrinas
en tu balcón sus nidos a col*gar*,
y otra vez con el ala a sus cristales
  jugando llamarán;

(2) *pero aquella*s que el vuelo refrenaban
tu hermosura y mi dicha al contemp*lar;*
*aquella*s que aprendieron nuestros nombres,
  esas... ¡NO *volverán!*

(3)   *Volverán* las tupidas madreselvas
de tu jardín las tapias a esca*lar,*
y otra vez a la tarde, aún más hermosas,
sus flores se abrirán;
(4)   *pero aquellas* cuajadas de rocío,
cuyas gotas mirábamos temb*lar*
y caer, como lágrimas del día...
esas... ¡NO *volverán*!

Otra diferencia entre la estrofa 1 y 2, así como entre la 3 y la 4, es el hecho de pasar de lo general a lo específico con el empleo de los pronombres y adjetivos demostrativos «aquellas» y «esas», señalados en las estrofas 2 y 4. Las estrofas 1 y 3 se distinguen de las otras dos y se agrupan entre sí por sus comienzos que se repiten con «volverán» que hemos indicado en la cita. Estos «volverán», del principio de las estrofas 1 y 3, contrastan con los finales exclamativos y precedidos por puntos suspensivos «¡No volverán!» de las estrofas 2 y 4.

Este proceso antagónico de pasar de lo general a lo específico se cumple sistemáticamente. Podemos agregar un ejemplo más para recalcar este hecho. Los verbos en infinitivo con que terminan los segundos versos de estas cuatro estrofas, que han quedado señalados en la cita anterior, mantienen este molde contrastante, y agregan algo más, de manera más sutil. Los infinitos de las estrofas 1 y 3 son verbos físicos, «colgar» y «escalar»; mas los de las estrofas 2 y 4 son más íntimos, internalizando y particularizando lo expuesto con «contemplar» y «temblar» [3].

Como sucedió en la rima III, que fue una ampliación de ciertos aspectos enunciados en la rima I, paralelamente se produce lo mismo aquí. La rima LIII desarrolla el pasaje de lo general a lo particular, de lo amplio a lo íntimo señalado en la rima I.

---

[3] DÁMASO ALONSO y CARLOS BOUSOÑO, *Seis calas en la expresión literaria española* (Madrid: Editorial Gredos, 1951). CARLOS BOUSOÑO en el capítulo V «Las pluralidades paralelísticas de Bécquer», pp. 189-227, lleva a cabo un estudio estilístico de la rima LIII y destaca las semejanzas. Bousoño concluye que esta sistematización casi hasta científica de correlaciones entre los vocablos en la expresión amorosa es una clara demostración de la razón y el aspecto cerebral imponiendo control y evitando el desborde de la emoción y lo sentimental.

Comparemos la similitud sorprendente del proceso en los últimos dos versos de la rima I con la misma lupa analítica que nos permite ampliar y destacar el mismo aspecto en las dos estrofas finales de la rima LIII:

I

....

(2)   Yo quisiera escribirle, del hombre
          domando el rebelde, mezquino idioma,
          con palabras que fuesen a un tiempo
          suspiros y risas, colores y notas.

(3)   Pero en vano es luchar, que no hay cifra
          capaz de encerrarlo, y apenas, ¡oh hermosa!,
          si, teniendo en mis manos las tuyas,
          pudiera, al oído, cantártelo a solas.

LIII

....

(5)   Volverán del amor en tus oídos
          las palabras ardientes a sonar;
          tu corazón, de su profundo sueño
                tal vez despertará;
(6)   pero mudo y absorto y de rodillas,
          como se adora a Dios ante su altar,
          como yo te he querido..., desengáñate:
                ¡así no te querrán!

La presencia de una receptora corpórea y concreta al final de la rima I por las referencias a las manos y su oído, vuelve de manera similar a sentirse presente hacia el final de la rima LIII. El hablante en el segundo verso de la cuarta estrofa al decir «cuyas gotas mirábamos temblar» implica la presencia de ambos amantes, y una experiencia mutua y exclusiva, tal como lo hizo con «yo quisiera escribirle» en la rima I. En la quinta estrofa de la rima LIII menciona sus oídos como lo había hecho al final de la estrofa tres en la rima I. Hasta ahora se ha preparado el escenario, hemos llegado a un ambiente íntimo y personal, una conversación de amantes, en pugna con uno más general y amplio del principio.

El proceso que extiende Bécquer en esta rima LIII es el

hecho de que el hablante se dirige coloquialmente a su amada diciéndole «desengáñate». Lo que quedaba enunciado que posiblemente sucedería en la rima I, aquí, en la rima LIII, ocurre. Al final de la rima I parece que se llega al comienzo de una conversación íntima que no se concreta, dado que el poema concluye. En la rima LIII, en efecto, presenciamos el desgarrador acto de desdén por parte de la amada y la expresión coloquial de despecho por parte del amante rechazado.

La culminación de este proceso que hemos buscado de mostrar meticulosamente en este análisis; es decir, el hecho de romper esas barreras del idioma poético para pasar al coloquial, indica la modernidad de Bécquer. Antes de Bécquer, la expresión lírica estaba circunscrita a un determinado vocabulario aceptado como poético y lo que se escapara de ese canon resultaba material inadecuado y, por lo tanto, desechable. Gustavo Adolfo rompe con este anquilosamiento lingüístico del material poético del siglo XIX y se desentiende de las restricciones impuestas hasta entonces, se desvía de esa rígida tradición. Bécquer abre la puerta a términos hasta entonces considerados estéticamente como no poéticos. El poeta de Sevilla va conformando una nueva estética; vocablos hasta entonces desdeñados por coloquiales encuentran acogida en las rimas y se ambientan en el entorno poético al que se integran, pasando a ser esas expresiones coloquiales parte del mundo lírico que las incorpora. Esta violación inaceptable en el siglo XIX se torna cada vez más común en los poetas del siglo XX. Bécquer es el nexo, la brecha precursora en esa trascendente transgresión lingüística, que aunque no es tan obvia y abundante como en los poemas de nuestro siglo, resulta ser la iniciación de tal tendencia. Hay también otras rimas en el volumen que proponen esta nueva línea lírica.

José Luis Cano subraya que lo conversacional aporta intimidad a la obra poética de Bécquer: «El gran acierto, pues, de Bécquer... es... el haber llevado su intimidad, en carne viva, a sus versos...» (27)[4].

---

[4] GUSTAVO ADOLFO BÉCQUER, *Rimas* (Madrid: Ediciones Cátedra, 1976), p. 27. José Luis Cano escribe una extensa introducción al volumen de poesías de Bécquer.

Tengamos en cuenta también que aunque sentimos la presencia del hablante y del receptor en la rima LIII, del pasaje de un lenguaje poético sencillo al coloquial, del desplazamiento de lo general a lo específico, todo esto es relativo. En realidad, lo que sucede en muchos de los poemas de Bécquer es que se vive la experiencia de una simultaneidad en el hecho de que algo aparentemente específico también resulta ser al mismo tiempo más amplio y general.

En la poesía de Bécquer, aunque hay un proceso de particularizar, esto no se lleva al extremo. Los nombres e identidades de los amantes en las rimas I y LIII no se revelan, se mantienen en el anonimato como en las demás rimas. Los poemas de Gustavo Adolfo se protegen de caer en lo anecdótico; lo que recogemos y vivimos en ellos es la experiencia profunda, particular y única que se expone. Por eso, paradójicamente, su arte, particularizándose, adquiere universalidad.

Lo sentimental, depurado del factor anecdótico, conecta al poeta de Sevilla con el arte lírico que lograría Juan Ramón Jiménez en su poesía pura, despojada de anécdotas. Además, el hecho de producir algo como una experiencia artística única a través del empleo del lenguaje une fuertemente a Gustavo Adolfo Bécquer, no sólo con Juan Ramón, sino también con Antonio Machado, Jorge Guillén, Federico García Lorca y los demás poetas de la Generación del 27.

En las tres rimas analizadas hemos visto la conjugación de la razón y la inspiración, lo cual separa a Bécquer del romanticismo. Las formas poéticas cuidadas y el empleo de un lenguaje depurado imponen un control a las emociones que no existía entre los románticos. También vimos que los efectos visuales y sonoros se unen a los verbales, y que el arte plástico y el musical se conjugan en su poesía. Esto, sumado al tratamiento de ciertas imágenes impresionistas, emparenta a Gustavo Adolfo con los parnasianos y simbolistas del movimiento modernista. Además, se ha observado que al lenguaje poético se agrega el coloquial produciendo una particular intimidad a sus poesías. Lo evanescente se aúna a lo concreto dotando a las rimas de un halo de misterio. Bécquer, gran innovador, hace poesía no vista en su tiempo. Tanto su poética propuesta en los primeros poemas del volumen, como así también los recursos estilísticos logrados que hemos enumerado, lo destacan como poeta.

Hoy miramos a Gustavo Adolfo Bécquer como precursor de lo hecho poéticamente en los comienzos de nuestro siglo. Vemos al escritor sevillano como profeta de lo que se haría y desarrollaría poéticamente; en las rimas hay indicios de las tendencias que se seguirían más tarde.

Hasta aquí comprobamos cómo funcionan en tres de sus rimas estos elementos modernos mencionados y hemos ido demostrando ideas muy aceptadas por los críticos de Bécquer en nuestros días, pero no suficientemente estudiadas como nos proponemos ir haciéndolo aquí. Una lectura cuidadosa nos confirma lo propuesto en este escrito: sus rimas son el mejor testimonio para verificar la modernidad del célebre poeta sevillano.

I. CUANDO EL ROMANTICISMO QUEDA OPERANDO DE FONDO: EL CONTROL DE LAS EMOCIONES EN LAS *RIMAS*.

A primera vista, la poesía de Bécquer nos parece totalmente romántica. Cuanto más la observamos empezamos a reconocer elementos fuera del romanticismo tradicional, y de esa forma, se nos va borrando esa primera impresión errónea de sus *Rimas*. Paso a paso, con una más detenida observación de sus poemas, se abre ante nuestros ojos un mundo más amplio. Nos damos cuenta que su poesía se desprende del mundo reducido y delimitado por los parámetros románticos. Bécquer nos suena a romántico, pero nunca del trillado. Este efecto se produce por la incorporación de otras técnicas que hacen que lo romántico que tienen sus poesías suene diferente. Estos recursos estilísticos revelan un mundo nuevo para el lector de sus poemas.

Algo esencial en este efecto general que se percibe en sus *Rimas* está dado por el control de las emociones. Bécquer no transita el viejo camino de la retórica hueca, de la verborragia caduca y del desborde emocional que saturó la lírica romántica hasta ya pasada la mitad del siglo XIX. Al desligarse de estos procedimientos, su poesía se abre a posibilidades renovadoras. Bécquer no es retórico, nunca cae en la verborragia y jamás presenta descontrol; su poesía es mesurada.

Gustavo Adolfo parece estar muy consciente de la disciplina que se impone para producir una creación lírica que contenga fuertes emociones matizadas por el control y la mesura. En *Cartas literarias a una mujer* nos explica su procedimiento:

> Yo no niego que suceda así. Yo no niego nada; pero, por lo que a mí me toca, puedo asegurarte que cuando siento no escri-

bo. Guardo, sí, en mi cerebro escritas, como en un libro misterioso, las impresiones que han dejado en él su huella al pasar;
estas ligeras y ardientes hijas de la sensación duermen allí agru-
padas en el fondo de mi memoria hasta el instante en que, puro,
tranquilo, sereno y revestido, por así decirlo, de un poder sobre-
natural, mi espíritu las evoca, y tienden sus alas transparentes,
que bullen con un zumbido extraño, y cruzan otra vez a mis ojos
como en una visión luminosa y magnífica.

Entonces no siento ya con los nervios que se agitan, con el
pecho que se oprime, con la parte orgánica material que se con-
mueve al rudo choque de las sensaciones producidas por la pasión y los afectos; siento, sí, pero de una manera que puede llamarse artificial; escribo como el que copia de una página ya
escrita; dibujo como el pintor que reproduce el paisaje que se
dilata ante sus ojos y se pierde entre la bruma de los horizon-
tes. (622-23)

Bécquer, ya por entonces, está consciente de una tradición
romántica que España absorbió de Europa y triunfó en la lírica declamatoria de Espronceda e hizo furor en la exageración
casi desaforada de los versos de Zorrilla. Gustavo Adolfo frena
el descontrol, sus rimas son un muro de contención para el
desbordante curso que traía el romanticismo. En otras palabras, Bécquer rechaza la sensiblería y propone un tratamiento
nuevo de las emociones. En Bécquer no se produce un apresu-
ramiento para expresar lo que siente. Impone calma a su corazón y sentimientos primero, y luego, una vez pasada la eu-
foria, conforma en versos su poesía medida. Siguiendo con
su explicación en *Cartas literarias a una mujer*, indica que es
en la maestría del control de este proceso donde radica la
elaboración de la verdadera poesía:

Todo el mundo siente. Sólo a algunos seres les es dado el
guardar como un tesoro la memoria viva de lo que han sentido.
Yo creo que estos son los poetas. Es más: creo que únicamente
por esto lo son. (623)

José Pedro Díaz hace un análisis soberbio del entorno romántico en el cual germinaron las *Rimas*. Aporta poemas de
poetas contemporáneos a Bécquer y va indicando coincidencias
en sus producciones líricas [1]. Enumerando a los que secundan
la sobresaliente obra becqueriana, Díaz resume:

[1] José Pedro Díaz, *Gustavo Adolfo Bécquer, vida y poesía* (Madrid: Editorial Gredos, 1958), pp. 171, 113, 114, 191 y 190. Con estas

Creo que en esta obra de depuración y de maduración del lirismo pueden advertirse dos etapas. La primera la cumplen, desde el «Correo de la Moda», Trueva, Barrantes y Selgas; la segunda se realiza sobre todo a partir de 1857 y desde «La América» (E. F. Sanz, G. Mata, G. Blest Gana, A. M. Dacarrete y A. Ferrán). Esta segunda etapa, en la que aquella doble enseñanza se funde en una intención unitaria, es la que determina el ámbito dentro del cual florecerán las *Rimas*. (171)

Aunque Bécquer tiene como base un grupo de poetas con intenciones similares, su poesía supera las expectativas de estas dos generaciones:

Uno de los problemas más interesantes que ofrece el estudio de la literatura española del siglo XIX es la aparición de esta lírica de Bécquer de tan depurada ejecución, tan desprendida aparentemente de su entorno y nacida para atravesar el siglo y salir indemne de él, ya que Bécquer es el más evidente apoyo que el siglo XIX ofrece a los primeros grandes españoles del XX. (113)

El mismo Díaz separa a Bécquer del romanticismo tradicional:

Y la obra de Bécquer no sólo es mejor, sino que además es diferente. A este respecto puede señalarse en él un cierto desplazamiento del romanticismo. La filiación de Bécquer en el conjunto resulta previsible sólo en cuanto a la prosa, en la que puede verse —sobre todo en las leyendas— el desarrollo de los temas y los tonos de su predecesores románticos. Pero su poesía, en cambio, determina nítidamente un clima nuevo. (114)

Díaz acentúa muy acertadamente el distanciamiento de Bécquer de lo romántico, enfatiza la separación que hay entre él y el romanticismo, recalcando el desprendimiento de las *Rimas* del pasado, y muestra su función precursora en la lírica española:

Si el romanticismo puede ser caracterizado como un fecundo estallido sentimental durante el cual, abolidas las reglas de una estética rígida y destronado el imperio de la razón, la creación literaria se realiza en un clima de espontaneidad poco rigurosa y sin contralores que la gobiernen, la situación no debe ser consi-

citas no es nuestro propósito repetir enteramente el análisis de Díaz, sino referir en forma somera a lo que ya ha dejado magníficamente expuesto el destacado crítico de Bécquer.

derada como un común denominador que valga también para
Bécquer. (191)

Díaz ve a Bécquer pasando por sobre la culminación del
romanticismo para ir a forjar un nuevo horizonte:

> De ese modo la obra de Bécquer hace culminar aquella co-
> rriente a la vez que asume su propio logro; pero al hacerlo de-
> termina, aún, nuevos caminos; cierra un ciclo y abre otro. Por-
> que esa tradición de la que deriva no sólo no lo ciñe ni lo limita,
> sino que, justamente, lo nutre y lo fecunda para nuevos des-
> arrollos. (190)

El libro de Martín Alonso es otro trabajo crítico de mucho
peso con referencia al desprendimiento que se produce en las
Rimas con respecto al romanticismo [2]. Alonso establece un
fuerte contraste entre las dos figuras principales de la poesía
española del siglo XIX: «A veces, en una orgía enfática y deses-
perada como Espronceda; otras, en una sinfonía nueva, apasionada, pero serena y transcendente, como en Bécquer» (249).
El mismo crítico resalta las diferencias entre estos dos poetas
e indica que Bécquer trae para el lector de su poesía una nueva dimensión lírica:

> Bécquer, en algún modo, al crear el «segundo estilo», o una
> nueva poética, se siente extraño en su tierra propia y desfasada
> de sus contemporáneos. Porque el poeta romántico ut sic, o por
> excelencia, era el que buscaba la embriaguez de lo sublime, lo
> que está sobre toda medida, como la rotundidad verbal del Te-
> norio, el tema del seductor sin perversidades demoníacas o la
> agitación desbordante de Espronceda que es un eco de Byron.
> Bécquer inaugura su poética en una expresión melancólica
> totalmente depurada, elevándola a lo más sencillo y elemental,
> capaz de asomar a los mundos armoniosos de la sensibilidad
> sincera e intimista. (249-50)

En cuanto al control de las emociones, tanto Díaz como
Alonso señalan la influencia germana en Bécquer. Henry Char-
les Turk indica la asociación especial del poeta con Heine [3].
Dámaso Alonso, por su parte, reconoce, en un análisis minu-

[2] MARTÍN ALONSO, *Segundo estilo de Bécquer* (Madrid: Ediciones
Guadarrama, 1972), pp. 249-50.
[3] HENRY CHARLES TURK, *German Romanticism in Gustavo Adolfo
Bécquer's Short Stories* (Lawrence, Kansas: The Allen Press, 1959).

cioso y erudito, la conexión entre Heine y Bécquer, pero al mismo tiempo muestra la independencia del poeta sevillano. Dámaso Alonso recalca lo auténtico y genuino de la expresión poética de Bécquer negando la más mínima imputación de plagio con respecto a lo escrito por el poeta alemán [4]. Lo que toma Bécquer de la tradición romántica germana es el tono popular, y principalmente, el control emotivo. Pero esto que adopta de lo germano lo adapta al ambiente meridional de sus *Rimas* y en el entorno de las mismas funciona de manera muy exclusiva.

Los románticos españoles en general absorbieron principalmente las tendencias de Francia e Inglaterra. Ya se mencionó en Espronceda la versificación rimbombante que es claro dejo de Byron, mientras que Víctor Hugo, Lamartine y demás franceses dejaron sus huellas de las luchas sociales de románticos españoles como Larra y Zorrilla. En este sentido, Bécquer se aparta de tal influencia anglo-francesa y, como excepción, acepta las tendencias germanas del control y la mesura. Antes que Bécquer escribiera sus *Rimas*, para 1857, Eulogio Florentino Sanz había traducido del alemán al castellano la poesía de Heine. Además de estar en contacto con tales traducciones, por esos años Bécquer estableció estrecha amistad con Augusto Ferrán, poeta español que residió en Alemania por un tiempo considerable, donde absorbió las tendencias germanas.

Bécquer nos trae en sus *Rimas* poemas que se desnudan de la retórica romántica y se despojan de la actitud rebelde, tanto en lo social como en lo político. Sus poesías no están cargadas de un tono de protesta, sino que expresan el intenso dolor en forma íntima. El joven crítico Carlos J. Barbáchano afirma [5]:

> Bécquer... elabora sus *Rimas* en un clímax cosmológico-dramático, con sencillez, claridad y una máxima exactitud en la ma-

---

[4] DÁMASO ALONSO, *Poetas españoles contemporáneos* (Madrid: Editorial Gredos, 1952), pp. 11-49. Alonso en el primer capítulo «Originalidad de Bécquer» con su análisis hace una soberbia defensa del poeta sevillano.

[5] CARLOS J. BARBÁCHANO, *Bécquer* (Madrid: Ediciones EPESA, 1970), p. 64.

nifestación de lo sentido... actualiza sus sentimientos, liberándolos de cualquier retórica, de cualquier complicación. No le importa la excesiva brillantez, sino la elegancia de su eficacia, la musicalidad del verso, el ritmo de la estrofa. (64)

El control de las emociones aísla a Bécquer del romanticismo en boga en su tiempo. Nuestro deseo será mostrar como se logra el control de las emociones en las *Rimas*. A través de varios de sus poemas evidenciaremos aspectos que son recurrentes, los cuales inciden en el control emotivo.

Uno de los aspectos que se repiten es el cuidado de la forma que impone orden al posible caos. La rima III nos había dejado ver esto anteriormente, y se pueden constatar efectos similares en otras rimas también, por ejemplo en la XI.

Otro aspecto que muestra el manejo de las emociones en las *Rimas* es el empleo de las exclamaciones que van firmemente frenadas y comprimidas, atenuando así su impacto emocional. La rima XXVII y otras nos dejarán ver este concepto.

El intenso dolor reprimido de las *Rimas* conlleva ecos «del dulce lamentar de los pastores» de las églogas de Garcilaso de la Vega. Tanto las poesías de Bécquer, como las de Garcilaso, son excelentes ejemplos de emociones controladas. Sus poemas nos traen emociones dispares que se reprimen por simple contraposición. El análisis de varias rimas nos permitirá explicar con más extensión este asunto.

Un cuarto aspecto que nos interesará elaborar es el tono prosaico en la poesía de Bécquer. Se han analizado exhaustivamente los elementos poéticos que contienen sus leyendas y los demás trabajos en prosa. El observar como funciona la prosa en las *Rimas*, es decir, el proceso inverso al llevado por la crítica en general, nos traerá un efecto digno de estudiarse con detenimiento en relación al control de las emociones. La rima XXXIV y muchas otras serán ejemplos apropiados de este recurso estilístico.

El quinto y último aspecto es la conciencia de Bécquer de estar al final del romanticismo. El poeta, con una actitud peculiar en sus poemas, numerosas veces se sirve de expresiones románticas trilladas para ironizarlas. De esta manera, las fuertes emociones quedan reprimidas bajo un manto de sarcasmo, cercano muchas veces al cinismo. En sus rimas, las expresiones gastadas del romanticismo funcionan como clichés, al mismo tiempo que le sirven para el control emotivo. Hacia el final de este capítulo, la rima LXVII y otras nos mostrarán lo aquí enunciado.

El control de las emociones en las *Rimas* de Gustavo Adolfo Bécquer produce una perspectiva llamativa que ubica lo que ellas tengan de romanticismo en un plano secundario. Por razón del control emotivo, lo que hay de romántico en sus poesías queda actuando de fondo. Al poner bajo control las emociones, afloran, en el rico escenario de sus poemas, elementos nuevos que adquieren relevancia. Son estos aspectos renovadores los que asumen un papel preponderante y los que queremos destacar en relación con la modernidad de las *Rimas* de Bécquer.

A. EL DOMINIO DE LAS EMOCIONES POR MEDIO DE FORMAS CUIDADAS.

El control de las emociones que se logra por la forma ordenada y cuidada que se encuentra en la concepción de las *Rimas* comenzó a evidenciarse en el análisis que hicimos de la rima III. La poesía de Bécquer nos trae el intenso dolor del amor no correspondido. Estas son fuertes emociones que al momento de expresarse poéticamente obra en ellas el elemento catalizador del orden y formas cuidadas, precipitando una expresión de lamento desesperado que actúa en un ambiente de sorprendente calma y quietud.

Bécquer, mientras comenta su poética en *Cartas literarias a una mujer,* muestra conciencia de la función preeminente del orden y cuidado formal en su expresión artística: «Hablemos como se habla. Procedamos con orden. ¡El orden! ¡Lo detesto, y, sin embargo, es tan preciso para todo!...» (625).

Concha Zardoya pone atención al balance que se produce

entre la forma y el contenido en las *Rimas*. En el caso de las poesías de Bécquer, entre el orden y el sentimiento: [6]

> Bécquer se salva y se salvará del olvido no sólo porque sus *Rimas* son la historia verdadera de una vida y de un alma, sino también porque supo forjarse —tras una enconada lucha con la expresión poética, lucha de su inspiración embridada por «la inteligente mano» (III, 42), de la razón que reúne y selecciona las palabras— una sabia técnica hecha de «silenciosa armonía» (XXXIV, 65), de ritmo, de medida, de sencillez, de concisión —a veces— lapidaria. Bécquer encabeza, justamente, la poesía contemporánea española porque tuvo plena conciencia de la íntima relación que existe en todo poema entre forma y contenido, según lo evidencia la rima V (62):
>
> > Yo soy el invisible
> > anillo que sujeta
> > el mundo de la forma
> > al mundo de la idea.
>
> ... Gustavo Adolfo Bécquer sentía, sin duda, una sincera y genuina reverencia por la perfección de la forma, íntimamente identificada con su contenido interior, con su carga anímica y sensorial, con su significado metafórico. (88-89)

Carlos Bousoño ve en el empleo del paralelismo una guía ordenadora en Bécquer que se opone diametralmente al proceder poético de los románticos:

> ... reiterar indefinidamente una postura es condenarla al fracaso. Bécquer debía huir de todo lo que ya se había hecho inexpresivo a fuerza de uso. Si hasta entonces el desorden había sido la actitud artística usual, el nuevo poeta necesitaba buscar una fórmula ordenadora. Y la encontró en los paralelismos. Y así, la técnica paralelística se nos aparece, en cierto modo, como el procedimiento con el que Bécquer acusadamente se sustrajo a un carácter muy destacado del romanticismo de escuela. (208)

Los estudios estilísticos de Zardoya y Bousoño muestran el control de las emociones por medio de las formas. Para más detalles, conviene referirse a estos trabajos críticos [7].

---

[6] CONCHA ZARDOYA, *Poesía española contemporánea* (Madrid: Ediciones Guadarrama, 1961), pp. 88-89. Zardoya en su capítulo introductorio «Las *Rimas* de Gustavo Adolfo Bécquer, a una nueva luz», pp. 21-89, realiza un magnífico análisis estilístico.

[7] DÁMASO ALONSO y CARLOS BOUSOÑO, *Seis calas en la expresión literaria española* (Madrid: Editorial Gredos, 1951), p. 208. Carlos Bousoño en el quinto capítulo «Las pluralidades paralelísticas de Bécquer» hace un estudio estilístico de rigor casi científico. En nuestro trabajo

En las *Rimas* se experimenta esa constante pugna entre forma y contenido. Paradójicamente, las emociones y el orden marchan en contraposición. Pero al mismo tiempo, milagrosamente, se transmite en sus poesías la sensación de una mágica amalgama de los opuestos. En sus poemas hay un ensamble inesperado de los extremos. De esta forma, la expresión del sentimiento en las *Rimas* de Bécquer adquiere niveles insuperables.

En las rimas se puede mostrar el equilibrio permanente entre las formas y el contenido, y cómo las emociones marchan bajo el orden organizador. En la rima XXI Bécquer establece una equivalencia entre la mujer y la poesía:

XXI

«¿Qué es poesía?», dices mientras clavas
en mi pupila tu pupila azul.
«¿Qué es poesía? ¿Y tú me lo preguntas?
Poesía... eres tú.» (419)

José Pedro Díaz agrega a esta ecuación poética de poesía = mujer el elemento del sentimiento que se desprende y

---

nos queremos desprender del rígido formato técnico de la estilística. Por otro lado, la férrea disciplina científica que impone Bousoño al texto de las *Rimas,* le permite descubrir algo muy significativo. Se nota, tras el análisis, que un orden matemático y preciso en las distribuciones formales de las rimas, a las cuales denomina «pluralidades paralelísticas», provee a los poemas de una expresión del sentimiento que aflora de manera muy cuidadosa. Bousoño concluye que esta mesura formal en la expresión de lo emotivo separa a Bécquer del desorden romántico:

Nuestro trabajo apunta a un conocimiento del estilo becqueriano. Pienso que, en parte, hemos alcanzado este norte inicial. Cierto que la semejanza paralelística de los conjuntos no es el único medio que Gustavo Adolfo utiliza en su lírica; pero es, sí, uno de los más peculiares. La frecuencia de su uso en las *Rimas* parece explicarse, sincrónicamente, por urgencias de intensidad expresiva; diacrónicamente, como oposición al desorden romántico (227).

El libro de Concha Zardoya, *Poesía española contemporánea,* 1961, amplía el estudio estilístico de las *Rimas,* pero sus conclusiones son similares a las de Bousoño. Zardoya muestra cómo la forma y el contenido se aúnan para lograr una expresión poética nueva en el poeta sevillano.

deriva de esta conversación íntima; es decir, poesía = sentimiento = mujer[8]. Y Jorge Guillén coincide en esta fórmula tripartita: «Mujer, sentimiento, poesía: es la trinidad esencial» (11)[9].

El cuidado formal de la rima XXI es llamativo. Bécquer, como en muchas otras rimas, emplea aquí la combinación de versos largos y breves intercalados. Miremos con atención los detalles formales de esta aparentemente sencilla rima:

> «¿Qué es *poesía?*», dices mientras clavas
> en mi pupila *tu* pupila azul.
> «¿Qué es *poesía?* ¿Y *tú* me lo preguntas?
> *Poesía...* eres *tú.*»

En forma insistente se presentan tres preguntas. Tres veces se menciona la poesía, mientras que tres veces también se refiere al «tú» de la amada. Con tres vocablos se insiste en preguntar «¿Qué es poesía?» De igual manera se contesta en forma concluyente con tres palabras: «Poesía... eres tú.» Los tres primeros versos van separados por hemistiquios, con tres palabras hacia cada lado. Esta simetría perfecta se disimula un tanto en el tercer verso con la segunda pregunta que contiene cinco elementos, pero bien podría prescindirse del «y» y del «lo» sin perder el significado, ni la equidistancia respetada hasta ese momento. En el cuarto verso los elementos «poesía» y «tú», separados antes por los hemistiquios, se combinan. Y al combinarse, las dos partes de tres vocablos cada una en los versos anteriores, se concentran y unen en las tres palabras finales: «Poesía... eres tú.»

Esta distribución perfecta de los elementos que se comparan se hace solamente consciente si ponemos atención a ella. Lo que sí impresiona desde un principio en el lector de la rima XXI es la expresión concentrada, sencilla y poderosa del sentimiento. Uno intuitivamente no se detiene a observar su equidistancia absoluta. Esta rima impresiona nuestros sentidos porque después de expresada tan perfecta comparación

---

[8] Díaz, p. 202.
[9] Jorge Guillén, *La poética de Bécquer* (Cuba: Ucar, García y Cía., 1943), p. 11.

parecería imposible decirlo de otra manera. La rima XXI minimiza, resume, concentra y puntualiza todo lo que pueda querer decirse del sentimiento amoroso en manos de la expresión poética. En este poema parece experimentarse la sensación de llegar al meollo de la combinación de la poesía, el sentimiento y la mujer. En esta rima se llega a la reducción máxima, se da en el centro de lo emotivo.

Deteniéndonos un poco más, nos damos cuenta que Bécquer, en la rima XXI, obtiene la síntesis más escueta posible donde se pone en juego el contenido y la forma, los sentimientos y el orden. Esta es una poesía clave en la producción artística becqueriana. Al hacernos ver el control de la emoción por medio del orden, parece que el contenido termina siendo domado por la forma, pero no ocurre así. El equilibrio entre ambos es tan perfecto que nunca tenemos la sensación de que uno prevalezca sobre el otro.

Además, la rima XXI es clave por esta aquivalencia que se establece entre la poesía y la mujer. De ahí en más, en otras rimas, cuando se refiere a la mujer podemos tomarlo al nivel mimético y literal como refiere Riffaterre [10], o bien, llevarlo al plano semiótico donde mujer signifique poesía [11]. Es decir,

---

[10] El crítico Riffaterre en «The Poem's Significance» dice que en la primera lectura y en la búsqueda de cierto significado en el texto, el lector arriba a un primer plano interpretativo, el mimético. En palabras de Riffaterre tenemos la descripción de este primer paso en la lectura del poema: «This first, heuristic reading is also where the first interpretation takes place, since it is during this reading that meaning is apprehended» (5). MICHAEL RIFFATERRE, *Semiotics of Poetry* (London: Indiana U. Press).

[11] En lecturas sucesivas del poema, según Riffaterre, el lector puede encontrar una correlación entre los signos que varíe del nivel mimético ya aceptado antes. El lector puede llegar a observar la coordinación de un nuevo sistema de correspondencias entre los signos del texto. Entonces, ya ha abandonado el nivel mimético de interpretación para sustituirlo por el semiótico. Este desarrollo o pasaje de un nivel al otro Riffaterre lo llama semiosis. Dejemos que el mismo teórico explique el proceso:
This transfer of a sign from one level of discourse to another, this metamorphosis of what was a signifying complex at a lower level of the text into a signifying unit, now a member of a more developed system, at a higler level of the text, this functional shift is the proper domain of semiotics. Everything related to

una interpretación llana y literal acepta a la amada simplemente como una mujer, mientras que una lectura más simbólica permite la equivalencia de amada = poesía. A partir de aquí, las *Rimas* nos permitirán, al menos, dos planos interpretativos. Uno, con significación literal; y el otro, que refiera al proceso poético, a una visión consciente del acto creador, a una actitud metapoética que entre a ser posible cada vez que se mencione a la amada en los poemas.

Igualmente, en la rima XI podemos por una parte experimentar la búsqueda de la mujer ideal; y por otra, ver como el poeta anhela dar con la expresión poética excelsa:

XI

—Yo soy ardiente, yo soy morena,
yo soy el símbolo de la pasión;
de ansia de goces mi alma está llena.
—¿A mí me buscas? —No es a ti, no.

—Mi frente es pálida; mis trenzas, de oro;
puedo brindarte dichas sin fin;
yo de ternura guardo un tesoro.
—¿A mí me llamas? —No; no es a ti.

—Yo soy un sueño, un imposible,
vano fantasma de niebla y luz;
soy incorpórea, soy intangible;
no puedo amarte. —¡Oh, ven; ven tú! (412)

Como muchos otros críticos, Carlos Barbáchano, comenta la rima XI en forma literal imponiéndole limitaciones que ella misma rechaza [12]. José Pedro Díaz amplía en forma acertada la interpretación del poema agregándole el plano metapoético, donde la elección de cierto tipo de mujer es equiva-

---

this integration of signs from the mimesis level into the higher level of significance is a manifestation of semiosis (4).
Así, las posibilidades de interpretación del poema se multiplican. En el caso de las *Rimas*, el signo mujer permite al nivel mimético la interpretación literal, mientras que al nivel semiótico podemos optar por el significado más simbólico de mujer = poesía.
[12] BARBÁCHANO, p. 168.

lente a la búsqueda por parte del poeta de su ideal estético
en el plano de la creación artística [13].

En la forma de la rima XI se observa una equilibrada contraposición:

> —Yo *soy ardiente*, yo *soy morena*,
> yo *soy* el símbolo de la pasión;
> de ansia de goces mi alma está llena.
> —¿A mí me buscas? —*No es a ti, no.*
>
> —Mi frente es *pálida*; mis trenzas, *de* oro;
> puedo brindarte dichas sin fin;
> yo de ternura guardo un tesoro.
> —¿A mí me llamas? —*No; no es a ti.*
>
> —Yo *soy* un sueño, un imposible,
> vano fantasma de niebla y luz;
> *soy* incorpórea, *soy* intangible;
> no puedo amarte. —*¡Oh, ven; ven tú!*

Los adjetivos son importantes en este contraste. La primera mujer (o tipo de poesía) es «ardiente» y se opone al blanco
desapasionado de «pálida» en la segunda estrofa. Mientras en
una fluye la sangre que trae calor y vida, en la otra se enfatiza la ausencia de vitalidad. Una es morena, que pudiera
apuntar a lo meridional y fogoso, en tanto que la otra es rubia
de «trenzas de oro», que connota lo nórdico y apacible. Hasta
podríamos aventurar que el poeta podría implicar un rechazo
tanto del romanticismo desbordante español, como también
el mesurado de influencia germana. Lo que acepta es una
combinación de ambas, que termina siendo algo muy diferente y exclusivo, que no es ni una, ni la otra. En la primera
estrofa se formula una posible expresión amorosa que el poeta
desdeña. En la segunda estrofa se tienta otra posible formulación que sufre igual definitivo rechazo.

En la primera estrofa se manifiestan ansias pasionales
de existencia y reconocimiento; «soy» se repite tres veces. En
la estrofa tercera y final «soy» se repite tres veces también.

---

[13] José Pedro Díaz, en su texto, lo expresa así:
   La rima XI (las tres mujeres), se desarrolla como una alegoría que nos revela esa misma condición fantasmal e imposible
de la mujer preferida, pero el ideal de amor romántico de Bécquer se superpone aquí a una concepción de su ideal poético (219).

En la primera estrofa los adjetivos y sustantivos tienden a lo inmaterial: «ardiente», «morena», «símbolo», «pasión», «ansia», «goces» y «alma». En la tercera estrofa los adjetivos y sustantivos también subrayan la inmaterialidad: «sueño», «imposible», «vano», «fantasma», «niebla», «luz», «incorpórea» e «intangible». La primera estrofa muestra denodada intención de obtener materialización y sufre el desdén. Al contrario, la última estrofa es la indiferencia absoluta y logra cautivar el corazón del poeta.

Hasta este punto hemos querido proseguir con una lectura de equivalencias lógicas, pero como lectores del poema llegamos a ciertos límites, sin poder alcanzar a explicarlo todo. En esta rima XI hay huecos insalvables, entramos en el terreno insondable de lo poético, se producen espacios inexplicables entre las comparaciones que quedan deambulando en el aire paradójico del poema. Nos encontramos aquí con el vagor indeterminado, nos movemos en un ambiente nebuloso y brumoso que resulta ininteligible. Todo resulta incierto desde el momento en que como lectores tratamos de racionalizarlo, y es en ese instante donde lo inefable y evasivo reinan, donde el sentimiento logra su expresión poética genuina [14].

---

[14] Una vez alcanzada la interpretación mimética y semiótica, Riffaterre destaca que el lenguaje poético resiste el proceso de reducción a un significado determinado: «Significance, and let me insist on this, now appears to be more than or something other than the total meaning deducible from a comparison between variants of the given» (12). El poema ha llegado así al nivel ininteligible, se establece un juego entre los dos planos que no permite una resolución:
  The effect of this disappearing act is that the reader feels he is in the presence of true originality, or of what he believes to be a feature of poetic language. a typical case of obscurity. This is when he starts rationalizing, finds himself unable to bridge the semantic gap inside the text's linearity, and so tries to bridge it outside of the text by completing the verbal sequence (13).
La realización del lenguaje poético en esta complejidad creemos haberla destacado con la lectura detenida de la rima XI, donde el texto resiste a un significado último; es más, destaca la ausencia de cierto preciso mensaje. Lo que nos queda, tras la lectura del poema, es la experiencia indefinida de una infinidad de interpretaciones válidas, o mejor dicho, la imposibilidad de llegar a una interpretación determinada o concluyente del poema.

Bécquer buscó una forma poética que aceptó como imposible de alcanzar. Trató de corporizar en sus poemas el sentimiento de encarnación imposible. No es el logro final lo que le apasiona, sino el intento denodado, la búsqueda ferviente de esa expresión poética [15]. En la empresa colosal de dar forma al sentimiento reside su grandeza [16].

Para insistir en lo aventurado de su misión como poeta leamos la rima XXXVIII:

XXXVIII

Los suspiros son aire y van al aire.
Las lágrimas son agua y van al mar.
Dime, mujer: cuando el amor se olvida,
¿sabes tú adónde va? (429)

El poeta se cuestiona lo efímero del amor y la falta de permanencia de los sentimientos. Si en los románticos teníamos la sobresaturación de la expresión amorosa, donde lo sentimental abundaba anegando y ahogando la lírica en un desprecio intencional de las formas, en Bécquer la experiencia es diferente. Gustavo Adolfo sigue un cuidado minucioso de las formas, como se ve en esta rima también, y como resultado, la expresión emotiva es volátil, se esfuma el sentimiento, se cuestiona hasta su propia esencia.

Bécquer, como nadie, tras las formas cuidadas de sus poemas impone control a la expresión sentimental logrando en sus rimas un ambiente formal donde germina el sentimiento en su pureza. Bécquer expresa la emotividad con la solemnidad y bajo el dominio formal que no alcanzó ningún otro poeta romántico del siglo XIX español.

---

[15] En la leyenda «Los ojos verdes», la narración de tonos poéticos funciona como una alegoría de esa persecución anhelante del poeta para encontrar la forma perfecta pp. 133-41.

[16] En la introducción a sus *Rimas*, Bécquer describe el proceso minucioso y delicado del artista para crear la forma que logre contener los sentimientos que se desean expresar: «Yo quisiera poder cincelar la forma que ha de conteneros como se cincela el vaso de oro que ha de guardar un preciado perfume» (40).

B. LAS EXCLAMACIONES CONTROLAN LO EMOTIVO.

Dentro de las formas de que se vale Gustavo Adolfo para
imponer moderación a las pasiones está el empleo particular
que hace de las frases exclamativas. Para los románticos las
exclamaciones resultaron un arma eficaz para indicar el éxtasis de la expresión amorosa. En Bécquer, por otra parte, los
versos encabezados por los signos exclamativos resultan una
herramienta útil para moderar en muchos casos la manifes-
tación emotiva.

Los románticos hicieron uso y abuso de la exclamación.
Tanto se puede observar en *Don Álvaro*, 1835, del Duque de
Rivas, donde los signos de admiración señalan la irrefrenable
tragedia; como también en los versos de Espronceda en *El
estudiante de Salamanca*, 1840, donde Don Félix lamenta a
Elvira. Luego, en Zorrilla, el *Don Juan Tenorio*, 1844, contiene
muchísimos versos exclamativos donde proliferan las declaraciones de amor. La exclamación en el romanticismo alimentó
el desborde pasional y emotivo. Núñez de Arce, con su poesía
grandilocuente, prosigue el mismo curso; y Campoamor, con
sus poemas declamatorios, extrema la tendencia en las décadas
de 1850 y 60. Echegaray lleva al teatro el empleo superlativo
de la exclamación en *El gran galeoto*, 1881, al punto que es
posible contar en su drama romántico más versos bajo el signo
de exclamación, que sin él. Aquí, los signos de admiración
exaltan las emociones de la tragedia del triángulo amoroso de
Don Julián, Teodora y Ernesto.

Las exclamaciones contribuyeron decididamente al tono
altisonante que trae la lírica romántica. Por otro lado, cuando
Bécquer emplea la exclamación, veremos que dota a sus rimas de diferentes matices emocionales, y no simplemente del
tono desesperado. Es más, veremos bajo la luz de sus poemas
que muchas exclamaciones producen, paradójicamente, calma y quietud. Los románticos y Bécquer utilizaron las exclamaciones, pero en muy diferente graduación y con fines
muy distintos.

Las exclamaciones, en las *Rimas* de Bécquer, por lo general se encuentran sólo al final de los poemas, muchas veces, únicamente en el último verso, como sucede en las rimas III, X, XI, XIII, XXXIX, etc. Concha Zardoya observa esto y las llama epifonemas, hace una clara explicación de su presencia en las *Rimas*, sin ahondar en las variaciones del empleo de las mismas [17].

En muchos casos el propósito de utilizar la exclamación es lograr contundencia en la afirmación que se hace en el último verso, pero no se emplea para exagerar lo emotivo. Como ejemplo, podemos mencionar las partes de la rima III que ya analizamos en detalle anteriormente. Al final de la primera sección se afirma: «¡Tal es la inspiración!» y la segunda parte concluye: «¡Tal es nuestra razón!» Así, se resaltan por medio de la exclamación los asuntos del poema, y no necesariamente el tono del mismo. Algo similar sucede con el estribillo de la rima IV:

IV

No digáis que agotado su tesoro,
de asuntos falta, enmudeció la lira.
Podrá no haber poetas, pero siempre
¡habrá poesía!

---

[17] Aquí traemos la definición de Zardoya de epifonema y su función en las *Rimas* de Bécquer:
Epifonema. Muchísimas rimas acaban con una exclamación final que intensifica su dramatismo: lo prolonga en el espíritu del lector y en él queda como un temblor del alma conmovida. Pero estos versos exclamativos sobrepasan la simple admiración, porque ellos son la reflexión final arrancada a nuestro ánimo, suspenso ante la consideración de lo que antecede. A causa de este matiz se convierten en epifonemas, que son términos de una anterior exposición. En tales epifonemas concentra Bécquer, muchas veces, el sentido más profundo de sus rimas, siendo sujeto, y a la par, conclusión de ellas. O en ellos vibra la súplica o grita el dolor, o se encubre el sarcasmo (33-34).
Al final de esta cita, vemos que la excelente crítica parece intuir la diferente gama anímica que se logra con el empleo de las exclamaciones. En nuestro trabajo deseamos profundizar en esta perspicaz intuición de Zardoya. Parece residir, en el empleo de las exclamaciones, un dominio digno de destacarse en relación al control emotivo en las *Rimas*.

> Mientras las ondas de la luz al beso
>   palpiten encendidas;
> mientras el sol las desgarradas nubes
>   de fuego y oro vista;
>
> mientras el aire en su regazo lleve
>   perfumes y armonías;
> mientras haya en el mundo primavera,
>   ¡habrá poesía!
>
> Mientras la ciencia a descubrir no alcance
>   las fuentes de la vida,
> y en el mar o en el cielo haya un abismo
>   que al cálculo resista:
>
> mientras la Humanidad, siempre avanzando,
>   no sepa a do camina;
> mientras haya un misterio para el hombre,
>   ¡habrá poesía!
>
> Mientras sintamos que se alegra el alma
>   sin que los labios rían;
> mientras se llore sin que el llanto acuda
>   a nublar la pupila;
>
> mientras el corazón y la cabeza
>   batallando prosigan;
> mientras haya esperanzas y recuerdos,
>   ¡habrá poesía!
>
> Mientras haya unos ojos que reflejen
>   los ojos que los miran;
> mientras responda el labio suspirado
>   al labio que suspira;
>
> mientras sentirse puedan en un beso
>   dos almas confundidas;
> mientras exista una mujer hermosa,
>   ¡habrá poesía! (405-06)

En la primera estrofa se introduce el asunto del poema con signos de exclamación: «Podrá no haber poetas, pero siempre / ¡habrá poesía!» En lo sucesivo, se prosigue con un delicado orden metonímico donde la razón y la inspiración contribuyen a la existencia de lo poético. Obsérvese que a lo largo del poema se mantiene un cuidado formal excelente de versos largos y cortos intercalados. Sistemáticamente se intercalan también estrofas donde su verso más reducido y final afirma: «¡habrá poesía!» La posible emotividad que pueda recargar este estribillo exclamatorio está diluida por el entorno ordenado y medido en que se expresa. Más que un tono exaltado, la rima IV trae a su lector un canto de afirmación de lo poético. Otra vez, el signo de admiración sirve para indicar el asunto del poema, más que para imprimir un tono de desbordante emoción como era en el caso de los románticos. Los signos de exclamación en Bécquer encierran muchas veces una idea, como vimos en las dos rimas anteriores. Lo que muchos críticos han notado en Gustavo Adolfo es la expresión concentrada y reducida de lo emotivo [18]. Muchas veces estas expresiones breves de la emoción vienen amuradas por los signos exclamativos. En muchos versos de las rimas se experimenta la sensación de que los signos de admiración están comprimiendo un concepto, están cerrando el escape a una idea o emoción que lucha por zafarse en busca de expansión, sin lograrlo. La exclamación opera así como muro de contención para la expresión pasional. Por ejemplo en la rima LXIX:

LXIX

Al brillar un relámpago nacemos,
y aún dura su fulgor cuando morimos,
¡Tan corto es el vivir!

La gloria y el amor tras que corremos,
sombras de un sueño son que perseguimos.
¡Despertar es morir! (445-46)

Hay otras rimas en donde se observa también que los signos

---

[18] GABRIEL CELAYA, *Gustavo Adolfo Bécquer* (Madrid: Ediciones Júcar, 1972). Este poeta denomina a la concentración de la expresión emotiva «brevedad eléctrica». Pone de relieve que esta manera comprimida de expresar el sentimiento separa y divide a Bécquer del estilo romántico altisonante:
¿Y a qué otra cosa sino a esto —sugerir lo que no se puede decir, evocar, provocar la imaginación del receptor con lo que, precisamente por sólo insinuado, más la estimula— apunta la «brevedad eléctrica»? Sobre lo que es esta brevedad, tan contraria al retumbo melodramático y sonoramente lleno del primer romanticismo, y no digamos hasta qué punto opuesta... (129).

exclamativos han acorralado al concepto o emoción, hasta
dejarlo algo inconcluso, como en la rima X:

X

Los invisibles átomos del aire
en derredor palpitan y se inflaman;
el cielo se deshace en rayos de oro;
la tierra se estremece alborozada.
Oigo flotando en olas de armonía
rumor de besos y batir de alas;
mis párpados se cierran... ¿Qué sucede?
¿Dime?... ¡Silencio!... ¡Es el amor que pasa! (411)

En la próxima rima, el lector recibe la impresión de que
el hablante se quedó sin palabras, y ya sin saber qué más
decir, suelta la exclamación del último verso:

XVII

Hoy la tierra y los cielos me sonríen;
hoy llega al fondo de mi alma el sol;
hoy la he visto..., la he visto y me ha mirado...
¡Hoy creo en Dios! (417)

En la siguiente rima, otra vez, el lector tiene la impresión
de que el hablante al no poder expresar más sobre lo que
siente por esa mujer, pronuncia una frase exclamativa algo
inconclusa al final del poema:

XXXIX

¿A qué me lo decís? Lo sé: es mudable,
es altanera y vana y caprichosa;
antes que el sentimiento de su alma,
brotará el agua de la estéril roca.

Sé que en su corazón, nido de sierpes,
no hay una fibra que al amor responda;
que es una estatua inanimada; pero...
¡Es tan hermosa! (429)

Los signos de admiración ponen un tope a la expresión emotiva. En vez de contribuir al descontrol verbal como sucedía en

la mayoría de los casos de la lírica romántica, en las *Rimas* de Bécquer las exclamaciones operan en sentido opuesto. Los exclamativos oponen una barrera para evitar el desenfreno verborrágico en la expresión emocional. En otras ocasiones las exclamaciones indican la falta de la palabra adecuada. Los signos de admiración señalan la imposibilidad de alcanzar la metáfora apropiada o el no poder dar con la expresión poética que encarne lo que el poeta siente. La rima XIII nos transmite esta frustración en su último verso:

XIII

Tu pupila es azul, y cuando ríes,
su claridad suave me recuerda
el trémulo fulgor de la mañana
que en el mar se refleja.

Tu pupila es azul, y cuando lloras,
las transparentes lágrimas en ella
se me figuran gotas de rocío
sobre una violeta.

Tu pupila es azul, y si en su fondo
como un punto de luz radia una idea,
me parece en el cielo de la tarde
¡una perdida estrella! (414-15)

Más que representar la manifetsación sentimental, esta metáfora final nos indica lo inadecuado del lenguaje para corporizar lo emotivo. Mientras que las comparaciones en las dos estrofas anteriores son más concretas, se evidencia que la imagen encerrada bajo los signos de admiración es más difusa, da el efecto de dispersión, nos produce la impresión de que lo que se quiere comparar se escapa de los labios del poeta y de sus posibilidades verbales. El poeta se encuentra ante el desafío de dejar expresado lo inefable. Gabriel Celaya cita una serie de reflexiones del poeta donde transmite esa sensación vacilante [19]:

Y apelando siempre a la inefabilidad: «Pensé entonces algo que no puedo recordar, y que, aunque lo recordase, no encontraría

---

[19] CELAYA, p. 125.

palabras para decirlo.» Y en otro lugar: «Ese silencio profundo, esa vaguedad sin nombre, imposible de explicar con palabras.» Y en otro: «Una voz insólita que murmura palabras desconocidas en un idioma extraño y celeste..» Y en otro: «Cantos celestes como los que acarician los oídos en los momentos de éxtasis; cantos que percibe el espíritu y no los puede repetir el labio.» Y en otro aún: «Esos fantasmas ligerísimos, fenómenos inexplicables de la inspiración, que al querer materializarlos pierden su hermosura.» (125)

La misma vacilación se nota en la rima XXIII:

XXIII

Por una mirada, un mundo;
por una sonrisa, un cielo;
por un beso..., ¡yo no sé
qué te diera por un beso! (419)

Si las exclamaciones en el romanticismo eran aplicadas para subrayar el desborde emotivo, en Bécquer no tienen la misma función. En estas dos últimas rimas analizadas las exclamaciones sirven como índice que señala la limitación verbal para expresar la emoción.

Hasta aquí hemos visto el dominio notable que ejerce Gustavo Adolfo en el empleo de las exclamaciones para producir diferentes gradaciones emotivas. Los signos de admiración sirven para concentrar y reprimir lo emocional dentro de versos muy cortos. También se utilizan en muchos casos para indicar el asunto, más que para incidir en el tono del poema; y en otras ocasiones, las exclamaciones difuminan las expresiones pasionales subrayando la imposibilidad lingüística de transmitir lo que se siente. En Bécquer encontramos una gama amplia en la utilización de la exclamación, mientras que en el romanticismo se producía un martilleo monótono y efecticista que Bécquer desdeña.

Gustavo Adolfo logra matices extraordinarios en el empleo calculado de las exclamaciones, y muchas veces va un poco más allá. En algunas rimas las exclamaciones logran imponer calma y quietud. Observemos este aspecto algo paradójico en la rima XXVII:

XXVII

Despierta, tiemblo al mirarte;
dormida, me atrevo a verte;
por eso, alma de mi alma,
yo velo mientras tú duermes.

Despierta ríes, y al reír, tus labios
inquietos me parecen
relámpagos de grana que serpean
sobre un cielo de nieve.

Dormida, los extremos de tu boca
pliega sonrisa leve,
suave como el rastro luminoso
que deja un sol que muere...
«¡Duerme!»

Despierta miras, y al mirar, tus ojos
húmedos resplandecen
como la onda azul, en cuya cresta
chispeando el sol hiere.

Al través de tus párpados, dormida,
tranquilo fulgor viertes,
cual derrama de luz templado rayo
lámpara transparente...
«¡Duerme!»

Despierta hablas, y al hablar, vibrantes,
tus palabras parecen
lluvia de perlas que en dorada copa
se derrama a torrentes.

Dormida, en el murmullo de tu aliento
acompasado y tenue
escucho yo un poema, que mi alma
enamorada entiende...
«¡Duerme!»

Sobre el corazón la mano
me he puesto porque no suene
su latido, y de la noche
turbe la calma solemne.

De tu balcón las persianas
cerré ya, porque no entre
el resplandor enojoso
de la aurora y te despierte...
«¡Duerme!» (422-23)

La primera estrofa de este poema establece que la vigilia acarrea la turbación, mientras que el sueño trae la quietud:

> *Despierta, tiemblo al mirarte;*
> *dormida, me atrevo a verte;*
> por eso, alma de mi alma,
> yo velo mientras tú duermes.

Luego, las demás estrofas van intercaladas por los encabezamientos «despierta» y «dormida». Así, la rima se desliza en un oleaje emocional de altos y bajos. La relectura del poema nos deja ver este vaivén emotivo. Cuando la amada está despierta se avivan las emociones, y cuando ella duerme, se hunden en la tranquilidad del sueño. Con una exclamación acompasada y soñolienta el poeta susurra al oído de su amada: «¡Duerme!» Esta es una exclamación queda que impone silencio a su corazón. El poema en general se desenvuelve en un ambiente calmo. «¡Duerme!» va cerrando el último hilo de luz, aquieta el más pequeño ruido perturbador. La exclamación «¡Duerme!» aplaca todo movimiento y sella la paz absoluta que se alcanza al fin del poema.

Así vemos que el poeta sevillano utiliza los signos de exclamación para el control emocional. Gustavo Adolfo, en sus *Rimas*, logra un dominio en el empleo de la exclamación que no lo ejercieron con la misma eficacia los románticos de su época. Si Bécquer logró dar el grito más agudo que se desprende del corazón herido en la rima LIII con su exclamación postrera: «como yo te he querido..., desengáñate: / ¡así no te querrán!», supo también otorgar un matiz variado a las exclamaciones de sus rimas hasta alcanzar el extremo opuesto. En la rima XXVII obtiene la supresión total de conmoción con otra exclamación: «¡Duerme!»

C. LAS EMOCIONES ENCONTRADAS SE REPRIMEN.

La relación entre Garcilaso de la Vega y Bécquer es estrecha. Los dos poetas centran su lamento en el amor no correspondido. Tanto Garcilaso como Bécquer se refieren a las emociones en base al recuerdo de ellas. Ambos poetas, en su visión retrospectiva de la experiencia amorosa, permiten que la turbulencia sedimente bajo el espacio temporal que da lugar a cierta calma y reflexión de lo vivido. En Garcilaso y en Bécquer el efecto de la memoria calma la ebullición emotiva. A través del tamiz cerebral del proceso de recomponer la experiencia amorosa se aplaca su efervescencia anterior. Ese espacio de tiempo amplio, que transcurre entre la pasión vivida y su plasmación en el objeto poético, tanto en Bécquer como en Garcilaso es semejante por el tono apacible con que recuerdan a la amada. Garcilaso es paralelo y modelo para Bécquer porque él también crea poesía que controla las emociones.

Juana de Ontañón se limita a conectar a Bécquer con Garcilaso sólo en su iniciación literaria [20]:

> Siempre le gustó escribir, desde muy pequeño; a los doce años dedica una oda a la muerte de su maestro Alberto Lista, y a los catorce habla de su predilección por Rioja y por Herrera, que nada influirán en su obra, más próxima a la del toledano Garcilaso. (XV)

Martín Alonso también reduce la posible conexión entre el poeta sevillano y el toledano a su primera faz interpretativa [21]: «Garcilaso fue uno de los poetas favoritos de Bécquer, acaso mejor en su primera etapa poética de Sevilla» (125). Por otro lado, si seguimos el curso biográfico de Bécquer, notamos en sus apuntes que la figura de Garcilaso cautivó su atención hasta el final de sus días. En su penúltimo año de vida está con su hermano Valeriano en Toledo, 1869. Allí, en el escenario medieval comenta al acercarse al sepulcro de Garcilaso: «Y aquel otro más alto y joven... proseguí pensando, ese es el que cantó el dulce lamentar de los pastores, tipo completo del siglo más brillante de nuestra Historia» (999).

En las *Rimas* se nota el dejo de Garcilaso. En la rima

---

[20] Gustavo Adolfo Bécquer, *Rimas, leyendas y narraciones*, 6.ª ed. (México: Editorial Porrúa. 1971), p. XV. Juana de Ontañón escribe un extenso prólogo a las obras de Bécquer.

[21] Martín Alonso, *Segundo estilo de Bécquer*, p. 125.

XXVII, que estuvimos considerando al final de la sección anterior, se observa el empleo de imágenes que contraponen efectos de conmoción y quietud: «relámpagos de grana que serpean / sobre un cielo de nieve.» La tormenta desenfrenada transcurre paradójicamente en un entorno estático y calmo; como la hiedra, de connotaciones siniestras, crece y se nutre en el ambiente agradable de la Egloga I [22]. Más adelante, en la misma rima, esta contraposición se encuentra en los términos opuestos: «...dormida, / *tranquilo fulgor* viertes», lo pacífico se asocia extrañamente con lo refulgente, y este encuentro contradictorio de diferentes tonos anímicos nos recuerda al «*dulce lamentar* de los pastores» [23], que coincidentemente mencionó Bécquer.

La rima XXVII no es la única donde es posible encontrar la reunión de extremos opuestos. La rima V, junto a las primeras del volumen, implica la actitud poética del autor. Aquí confluyen también imágenes en pugna: «Yo soy la ardiente nube / que en el ocaso ondea». En estos versos encontramos otra vez lo candente frente y junto a lo sereno. Sin extremar los procedimientos, estos versos traen eco del anochecer apacible que sirve de escenario en la Egloga I, mientras Salicio y Nemoroso nos comunican sus hondas penas amorosas. El ambiente apacible se opone al fluir de la desesperación angustiosa de los pastores. Por contraposición, las emociones emergen con relativa calma. Las imágenes opuestas se asocian conjugando la inesperada combinación que se hace de emociones ambivalentes.

En la próxima estrofa de la rima V leemos: «Yo soy nieve en las cumbres, / soy fuego en las arenas», que connota un ajuste emocional por parte de quien expresa sus dolores ínti-

---

[22] La hiedra es metáfora de la triste muerte de la amante en el canto de Nemoroso y es símbolo de la infidelidad de la otra amante, en el canto de Salicio. La hiedra, recordatorio del fin trágico del amor amargo de ambos pastores que se lamentan, paradójicamente crece y habita en un ambiente placentero.

[23] El dulce lamentar resulta ser dulce porque refiere a recuerdos amorosos una vez muy gratos y caros para los dos hablantes. Pero es un lamentar al mismo tiempo por los resultados trágicos de estos amores evocados. Los términos opuestos transmiten también una sensación de ambivalencia anímica en las *Rimas* de Bécquer.

mos en armonía con el entorno donde quedan plasmados esos dolores.

Hasta aquí hemos comprobado que Bécquer, al igual que Garcilaso, enfría lo candente del sentimiento tamizando la emoción vivida a través del velo apaciguante de la memoria y el recuerdo. Comprobamos también que hay un balance entre el ambiente exterior y el interior de los hablantes de los poemas. Sus emociones marchan bajo cotnrol en acuerdo con el entorno.

Otro punto de contacto entre Garcilaso y Bécquer, que es una constante a lo largo de sus poemas, es el profundo sentimiento amoroso por parte de quien canta que se estrella contra la fría indiferencia de la destinataria del canto. El apasionado corazón del «yo» en ambos casos se contrabalancea con el indiferente «tú» en quien vuelca sus deseos amorosos. En Garcilaso y en Bécquer el «yo» se desvive en la pasión, mientras el «tú» de la amada parece no sentir nada. El caudal emotivo del «yo» de los poemas se ve frenado por la actitud cortante de la indiferencia del «tú» de la amada que no responde al calor del cariño que se le ofrece. La rima XXXI señala el contraste en la actitud sentimental entre el «tú» y el «yo»:

XXXI

Nuestra pasión fue un trágico sainete
en cuya absurda fábula
lo cómico y lo grave confundidos
risas y llanto arrancan.

Pero fue lo peor de aquella historia
que, al fin de la jornada,
a ella tocaron lágrimas y risas,
¡y a mí sólo las lágrimas! (425-26)

En esta rima, otra vez, las emociones de diferente índole y tono, se mezclan: «lo *cómico* y lo *grave* confundidos / *risas* y *llanto* arrancan.»

Las emociones encontradas en la rima LXVIII tienen el efecto de reprimirse por propia contraposición:

LXVIII

No sé lo que he soñado
en la noche pasada;
triste, muy triste debió ser el sueño
pues despierto la angustia me duraba.

Noté, al incorporarme,
húmeda la almohada,
y por primera vez sentí, al notarlo,
de un amargo placer henchirse el alma

Triste cosa es el sueño
que llanto nos arranca;
mas tengo en mi tristeza una alegría.
¡Sé que aún me quedan lágrimas! (445)

Podemos notarlo en el verso «de un *amargo placer* henchirse el alma» o en la paradoja emocional en que termina
el poema: «mas tengo en mi *tristeza* una *alegría*. / ¡Sé que aún
me quedan lágrimas!»

La represión emotiva se repite en la serie de emociones
contrapuestas en un solo verso de la rima LXXV: «¿Y *ríe* y
llora, y *aborrece* y *ama*», y en el próximo verso la contradicción emotiva continúa: «y guarda un rastro del *dolor* y el
gozo».

En la rima XXXV se observan los dos elementos que hemos visto unen a Bécquer con Garcilaso. En esta rima el hablante se refiere a su pasión retrospectivamente, y también
se advierte el contraste del «yo» del poeta, desesperado y frenado a un mismo tiempo por la indiferencia del «tú» de la
amada:

XXXV

¡No me admiró tu olvido! Aunque de un día,
me admiró tu cariño mucho más;
porque lo que hay en mí que vale algo,
eso... ¡ni lo pudiste sospechar! (427)

Muchas de las rimas son una flecha sin dirección, un que-
jido que se pierde en el aire, un grito de dolor que se difu-

mina y esparce al no encontrar eco emocional de quien debería ser receptora afectiva de la expresión poética.

Una rápida lectura de las rimas XXXIX, XLVI, LXIV y LXXVII nos dejará ver el mismo concepto.

En la lectura de la rima XXXIX vemos que la pasión amorosa y fogosa del hablante se ve frenada por la indiferencia de ella:

XXXIX

¿A qué me lo decís? Lo sé: es mudable,
es altanera y vana y caprichosa;
antes que el sentimiento de su alma,
brotará el agua de la estéril roca.

Sé que en su corazón, nido de sierpes,
no hay una fibra que al amor responda;
que es una estatua inanimada; pero...
¡Es tan hermosa! (429)

En la rima XLVI salta a la vista del lector la contraposición de reacciones en cuanto a lo amoroso, él sufre mientras ella sigue su curso alegre; y así se produce un canto reprimido:

XLVI

Me ha herido recatándose en las sombras,
sellando con un beso su traición.
Los brazos me echó al cuello, y por la espalda
partióme a sangre fría el corazón.

Y ella prosigue alegre su camino,
feliz, risueña, impávida; ¿y por qué?
Porque no brota sangre de la herida...
¡Porque el muerto está en pie! (433)

Una vez más, en la rima LXIV, las emociones se contraponen, la fidelidad eterna de él choca contra el goce pasajero y la indiferencia de ella:

LXIV

Como guarda el avaro su tesoro,
guardaba mi dolor;

yo quería probar que hay algo eterno
a la que eterno me juró su amor.

Mas hoy le llamo en vano, y oigo al tiempo,
que lo agotó, decir:
«¡Ah barro miserable, eternamente
no podrás ni aun sufrir!» (443)

En la rima LXXVII el lector percibe en el hablante el true-
que del amor en rencor, emociones opuestas se entrecruzan
por despecho a la indiferencia de su amada:

LXXVII

Dices que tienes corazón, y solo
lo dices porque sientes sus latidos.
Eso no es corazón...; es una máquina
que al compás que se mueve hace ruido. (457)

Las emociones encontradas se reprimen. En muchas rimas el amor pasa a ser rencor, la fidelidad se frustra con la
traición y el deseo pasional se reprime ante la indiferencia.
Si hemos insistido en analizar esta represión de su canto repetidas veces en diferentes rimas, es porque este aspecto resulta clave en la poesía de Bécquer y en su relación con Garcilaso [24].

---

[24] En estas notas deseamos incluir una rima que se atribuye a
Bécquer:

1
Soy yo

Si copia tu frente
del río cercano la pura corriente
y miras tu rostro de amor encendido,
soy yo, que me escondo
del agua en el fondo
y, loco de amores, a amar te convido;
soy yo, que en tu pecho buscando morada,
envío a tus ojos la ardiente mirada,
mi llama divina...,
y el fuego que siento la faz te ilumina.
Si en medio del valle
en tardo se trueca tu andar animado,
vacila tu planta, se pliega tu talle...
soy yo, dueño amado,
que en no vistos lazos

Por último, pongamos atención a cierta coordinación entre las formas poéticas y las emociones que es algo más exclusivo de Bécquer en sí. Ya habíamos aceptado en «poesía eres tú» una equivalencia que nos transportaba en la lectura de las *Rimas* a un nivel semiótico o metapoético. Bécquer aceptó esta propuesta de mujer = poesía: «En la mujer, sin embargo, la poesía está como encarnada en su ser... es, en una palabra, el verbo poético hecho carne» (620). En las rimas de Gustavo Adolfo la mujer y la forma poética son una misma

> de amor anhelante te estrecho en mis brazos;
> soy yo quien te teje la alfombra florida
> que vuelve a tu cuerpo la fuerza y la vida;
> soy yo que te sigo
> en alas del viento soñando contigo.
> Si estando en tu lecho
> escuchas acaso celeste armonía,
> que llena de goces tu cándido pecho,
> soy yo, vida mía...;
> soy yo, que, elevando
> al cielo tranquilo mi férvido canto;
> soy yo, que los aires cruzando ligero
> por un ignorado movible sendero,
> ansioso de calma,
> sediento de amores, penetro en tu alma. (493-94)

El ambiente de: «Si copia tu frente / del río cercano la pura corriente» recuerda a la Egloga I en el siguiente pasaje: «Corrientes aguas puras, cristalinas, / árboles que os estáis mirando en ellas». También hay fuerte eco de la égloga de Garcilaso en la acción de ver el reflejo de las aguas como fuente de donde emanan las emociones. El ambiente de «en medio del valle» trae remembranzas del plácido entorno del «verde prado de fresca sombra lleno» de la Egloga I.

El pasaje: «soy yo quien te teje la alfombra florida», refiriendo al canto del poeta, recuerda al tejido de las ninfas en la Egloga III de Garcilaso. Ambas imágenes conllevan un plano metapoético del proceso artístico de elaborar el verso como el entretejimiento de palabras. El colorido tejido que en realidad le ofrece el poeta a la amada en esta rima es su poema: «soy yo, que, elevando / al cielo *tranquilo* mi *férvido* canto». Obsérvese la contraposición emotiva de los vocablos subrayados. Este aspecto se repite al final en: «*ansioso de calma*, / sediento de amores, penetro en tu alma.» Estas son contradicciones anímicas que abundan también en las églogas de Garcilaso de la Vega.

Esta rima citada es extensa, a la manera de las églogas de Garcilaso. La rima XVI parece ser una reducción de ésta, dejando el verso más irregular y ciñéndose a las medidas métricas más típicas de Bécquer. Dentro de las poesías atribuidas a Bécquer, la rima 1 titulada «Soy yo», es quizá la que más fuertemente se conecta tanto en forma, como en tono, a las églogas de Garcilaso.

cosa. Por otro lado, el «yo» del poeta en las poesías becquerianas es masculino. El «yo» del poeta, el «yo» poético del
creador en la tarea difícil de hacer aflorar sus intensas emociones ve que éstas se refrenan, se apaciguan al momento de
dejarlas plasmadas en el «tú» de la creación, en el «tú» feme-
nino, en la poesía en sí. El «yo» del creador trata de manifestar su emoción que se ve reprimida al encarnarse en la
forma del «tú» de su poesía. Las emociones de este «yo» poético y creador quedan menguadas al encontrar forma *en la
rima*. Así se llega a un equilibrio emotivo en el proceso creador
que es muy peculiar en Bécquer.

Como conclusión de esta sección, reafirmemos que las emociones encontradas en las *Rimas* de Bécquer dejan un extraño
sabor de «amargo placer» (rima LXVIII) que nos recuerda el
paradójico dolor amoroso del «dulce lamentar de los pastores» (Egloga I) de Garcilaso de la Vega. Una vez ocurridos los
hechos que exaltaron los ánimos en el plano amoroso transcurre un tiempo que permite reposar la emoción. Luego, la
memoria reencarna en el recuerdo una expresión poética mesurada en base a lo vivido. El otro aspecto que controla las
emociones es el de los estados anímicos que marchan en direcciones opuestas y que al encontrarse paradójicamente en
los versos reprimen y evitan entre sí la exageración de la expresión emocional, dotando a los poemas de calma y mesura
en la interpretación de las pasiones humanas.

D. La función de los elementos de prosa

El tono coloquial y la utilización de la prosa en las *Rimas*
es otro recurso formal para imponer control a las emociones.
Como se mencionó en la introducción de este capítulo, mucha
de la crítica hecha sobre Bécquer ha destacado las cualidades
poéticas de su prosa. El proceso inverso, es decir, poner atención al tinte de prosa y tono coloquial que envuelve la mayoría de sus poesías, ha sido un aspecto que ha quedado sor-
prendentemente desatendido. Por otro lado, el observar la
influencia de la prosa y su timbre conversacional en la poesía

de Bécquer resulta algo totalmente lógico dado que vinieron primero las publicaciones de sus trabajos en prosa, y más tarde, al final de sus días, salieron a luz los poemas.

Su trabajo literario podría dividirse, para ganar practicidad, en quinquenios. Para detalles de fechas puede consultarse el ordenamiento en tablas cronológicas en los libros de José Pedro Díaz [25] y Martín Alonso [26]. Una división quinquenal nos permitirá ver rápidamente la actividad literaria de Bécquer.

A fines del año 1848, cuando sólo tenía 12 años, se registra su primera obra en honor de su maestro fallecido: «Oda a la muerte de don Alberto Lista» (464). De 1849 a 1854 son los años de transición en el joven artista. Deja definitivamente Sevilla, va a Madrid, se desprende de la pintura y asume su vocación por las letras. En compañía de Nombela y Campillo enfrenta el difícil mundo de la capital. De 1855 a 1859 saca sus primeras publicaciones, iniciándose en el periodismo. En esos años, escribe algunos trabajos en prosa, biografías, corrige y adapta obras de teatro y algunas zarzuelas. También por aquellos años acomete el proyecto que le alentó a ir a Madrid; la

---

[25] José Pedro Díaz, en *Gustavo Adolfo Bécquer, vida y poesía*, 1958, dedica toda la primera parte del libro (pp. 2-109), a la vida del poeta. En esa sección va minuciosamente detallando fechas de las publicaciones. Por ejemplo, en la página 101 describe el período principal de su producción en prosa, perteneciente al quinquenio 1860-1865:
Desde el punto de vista de su creación literaria en prosa, su período de mayor fecundidad es este que va de 1860 a 1865. Véase a continuación las fechas de las publicaciones más significativas. De 1860 es «La cruz del diablo». De 1861: *Cartas literarias a una mujer*, «La creación», «Maese Pérez», «Los ojos verdes», «El monte de las ánimas», «¡Es raro!», el prólogo a *La soledad* de Augusto Ferrán, «Creed en Dios», y «El Cristo de la calavera». De 1862: «El aderezo de esmeraldas», «El miserere», «El rayo de luna», «Tres fechas», «La venta de los gatos», y el pequeño trabajo «Un drama». De 1863: «El beso», «La corza blanca», «La cueva de la mora», «El gnomo», «La promesa» y los trabajos menos importantes «La ridiculez», «La pereza», «Las perlas» y «Apólogo». De 1864 sólo *Desde mi celda* y «La rosa de pasión». En 1865 la intensidad de su trabajo parece ya haber decaído sensiblemente. Son de ese año «La noche de difuntos», «Memorias de un pavo» y algunas crónicas. (101)
[26] Martín Alonso, en *Segundo estilo de Bécquer*, 1972, en las páginas 445 a 451, tiene las tablas cronológicas de las prosas becquerianas.

posible publicación de la *Historia de los templos de España*
(767-947). Este es un plan muy ambicioso, que al carecer de
apoyo financiero no llega a realizarse. De 1860 a 1864, Bécquer consigue cierta estabilidad profesional. Todos esos años
trabaja en el periódico «El Contemporáneo». Allí escribe y sa-
len publicadas la mayoría de las leyendas, su trabajo principal
en prosa. También, por esos años, publica sus otras obras en
prosa: *Desde mi celda* (497-614), y los ensayos sobre poesía en
Cartas literarias a una mujer (615-635) y el prólogo para el
libro de poesías: *La soledad* (Colección de cantares por Agusto
Ferrán y Fornies) (1184-95). Entre 1865 y 1870 va dejando
gradualmente la prosa. Aunque cumple el cargo de censor de
novelas desde 1865 hasta 1868, su interés se va centrando en
la poesía. Entre 1866 y 1868 termina el manuscrito *Rimas del
libro de los gorriones* (399-496) que contiene sus poesías. Es
verdad que resulta imposible determinar con exactitud cuán-
do escribió cada una de ellas, pero sí se sabe que es recién en
junio de 1868 que las termina de reunir en un solo volumen,
tras un trabajo cuidadoso de dos años.

Hay otro detalle más que es significativo en este recuento
histórico de su producción literaria. Bécquer dejó el manuscrito de sus poesías en manos de su amigo González Bravo,
ministro del gobierno conservador de Isabel II. En la revolución liberal de septiembre de 1868 se pierden estos folios;
posiblemente fueron quemados. Arduamente, en el año 1869
Bécquer recompone de memoria su volumen de poesías. En
1870 termina esta labor y pocos días antes de morir da a su
amigo Campillo el manuscrito de las rimas que los amigos
publicarán más tarde, en 1871, un año después de su muerte.

De este resumen destacamos que Gustavo Adolfo Bécquer
escribió su prosa primero, y luego su poesía. Aun dejó escritos
sus pensamientos poéticos en prosa antes de dar a luz sus rimas. Por eso resulta lógico encontrar posibles rasgos de prosa
en su poesía. Aunque no se pueden determinar los años de sus
poesías, sabemos que las reescribió y terminó de darles la
forma tal cual tienen hoy día en sus dos últimos años de vida.
Podemos concluir que, en general, el trabajo en prosa precede
al poético. También deducimos de este breve resumen que te-

nemos en Bécquer un poeta maduro en el momento que da forma final a sus *Rimas*. Para entonces había dejado atrás la fogosidad de sus años adolescentes y era ya un escritor formado a través de años de experiencia literaria. Por lo tanto, el esfuerzo de ver los rasgos de prosa y su efecto en las *Rimas*, será totalmente legítimo, al mismo tiempo que instructivo.

La inclusión de la prosa en lo poético se produce varias veces en las rimas, haciendo variar los tonos anímicos. La rima XXXIX es un buen ejemplo:

XXXIX

¿A qué me lo decís? Lo sé: es mudable,
es altanera y vana y caprichosa;
antes que el sentimiento de su alma,
brotará el agua de la estéril roca.

Sé que en su corazón, nido de sierpes,
no hay una fibra que al amor responda;
que es una estatua inanimada; pero...
¡Es tan hermosa! (429)

El poema comienza, en sus dos primeros versos, con un tono puramente coloquial que impone una máscara de frialdad en el hablante, que aparentemente acepta la indiferencia de ella: «¿A qué me lo decís? Lo sé: es mudable, / es altanera y vana y caprichosa». En los próximos dos versos, con el hipérbaton, la anticipación del adjetivo «estéril», y la comparación metafórica de los términos corazón = roca, el hablante pasa al estilo poético. Con este cambio de estilo, del conversacional al poético, consecuentemente hay una transición emocional en el hablante. Si en los dos primeros versos aprueba la indiferencia de ella con igual indiferencia por parte de él, en el tercer y cuarto verso el hablante parece implicar al menos cierta queja que no había al principio: «antes que el sentimiento de su alma, / brotará el agua de la estéril roca.» De haber continuado con la forma en prosa no se hubiera quizás señalado adecuadamente el cambio emocional. Observemos este parafraseo posible: ¿A qué me lo decís? Lo sé: es mudable, es altanera y vana y caprichosa; posiblemente, brotará agua de la roca estéril antes de que el sentimiento emane de su alma. Los prosaico habría ahogado la emoción que se dispersa en la palabrería, y el poema hubiera caído en lo pedestre. La mezcla de lo poético y lo prosaico hace un contrabalanceo de lo estético y emocional. Cuando se utiliza el estilo poético la emoción se intensifica por efecto de la concentración verbal; cuando se usa la prosa, se diluye por efecto de la dispersión.

La segunda estrofa da comienzo con «*sé*» que proviene y se deriva del inicio coloquial de la primera estrofa: «¿A qué me lo decís? Lo *sé*...» La queja del hablante sube de tono en la emoción del estilo poético de esta siguiente estrofa: «Sé que en su corazón, nido de sierpes, / no hay una fibra que al amor responda». El penúltimo verso: «...*es* una estatua inanimada; pero...» trae ecos de la enumeración de tono conversacional del principio de la rima: «¿A qué me lo decís? Lo sé: *es* mudable, / *es* altanera y vana y caprichosa». Pero si nos fijamos con cuidado, estas enumeraciones del principio de la rima consisten de adjetivos calificativos a modo de prosa, mientras que «es una estatua inanimada» desarrolla una metáfora de la mujer a modo poético. Hacia el final de la rima el nivel poético y el de la prosa se han conjugado. Así llegamos al final con: «¡Es tan hermosa!» Aquí tenemos una expresión de admiración algo común, pero lo prosaico ya ha adquirido kilates poéticos. Como en muchas rimas, aquí el lenguaje coloquial trasciende sus límites y adquiere valor y altura poética. «¡Es tan hermosa!» conjuga en el plano emocional esa actitud pasiva del hablante en un comienzo y la profunda admiración por la mujer al final.

Aun una rápida lectura de algunas rimas puede hacernos percibir como la inclusión de lo coloquial y prosaico impone cierto control emocional a los poemas. Los románticos mezclaron los estilos de prosa y poesía, pero lo hicieron con una actitud rebelde para romper con las férreas restricciones neoclásicas. En cambio, Bécquer mezcla la prosa en sus rimas para producir y hacer variar los matices anímicos. Con esto en mente, léanse por ejemplo las rimas: XI, XII, XXI, XXIII, XXVI, XXXIII y XXXIV, entre las más notables.

Hagamos una lectura detenida de la rima XXXIV, y veremos con más claridad el contraste entre el plano poético y el prosaico, y, por consecuencia, los efectos distintos de ambos estilos:

XXXIV

Cruza callada, y son sus movimientos
      silenciosa armonía;
suenan sus pasos, y al sonar recuerdan
del himno alado la cadencia rítmica.

Los ojos entreabre, aquellos ojos
      tan claros como el día;
y la tierra y el cielo, cuanto abarcan,
arden con nueva luz en sus pupilas.

Ríe, y su carcajada tiene notas
      del agua fugitiva;
llora, y es cada lágrima un poema
de ternura infinita.

Ella tiene la luz, tiene el perfume,
      el color y la línea;
la forma, engendradora de deseos,
la expresión, fuente eterna de poesía.

¿Que es estúpida? ¡Bah! Mientras, callando,
      guarde oscuro el enigma,
siempre valdrá, a mi ver, lo que ella calla
más que lo que cualquiera otra me diga. (427)

En las primeras cuatro estrofas lo poético exalta el amor. Algunos de los términos indicados señalan la atención que se da al elemento poético, mientras que «arden», «lágrima», «ternura» y «de deseos» subrayan la faz emotiva:

Cruza callada, y son movimientos
      silenciosa *armonía;*
suenan sus pasos, y al sonar recuerdan
del *himno* alado la *cadencia rítmica.*

Los ojos entreabre, aquellos ojos
      tan claros como el día;
y la tierra y el cielo, cuanto abarcan,
arden con nueva luz en sus pupilas.

RÍE, y su carcajada tiene *notas*
  del agua fugitiva;
LLORA, y es cada *lágrima* un *poema*
  de *ternura* infinita.

Ella tiene la luz, tiene el perfume,
  el color y la línea;
la forma, engendradora *de deseos*,
la expresión, fuente eterna *de poesía*.

¿Que es estúpida? ¡Bah! Mientras, callando,
  guarde oscuro el enigma,
siempre valdrá, a mi ver, lo que ella calla
más que lo que cualquiera otra me diga.

En la estrofa central del poema subrayamos «ríe» y «llora».
El valor emocional de ambos verbos es obvio, y al compararlos con «notas» y «poema», el estilo poético queda presente igualmente en las dos palabras. En el centro de la rima se han conjugado el estilo poético con las manifestaciones anímicas extremas de la risa y el llanto.

Algo interesante que sucede en esta rima es que en la quinta estrofa, cuando no nos es posible señalar ningún término refiriendo a lo poético, tampoco nos es posible detectar ningún término que refiera a lo anímico. Parece que los términos poéticos ahondan en la expresión emotiva, mientras que los puramente coloquiales aplacan las emociones evitando mencionarlas.

Cuando llega la sensación de casi experimentar un desborde emotivo tras la expresión poética, se frena la pasión repentinamente:

Ella tiene la luz, tiene el perfume,
  el color y la línea;
la forma, engendradora de deseos,
la expresión, fuente eterna de poesía.

¿Que es estúpida? ¡Bah! Mientras, callando,
  guarde oscuro el enigma,
siempre valdrá, a mi ver, lo que ella calla
más que lo que cualquiera otra me diga.

Cuando parecíamos haber llegado a la realización total en lo poético y sentimental en la comparación de la mujer, el sentimiento y la poesía: «...fuente eterna de poesía», se revierte bruscamente el proceso con términos burdamente prosaicos al comienzo de la estrofa final: «¿Que es estúpida? ¡Bah! ...» Lo coloquial se ha entrometido inesperadamente, ha frenado las emociones sin anularlas. El resto del poema se expresa en estilo de prosa, con un lenguaje común, pero que carga tanto enigma que conserva sus ciertos valores poéticos en relación al entorno lírico. Además, el empleo de vocales abiertas (e, a) y las aliteraciones dotan a este lenguaje obviamente conversacional de elementos poéticos.

La prosa en esta poesía frenó el posible desborde emocional y se conjugó con lo poético. En los románticos, la inclusión de la prosa en la poesía no varía en los términos que se utilizan, como delirio, relámpagos, suspiros, éxtasis, etc., que se emplean tanto en la prosa como en la poesía indistintamente, y por consiguiente, el tono exagerado no varía tampoco. Los románticos sólo mezclaron los géneros como acto de rebeldía contra el neoclasicismo compartimentado sin distinguir estilos o palabras que los diferenciaran. Cuando Bécquer pasa de la poesía a la prosa, los vocablos que selecciona son muy diferentes, y el tono que les imprime también.

Bécquer indudablemente estaba consciente de este método en sus rimas. Sabía que una manera de poderse separar del romanticismo exagerado era incorporando cierta clase de prosa a sus poemas y poner, de este modo, rienda a las emociones. Así adquiere relevancia el comentario suyo que aparece en *Cartas literarias a una mujer* y que ha pasado desapercibido por la mayoría de los críticos, pero que es de tremenda relevancia con respecto a lo que estamos analizando aquí. En este pasaje, en el primer párrafo, Bécquer se burla del proceder desesperado de los románticos, y en contraposición, ofrece luego una fórmula nueva de hacer poesía:

> Efectivamente, es más grande, más hermoso, figurarse al genio ebrio de sensaciones y de inspiración, trazando a grandes rasgos, temblorosa la mano con la ira, llenos aún los ojos de lágrimas o profundamente conmovidos por la piedad esas tiradas de poesía que más tarde son la admiración del mundo; pero ¿qué quieres?, no siempre la verdad es lo más sublime.
> ¿Te acuerdas? No hace mucho que te lo dije a propósito de una cuestión parecida.

Cuando un poeta te pinte en magníficos versos su amor,
duda. Cuando te lo dé a conocer en prosa, y mala, cree. (623)

Sin duda, la prosa, hasta algo descuidada en algunos casos,
es un recurso formal presente en las *Rimas* de Bécquer que
contribuye al control emotivo.

La rima XL nos permitirá ilustrar una vez más el proceso
de las emociones que afloran en la sección donde prima lo
lírico y la sujeción emotiva que se evidencia en los trozos de
poesía donde lo coloquial prevalece. Lo poético y sentimental
se destacan en los diez primeros versos. Luego, lo conversa-
sional y reprimido prevalece en los próximos dieciocho versos
del poema. Más tarde, luego de un hiato de sosiego, en los
primeros seis versos vuelve a predominar lo sentimental junto
a lo poético:

XL

Su mano entre mis manos,
sus ojos en mis ojos,
la *amorosa* cabeza
apoyada en mi hombro,
¡Dios sabe cuántas veces,
con paso perezoso,
hemos vagado juntos
bajo los altos olmos
que de su casa prestan
misterio y sombra al pórtico!
Y ayer..., un año apenas
pasado *como un soplo,*
con qué exquisita gracia,
con qué admirable aplomo,
me dijo, al presentarnos
un amigo oficioso:
«Creo que en alguna parte
he visto a usted.» ¡Ah!, *bobos,*
que, sois de los salones
comadres de buen tono
y andáis por allí a caza
de galantes *embrollos:*
¡Qué historia habéis perdido!
¡Qué manjar tan sabroso
para ser devorado
sotto voce en un corro,
detrás del abanico
de plumas y de oro!
....

> ¡*Discreta* y *casta* luna,
> copudos y altos olmos,
> paredes de su casa,
> umbrales de su pórtico,
> callad, y que el secreto
> no salga de vosotros!
> Callad, que por mi parte
> lo he olvidado todo;
> y ella..., ella, ¡no hay máscara
> semejante a su rostro! (429-31)

El poema, en sus primeros diez versos, refiere al recuerdo emotivo del hablante y su amada en un pasado añorado que se enmarca en un estilo lírico. Luego viene una pausa, y con: «Y ayer..., un año apenas / pasado como un soplo» nos adentramos al estilo coloquial. Junto a esta transición en el estilo, del poético al conversacional; en lo emocional, se pasa del amor soñado antes por el hablante, al tono irónico y quejoso después. Es más, el hablante llega al punto de desprenderse de la palabra y concede a su amada indiferente la expresión más llanamente conversacional cuando procede a citarla directamente: «Creo que en alguna parte / he visto a usted.» Luego, asistimos al hecho de que la pureza de los sentimientos del hablante es rebajada al nivel de chisme y los términos se vuelven vulgares, otra vez, para describir la ausencia de sentimientos. Hacia el final, el hablante reasume su postura emocional del principio del poema y el verso, consecuentemente, fluye otra vez poéticamente como sucedió al comienzo. Pero en los últimos versos, el hablante, por despecho, acepta el embuste del lenguaje coloquial para esconder sus emociones: «Callad que por mi parte / lo he olvidado todo». Pero al referirse en los dos últimos versos al objeto de su amor, su expresión vacila entre lo prosaico y lo poético, entre las emociones que se escapan, y el disimularlas y ahogarlas a tiempo: «y ella..., ella, ¡no hay máscara / semejante a su rostro! »

En este poema vemos claramente que cuando se emplea el estilo poético, con términos de tono lírico, las emociones se desatan. Pero cuando se aplica el estilo conversacional, el tono cambia en los términos coloquiales que se emplean: «como un soplo», «un amigo oficioso», «bobos», «comadres» y «embrollos»; así, consecuentemente, las emociones se esconden.

Las emociones, en las *Rimas* de Gustavo Adolfo Bécquer, están bajo control. La incorporación consciente de elementos de prosa con un tono conversacional aporta hábilmente a la sujeción emotiva de los poemas.

E.   EL PECULIAR EMPLEO DEL CLICHÉ ROMÁNTICO.

Quizás el elemento que evidencia más el desprendimiento de Bécquer del movimiento que lo precedió, el romanticismo, sea el esfuerzo de controlar las emociones por medio del tono irónico. Este tono está dado en algunas ocasiones por el empleo de frases románticas gastadas. Con el uso irónico del cliché romántico Gustavo Adolfo da la espalda a ese movimiento ya algo caduco para entonces. Con el cliché se desliga, se desasocia de lo anterior. El poeta de Sevilla se sirve del cliché para decir basta al romanticismo desenfrenado. Bécquer incluye en sus rimas expresiones que siguen los cánones románticos, y luego, con un lenguaje prosaico las ironiza.

La rima XXXIV nos dejó ver este contraste estilístico entre lo poético y lo prosaico:

XXXIV

(1)   Cruza callada, y son sus movimientos
                     silenciosa armonía;
            suenan sus pasos, y al sonar recuerdan
            del himno alado la cadencia rítmica.

(2)   Los ojos entreabre, aquellos ojos
                     tan claros como el día;
            y la tierra y el cielo, cuanto abarcan,
            arden con nueva luz en sus pupilas.

(3)   Ríe, y su carcajada tiene notas
                     del agua fugitiva;
            llora, y es cada lágrima un poema
            de ternura infinita.

(4)   Ella tiene la luz, tiene el perfume,
                     el color y la línea;
            la forma, engendradora de deseos,
            la expresión, fuente eterna de poesía.

(5)   ¿Qué es estúpida? ¡Bah! Mientras, callando,

> guarde oscuro el enigma,
> siempre valdrá, a mi ver, lo que ella calla
> más que lo que cualquiera otra me diga. (427)

Las primeras cuatro estrofas exaltan a la mujer hasta alcanzar un desborde verbal que nos pone en duda si realmente pertenece a la postura becqueriana: «Ella tiene la luz, tiene el perfume, / el color y la línea; / la forma, engendradora de deseos». Cuando comenzamos la última estrofa, la pregunta burda: «¿Qué es estúpida? ¡Bah!...» sí cuestiona más hondamente todo lo expresado antes, no sólo de la mujer, sino de la materia poética y su manejo descuidado. El cuestionamiento irónico de la quinta estrofa enjuicia la verborragia de la cuarta y propone silenciar la expresión rimbombante: «...Mientras, *callando*, / guarde oscuro el enigma, / siempre valdrá, a mi ver, *lo que ella calla* / más que lo que cualquiera otra me diga.» El valor de esta mujer (o de la nueva poesía) reside en saber callar. El poeta la elige por saberse medir, en contraste con las demás que tanto hablan sin decir nada. El oscuro enigma de su silencio atrae al poeta, y es este tipo de mujer (o de poesía) el que gana su atención.

En la rima XXVI se ataca más frontalmente el tipo de poesía romántica hueca que tenía sus fieles seguidores en los días de Bécquer:

XXVI

> Voy contra mi interés al confesarlo;
>   pero yo, amada mía,
> pienso, cual tú, que una oda sólo es buena
> de un billete de Banco al dorso escrita.
> No faltará algún necio que al oírlo
>   se haga cruces y diga:
> «Mujer, al fin, del siglo diecinueve,
> material y prosaica...» ¡Bobería!
> ¡Voces que hacen correr cuatro poetas
> que en invierno se embozan con la lira!
> ¡Ladridos de los perros a la luna!
> Tú sabes y yo sé que en esta vida,
> con genio, es muy contado quien la escriba
> y con oro, cualquiera hace poesía. (421-22)

Con esta rima Bécquer lleva a cabo un duro ataque a la

proliferación de poesía romántica de mala calidad. Aquí se critica el hecho de adoptar una postura gastada, que después de tanto efecticismo cayó en lo ridículo. Pongamos atención al tono irónico y sarcástico de estos versos: «¡*Voces* que hacen correr cuatro *poetas* / que en *invierno* se *embozan* con la *lira*!» Gustavo Adolfo critica la aparatosidad de ese romanticismo que de tanto adorno y ornamentación perdió sus esencias. Junto a Bécquer nos reímos de la vociferación de estos pseudo-poetas que con lira en mano, encubiertos por la capa, producen o «hacen» poesía comercializada. Como culminación de esta parodia utiliza un verso que es ejemplo de esta poesía hueca: «¡Ladridos de los perros a la luna!» El ambiente, el tono y los elementos de este verso son tan románticos y tan repetidos, que funcionan como cliché.

Bécquer, consciente de estar al fin de un proceso, mira a éste con cierto desdén. Las expresiones románticas exageradas funcionan como cliché. Al comienzo de este capítulo dijimos que la poesía de Gustavo Adolfo suena a romántica, pero no de la trillada. El uso del cliché contribuye a establecer una diferenciación entre el romanticismo y su poesía. El tono irónico de algunas rimas coloca en el rango de cliché a las expresiones románticas demasiado repetidas. La rima XXVI es un alegato contra los convencionalismos románticos, cuyas expresiones y posturas, por exageradas, perdieron impacto emotivo. Es más, esas expresiones, de tan usadas, dejaron atrás la originalidad, y permiten que se las parodien en función del cliché. Con el empleo del cliché en las *Rimas* se establece una separación entre lo hecho en materia poética hasta ese momento y el nuevo horizonte que propone el poeta sevillano. El cliché romántico en Gustavo Adolfo Bécquer es un hito que marca el cierre de una época para dar espacio a una retórica nueva.

La rima LXVII nos dejará ver en detalle lo explicado en este párrafo anterior:

LXVII

(1)   ¡Qué hermoso es ver el día
coronado de fuego levantarse,

y a su beso de lumbre
brillar las olas y encenderse el aire!

(2)   ¡Qué hermoso es, tras la lluvia,
del triste otoño en la azulada tarde,
de las húmedas flores
el perfume aspirar hasta saciarse!

(3)   ¡Qué hermoso es, cuando en copos
la blanca nieve silenciosa cae,
de las inquietas llamas
ver las rojizas lenguas agitarse!

(4)   ¡Qué hermoso es, cuando hay sueño,
dormir bien... y roncar como un sochantre...
y comer, y engordar! ¡Y qué desgracia
que esto solo no baste! (444-45)

Ya hemos visto que Bécquer hace un empleo mesurado de los signos de admiración. En ese sentido, esta rima es una excepción. Nótese que en ella no se puede contar ni un solo verso que no quede encerrado dentro de los signos de exclamación. Este desorden formal no se identifica con Bécquer, sino que se asemeja más a lo puntualizado en los versos de Espronceda, Zorrilla, etc.

Los comienzos de cada estrofa, en vez de recordarnos los paralelismos formales cuidadosamente ordenados y distribuidos como estudió Carlos Bousoño en el análisis de los poemas de Bécquer, nos chocan por su insistencia inusitada. La repetición tediosa de: «¡Qué hermoso es...!» no se asocia con los paralelismos conceptuales que estudia Bousoño en otras rimas de Bécquer. Estas exclamaciones, más bien, nos recuerdan el martilleo monótono y efecticista del tipo de romanticismo que Gustavo Adolfo rechazó. Esta reincidencia exclamativa algo ingenua de: «¡Qué hermoso es...!», en cada estrofa, nos pone en alerta, nos hace pensar en su posible connotación paródica.

Los elementos que se describen en las tres primeras estrofas parecen enumerar ciertos arquetipos románticos: el esplendoroso amanecer, la lluvia en un *triste otoño* y la *blanca nieve*. Si nos detenemos en estos dos últimos elementos subrayados, vemos que los adjetivos preceden a los sustantivos, en ambos casos por su valor ya dado. Más que modificar emotiva o visualmente a sus respectivos sustantivos, «triste» y «blanca» categorizan al «otoño» y a la «nieve» en una apreciación más que arquetípica. El «triste otoño» y «la blanca nieve» son expresiones que suenan a cliché.

Si nos fijamos detenidamente en las primeras tres estrofas, advertiremos que hay otra repetición que insiste en cierta fervorosidad emotiva que no aparece en el Bécquer de sus otras rimas: «encenderse», «saciarse» y «agitarse». Esta repetición, asociada con el comienzo de cada estrofa, subraya lo estéril de la búsqueda del desborde emocional: « ¡Qué hermoso es... encenderse...»; « ¡Qué hermoso es... saciarse! » y « ¡Qué hermoso es... agitarse! »

El empleo exagerado de los signos exclamativos; la tediosa repetición de los comienzos emotivos con cierta admiración ingenua: «¡Qué hermoso es...!»; la descripción de elementos arquetípicos y trillados: «triste otoño» y «blanca nieve»; y la búsqueda redundante de la expresión emotiva: «encenderse», «saciarse» y «agitarse»; son recursos que enmarcan a estas tres primeras estrofas de la rima LXVII dentro de la categoría del cliché de la poesía romántica. A continuación señalamos en la rima todos estos aspectos observados:

> *¡Qué hermoso es* ver el día
> *coronado de fuego* levantarse,
>   y a su beso de lumbre
> brillar las olas y *encenderse* el aire!

>   *¡Qué hermoso es,* tras la lluvia,
> del *triste otoño* en la azulada tarde,
>   de las húmedas flores
> el perfume aspirar hasta *saciarse!*

>   *¡Qué hermoso es,* cuando en copos
> la *blanca nieve* silenciosa cae,
>   de las inquietas llamas
> ver las rojizas lenguas *agitarse!*

>   *¡Qué hermoso es,* cuando hay sueño,
> dormir bien... y roncar como un sochantre...
>   y comer, y engordar! ¡Y qué desgracia
>   que esto solo no baste!

La cuarta estrofa tiene exactamente el mismo comienzo que las demás: «¡Qué hermoso es...!» Luego, el resto del primer verso podría entrar todavía dentro de los mismos parámetros románticos de las estrofas anteriores: «¡Qué hermoso es, cuando hay sueño». Pero, el comienzo del segundo verso suena ya algo desacompasado con lo anterior: «...cuando hay sueño, / dormir bien...» Al terminar de leer este verso comprobamos que el lenguaje vulgarmente conversacional del resto tira abajo todo el escenario emotivo que se había venido formando hasta ese entonces en el poema: «...y roncar como un sochantre...» En el tercer verso de esta última estrofa se insiste en el ataque demoledor que da por tierra al andamiaje romántico que se había venido construyendo en la rima: «y comer, y engordar!...» Si el poema venía tiñéndose de tono irónico, ahora ya llegó al sarcasmo y burla. La rima concluye con una observación hasta cínica, indicando las limitaciones de este tipo de expresión poética: «...¡Y qué desgracia / que esto solo no baste!» Bécquer parodia los vocablos y lugares comunes románticos no sólo de por sí, sino como una manera de hacernos ver que su visión emotiva no es un desborde pueril, pero más bien una visión consciente de alguien que sabe acerca de los excesos, y de cómo evitarlos.

Bécquer emplea esporádicamente el cliché romántico en sus rimas para burlarse de esa retórica gastada. El cliché es un signo de rechazo de lo anterior; sabiamente, no reincide con redundancia en el uso de este recurso, pero sí lo emplea suficientemente, como hemos visto, para manifestar una desaprobación de ese tipo de poesía. Cuando Bécquer deja a un lado el empleo del cliché romántico, entonces nos señala en sus rimas un nuevo camino lírico, con una retórica diferente.

F. CONCLUSIONES.

Las *Rimas* de Gustavo Adolfo Bécquer, únicamente con la primera impresión de su lectura, podrían parecer sumergidas en el ambiente romántico. Pero leídas detenidamente evidencian que contienen recursos estilísticos que se contraponen al movimiento anterior. Cuando el romanticismo se venía deformando en una verborragia descontrolada de la pasión, las *Rimas* traen sujeción a lo emotivo con su verso mesurado y la incorporación de técnicas nuevas.

Los románticos buscaban que la forma de sus poemas se sujetara al asunto tratado. Si el contenido emocional de las poesías demandaba un descuido formal que reflejara las pasiones en desorden, tal ajuste de la forma al contenido se producía. En contraste, en Bécquer se nota una más equilibrada interdependencia entre contenido y forma. Vimos que la forma, en las *Rimas*, evita el desborde de los sentimientos. Forma y contenido se contrabalancean mutuamente lográndose así una expresión poética más cuidada.

El dominio de la exclamación se analizó dentro de los elementos empleados en las *Rimas* para imponer cierto control emocional. Mientras que en los románticos el signo de admiración señalaba el desenfreno, en las poesías becquerianas se lo emplea para lograr una gama amplia de niveles anímicos, desde lo muy exaltado, hasta la calma más absoluta.

También vimos en este capítulo que en las *Rimas* se amalgaman, paradójicamente, emociones contrapuestas. El tema del amor no correspondido y la expresión íntima del dolor amoroso tienen dejos de Garcilaso. La Generación del 27 miró hacia Góngora y los poetas del Siglo de Oro como fuente de inspiración. Bécquer, como precursor de la poesía del siglo xx, puso sus ojos en el clásico Garcilaso. Si Garcilaso de la Vega dio base con su poesía al renacimiento en el Siglo de Oro, paralelamente, Gustavo Adolfo Bécquer con sus rimas provee los cimientos para la gran renovación de la poesía española producida a partir del siglo xx.

En otra sección de este capítulo obsevamos que otro procedimiento que contribuye al control emotivo en los poemas becquerianos es la mezcla del estilo conversacional con el poético. Los románticos habían combinado la poesía con la prosa, sin variar mayormente el tono desesperado de su lírica. Bécquer, tras una selección cuidadosa de vocablos, utiliza el tono conversacional de la prosa en sus rimas para frenar las emociones. La inclusión de prosa para producir variación anímica en los poemas es otra innovación becqueriana que lo desliga de sus contemporáneos. Más adelante, en su oportunidad, veremos que la aceptación de lo coloquial en las *Rimas*, no sólo sirve para dominar las emociones, sino que es un rasgo que emparenta al poeta sevillano con la poesía del siglo xx.

Dentro de todos estos aspectos estilísticos mencionados, como el balance entre la forma y el contenido, el dominio de los signos de admiración, las emociones encontradas y lo conversacional en sus rimas, el aspecto que más lo separa del movimiento romántico es el empleo del cliché.

Más que la conciencia de estar al final de un movimiento, como muchos críticos ven a Bécquer todavía, el cliché detecta en las *Rimas* una sonrisa socarrona hacia las expresiones lacrimógenas de los románticos. En algunos instantes, Bécquer parodia esos convencionalismos, y tras la parodia, viene el firme rechazo de esa retórica gastada.

Así arribamos a un punto crucial del análisis que estamos realizando de las *Rimas*. Hasta aquí hemos hecho un estudio estilístico del artista sevillano, donde nos hemos impuesto la disciplina de concentrarnos exclusivamente en los elementos no románticos, sino modernos, de Gustavo Adolfo Bécquer, para destacar la relevancia de ellos en las *Rimas*.

De esta manera, a través del análisis llegamos a la conclusión de que el romanticismo sólo queda operando de fondo en las *Rimas*. Definitivamente se hace necesario romper con esa manera tradicional de mirar la poesía becqueriana con el romanticismo en un primer plano. En vez de llevar a cabo una aproximación de atrás hacia adelante, con el romanticismo en frente de las *Rimas*, revertiremos el proceso. Para realzar la modernidad de Bécquer, buscaremos una visión de su poesía desde el punto de vista del lector de nuestros días. Esta perspectiva renovadora, mirando desde adelante hacia atrás en el tiempo y evolución poética, nos permitirá situar el romanticismo operando sólo de fondo con respecto a las *Rimas*. Entonces, en el primer plano, se destacarán los elementos modernos de Bécquer en la observación que hace del texto el lector de hoy día. Ya es tiempo que dejemos el romanticismo atrás, y nos concentremos más y más en la modernidad de su obra poética.

II. VISIÓN PANORÁMICA DE CIERTAS ACTITUDES MODERNISTAS EN LOS POEMAS DE BÉCQUER.

El modernismo se va tratando cada vez más bajo el concepto de una época que abarca las últimas décadas del siglo XIX y los comienzos del XX [1]. Los críticos van aceptando también la idea de que el modernismo constituye la confluencia de muchas tendencias culturales y cierta heterogénea mezcla de trayectorias literarias, en lugar de observarlo como un movimiento monolítico [2]. Esta visión amplia del modernismo es la que va prevaleciendo más y más entre los críticos de nuestros días [3].

---

[1] RICARDO GULLÓN, *Direcciones del modernismo* (Madrid: Editorial Gredos, 1963). En las primeras páginas de este libro el autor presta atención a las observaciones de Juan Ramón para cimentar su estudio del modernismo como época amplia: «Juan Ramón Jiménez sostiene que el modernismo no es una escuela ni un movimiento artístico, sino una época. Probablemente esta idea es exacta.» (7). Este concepto de época es el que prima en el estudio de Gullón.

[2] Gullón al comienzo de su estudio propone lo siguiente:
... el modernismo literario no debe ser considerado como un bloque, monolito en que las tendencias y las personalidades se reduzcan a un programa y una actitud. ... La tendencia simplista a reducir el modernismo a dos o tres de sus elementos más característicos, o que, sin serlo, pasan por tales, constituye uno de los males de nuestra historiografía literaria. (8)

[3] NED J. DAVISON, *The Concept of Modernism in Hispanic Criticism* (Boulder, Colorado: Pruett Press, 1966). El autor de este estudio reúne muy ordenadamente diferentes interpretaciones en la definición del modernismo, y destaca que la corriente que considera al modernismo como época es la más popular entre los críticos:
The inclusiveness of this interpretation is shared, as has been intimated, by other critics, Angel del Río being perhaps the most influential through his excellent and newly revised *Historia de la literatura española*. As was noted earlier, Del Río suggests that Gullón's views are not only the most accurate but the most widely accepted today. ... it may be true that opinion on the Spa-

Las separaciones hechas por Pedro Salinas y Guillermo Díaz-Plaja [4] entre el modernismo de Latinoamérica y la Generación del 98 española, son ya comparticiones inaceptables. La visión unificadora del modernismo es compartida por Max Henríquez Ureña [5], Iván A. Schulman [6], Federico de Onís, Enrique Anderson Imbert y Ángel del Río, entre muchos otros. Esta apreciación del modernismo como época que abarca aproximadamente desde los años 1880 a 1920 es lo suficientemente flexible como para contemplar la posibilidad de la influencia de ciertos autores anteriores a esos años donde los gérmenes modernistas ya estaban incubándose.

Bajo esta visión amplia comenzamos a vislumbrar una transición natural que se establece entre el romanticismo y el modernismo [7]. Algunos poetas se van desprendiendo por esos

---

nish aspects of the movement may be moving toward Gullón's epochal interpretation. (54-55)

[4] GUILLERMO DÍAZ-PLAJA, *Modernismo frente a noventa y ocho* (Madrid: Editorial Espasa-Calpe, 1951). Este crítico lleva a cabo un trabajo analítico en el esfuerzo de contrastar, diferenciar y separar ambos movimientos. Esta teoría ha sido muy cuestionada, y generalmente rechazada últimamente.

[5] MAX HENRÍQUEZ UREÑA, *Breve historia del modernismo*, 2.ª ed. (México: Fondo de Cultura Económica, 1962). Henríquez Ureña tiene una actitud crítica muy flexible, que mira al modernismo como una confluencia de muchas y diversas tendencias guiadas por el mismo objetivo de buscar el perfeccionamiento artístico:
... en el movimiento modernista cabían todas las tendencias, con tal de que la forma de expresión fuese depurada, esto es, con tal de que el lenguaje estuviera trabajado con arte, que es, por excelencia, el rasgo distintivo del modernismo. (19)

[6] LILY LITVAK, *El modernismo* (Madrid: Taurus Ediciones, 1975), pp. 65-95. La crítica reúne una serie de estudios referentes a este asunto. En su artículo «Reflexiones en torno a la definición del modernismo», 1966, Iván A. Schulman juzga el modernismo como el estilo de toda una época: «No hay una definición capaz de precisar todos sus atributos estilísticos e ideológicos, precisamente porque el modernismo es el estilo de una época.» (78)

[7] Ned J. Davison cita la opinión de varios críticos para indicar una continuación nada abrupta en el pasaje del romanticismo al modernismo:
Max Henríquez Ureña expresses... «did not go against romanticism in essence but against its excesses, and especially against the triteness of form and the repetition of commonplaces and over-worked images». ... Lamothe: «a real break between romanticism and Modernism does not exist»; Del Río, speaking of Spain and Spanish America, «perhaps it would be more exact to speak

años de las tendencias románticas y empiezan conscientemente a elaborar rasgos renovadores en sus poéticas. Esta actitud revitalizante de modernizar la poesía española se encuentra en Bécquer. Bernardo Gicovate en 1974, en un artículo tan reciente como revelador, afirma [8]:

> Pero el Bécquer que va a guiar al modernismo posterior no será sólo el de los sepulcros, ni siquiera el de las armonías filosóficas... Este Bécquer de las musicalidades extrañas, de las combinaciones métricas novedosas y sutiles y de los asonantes imperceptibles es el que guía la iniciación modernista... (197)

Una década antes, en 1963, Ricardo Gullón previó el enlace de Bécquer con el modernismo [9]:

> ... Bécquer era un poniente: el del romanticismo; desde entonces, pasa a ser una aurora: la de la poesía moderna (aurora: tintes indecisos, pero anuncio inequívoco del nuevo día). En lo mejor del modernismo sigue vigente el impulso interiorizante y sentimental de la poesía becqueriana... (28)

Retrocediendo diez años más, en 1954, Max Henríquez Ureña indica que la poesía de Bécquer es precursora de la modernista [10]:

> La influencia... de Bécquer, que alcanzó enorme boga en la América española y que los modernistas, aunque sólo ocasionalmente

---

of a surpassing or evolution rather than a reaction»; Valbuena Prat: «as a reaction to Realism on the one hand and at the same time a stylization of Romantic currents», Anderson Imbert: «the Modernists learned to write observing what was elegant in romanticism, not what was passionate»... (19-20)

[8] HOMERO CASTILLO, *Estudios críticos sobre el modernismo* (Madrid: Editorial Gredos, 1974), pp. 190-202. Castillo incluye el ensayo de Bernardo Gicovate «Antes del modernismo» citado en el texto.

[9] Gullón, en su libro mencionado en las notas 1 y 2 de este capítulo, ve a Bécquer como precursor tanto del parnasianismo y simbolismo como del modernismo en general:

De momento, quiero señalar que, como hizo notar Juan Ramón Jiménez, en el modernismo hay una tendencia parnasiana y otra simbolista. No creo que aquella preceda a esta, pues si la voluntad de sugerir en la poesía algo inefable, indefinible, es una de las notas distintivas del simbolismo, el más caracterizado precursor del modernismo, Gustavo Adolfo Bécquer, es testimonio de que, desde hace casi cien años, antes del parnasiomodernismo, en la poesía de lengua española se manifestaba esa pretensión. (11-12)

[10] HENRÍQUEZ UREÑA, p. 31.

siguieron sus huellas, especialmente Darío y Silva, siempre tuvieron en alto aprecio su sensibilidad refinada y por su forma clara y pulcra. En Bécquer encontramos, además, a cada instante, procedimientos típicamente impresionistas, que los modernistas supieron aprovechar. (31)

Como se aprecia en estas tres citas, la idea de Gustavo Adolfo como precursor de ciertos aspectos modernistas es algo que ha estado ya en la mente de los críticos durante las últimas tres décadas. Bécquer es uno de los iniciadores del proceso modernista [11]. Por otro lado, después de estas acertadas apreciaciones sobre la trascendencia del poeta sevillano, todavía queda por hacer el esfuerzo analítico que detecte esas actitudes modernistas en sus poemas. Si aceptamos al modernismo como un movimiento polifacético nos será posible tomar varias de sus características, aunque no todas, para ir demostrando su presencia en las *Rimas*. La incidencia de Bécquer en el modernismo parece ser ya incuestionable, aunque sí queda por realizarse un estudio que confirme lo enunciado, tarea que decididamente nos disponemos a llevar a cabo a continuación.

Si hay un elemento unificante y central del modernismo éste es, sin dudas, el cuidado que se da al manejo del lenguaje. En el modernismo se produce una elaboración consciente del estilo, se desarrolla una «voluntad de estilo» que difiere de la espontaneidad romántica anterior. Bécquer, en relación con sus contemporáneos, parece estar más consciente de la composición artística. En 1972 se publica un ensayo estilístico de

---

[11] UNIVERSIDAD NACIONAL DE LA PLATA, *Gustavo Adolfo Bécquer* (Estudios reunidos en conmemoración del centenario) (La Plata, Argentina: Facultad de Humanidades y Ciencias de la Educación, Universidad de La Plata, 1971), pp. 143-56. En esta publicación aparece un trabajo de Juan Carlos Ghiano «Para la fortuna de Bécquer en nuestra América». Ghiano, después de un recuento histórico a modo panorámico, arriba a las siguientes conclusiones:

De esta manera se cierra el ciclo de la influencia becqueriana directa en los iniciadores del modernismo. ...Bécquer interesó a los jóvenes de esta América en la medida en que se había alejado de las condiciones habituales en el romanticismo de lengua española. (156)

Juan Antonio Tamayo donde se resalta esto [12]. Además de ver en Bécquer un trabajador del estilo, Tamayo demuestra en forma muy convincente la secuencia prosa-poesía en las obras de Gustavo Adolfo [13]. En el paso de la prosa a la poesía existe en el poeta sevillano un proceso de reducción y síntesis. En esta transición de la narrativa a los poemas se realiza una selección y tamización donde los elementos de mayor relieve artístico se conservan. Sus poesías constituyen un esfuerzo estético seleccionador donde lo irrelevante se desecha y permanecen los signos de alto valor sugestivo y creador.

Bécquer escribe en prosa su proyecto artístico que luego concreta en sus versos. Muchas de sus leyendas en tema y forma preceden a las *Rimas* [14]. Las *Cartas literarias a una mujer* constituyen una serie de seis ensayos de su pensamiento poé-

---

[12] Consejo Superior de Investigaciones Científicas, *Estudios sobre Gustavo Adolfo Bécquer* (Madrid: Sucesores de Rivadeneyra, 1972), pp. 17-51. Entre estos artículos se encuentra «Contribución al estudio de la estilística de Gustavo Adolfo Bécquer», de Juan Antonio Tamayo que afirma:

> Hay que pensar, y mas si estamos convencidos de que Bécquer era un gran creador consciente de su arte y poseedor indudable de los secretos de la técnica, que estas diferencias estilísticas son intencionadas. Cuando el gran poeta sevillano, como veremos más adelante, convierte en poema un pasaje de sus obras en prosa, lejos de proceder por acumulación de elementos ornamentales procede por eliminación para dejar solamente lo esencial poético. (20)

[13] Tamayo sostiene que en la mayoría de los casos es posible demostrar que la prosa precedió a la poesía:

> Por lo que se refiere a las relaciones entre verso y prosa de Bécquer, estimamos que, en la mayor parte de los casos, la redacción en prosa precedió a la redacción en verso. Pero no todos los casos son de igual importancia. Hay coincidencias que no son otra cosa que la aparición en ambos textos de formas habituales de expresión; otras veces existe una deliberada reiteración metafórica y, finalmente, en los casos más importantes, la redacción en verso es una verdadera reelaboración perfeccionada que conduce a una versión poética de mayor concentración. (50)

[14] Como ejemplo de este aspecto podríamos mencionar las siguientes correlaciones entre prosa y poesía: La leyenda «Los ojos verdes» (133-41), es reducida a la enfatuación que sufre el poeta en la rima XIV. La leyenda aragonesa «El gnomo» (216-33), viene condensada en la serie de imágenes sugestivas de la magnífica rima V. La leyenda toledana «El beso» (275-90) resurge en el ambiente medieval decadente de la rima LXXVI.

tico en prosa que más tarde respeta en los poemas [15]. En el
prólogo al volumen de poesías *La soledad* de Augusto Ferrán,
Bécquer formula su propio procedimiento creativo. Aún en el
prólogo de las *Rimas* sus intenciones estéticas quedan enunciadas. Tanto las *Leyendas*, como las *Cartas literarias a una
mujer*, el prólogo a *La soledad* y la «Introducción» a su volumen de poesías constituyen escritos en prosa que describen
un plan de trabajo previo a las *Rimas*, son un planteamiento
premeditado y consciente de la elaboración artística de los
poemas. Inclusive sus primeras rimas del volumen revelan
una programación finamente orquestada de su poética y auto-
conciencia creadora. Bécquer es un poeta preocupado de su
arte y consciente de su estilo poético. Todas estas evidencias
rompen con la imagen errónea de un Bécquer espontáneo en
la expresión sentimental de sus poesías. En Gustavo Adolfo, a
diferencia de sus contemporáneos, existe un esfuerzo deno-

---

[15] En la carta II, Bécquer cuestiona: «¿Cómo la palabra, cómo un
idioma grosero y mezquino, insuficiente a veces para expresar las
necesidades de la materia, podrá servir de digno intérprete entre dos
almas?» (624). Este cuestionamiento tiene definido enlace con lo que
se propone en la rima I, estrofas 2 y 3:
Yo quisiera escribirle, del hombre
domando el rebelde, mezquino idioma,
con palabras que fuesen a un tiempo
suspiros y risas, colores y notas.
Pero en vano es luchar, que no hay cifra
capaz de encerrarlo, y apenas, ¡oh hermosa!,
si, teniendo en mis manos las tuyas,
pudiera, al oído, cantártelo a solas. (401)
En la carta III vemos un preámbulo teórico de lo que luego lleva
a la práctica en la composición de la rima III en lo relativo a la inspiración. Una lectura de la rima nos dejará ver en verso lo antes for-
mulado y programado en prosa. Bécquer dice en la carta III: «¡Imágenes confusas, que pasáis cantando una canción sin ritmo ni palabras, que sólo percibe y entiende el espíritu! ¡Febriles exaltaciones
de la pasión, que dais colores y forma a las ideas más abstractas!»
(630)
En otra ocasión, el detenido planteo de un programa poético queda velado tras la aparente espontaneidad de la conversación del poeta y su amada. En la carta I leemos: «Después lo he pensado mejor,
y no dudo al repetirlo; la poesía eres tú. ¿Te sonríes? Tanto peor
para los dos. Tu incredulidad nos va a costar: a ti, el trabajo de leer
un libro, y a mí, el de componerlo.» (618). Este plan se concreta en el
volumen de las *Rimas*, y especialmente en la rima XXI que ya analizamos en detalle.

dado de depuración, de cuidado formal y cultivo de un estilo que lo identifica con las filas de los modernistas [16].

En las *Rimas* se aúnan las cualidades plásticas, musicales y literarias del poeta sevillano. En «un himno gigante y extraño» se entrelazan armoniosamente los «colores y notas» (rima I). En sus poesías se produce un «armonioso ritmo» que se conjuga con «la belleza plástica» (rima III). Todo esto coincide con el programa de los inicios modernistas que propone Charles Baudelaire (1821-1867) en su poema «Correspondances» de 1857: «Vaste comme la nuit et comme la clarté, / Les parfums, les couleurs et les sons se répondent» [17] (488).

En las *Rimas* se combinan los efectos visuales con los sonoros alcanzándose una perfección formal inusitada para esos días del romanticismo tardío en España.

La rima LXXIII es un ejemplo apropiado para observar la sonoridad del canto unida a las imágenes que se proyectan en el poema. En esta poesía se pone de relieve el talento acústico y el don pictórico de Bécquer:

LXXIII

(1)   Cerraron sus ojos,
             que aún tenía abiertos;
             taparon su cara
             con un blanco lienzo;
             y unos sollozando,

---

[16] En *Gustavo Adolfo Bécquer* (Estudios reunidos en conmemoración del centenario), 1971, Arturo Berenguer Carisomo en su artículo «Bécquer en la prosa española del siglo XIX» (131-42), afirma algo sobre la prosa becqueriana que también podría aplicarse a su poesía:
Ya hemos dicho algo sobre este punto; conviene, sin embargo, insistir; se trata de uno de los rasgos más «fuera de serie» en la prosa española de hace cien años. Todo escritor tiene un estilo; lo tiene por el solo hecho de escribir... lo que no todos tienen es esa «voluntad» de someterlo a una conducta estética determinada... Bécquer la tuvo y la sostuvo. Colma toda su prosa imaginativa o especulativa una morosidad, un cuidado de verdadera «ecriture artiste», de auténtica conciencia creadora. ...un tesonero castigo de lima, una brava tarea para domeñar y estilizar su propia lengua literaria. (138)
[17] ALBERT SCHINZ, *Nineteenth Century French Readings* (New York: Holt, Renehart and Winston, 1965), p. 488. El capítulo XVIII, pp. 466-501, está dedicado a Charles Baudelaire.

y otros en silencio,
de la triste alcoba
todos se salieron.

(2)   La luz, que en un vaso
ardía en el suelo,
al muro arrojaba
la sombra del lecho;
y entre aquella sombra
veíase, a intérvalos,
dibujarse rígida
la forma del cuerpo.

(3)   Despertaba el día,
y a su albor primero,
con sus mil ruidos
despertaba el pueblo;
ante aquel contraste
de vida y misterios,
de luz y tinieblas,
medité un momento:
¡Dios mío, qué solos
se quedan los muertos!

(4)   De la casa en hombros
lleváronla al templo,
y en una capilla
dejaron el féretro.
Allí rodearon
sus pálidos restos
de amarillas velas
y de paños negros.

(5)   Al dar de las ánimas
el toque postrero,
acabó una vieja
sus últimos rezos;
cruzó la ancha nave,
las puertas gimieron,
y el santo recinto
quedóse desierto.

(6)   De un reloj se oía
compasado el péndulo
y de algunos cirios
el chisporroteo.
Tan medroso y triste,
tan oscuro y yerto
todo se encontraba...,
que pensé un momento:
¡Dios mío, qué solos
se quedan los muertos!

(7)   De la alta campana
la lengua de hierro
le dio, volteando,
su adiós lastimero.
El luto en las ropas,
amigos y deudos
cruzaron en fila
formando el cortejo.

(8)   Del último asilo,
oscuro y estrecho,
abrió la piqueta
el nicho a un extremo.
Allí la acostaron,
tapiáronle luego,
y con un saludo
despidióse el duelo.

(9)   La piqueta al hombro,
el sepulturero
cantando entre dientes
se perdió a lo lejos.
La noche se entraba,
reinaba el silencio;
perdido en las sombras,
medité un momento:
¡Dios mío, qué solos
se quedan los muertos!

(10)   En las largas noches
del helado invierno,
cuando las maderas
crujir hace el viento
y azota los vidrios
el fuerte aguacero,
de la pobre niña
a veces me acuerdo.

(11)   Allí cae la lluvia
con un son eterno;
allí la combate
el soplo del cierzo.
Del húmedo muro
tendida en el hueco,
¡acaso de frío
se hielan sus huesos!...
....

(12)   ¿Vuelve el polvo al polvo?
¿Vuela el alma al cielo?
¿Todo es, sin espíritu,
podredumbre y cieno?
¡No sé; pero hay algo

que explicar no puedo,
algo que repugna,
aunque es fuerza hacerlo,
a dejar tan tristes,
tan solos, los muertos! (449-52)

Sabido es que Gustavo Adolfo, mientras componía sus rimas, al margen del papel que utilizó dibujaba bosquejos que nutrían su imaginación [18]. La labor musical de componer el poema y el ejercicio plástico de objetivar su imaginación en dibujos eran tareas simultáneas en Bécquer. Este poema descriptivo que analizaremos a continuación lo evidencia.

En la primera estrofa, por sobre la imagen presentada, hay un efecto sonoro que prevalece: «Cerraron sus ojos... unos sollozando, / otros en silencio... todos se salieron.» El susurro de las eses y ces, sumado a la reiteración de la vocal «o», impregna al ambiente de una intrigante solemnidad. En la segunda estrofa el efecto visual toma mayor preponderancia terminando en el «dibujarse rígida / la forma del cuerpo.» La tercera conjuga sonido e imagen.

En la cuarta estrofa son las imágenes las que se utilizan para comunicarnos los hechos, y en la quinta, los sonidos. En la sexta los efectos visuales y sonoros se entremezclan: «De un reloj se oía / compasado el péndulo / y de algunos cirios / el chisporroteo.» Destaquemos «chisporroteo» dado que en ese signo hay una perfecta amalgama del efecto sonoro y del visual. Luego, de nuevo nos encontramos con la aliteración como sucedió en la primera estrofa, pero esta vez resulta más tenebrosa con el sonido de las tes: «Tan medroso y triste, / tan oscuro y yerto / todo se encontraba...» También hemos señalado la mezcla de las eres con otras con-

---

[18] En *Gustavo Adolfo Bécquer* (Estudios reunidos en conmemoración del centenario), 1971, bajo el título «Bécquer en Buenos Aires», pp. 31-39, Angel J. Battistessa señala la correspondencia de la elaboración pictórica y poética en el genio sevillano:
    Lo que sobremanera importa, aparte los versos, es el valor de estos dibujos porque ilustran uno de los modos del trabajo de Bécquer: en la composición de algunas de sus *Rimas* el poeta solía «ayudarse» con el estímulo de imágenes gráficas. (35).

sonantes en las mismas sílabas que sirven para aumentar el efecto tétrico.

En los cuatro primeros versos de la séptima estrofa parece prevalecer el sonido, pero en los próximos cuatro tenemos el efecto visual que continúa en la estrofa octava. En el comienzo de la nueve sigue la descripción de los detalles del funeral donde la presencia de las pes y tes forma un golpeteo sonoro que espanta: «La *pique*ta al hom*br*o, / el se*pul*turero / can*t*ando en*tr*e dien*t*es / se *perd*ió a lo lejos.» La mezcla de las eres con otras consonantes nuevamente aumentan el efecto siniestro. Más tarde, entre «el silencio» y «las sombras», que sirven justamente para denotar la ausencia de sonido e imagen, se cierra el proceso del funeral que se describió hasta aquí.

En las estrofas diez y once los efectos sonoros son ecos que recuerdan las imágenes anteriores. La última estrofa del poema culmina con el estribillo final de la tercera, sexta y novena estrofa. La contundencia emocional de la repetición sentenciosa se hace absoluta en la modificación leve, pero significativa, de esos dos últimos versos: «a dejar *tan tristes*, / *t*an *s*olos, los *muertos*!»

En la rima LXXIII sonido y color, notas y objetos, música e imagen conforman un mundo solemnemente tétrico. Gustavo Adolfo maneja su pincel y arranca sonidos de su lira embozada con la maestría singular de la pluma más diestra entre los poetas españoles del siglo XIX [19]. Bécquer es un esteta [20],

---

[19] BENJAMÍN JARNÉS, *Doble agonía de Bécquer* (Madrid: Talleres Espasa-Calpe, 1936). Jarnés comenta: «Y acabará por pintar, eso sí, pero con la metáfora. Será un escritor preferentemente plástico.» (35). Más adelante agrega: «La virtud plástica de Bécquer, su agilidad descriptiva, se ponen de relieve en otras muchas páginas ya más conocidas.» (209). Y luego dice: «Siempre el gozador de lo plástico junto al intérprete de lo más íntimo. Pobablemente Bécquer no acaba de decidirse por una forma de expresión. Desde niño el arte de escribir y el de pintar le seducen igualmente.» (218)
Bécquer asocia la pintura con su función creativa en el orden literario continuamente, como podría verse en las páginas 202, 249, 271, 282, 308, 317, 349, 353, 357, 359 y 550 de sus *Obras completas*, 1969.
[20] VIDAL BENITO REVUELTA, *Bécquer y Toledo* (Madrid: Artes Gráficas Benzal, 1972). Revuelta subraya el esfuerzo estético como una constante en Bécquer:

un exquisito cultivador del estilo; es un poeta con firme vocación modernista.

A. BÉCQUER Y LOS PARNASIANOS.

El modernismo recibió en gran parte del parnasianismo
el deseo de perfeccionar la forma. En este sentido el parnasianismo fue una guía para el modernismo en cuanto a la preocupación de lograr una forma depurada. El impulso inicial del
modernismo se concentró en el ansia de la renovación y su-
peración formal [21]. En Bécquer, como ya observamos en el
capítulo anterior, el equilibrio formal de sus rimas difiere de
las tendencias románticas. Ya indicamos en la balanceada simetría de la rima XXI un cuidado de la forma y una pulida
precisión. También nos referimos en ese capítulo a los paralelismos analizados por Bousoño y la llamativa exactitud de
sus correspondencias. Gustavo Adolfo trabajó la forma de sus
poemas con tesón y constancia.

Ninguno de los biógrafos de Bécquer pone en duda su conocimiento del francés. El joven poeta, en sus primeros años
en Madrid, de 1854 a 1860, se ganó la vida haciendo traducciones del francés al castellano, actividad que menguó más tarde,
pero que nunca abandonó por completo. Son justamente estos
sus años de maduración literaria y los mismos en que coincidentemente Baudelaire, el más importante poeta francés en
ese período de transición, escribe sus poemas y publica *Les
fleurs du mal*, 1857. A la par de las poesías de Baudelaire, las

---

¡Si fue lo que hizo toda su vida, a lo largo de toda su obra: em-
bellecer la cotidiana realidad! Como un Midas de la poesía, su
prosa o su verso tuvo, tiene, entre otras virtudes y valores, la
de hermosear lo circundante. (63)

[21] Henríquez Ureña en su libro señala:
Del parnasismo francés recibió el modernismo, en buena parte, el anhelo de perfección de la forma. ... lo que importa tener
en cuenta es que el parnasismo sirvió de guía al movimiento
modernista en lo que atañe a la preocupación de la forma. (13)
Un poco más adelante insiste en aclarar: «El impulso inicial del modernismo se tradujo, por lo tanto, en un ansia de novedad y de supera-
ción en cuanto a la forma.» (16)

Rimas muestran un arte controlado, calculado, pensado y más consciente que el de los románticos, contra quienes ambos reaccionan. Tanto Baudelaire como Bécquer fueron devotos admiradores de Edgar Allan Poe y Wagner. Théophile Gautier (1811-1872), teorizador del parnasianismo, ya había para entonces publicado sus postulados parnasianos en «L'Art». Sin duda, en los años de la década de 1860 Gustavo Adolfo tuvo conciencia del desarrollo del parnasianismo francés.

Otra nota histórica a tener en cuenta es que luego de la revolución liberal del mes de septiembre de 1868, Bécquer pierde su trabajo y viaja a París con su protector y amigo el Ministro Luis González Bravo que fue expatriado a Francia. Recordemos que en estas circunstancias inestables se pierden los originales de sus poesías y que éstos (1865-1876) son los años de auge del parnasianismo francés. Gustavo Adolfo pasa unos meses en París, seguramente se impregna del ambiente literario allí, y vuelve a Madrid recién a principios del año 1869. Es entonces que comienza su labor de reconstrucción de las rimas que le llevará todo ese año. El estudio del grado de incidencia de las tendencias francesas del momento en la reconstrucción de sus poemas es algo que todavía no se ha analizado. Pero de lo que sí podemos estar seguros, tras estos datos históricos, es que Bécquer tenía clara conciencia del impacto del parnasianismo en la literatura francesa entre los años finales de los cincuenta y la década de 1860.

Bécquer tuvo siempre dotes para la expresión pictórica, musical y literaria. La pintura y el dibujo los desarrolló desde niño bajo la tutela de su padre, pintor renombrado, y también bajo la influencia de su hermano mayor Valeriano, artista reconocido. En sus primeros años en Madrid el poeta sevillano compuso zarzuelas, asistió regularmente a la ópera, y si bien no desarrolló su talento musical en forma profesional, conocía muy de cerca el ambiente. Ya dijimos que admiraba a Wagner que combinaba las artes en sus sinfonías de principio de los años sesenta; relacionaba el escenario (lo visual) con la música y la poesía. La pintura y la música vimos que tu-

vieron un papel fundamental en las imágenes y los efectos
sonoros en la composición de las rimas becquerianas.

Simultáneamente con esta convergencia de diferentes disciplinas en sus versos, en Bécquer se vislumbra un delicado
orfebre de la poesía, un escultor cuidadoso de su canto, acti·
tud esta que lo emparenta con los parnasianos.

En la introducción a sus rimas está expresada esa misión
escultórica al versificar y que menciona Adolfo de Sandoval [22]:
«Fue un escultórico; fue un poeta... sonoro, musical» (65).
En su introducción Bécquer nos habla de sus ansias de perfección formal: «Yo quisiera poder cincelar la forma que ha
de conteneros, como se cincela el vaso de oro que ha de guardar un preciado perfume» (40). En las *Leyendas* aparece también esa preocupación por la forma [23]. En los artículos escritos
en su retiro en el monasterio de Veruela titulados *Desde mi
celda*, Bécquer muestra conciencia de unir la forma a los
efectos visuales y sonoros de sus composiciones [24]. En *Cartas
literarias a una mujer* la labor del poeta de dar forma a sus
ideas es una de las mayores preocupaciones [25].

En Bécquer, al igual que en los parnasianos, el poeta cumple la función de dar forma a su pensamiento. En la rima V,
estrofa 18, establece:

---

[22] ADOLFO DE SANDOVAL, *El último amor de Bécquer*, 1.ª ed. (Barcelona: Talleres Gráficos Agustín Núñez, 1941), p. 65.

[23] En la leyenda «El beso» leemos: «Yo no creo, como vosotros,
que esas estatuas son un pedazo de mármol tan inerte hoy como el día
en que lo arrancaron de la cantera.» (289)

[24] En la carta V desde la celda, Bécquer dice:
A donde no alcanza, pues, ni la paleta del pintor con sus infinitos recursos, ¿cómo podrá llegar mi pluma sin más medios que
las palabras, tan pobres, tan insuficientes para dar idea de lo que
es todo un efecto de líneas, de claroscuro, de combinación de
colores, de detalles que se ofrecen junto a la vista, de rumores
y sonidos que se perciben a la vez. ... Cuando se acomete la difícil empresa de descomponer esa extraña armonía de la forma,
el color y el sonido... (550-51)

[25] En la carta literaria II Bécquer menciona:
... una preocupación bastante generalizada, aun entre las perso-
nas que se dedican a dar forma a lo que piensan, que, a mi modo
de ver, es sin parecerlo, una de las mayores. (622)
Luego, en las *Cartas literarias a una mujer*, formula más extensamente
su teoría poética entre el pensamiento y la forma artística.

> Yo soy el invisible
> anillo que sujeta
> el mundo de la forma
> al mundo de la idea. (409)

Gustavo Adolfo, a la par de los parnasianos, admira el trabajo escultórico no sólo por su perfección formal y por considerarlo un arte superior («Oui, l'oeuvre sort plus belle / D'une forme au travail / Rebelle, / Vers, marbre, onyx, émail» (297), diría Gautier en «L'Art») [26]; sino también por su permanencia en el tiempo («Tout passe. —L'art robuste / Seul a l'éternité, / Le buste / Survit à la cité.» (298), predicaría Gautier también en «L'Art»). En la rima LXXVI se recoge la impresión de que el trabajo escultórico de «una mujer hermosa... del cincel prodigio» vence al tiempo; el arte en la escultura se eterniza. El poeta sevillano se aúna a los parnasianos franceses en la búsqueda de la forma perfecta del canto como si fuera a cincelarlo y modelarlo («Sculpte, lime, cisèle, / Que ton rêve flottant / Se scelle / Dans le bloc résistant!» (298), demandaría Gautier en su postulado); en la rima III declara:

> cincel que el bloque muerde
> la estatua modelando,
> y la belleza plástica
> añade a la ideal; (404)

Otro aspecto que Bécquer comparte con los parnasianos es el esfuerzo por controlar las emociones. Esto lo discutimos con suficiente extensión en nuestro capítulo anterior. En las *Rimas* notamos cierta frialdad en el objeto observado, la mujer, equivalente muchas veces a su poesía. El parnasianismo no es una constante a través de todas las poesías becquerianas. Pero si los parnasianos se distinguieron principalmente por una preocupación formal que luego nutrió al modernismo, Bécquer definitivamente comparte los mismos ideales artísticos que aquéllos.

Pensando en otras actitudes modernistas podríamos men-

---

[26] ALBERT SCHANZ, *Nineteenth Century French Readings*. El capítulo X, pp. 286-321, está dedicado a Théophile Gautier.

cionar el exotismo y las referencias a objetos preciosos. En
Bécquer estos dos aspectos no abundan.

Durante sus primeros años en Madrid compone la leyenda
«El caudillo de las manos rojas» (45-94). En esta tradición de
la India se nota a Bécquer atraído por el Oriente, como sucedería después con muchos modernistas, especialmente en el
caso de José Juan Tablada. Pero esta fascinación con los temas
orientales es pasajera en el poeta sevillano y la abandona más
tarde. La tendencia hacia el exotismo no tiene mayor impacto
en las *Rimas* como lo tuvo en muchos poemas modernistas
posteriores.

En cuanto a la descripción de objetos preciosos es un rasgo
que se ve más asiduamente en sus leyendas y trabajos en prosa [27]. En las *Rimas* se nota la presencia de diversos objetos
valiosos como el oro especialmente, pero también las perlas,
rubíes y esmeraldas entre otros más. En las rimas III, V, IX,
X, XII, XV, XVIII, XIX, XXV, XXVII, XL y LXXII se pueden localizar estos objetos finos, pero hay que señalar que
su inclusión, considerando las *Rimas* en general, es sólo es-
porádica. En las poesías de Bécquer se mantiene cierta so-
briedad en contraste con lo que sucede en el modernismo,
donde la ornamentación de los poemas con objetos preciosos
se torna en el foco de atención por su abundancia, llegándose
casi a un manierismo descriptivo, especialmente en la primera fase modernista. Tanto el exotismo como la atracción
hacia objetos preciosos son tendencias leves en Gustavo Adolfo Bécquer y que tendrían mucha mayor preponderancia en
los modernistas.

B. BÉCQUER Y LOS SIMBOLISTAS.

Otra fuente importante de donde tomó vigor el modernismo fue el simbolismo. Baudelaire, en realidad, es un poeta

---

[27] Una lectura de las leyendas y narraciones en las páginas 119,
140, 203, 219, 220, 272, 342 y 625 de las *Obras completas*, 1969, eviden-
ciaría claramente la referencia a objetos preciosos como una atracción particular de la prosa becqueriana.

de transición, mientras que Paul Verlaine (1844-1896), que luego de sus inicios en el parnasianismo hasta «Poemes satur-
niens» de 1866, abandona esa tendencia para asumir de ahí
en adelante la directriz del simbolismo. Stephane Mallarmé
(1842-1898), otro simbolista de esos años, lo llamó afectuo-
samente el padre del simbolismo. Verlaine fue admirado por
la musicalidad de sus poemas. A Bécquer, por la intimidad
de sus poesías, lo vemos más cerca de Verlaine que de su contemporáneo Baudelaire.

El simbolismo aportó al modernismo la musicalidad. El
sonido cobró mayor importancia en la poesía. Los poemas se
enriquecieron en ritmo. Los simbolistas pusieron gran énfasis
en la cualidad musical de la poesía y produjeron poemas especialmente para ser escuchados. Este es un factor presente
en las *Rimas* y que queda algo descuidado por los críticos que
se dejan llevar demasiado por los efectos visuales de los
poemas [28].

Charles Chadwick puntualiza la transición del parnasianismo al simbolismo [29]:

... one of the tenets of Symbolism, both of human and of the
transcendental kind, that further help to define its meaning more

---

[28] JOSÉ M. MONNER SANS, *Rimas e ideario de sus obras* (Montevideo: Editores Claudio García y Cía., 1937). Monner Sans en el centenario del nacimiento de Bécquer (1836-1936) prologa una edición
de las *Rimas* donde destaca lo pictórico por sobre lo musical: «Es
poeta más plástico que auditivo.» (24). Como otros críticos, Sans,
para enfatizar una característica, erróneamente rebaja la otra. Como
muchos otros, al recalcar lo visual en Bécquer, equivocadamente trata de disminuir la importancia de su armonía musical, que también
es fundamental. Y ya que nos referimos a este tema, aprovechamos
para reconocer que Bécquer no desarrolló tanto la sinestesia como
lo hicieron luego los simbolistas y modernistas. En cuanto a las imágenes, símiles y metáforas de sus poemas, cobran un interés por lo
visual que se acrecentará en el modernismo. Pero estos efectos visuales en Gustavo Adolfo son más bien tradicionales con respecto a la
experimentación modernista que culmina en la sofisticada forma de
usar las metáforas, como en el caso de Leopoldo Lugones y Julio He-
rrera y Reissig. Entre ellos y Bécquer existe un abismo. Por otro
lado, insistimos, Gustavo Adolfo Bécquer es uno de los primeros poetas del siglo XIX que resalta lo visual en su poesía, actitud que lo
emparenta con los modernistas.
[29] CHARLES CHADWICK, *Symbolism* (London: Methuen and Co., Ltd.,
1971), pp. 4-5.

closely, was the equation between poetry and music in preference to the equation between poetry and sculture, or poetry and painting that had been current in the middle of the nineteenth century in France. (4-5)

Ya hemos visto el aspecto musical en Bécquer, pero en relación a los simbolistas quedan detalles importantes para agregar [30]. La pasión musical en el poeta sevillano parece innata [31]. Para mostrar los dones musicales de Gustavo Adolfo en su creación artística podríamos remitirnos a la lectura de la leyenda «Maese Pérez el organista» (142-159) donde en algunos pasajes se envuelve la prosa de un acústico simbolismo excepcional [32]. La leyenda «El Miserere» (189-200) tiene momentos

---

[30] Carisomo, en el artículo citado en nuestra nota 16, se refiere a la musicalidad de la prosa de Bécquer:

Carecemos de datos suficientes para informarnos acerca de los conocimientos musicales del poeta; el anecdotario sí nos dice le apasionaban Donizzetti y Bellini; sea como fuere, el oído para el ritmo del período acredita un fino deleite, una sensual complacencia en la armonía y cadencia prosísticas anticipada en un cuarto de siglo a parecidos ensayos acústicos del modernismo... (139)

[31] En el prólogo de S. y J. Alvarez Quintero, pp. 15-36, a las *Obras completas*, 1969, se describe la fascinación que sufre Bécquer por la música:

La música le producía embriaguez inefable. No había que pensar en comer ni en dormir; no había que hacer nada ni ver a nadie, por importante que ello fuese, mientras le hablaban a su alma Beethoven o Bellini. Este vivo sentimiento musical, nativo y cultivado, llena toda su obra de una íntima y lejana melodía apenas perceptible, que no se sabe de dónde nace, pero que presta a sus páginas un secreto hechizo, un escondido encanto. (30)

[32] Las palabras de la leyenda «Maese Pérez el organista», pp. 142-59, parecen contener música en sí mismas. Vaya aquí un ejemplo:

Cantos celestes como los que acarician los oídos en los momentos de éxtasis, cantos que percibe el espíritu y no los puede repetir el labio, notas sueltas de una melodía lejana que suena a intervalos, traídas en las ráfagas del viento; rumor de hojas que se besan en los árboles con un murmullo semejante al de la lluvia, trinos de alondras que se levantan gorjeando de entre las flores como una saeta despedida a las nubes; estruendos sin nombre, imponentes como los rugidos de una tempestad, coros de serafines sin ritmo ni cadencia, ignora música del cielo que solo la imaginación comprende, himnos alados que parecían remontarse al trono del Señor como una tromba de luz y de sonidos..., todo lo expresaban las cien voces del órgano con más pujanza, con más misteriosa poesía, con más fantástico color que lo habían expresado nunca. (154)

en que la palabra y los efectos musicales se mueven acordes, conjugándose a la manera en que lo harían los simbolistas más tarde [33].

La poesía de Bécquer contiene una melodía íntima cautivante. Más allá de las imágenes nos queda resonando en los oídos esa acompasada música de sus *Rimas*. La rima XII, como todas las demás, es para leer en voz alta. Por detrás del engarzamiento exquisito de imágenes marcha ese rítmico efecto musical que hace del poema una obra de arte excepcional:

XII

Porque son, niña, tus ojos
verdes como el mar, te quejas:
verdes los tienen las náyades,

---

[33] En la leyenda «El Miserere», pp. 189-200, el compás de la música y las voces se entremezclan, al igual que en el ideal estético de los poemas simbolistas; las palabras se transforman en música. ANNA BALAKIAN, *El movimiento simbolista*, trad. José-Miguel Velloso, Ediciones Guadarrama (Nueva York: Randon House, 1967). Ella comenta sobre la poesía de Verlaine, guía del simbolismo francés:

En la poesía de Verlaine, no es la palabra aislada la que pone en movimiento asociaciones de imágenes en la mente del lector, o provoca vagas emociones con la música, sino que las asociaciones de combinaciones especiales de palabras, que contienen inflexiones de sonido, como «il pleure dans mon coeur», suenan en efecto como música. Hacen música del mismo modo que la armonía de una serie de sonidos musicales. La poesía se convierte en música porque se dirige al oído y no por su función inherente o por su efecto sobre las asociaciones mentales. (84).

Este mismo efecto se puede ver en ciertos pasajes de la leyenda «El Miserere», como en muchas de las poesías becquerianas. De la leyenda extraemos a continuación este fragmento:

Cuando los monjes llegaron al peristilo del templo, se ordenaron en dos hileras y, penetrando en él, fueron a arrodillarse en el coro, donde, con voz más levantada y solemne, prosiguieron entonando los versículos del salmo. La música sonaba al compás de sus voces: aquella música era el rumor distante del trueno, que, desvanecida la tempestad, se alejaba murmurando; era el zumbido del aire que gemía en la concavidad del monte; era el monótono ruido de la cascada que caía sobre las rocas, y la gota de agua que se filtraba, y el grito del búho escondido, y el roce de los reptiles inquietos. Todo esto era la música y algo que no puede explicarse ni apenas concebirse; algo más que parecía como el eco de un órgano que acompañaba los versículos del gigante himno de contrición del rey salmista con notas y acordes tan gigantes como sus palabras terribles. (197).

verdes los tuvo Minerva,
y verdes son las pupilas
de las hurís del Profeta.

El verde es gala y ornato
del bosque en la primavera.
Entre sus siete colores,
brillante el iris lo ostenta.

Las esmeraldas son verdes,
verde el color del que espera,
y las ondas del Océano,
y el laurel de los poetas.

★

Es tu mejilla temprana
rosa de escarcha cubierta,
en que el carmín de los pétalos
se ve al través de las perlas.

Y, sin embargo,
sé que te quejas
porque tus ojos
crees que te afean.

Pues no lo creas;
que parecen tus pupilas,
húmedas, verdes e inquietas,
tempranas hojas de almendro,
que al soplo del aire tiemblan.

Es tu boca de rubíes
purpúrea granada abierta,
que en el estío convida
a apagar la sed en ella.

Y, sin embargo,
sé que te quejas
porque tus ojos
crees que la afean.

Pues no lo creas;
que parecen, si enojada
tus pupilas centellean,
las olas del mar que rompen
en las cantábricas peñas.

★

> Es tu frente, que corona
> crespo el oro en ancha trenza,
> nevada cumbre en que el día
> su postrera luz refleja.
>
> Y, sin embargo,
> sé que te quejas
> porque tus ojos
> crees que la afean.
>
> Pues no lo creas;
> que entre las rubias pestañas,
> junto a las sienes, semejan
> broches de esmeralda y oro
> que un blanco armiño sujetan.
>
> Porque son, niña, tus ojos
> verdes como el mar, te quejas;
> quizás, si negros o azules
> se tornasen, lo sintieras. (412-14)

La experiencia de una lectura en voz alta dice mucho más de lo que podríamos agregar en un esfuerzo crítico para destacar los efectos musicales del poema. Esa reiteración acompasada del verde en los primeros versos, que luego se transforma en la repetición del estribillo, es magistral. Ese vaivén emocional entre el elogio y el desprecio, que se consustancia con la variación en la versificación, es deleitable. Como si nos moviéramos a través de una sinfonía, al sonido entrecortado de la estrofa de versos breves para el reproche: «Y, sin embargo, / sé que te quejas / porque tus ojos / crees que la afean», le sigue el remanso sonoro del elogio: «Pues no lo creas; / que entre las rubias pestañas, / junto a las sienes, semejan / broches de esmeralda y oro / que un blanco armiño sujetan.»

¡Qué maestría de la acústica cuando la emoción se enciende y las palabras fonéticamente van marcando esa agitación!:

> Pues no lo creas;
> que parecen, si enojada
> tus pupilas centellean,
> las olas del mar que rompen
> en las cantábricas peñas.

El prólogo que escribe Bécquer para las *Rimas* en algunas

ediciones se titula «Introducción sinfónica» y es un adecuado preámbulo a este mundo de colores y sonidos que crean sus poesías.

Las rimas XXVII, LII y LVI son finísimos ejercicios acústicos donde los sonidos nos sugieren y comunican los diferentes estados anímicos de paz, angustia y hastío. De la rima XXVII dejamos puntualizados los efectos sonoros en el capítulo anterior cuando pusimos atención a las exclamaciones. En la rima LII el retumbe de las erres nos transmite el desgarrado dolor del poeta en su angustioso aislamiento:

LII

Olas gigantes que os *rompéis br*amando
en las playas desie*r*tas y *remotas;*
envuelto en*tr*e la sábana de espumas,
¡llevadme con voso*tr*as!

Ráfagas de huracán, que *arrebatáis*
del alto bosque las ma*rch*itas hojas;
arrastrado en el ciego to*r*bellino,
¡llevadme con voso*tr*as!

Nubes de tempestad que *rompe* el *rayo*
y en fuego o*r*náis las de*spr*endidas o*r*las,
arrebatado entre la niebla oscura,
¡llevadme con vosotras!

Llevadme, por *p*iedad, a donde el vé*r*tigo
con la *razón* me *arranque* la memoria...
¡Por *p*iedad!... ¡Tengo miedo de queda*r*me
con mi dolo*r* a solas! (436)

También es importante poner atención al efecto de las eres combinadas con otras consonantes, como habíamos señalado en el caso de la rima LXXVIII. Además, los acentos recalcan la desesperación.

En la rima LVI el repetir sistemático nos comunica el hastío del vivir. Muchas veces, en Bécquer, el efecto sonoro y el asunto del poema están más directamente relacionados a diferencia de los simbolistas que preferían dejarlo sugerido:

LVI

(1)   Hoy como ayer, mañana como hoy,
            ¡y siempre igual!
        Un cielo gris, un horizonte eterno,
            ¡y andar..., andar!

(2)   Moviéndose a compás, como una estúpida
            máquina, el corazón;
        la torpe inteligencia, del cerebro
            dormida en un rincón.

(3)   El alma, que ambiciona un paraíso,
            buscando sin fe;
        fatiga sin objeto, ola que rueda
            ignorando por qué.

(4)   Voz que incesante con el mismo tono
            canta el mismo cantar;
        gota de agua monótona que cae
            y cae sin cesar.

(5)   Así van deslizándose los días,
            unos de otros en pos,
        hoy lo mismo que ayer..., y todos ellos
            sin goce ni dolor.

(6)   ¡Ay!, a veces me acuerdo suspirando
            del antiguo sufrir...
        Amargo es el dolor; pero siquiera
            ¡padecer es vivir! (438-39)

El golpe repetitivo de la cuarta estrofa es una maravillosa réplica del goteo, no sólo por la repetición, sino también por el efecto sonoro de las palabras utilizadas que transmiten la monotonía, hastío y abulia del vivir:

> Voz que incesante con el *mismo tono*
>   *canta* el *mismo cantar;*
> gota de agua monótona que *cae*
>   y *cae* sin cesar.

Bécquer admiró a Espronceda y Zorrilla por la sonoridad de sus cantos. Pero en estos poetas brota la nota musical espontáneamente, mientras que en Bécquer, como vimos en los casos estudiados, la armonía de sus poemas está más cuidadosamente trabajada. La musicalidad de las *Rimas* no copia del romanticismo, Gustavo Adolfo no mira hacia atrás para reproducir; de lo hecho por Espronceda y Zorrilla aprende, pero a partir de ahí evoluciona e innova. La musicalidad de las *Rimas* se proyecta hacia adelante, hacia lo que aspirarían los simbolistas en materia poética.

Otro indicio simbolista que se prevé en Bécquer es su convicción en cumplir una misión trascendente con su arte. En la leyenda «El beso» dice:

> Indudablemente, el artista, que es casi un dios, le da a su obra un soplo de vida que no logra hacer que ande y se mueva, pero que le infunde una vida incomprensible y extraña, vida que yo no me explico bien... (289)

Los simbolistas veían al poeta como a un profeta. Chadwick indica:

> It was Baudelaire and his successors who elevated the poet to the rank of priest or profet or what Rimbaud called «le poete-voyant» —«the poet-seer»— endowed with the power to see behind and beyond the objects of the real world to the essences concealed in the ideal world. (3)

Coincidiendo con los simbolistas leemos en la rima V, estrofas 15, 16 y 17, similar formulación predicada por Bécquer:

> Yo sigo en raudo vértigo
> los mundos que voltean,
> y mi pupila abarca
> la creación entera.
>
> Yo sé de esas regiones
> a do un rumor no llega,
> y donde informes astros
> de vida un soplo esperan.
>
> Yo soy sobre el abismo
> el puente que atraviesa;
> yo soy la ignota escala
> que el cielo une a la tierra. (408-9)

A esa elevación mítica del poeta al rango de profeta se une en Bécquer, al igual que en los simbolistas después, un mundo circundante donde no es posible separar lo tangible de lo abstracto, lo real de lo ideal [34]. Gustavo Adolfo dice en su introducción a las *Rimas*:

> Deseo ocuparme un poco del mundo que me rodea, pudiendo, una vez vacío, apartar los ojos de este otro mundo que llevo dentro de la cabeza. El sentido común, que es la barrera de los sueños, comienza a flaquear, y las gentes de diversos campos se mezclan y confunden. Me cuesta trabajo saber qué cosas he soñado y cuáles me han sucedido. Mis afectos se reparten entre fantasmas de la imaginación y personajes reales. Mi memoria clasifica revueltos nombres y fechas de mujeres y días que han muerto, o han pasado, con los días y mujeres que no han existido sino en mi mente. (41)

La rima LXXV sirvió para darle a Bécquer el tilde de «huésped de las tinieblas». Con este poema nos sumergimos en ese mundo de aire enrarecido que reina en sus poesías en general. Gustavo Adolfo nos abre la puerta al mundo de los sueños que los simbolistas incursionarán más tarde, y será materia prima para la composición literaria de los escritores surrealistas de nuestro siglo:

LXXV

¿Será verdad que cuando toca el sueño
con sus dedos de rosa nuestros ojos,

---

[34] En la leyenda «Los ojos verdes», pp. 131-41, además de ver al poeta como ser superior, al modo de los simbolistas, la mujer está hecha de la misma sustancia evanescente del mundo poético:
—Fernando— dijo la hermosa entonces con una voz semejante a una música—, yo te amo más aún que tú me amas; yo, que desciendo hasta un mortal siendo un espíritu puro. No soy una mujer como las que existen en la Tierra; soy una mujer digna de ti, que eres superior a los demás hombres. Yo vivo en el fondo de estas aguas, incorpórea como ellas, fugaz y transparente: hablo con sus rumores y ondulo con sus pliegues. Yo no castigo al que osa turbar la fuerza donde moro; antes lo premio con mi amor, como a un mortal superior a las supersticiones del vulgo, como a un amante capaz de comprender mi cariño extraño y misterioso. (140)
Este pasaje nos recuerda al tipo de mujer, o poesía, que atrae al poeta en la última estrofa de la rima XI:
—Yo soy un sueño, un imposible,
vano fantasma de niebla y luz;
soy incorpórea, soy intangible;
no puedo amarte. —¡Oh, ven; ven tú! (412)

de la cárcel que habita huye el espíritu
    en vuelo presuroso?

    ¿Será verdad que, huésped de las nieblas,
de la brisa nocturna al tenue soplo
alado sube a la región vacía
    a encontrarse con otros?

        ¿Y allí desnudo de la humana forma,
allí, los lazos terrenales rotos,
breves horas habita de la idea
    el mundo silencioso?

        ¿Y ríe y llora, y aborrece y ama
y guarda un rastro del dolor y el gozo,
semejante al que deja cuando cruza
    el cielo un meteoro?

        ¡Yo no sé si ese mundo de visiones
vive fuera o va dentro de nosotros;
pero sé que conozco a muchas gentes
    a quienes no conozco! (453-54)

Sin duda, Bécquer fue, en su labor de poeta, un vidente de la
materia literaria que atraería a escritores posteriores.

    La rima VIII también configura un mundo híbrido en la
mezcla de lo espiritual y lo físico:

                            VIII

            Cuando miro el azul horizonte
                perderse a lo lejos,
            al través de una gasa de polvo
                dorado e inquieto,

            me parece posible arrancarme
                del mísero suelo,
            y flotar con la niebla dorada
                en átomos leves,
                cual ella deshecho.

            Cuando miro de noche en el fondo
                oscuro del cielo
            las estrellas temblar, como ardientes
                pupilas de fuego,

            me parece posible a do brillan
                subir en un vuelo,
            y anegarme en su luz, y con ellas
                en lumbre encendido
                fundirme en un beso.

> En el mar de la duda en que bogo,
> ni aun sé lo que creo;
> ¡sin embargo, estas ansias me dicen
> que yo llevo algo
> divino aquí dentro! (410-11)

En la manera simbolista más auténtica, el poeta que se siente envuelto en su misión profética, cierra el poema con esta convicción: «...yo llevo algo / divino aquí dentro!»

En Verlaine, al igual que en otros simbolistas, el sensualismo, muchas veces rayante en lo erótico, se hace parte del material con que trabaja. En Bécquer la sensualidad no desborda, pero se siente su presencia. Joaquín de Entrambasaguas, en un estudio freudiano de las *Rimas*, destaca este aspecto no tan relevante en Gustavo Adolfo como lo fue para los modernistas-simbolistas [35].

Otra actitud que se yuxtapone al simbolismo es la visión del mundo o ideología que traen los decadentes. En la segunda mitad del siglo XIX se crean preocupaciones sociales e intelectuales que Hans Hinterhäuser describe y sintetiza con el rótulo de «mal del siglo» [36]. Este inconformismo social se tradujo a la literatura en las tendencias decadentistas. Pero no todo se reduce a una postura negativa contra el ambiente burgués adverso que rodea a los poetas. Los decadentes encontrarán refugio en el pasado. Roma antigua será su imán. Bécquer dice: «Yo busco de los siglos / las ya borradas huellas» (rima V) y encuentra en Toledo el material decadente (término este último de connotación positiva en la literatura que designa el grupo de poetas que resucitan las artes de las ruinas) para sus *Leyendas* y *Rimas* [37].

---

[35] JOAQUÍN DE ENTRAMBASAGUAS PEÑA, *La obra poética de Bécquer en su discriminación creadora y erótica* (Madrid: Gráfica Clemares, 1974). El crítico ordena las rimas en base a la vida erótica del poeta, enfatizando este aspecto.

[36] HANS HINTERHÄUSER, *Fin de siglo: figuras y mitos* traducido por María Teresa Martínez (Madrid: Taurus Ediciones, S. A., 1980).

[37] HINTERHÄUSER cita a GREGORIO MARAÑÓN, *Elogio y nostalgia de Toledo*, Madrid, 1951, p. 19:
«Pues Toledo, en su cacerío milenario, hecho de ruinas que se hacen ruinas... ser ruinas; y al lado de ellas, obras de arte que perduran, con aliento inmortal...» (50)

El mundo en ruinas y artístico de Toledo y la idea de la muerte

En la leyenda «El beso» (275-90) el guerrero cincelado en piedra cobra vida. En las ruinas de Toledo, dentro de su decadencia, corre un hilo vigorizante en su arte milenario e intacto que cautiva al poeta sevillano. La rima LXXVI tiene dejos de la leyenda «El beso», donde de lo inerte parece emanar vida, donde el arte rompe los lazos de la muerte:

LXXVI

En la imponente nave
del templo bizantino,
vi la gótica tumba, a la indecisa
luz que temblaba en los pintados vidrios.

Las manos sobre el pecho,
y en las manos un libro,
una mujer hermosa reposaba
sobre la urna, del cincel prodigio.

Del cuerpo abandonado
al dulce peso hundido,
cual si de blanda pluma y raso fuera,
se plegaba su lecho de granito.

De la última sonrisa,
el resplandor divino
guardaba el rostro, como el cielo guarda
del sol que muere el rayo fugitivo.

Del cabezal de piedra,
sentados en el filo,
dos ángeles, el dedo sobre el labio,
imponían silencio en el recinto.

No parecía muerta;
de los arcos macizos

---

atraen a Bécquer, como sucedería en los poetas decadentes más tarde. Gustavo Adolfo en la carta III desde la celda dice:
    ¡Cuántas veces, después de haber discurrido por las anchurosas naves de alguna de nuestras inmensas catedrales góticas o de haberme sorprendido la noche en uno de esos imponentes y severos claustros de nuestras históricas abadías, he vuelto a sentir inflamada mi alma con la idea de la gloria, pero una gloria más ruidosa y ardiente que la de poeta!... a encontrar la paz del sepulcro en el fondo de uno de esos claustros santos donde vive el eterno silencio y al que los siglos prestan su majestad y su color misterioso e indefinible. (535-36)
Del mundo artístico yacente y en ruinas, los decadentes buscan el vigor y la vitalidad de esas civilizaciones pujantes de antaño.

> parecía dormir en la penumbra,
> y que en sueños veía el paraíso.
>
>   Me acerqué de la nave
>   al ángulo sombrío,
> con el callado paso que se llega
> junto a la cuna donde duerme un niño.
>
>   La contemplé un momento,
>   y aquel resplandor tibio,
> aquel lecho de piedra que ofrecía,
> próximo al muro, otro lugar vacío,
>
>   en el alma avivaron
>   la sed de lo infinito,
> el ansia de esa vida de la muerte,
> para la que un instante son los siglos...
> ....
>
>   Cansado del combate
>   en que luchando vivo,
> alguna vez me acuerdo con envidia
> de aquel rincón oscuro y escondido.
>
>   De aquella muda y pálida
>   mujer me acuerdo y digo:
> «¡Oh, qué amor tan callado, el de la muerte!
> ¡Qué sueño el del sepulcro tan tranquilo! (454-56)

La vida y la muerte se entremezclan por milagro del arte. De «la gótica tumba» parece levantarse la vida. El poeta nos dice que «no parecía muerta» y aún queda en «el rostro», «del cincel prodigio», la huella «de la última sonrisa». El poeta se acerca al «lecho de piedra» de la «mujer hermosa» con la reverencia que impone aquello que aún tiene indicios de vida; porque claramente nos indica que «parecía dormir en la penumbra». Ahora «la gótica tumba» semeja «la cuna donde duerme un niño», pues aparentemente emana de ella el «resplandor tibio» originando, a través del arte, «vida de la muerte».

Bécquer compartió la paradoja de la decadente vitalidad que encuentran los poetas fineseculares en las ruinas que exploran [38]. En el último tercio del volumen de las *Rimas*, Béc-

---

[38] A Baudelaire y Verlaine les atrajo lo decadente. Anna Balakian dice en su libro:
   Finalmente, de cuando en cuando en su «chanson grise», Verlaine introduce el sentido de la muerte, el temblor de lo efí-

quer toma una actitud decadente y contemplativa de «esa vida de la muerte».

Hay ciertas pautas simbolistas que difieren de la poesía de Gustavo Adolfo y de su concepción simbólica. El simbolismo del poeta sevillano se entremezcla más con la realidad, en vez de producirse en los poemas un mundo totalmente idealizado, a la manera de los franceses. Al simbolismo becqueriano lo veremos resurgir en el tipo de poesía que practicarán Juan Ramón Jiménez y otros en nuestro siglo. Pero esto será tema del próximo capítulo, donde veremos las relaciones entre Bécquer y el poeta de Moguer.

C. Bécquer y Rubén Darío.

La conexión de Gustavo Adolfo Bécquer con el modernismo no se puede limitar a apuntar ciertos paralelismos y semejanzas entre las actitudes poéticas becquerianas y el parnasismo y el simbolismo. Más importante aún que esto es mostrar cómo las *Rimas* entroncan con el eje conductor del modernismo hispánico, Rubén Darío. Bernardo Gicovate en su estudio «Antes del modernismo», citado al principio de este capítulo, puntualiza el trabajo preparatorio de Bécquer como premodernista:

> Nadie en español había proclamado tan claramente la necesidad de un trabajo de persecución de la forma: el ideal romántico-simbolista de transformar en música y color las palabras poéticas... Ecos de estos deseos de transformación de los sentidos se van a dar en Silva y en Darío, y aunque en ellos actúe ya el programa sinestésico de Baudelaire o de Verlaine, son las palabras sencillas de Bécquer las que han preparado el terreno y las que ofrecen el hilo conductor dentro de la tradición. (197)

----

mero, el olor de la decadencia. Pronuncia la palabra «mourir» con una arrebato de saciedad y plenitud. En este sentido añadió algunas notas al retrato del «decadente» y al espíritu de la decadencia que ya hemos discernido vagamente en Baudelaire. Al definirlo, dice: «Me gusta la palabra «decadencia» con sus reflejos de púrpura y oro.» Esta palabra sugería los pensamientos refinados del hombre extremadamente civilizado en posesión de delicados sentidos, alma capaz de intensas voluptuosidades. La decandencia es «el arte de morir en belleza». (85)

La influencia de Bécquer se hace más obvia en las primeras composiciones de Darío, años de la maduración artística del poeta nicaragüense, hasta *Azul*, 1888.

En las primeras páginas de las *Obras completas* de Rubén Darío [39] se leen poesías del período de 1880 a 1886, *La iniciación melódica*, hasta que viaja a Chile. El primer poema data del 10 de julio de 1881 y sólo hace falta transcribirlo para dejar escuchar en él el eco de las rimas becquerianas:

AL LECTOR

Lector: si oyes los rumores
de la ignorada arpa mía,
oirás ecos de dolores;
mas sabe que tengo flores
también, de dulce alegría. (21)

La rima XV de Bécquer combina un ejercicio visual y sonoro de la más delicada forma modernista:

XV

Cendal flotante de leve bruma
rizada cinta de blanca espuma,
rumor sonoro
de arpa de oro,
beso del aura, onda de luz,
eso eres tú.

Tú, sombra aérea, que cuantas veces
voy a tocarte te desvaneces
como la llama, como el sonido,
como la niebla, como el gemido
del lago azul.

En mar sin playas onda sonante;
en el vacío, cometa errante;
largo lamento
del ronco viento,
ansia perpetua de algo mejor,
eso soy yo

---

[39] RUBÉN DARÍO, *Obras completas* (Madrid: Ediciones Castilla, 1953), V. Todas las citas de Rubén Darío indicadas en el texto provendrán de este volumen.

¡Yo, que a tus ojos, en mi agonía,
los ojos vuelvo de noche y día;
yo, que incansable corro y demente
tras una sombra, tras la hija ardiente
de una visión! (416)

Darío, a los 13 años de edad, en 1880, compone el
poema «A ti», donde, teniendo en mente la rima anterior, el
referente becqueriano es fácilmente perceptible [40]:

A TI

Yo vi una ave
que suave
sus cantares
a la orilla de los mares
entonó,
y voló...
Y a lo lejos,
los reflejos,
de la luna en alta cumbre,
que argentando las espumas,
bañaba de luz sus plumas
de tisú...
¡Y eras... tú!

Y vi un alma
que sin calma
sus amores
cantaba en triste rumores
y su ser
conmover
a las rocas parecía;
miró la azul lejanía,
tendió su vista anhelante,
suspiró,
y cantando pobre amante:
prosiguió...
¡Y era... yo! (21-22)

---

[40] Carisomo, en el mismo artículo citado en nuestras notas 16 y 30
de este capítulo, indica que Bécquer ya había formado escuela en el
momento en que Darío se inicia:
    Puntualicemos antes un conocido fenómeno: las *Rimas* de
    Gustavo Adolfo, a medida de su creciente difusión, digamos
    desde 1880, se convirtieron no sólo en lectura de todos y para
    todos, sino en una especie particular de «escuela lírica» llega-
    da intacta hasta los modernistas y, sin desmedro, hasta los
    «ismos» de la primera posguerra. (136)

Tanto el asunto como los ejercicios sonoros y visuales de esta poesía, aunque mucho menos sofisticados, recuerdan a la rima XV.

Se haría demasiado extenso mostrar punto por punto la influencia de Bécquer en Darío en sus primeros años de desarrollo artístico. De todas maneras, vale la pena señalar que muchas veces Darío nombra a Bécquer en sus poemas. En uno de 1884 nos encontramos con lo siguiente:

> ....
> Juzga el amor como dolencia sacra
> que martiriza al par que infunde llama
> de calor infinito; la pureza,
> la virtud, la honradez, muy naturales
> cosas. Gustavo Adolfo
> Bécquer estuvo enfermo de esa fiebre.
> .... (223)

En otro poema juvenil Darío cita la rima XXVI de Bécquer:

> ....
> Es verdad que el dinero
> es soberbia palanca
> para llegar a ser gran caballero,
> para ganarse hasta el mejor lucero,
> por más que digan los que están sin blanca
> (como ciertos poetas arrancados
> que en invierno se embozan en la lira,
> como Bécquer nos dice); y no es mentira,
> .... (259)

Una vez en Chile, en 1887, Rubén Darío, cuando tenía ya veinte años, escribe para un concurso sus *Rimas* de definido corte becqueriano [41]. La rima VI de Darío refiere a la rima I de Bécquer:

> ....
> ¡Y flotando en la luz el espíritu,

---

[41] RICARDO GULLÓN en su libro *Direcciones del modernismo*, 1963, subraya la conexión de las *Rimas* de Bécquer con las de Darío:
Sus *Rimas* no son becquerianas solamente por el título, sino imitación del tono, acento y lenguaje del poeta sevillano, realizada para presentarse a un concurso poético convocado en Chile con el fin de recompensar «una colección de doce a quince poesías del género subjetivo de que es tipo el poeta Bécquer». (13)

> mientras arde en la sangre la fiebre,
> como «un himno gigante y extraño»
> arrancar a la lira de Bécquer! (615)

El comienzo de la rima VIII de Darío: «Yo quisiera cince-
larte / una rima / delicada y primorosa / como una áurea mar-
garita...» (616) es una réplica del ideal poético que expresa
Bécquer en la introducción a sus *Rimas*: «Yo quisiera poder
cincelar la forma que ha de conteneros, como se cincela el
vaso de oro...» (40).

Un año más tarde, en 1888, Rubén Darío publica *Azul*, que
para muchos es el comienzo definitivo del programa modernista en Hispanoamérica. En *Azul* hay claros tonos del parnasianismo francés. Dentro de ese volumen de cuentos y poesías viene el relato breve «El rubí» que tiene evidente conexión
con la leyenda «El gnomo» que había escrito Bécquer aproximadamente veintéséis años antes [42]. Al principio de la década
de 1860 Gustavo Adolfo deja un catálogo modernista que se
adelanta un cuarto de siglo al libro *Azul* de Darío. Nos estamos refiriendo a la rima V que hemos citado fragmentaria-
mente a través de este capítulo. En esta poesía se conglomera
una gama amplia de las tendencias y actitudes modernistas.
En la rima V Gustavo Adolfo Bécquer no sólo sintetiza su leyenda «El gnomo», sino que reúne los rasgos modernistas que
hemos ido señalando en sus otros poemas también:

V

(1)   Espíritu sin nombre,
             indefinible esencia,
             yo vivo con la vida
             sin forma de la idea.

---

[42] Carisomo parece implicar este posible punto de contacto entre «El gnomo» de Bécquer y «El rubí» de Darío, pero no lo especifica:
    ... en eso se anticipó en treinta años a la prosa del simbolismo;
    para acreditarlo fehacientemente queda el testimonio de «El
    gnomo» —1862— que, sin reparos, podrían haber firmado cómo-
    damente Maeterlinck o Darío. (137)

(2)   Yo nado en el vacío,
del sol tiemblo en la hoguera,
palpito entre las sombras
y floto con las nieblas.

(3)   Yo soy el fleco de oro
de la lejana estrella;
yo soy de la alta luna
la luz tibia y serena.

(4)   Yo soy la ardiente nube
que en el ocaso ondea;
yo soy del astro errante
la luminosa estela.

(5)   Yo soy nieve en las cumbres,
soy fuego en las arenas,
azul onda en los mares
y espuma en las riberas.

(6)   En el laúd soy nota,
perfume en la violeta,
fugaz llama en las tumbas,
y en las ruinas hiedra.

(7)   Yo canto con la alondra
y zumbo con la abeja,
yo imito los ruidos
que en la alta noche suenan.

(8)   Yo atrueno en el torrente,
y silbo en la centella,
y ciego en el relámpago,
y rujo en la tormenta.

(9)   Yo río en las alcores,
susurro en la alta yerba,
suspiro en la onda pura
y lloro en la hoja seca.

(10)   Yo ondulo con los átomos
del humo que se eleva
y al cielo lento sube
en espiral inmensa.

(11)   Yo, en los dorados hilos
que los insectos cuelgan,
me mezco entre los árboles
en la ardorosa siesta.

(12)   Yo corro tras las ninfas
que en la corriente fresca
del cristalino arroyo
desnuda juguetean.

(13)   Yo, en bosques de corales
                que alfombran blancas perlas,
                persigo en el Océano
                las náyades ligeras.

(14)   Yo, en las cavernas cóncavas,
                do el sol nunca penetra,
                mezclándome a los gnomos,
                contemplo sus riquezas.

(15)   Yo busco de los siglos
                las ya borradas huellas,
                y sé de esos imperios
                de que ni el nombre queda.

(16)   Yo sigo en raudo vértigo
                los mundos que voltean,
                y mi pupila abarca
                la creación entera.

(17)   Yo sé de esas regiones
                a do un rumor no llega,
                y donde informes astros
                de vida un soplo esperan.

(18)   Yo soy sobre el abismo
                el puente que atraviesa;
                yo soy la ignota escala
                que el cielo une a la tierra.

(19)   Yo soy el invisible
                anillo que sujeta
                el mundo de la forma
                al mundo de la idea.

(20)   Yo, en fin, soy ese espíritu,
                desconocida esencia,
                perfume misterioso
                de que es vaso el poeta. (406-9)

Las primeras cinco estrofas desarrollan una serie de imágenes simbolistas-impresionistas que conforman el mundo etéreo y vago que reina en las *Rimas*.

La sexta estrofa, en su primer verso, pone atención a la
musicalidad: «En el laúd soy nota», efecto sonoro que se desarrolla después en las próximas tres estrofas con los comienzos de cada verso: «yo canto», «y zumbo», «yo imito los ruidos», «yo atrueno», «y silbo», «y rujo», «yo río», «susurro»,
«suspiro», «y lloro».

En las estrofas diez y once el poeta vuelve a los efectos
visuales de los primeros versos, pero sus imágenes esta vez
son un tanto más reales; a diferencia de los simbolistas franceses, aquí el espíritu poético se entremezcla con un mundo
algo más tangible.

En la estrofa doce se han mezclado el mundo fantástico y
el real, también se combinan las imágenes con los sonidos.
Además, en esta sección del poema, se inyecta cierto sensualismo:

> Yo corro tras las ninfas
> que en la corriente fresca
> del cristalino arroyo
> desnudas juguetean.

Las ninfas desnudas abrieron nuestra imaginación para
que en las estrofas trece y catorce nos internemos en el mundo donde habitan esas «ninfas», «las náyades ligeras» y «los
gnomos». En estos versos de la rima V llegamos a dar con un
ambiente adornado de «bosques de corales», alfombrado de
«blancas perlas», lleno de objetos preciosos y «riquezas».

La estrofa quince sintetiza un postulado decadente, actitud
que ya había quedado latente en ciertas imágenes de algunos
versos anteriores: «fugaz llama en las tumbas, / y en las ruinas
hiedra.»

El resto del poema conforma una visión del artista como
profeta:

> ....
> Yo sigo en raudo vértigo
> los mundos que voltean,
> y mi pupila abarca
> la creación entera.
>
> Yo sé de esas regiones
> a do un rumor no llega,
> y donde informes astros
> de vida un soplo esperan.
>
> Yo soy sobre el abismo
> el puente que atraviesa;
> yo soy la ignota escala
> que el cielo une a la tierra.

> Yo soy el invisible
> anillo que sujeta
> el mundo de la forma
> al mundo de la idea.
>
> Yo, en fin, soy ese espíritu,
> desconocida esencia,
> perfume misterioso
> de que es vaso el poeta.

Rubén Darío abrevió este mismo concepto místico de la misión poética dejando escrito en *Cantos de vida y esperanza*, 1905, canto IX:

> ¡Torres de Dios! ¡Poetas! (880)

Un tiempo después, en *El canto errante* de 1907, Rubén Darío parece ir repitiendo los preceptos formulados al final de la rima V:

> Pienso que el don del arte es aquel que de modo superior hace que nos reconozcamos íntima y exteriormente ante la vida. El poeta tiene la visión directa e introspectiva de la vida y una supervisión que va más allá de lo que está sujeto a las leyes del general reconocimiento. (955)

A pesar de estos puntos coincidentes entre Bécquer y Darío, justo es reconocer que este último trabajó más extensamente en la sinestesia y también experimentó más la variación métrica. La poesía del poeta nicaragüense fue más lejos en estos aspectos que la de Bécquer, especialmente en la renovación lingüística. Además, sus poesías contienen mayor exotismo en el resurgir del mundo mitológico. De todas maneras, si bien Rubén Darío, después de sus inicios literarios va incursionando en una renovación poética sin precedentes, tampoco abandona totalmente ciertos rasgos becquerianos que dieron forma a su canto [43].

---

[43] En *Estudios sobre Gustavo Adolfo Bécquer*, 1972, ENRIQUE RULL en su artículo titulado «'Pensamientos' de Bécquer y 'Nocturnos' de Darío», pp. 563-79, hace un estudio muy interesante de la relación entre estos dos textos, y concluye aclarando.
   Toda esta arquitectura de sentido y expresión no significa, sin embargo, más que el momento de incidencia del pensar poético becqueriano en la materia que elabora Rubén Darío,

Rubén Darío escribirá en su pináculo modernista *Prosas profanas*, en 1896. En el último poema del libro, el nicaragüense comienza diciendo: «Yo persigo una forma que no encuentra mi estilo» (856) que parece espejo de lo dicho por Bécquer en junio de 1868: «Yo quisiera poder cincelar la forma... Mas es imposible» (40). Ambos genios coinciden en las mismas actitudes y ansias modernistas de encontrar la forma perfecta para sus cantos y su arte.

Darío nunca olvidó los ideales estéticos del maestro sevillano de su juventud. En *El canto errante* deposita su fe en la renovación constante de la forma artística, actitud fundamentalmente modernista, pasión esta que tiene sus orígenes en Bécquer:

> No. La forma poética no está llamada a desaparecer, antes bien a extenderse, a modificarse, a seguir su desenvolvimiento en el eterno ritmo de los siglos. Podrá no haber poetas, pero siempre habrá poesía. dijo uno de los puros (rima IV). Siempre habrá poesía y siempre habrá poetas. (946-47)

Si el modernismo fue el mayor esfuerzo artístico emprendido en pos de la renovación poética hispánica desde el Siglo de Oro, es indiscutible que Rubén Darío fue su máximo conductor, y tiene en Gustavo Adolfo Bécquer su más claro y auténtico precursor.

> sin menoscabo de la particular concepción y expresión de este último en el sentido general de los poemas... Nuestra intención ha sido señalar no sólo el influjo del texto becqueriano en el segundo «Nocturno» y la prolongación y reminiscencia en el tercero, sino también mostrar que la unidad y cohesión de ellos radica en una concepción poética esbozada por Bécquer en un sentido global y en múltiples aspectos de detalle. (578)

En las palabras finales del artículo, Rull reafirma que la influencia de Bécquer en Darío se puede reconocer en toda su obra, idea que deseamos extender con nuestro estudio:

> Este recorrido nos ha servido, creemos, para mostrar varios hechos. Uno de ellos es que el becquerianismo de Rubén es profundo, que pasada la época de intencionada imitación no desaparece, como se suele decir, sino que, resuelto desde su origen en patética participación vivencial, informa ya luego la poesía de Rubén en los momentos de más honda interioridad de su vibración lírica. (579)

III. RESONANCIAS BECQUERIANAS EN LA POESÍA DE JUAN RAMÓN JIMÉNEZ Y ANTONIO MACHADO.

El modernismo no prosperó en España con la magnitud que lo hizo en Hispanoamérica. La influencia de Bécquer como poeta precursor la vemos más inmediatamente en los versos de Rubén Darío, tal como se analizó en el capítulo anterior. Hacia fines del siglo XIX, en España, las *Rimas* quedan algo relegadas; su canto suave es ahogado por la rimbombante poesía de Núñez de Arce y Campoamor. El poeta sevillano no forma escuela en ese entonces y permanece un tanto desatendida su obra. Hasta que no pasa esa ola avasalladora de poesía altisonante, vacía y hueca, no hay respiro. Transcurren unos treinta años de la muerte de Gustavo Adolfo hasta que en las postrimerías del siglo XIX y comienzos del nuevo vuelve a ser reconsiderado. Los de la generación del 98 lo admiran, Miguel de Unamuno, dentro de su labor de poeta, deja escritas sus *Rimas* [1].

---

[1] JUAN RAMÓN JIMÉNEZ, *El modernismo*, 1.ª ed. (México: Gráfica Cervantina, 1962). En el prefacio de este libro de Juan Ramón, Ricardo Gullón destaca la presencia de Bécquer tanto en el modernismo como en la generación del 98:

Bécquer y Rosalía estaban allí, trayendo con su fragante sencillez a los más puros, y cuando pasa el cortejo, cuando se diluyen en el aire los sones de la marcha triunfal, vuelven a oírse en el aire limpio de la espaciosa y triste España (y mucho más lejos, también), las palabras dichas, un día, por los dos grandes románticos de poco antes. Y no se entenderá el modernismo si no se entiende cuanto hay en él, en los más grandes —Martí, Darío, Silva, Unamuno, Machado, Juan Ramón— de confidencia apasionada, es decir, de lirismo becqueriano. En todos los poetas citados reaparece el acento de las *Rimas...*, dejando irrumpir en campo abierto el agua remansada e impaciente de la intimidad. (19)

A principios de siglo Antonio Machado y Juan Ramón Jiménez son los poetas principales. Juan Ramón en 1902 escribe
también sus *Rimas*[2]. Francisco Garfias indica que la influencia de Bécquer en Juan Ramón no se limita sólo a este volumen citado, sino que se ve también en las otras obras de formación del poeta de Moguer (1900-1916)[3].

---

[2] En el mismo libro de la nota anterior, Juan Ramón Jiménez también tiene un prólogo que titula «Los que influyeron en mí», pp. 54-58.
La forma de confesión íntima de un diario nos revela que en su juventud Bécquer le influyó:

> Yo empecé a escribir a mis 15 años, en 1896. Mi primer
> poema fue en prosa y se titula «Andén»; el segundo, improvi-
> sado una noche febril en que estaba leyendo las *Rimas* de Béc-
> quer, era una copia auditiva de alguna de ellas, alguna de las
> típicas rimas con agudos; y lo envié inmediatamente a «El
> Programa», un diario de Sevilla, donde me lo publicaron al
> día siguiente. ... Mis lecturas de esa época eran Bécquer, Ro-
> salía de Castro... (54)

[3] JUAN RAMÓN JIMÉNEZ, *Primeros libros de poesía* (Madrid: Aguilar, S. A. dye Ediciones, 1958). Francisco Garfias hace la recopilación
y prólogo a esta edición, pp. 15-65, donde destaca las *Rimas* de Juan
Ramón: «*Rimas* es un libro más ponderado que los anteriores... Bécquer es en este libro un eco permanente.» (28). No sólo las *Rimas* de
Juan Ramón coinciden con el gusto becqueriano, sino también otro
de sus volúmenes:

> Si en *Rimas* se prefilaba, en algún instante, la personalidad
> de Juan Ramón, *Arias tristes* marca el momento de su primera
> plenitud. Un vago acento becqueriano, de un Bécquer imposi-
> ble pasado por Heine y Verlaine, y por el canto popular anda-
> luz, se derrama melancólicamente por todo el libro, triste y be-
> llo como un otoño. El sentimiento musical, superviviente en
> libros sucesivos, da una dorada entonación a estas arias de
> aparente sencillez que traían a la poesía española un anhelo
> de perfección, un gusto inusitado por la belleza pura. (30)

Garfias cita una carta de Antonio Machado a Juan Ramón donde, tras
el elogio sincero, resalta la vena becqueriana en los versos del poeta de Moguer. Además, esta carta revela la conciencia que tenía Machado de la trascendencia de los poemas de Bécquer:

> De estos años es una carta de Antonio Machado al poeta en la
> que le dice: «Una tan fina sensibilidad como la de usted no
> existe, creo yo, entre poetas castellanos; tal dulzura de ritmo
> y delicadeza para las armonías apagadas, tampoco. Suavidad
> de sonidos, de tonos, de imágenes, de sentimiento. Sedas mar-
> chitas o frondas a través de un cristal algo turbio o a través
> de la lluvia. Usted ha oído los violines que oyó Verlaine y a
> traído a nuestras almas violentas, ásperas y destartaladas, otra
> gama de sensaciones dulces y melancólicas. Usted continúa a
> Bécquer, el primer renovador del ritmo interno de la poesía
> española...» (36)

Al igual que Bécquer, Juan Ramón crea una poesía íntima, donde el sentimiento se expresa fuertemente, pero sin caer en el desborde emocional. Tanto en la poesía de Gustavo Adolfo como en la de Jiménez queda expresado el sentimiento sin caerse en el sentimentalismo. Como ejemplo de esto podríamos citar uno de sus poemas tempranos titulado «Adolescencia». Aquí, al igual que en Bécquer, la emoción se reprime por ser recordada en vez de vivida [4]:

> En el balcón, un momento
> nos quedamos los dos solos;
> desde la dulce mañana
> de aquel día, éramos novios.
>
> El paisaje soñoliento
> dormía sus vagos tonos
> bajo el cielo gris y rosa
> del crepúsculo de otoño.
>
> Le dije que iba a besarla;
> la pobre bajó los ojos
> y me ofreció sus mejillas
> como quien pierde un tesoro.
>
> Las hojas muertas caían
> en el jardín silencioso,
> y en el aire fresco erraba
> un perfume de heliotropo.
>
> No se atrevía a mirarme;
> le dije que éramos novios,
> y las lágrimas rodaron
> de sus ojos melancólicos. (28-29)

---

[4] JORGE GUILLÉN, *Lenguaje y poesía* (Madrid: Artes Gráficas Clavileño, S. A., 1962). Guillén tiene una sesión titulada «Lenguaje insuficiente, Bécquer o lo inefable soñado», pp. 143-82. En el capítulo IV el autor atiende al factor de recordar los sentimientos para imponer control a las emociones como uno de los recursos becquerianos:

> El acto de escribir es posterior a la vida que evoca aquella escritura. El escritor recuerda, y si la memoria es la cuna de la poesía, los materiales vividos reaparecerán serenados por el recuerdo... Opinaba Friedrich Schlegel que «cuando el artista se encuentra bajo el poder de la imaginación y del entusiasmo, no está en las debidas condiciones para comunicar lo que tiene que decir... En esa situación desearía decirlo todo. Quien cae en tentación semejante no acierta a reconocer el valor y el mérito de la autocontención.» (160)

En el capítulo VI, pp. 174-77, Guillén vuelve a esa característica becqueriana que lo emparenta con poetas posteriores.

Gustavo Adolfo aporta a la poesía del siglo XX su nueva retórica del sentimiento amoroso, despojada de exageraciones y desprendida del sentimentalismo. En esto, el citado poema de Juan Ramón es reflejo de ese nuevo lenguaje lírico que nace con las *Rimas* de Bécquer.

Ya se vio en el capítulo anterior la conexión de Gustavo Adolfo con los simbolistas. Juan Ramón está estrechamente ligado a Bécquer en este aspecto. Ambos hacen poesía amorosa donde la anécdota se borra, donde se sugiere en vez de enunciar. En cuanto a esta característica de evitar una relación directa entre el poema y un hecho anecdótico, vale hacer notar que Bécquer sólo enumeró las rimas sin darles títulos que las pudieran encuadrar dentro de una determinada anécdota. Algo que posiblemente sea anecdótico, en Bécquer se encuentra voluntariamente escondido. Como ejemplo se podría dar la rima XLII:

XLII

Cuando me lo contaron sentí el frío
de una hoja de acero en las entrañas;
me apoyé contra el muro, y un instante
la conciencia perdí de dónde estaba.

Cayó sobre mi espíritu la noche;
en ira y en piedad se anegó el alma...
¡Y entonces comprendí por qué se llora,
y entonces comprendí por qué se mata!

Pasó la nube de dolor..., con pena
logré balbucear unas palabras...
y... ¿qué había de hacer?... era un amigo...
me había hecho un favor... Le di las gracias. (432-33)

La rima no tiene título que la defina. Aunque tomamos conciencia de que algo trágico le sucedió al hablante es imposible determinar qué es lo que le ocurrió. En esta poesía, como en muchas, no hay nombres, no hay referencias ni a lugares ni a momentos en particular. Al borrar y obscurecer el hecho anecdótico lo que queda en primer plano e impresiona la percepción del lector son los factores anímicos que perduran en la lectura del poema. Al negar la exclusividad de la experiencia

referida tras el proceso consciente de eliminar detalles anec-
dóticos, tal experiencia se universaliza. Los sentimientos que
se desprenden del poema no sólo evocan algo propio del hablante, sino que alcanzan al mundo íntimo del lector.
Hay muchas otras rimas que podrían considerarse bajo
una aproximación similar a ésta dado que es una constante
en el volumen. Por ejemplo léanse las rimas XXXI, XXXIII,
XXXVI, XLI, XLIV, XLIX, L, LI, LIV y LVIII. Todas ellas
son rimas de tono confesional e íntimo que al habérseles des-
dibujado el factor anecdótico reciben acogimiento universal.
Esto parece explicar la extensa popularidad de que gozan las
Rimas de Gustavo Adolfo Bécquer en diferentes generaciones y
en distintas latitudes; éste también es un hecho constante de
su poesía. La rima XXXII resulta otro buen ejemplo de lo
comentado aquí. Los puntos suspensivos al final del poema
abren un margen amplio en el espectro de interpretaciones
para que el lector juegue con tales posibilidades:

XXXII

Pasaba arrolladora en su hermosura,
   y el paso le dejé;
ni aun a mirarle me volví, y, no obstante,
   algo a mi oído murmuró: «Esa es.»

   ¿Quién reunió la tarde a la mañana?
     Lo ignoro; sólo sé
que en una breve noche de verano
   se unieron los crepúsculos y... fue. (426)

El poema comienza con un lenguaje coloquial que posiblemente nos invite a enterarnos de una anécdota amorosa que
se nos narra. Pero ya al final de la primera estrofa, el último
verso comienza a cerrarnos las puertas de esa posible sencilla experiencia sentimental, y con sus términos algo escurri-
dizos «algo a mi oído murmuró: «Esa es» nos abre el camino
a muchas posibles interpretaciones que quedan sugeridas por
lo ambiguo y esquivo de la expresión.
El comienzo de la segunda estrofa avanza en el campo
de la especulación. Con la pregunta: «¿Quién reunió la tarde

a la mañana?» se nos arranca de ese mundo literal y reducido de la primera estrofa y se nos lleva a uno más universal con los términos «tarde» y «mañana», que resultan más generales. Nótese también que la alteración de la secuencia normal mañana-tarde por tarde-mañana nos despega aún más de lo circundante y reconocible; se quiebra así con lo común, cíclico y rutinario de todos los días.

Lo que podría sonar a un encuentro casual en los primeros versos del poema, va abarcando una experiencia más total, amplia y compleja, más tarde. El hablante confiesa «lo ignoro» y nosotros nos encontramos como lectores pisando ese mismo terreno de lo desconocido, intuible, pero imposible de definir.

En el resto del poema, aunque se vuelve al tono familiar y conversacional del principio, ya no tiene el mismo efecto: «...solo sé / que en una breve noche de verano / se unieron los crepúsculos y... fue.» La imagen final del poema, aunque lleva ese tono coloquial y parece relacionarse a un mundo concreto, si se la trata de explicar literalmente no tiene solución posible. En este momento nos encontramos en la situación de aceptar que tanto el lenguaje coloquial como las imágenes no nos indican ninguna experiencia definitiva, pero nos sugieren muchas.

Con los puntos suspensivos finales sentimos la sensación de que en lo inconcluso del poema se completa su creación; allí se forma un espacio que se venía creando y conformando desde antes en la ambigüedad expresiva del poema para que como lectores quedamos en manos de las innumerables sugerencias propuestas. De esta forma, el «...fue» solitario del final no es conclusivo; es verdad que como tiempo verbal pasado, indica un hecho concluido, pero es una forma verbal que aparece aislada en el poema, que sin sujeto y sin predicado no logra concluir en algo definitivo. Nosotros, una vez más, como lectores debemos proveerle sujeto y posible predicado, tarea que cumplimos en manos de la intuición, dado que de otra manera no podría hacerse por carecer el poema de los elementos básicos para justificarlo y resolverlo en forma lógica.

En esta rima se ha creado por medio del lenguaje una experiencia intransferible que no se puede comunicar lógicamente. La imagen final comunica lo inexpresable. Al igual que los simbolistas y Juan Ramón, Bécquer nos pone en contacto con lo inefable e indescifrable.

Tal como Gustavo Adolfo, Juan Ramón Jiménez en muchos de sus poemas parte de la realidad cotidiana, pero en seguida las imágenes nos transportan a un mundo poético amplio y trascendente, como sucede con esta rima de Bécquer, donde nos encontramos ante una experiencia no reductible e imposible de conceptualizar en un mensaje determinado [5].

El poeta sevillano despoja a sus rimas de los ropajes del recargado romanticismo español, aligera sus versos para que estos logren elevarse a un nivel poético inusitado. Paralelamente a este fenómeno, años más tarde, Juan Ramón desnuda a sus poemas de los adornos modernistas y busca una poesía pura, breve y concentrada. Partiendo de una realidad concreta desprende a su obra artística de toda impureza, lo trivial o circunstancial se elimina, sólo lo esencial se retiene para que la poesía, en forma corta, simple y escueta, emprenda vuelo hacia un plano estético renovador. Gustavo Adolfo inicia esa técnica que consiste en quitar lo irrelevante, reducir y simplificar. Bécquer anhela captar la esencia poética en todas las cosas y Juan Ramón continúa esa misma búsqueda con su lírica.

El esfuerzo por lograr precisión en la expresión poética y cuidado exquisito de la forma tiene su antecedente en Bécquer [6]. Esta vertiente se ahonda con la poesía de Juan Ramón,

---

[5] En este asunto podríamos remitirnos al poema «Desvelo», que ya he analizado en el trabajo que se titula «La elaboración de una experiencia trascendente en la poesía 'Desvelo' de Juan Ramón Jiménez». La tesis que defiendo en ese estudio es que el juego de imágenes dentro del poema «Desvelo» parte de la realidad; pero en su disposición lingüística tan perfecta esas imágenes llegan a conformar una experiencia trascendente, propia del poema y que va por sobre la realidad cotidiana. En el manejo de imágenes y metáforas el poema trasciende lo ordinario y se remonta a un plano estético superior creado por su propio contexto.

[6] FRANCISCO RICO, *Historia y crítica de la literatura española;* VÍCTOR G. DE LA CONCHA, *Época contemporánea: 1914-1939* (Barcelona:

que será línea rectora para la Generación del 27, especialmente para Jorge Guillén [7]. Si bien Bécquer no hizo escuela en sus días, renace con fuerza más tarde, y es posible trazar una línea directriz que nace en Gustavo Adolfo, prosigue en Juan Ramón y enlaza a Jorge Guillén. A través de esta sucesión se logra gestar una nueva retórica lírica enfocada hacia la exactitud de la expresión.

La poesía de Bécquer no es una mera copia de la realidad, sino que resulta ser una creación superior objetivada a través del lenguaje. En esta orientación, en los comienzos del siglo XX, Antonio Machado continúa el surco abierto por Bécquer. En sus poemas *Campos de Castilla*, 1907-1917, describe esa región de España y nos recrea la Soria milenaria que había sido material de inspiración para muchas de las leyendas de Gustavo Adolfo. La obra temprana de Machado (1900-1917) es la que refleja más claramente la influencia becqueriana; por ejemplo, su destacado libro *Soledades*, 1899-1907, contiene algunos poemas que nos recuerdan ciertas rimas [8]. En el poema IV los efectos visuales y luego los sonoros, que al final del mismo terminan asociados, nos hacen pensar en la rima LXXIII que analizamos en detalle en el capítulo anterior:

Editorial Crítica, 1984). En esta obra, publicada recientemente, FRANCISCO JAVIER BLASCO tiene un artículo titulado «La pureza poética juanramoniana», pp. 174-78. Blasco propone que la pureza de Juan Ramón tiene su origen en Bécquer:

> Basta añadir que, si la poesía pura española pretende romper con los restos del romanticismo, vivo todavía en la herencia modernista, el ideal de pureza juanramoniano busca, precisamente, todo lo contrario: profundizar en los hallazgos del modernismo —es decir, del simbolismo—, a través de la dirección intimista marcada por Bécquer. (175)

[7] Jorge Guillén, en el mismo libro citado en la nota 4 de este capítulo, emparenta a Bécquer con los poetas puros por el proceso selectivo de su poesía:

> Junto al Bécquer bonito y muy popular —con sus lágrimas frágiles— se disimula un poeta muy puro... ha compuesto una poesía tan breve como intensa, donde la frase adquiere una forma que parece vaporosa: a tal extremo es radiante la materia de aquellos vocablos conductores de visión en la luz. (180)

[8] MANUEL y ANTONIO MACHADO, *Obras completas* (Madrid: Editorial Plenitud, 1947). Todas las citas de Antonio Machado indicadas en el texto provienen de este volumen.

IV. EN EL ENTIERRO DE UN AMIGO

Tierra le dieron una tarde horrible
del mes de julio, bajo el sol de fuego.

A un paso de la abierta sepultura,
había rosas de podridos pétalos,
entre geranios de áspera fragancia
y roja flor. El cielo
puro y azul. Corría
un aire fuerte y seco.

De los gruesos cordeles suspendido,
pesadamente, descender hicieron
el ataúd al fondo de la fosa
los dos sepultureros...

Y al reposar sonó con recio golpe,
solemne, en el silencio.

Un golpe de ataúd en tierra es algo
perfectamente serio.

Sobre la negra caja se rompían
los pesados terrones polvorientos...

El aire se llevaba
de la honda fosa el blanquecino aliento.

Y tú, sin sombra ya, duerme y reposa,
larga paz a tus huesos...

Definitivamente,
duerme un sueño tranquilo y verdadero. (852-53)

No sólo el tema del funeral narrado nos evoca la rima LXXIII, sino también el hecho de ver esa emoción contenida en estrofas de dos versos y la tragedia de la muerte que
encuentra el remanso en las dos últimas estrofas breves. La
técnica se une a la manera de presentar el asunto en el poema,
los efectos visuales y sonoros de: «Un golpe de ataúd en tierra es algo / perfectamente serio. / Sobre la negra caja se
rompían / los pesados terrones polvorientos...» son ecos y
espejos de la rima LXXIII: «La piqueta al hombro, / el sepulturero / cantando entre dientes / se perdió a lo lejos.» El
sonido quebradizo y contundente de las pes, tes y eres coin-

cide con las imágenes macabras que se describen tanto en el
poema de Machado como en la rima de Bécquer.

El efecto repetitivo de la anáfora en la rima LXXIII se
encuetnra en otro poema de Machado, el XII de *Soledades*:

XII

Amada, el aura dice
tu pura veste blanca...
No te verán mis ojos;
¡mi corazón te aguarda!

El viento me ha traído
tu nombre en la mañana;
el eco de tus pasos
repite la montaña...
No te verán mis ojos;
¡mi corazón te aguarda!

En las sombrías torres
repican las campanas...
No te verán mis ojos;
¡mi corazón te aguarda!

Los golpes del martillo
dicen la negra caja;
y el sitio de la fosa,
los golpes de la azada...
No te verán mis ojos;
¡mi corazón te aguarda! (861)

Ambos poetas evitan el desahogo de tipo romántico, sus
cantos están cargados de emoción, pero la pasión va refre-
nada en la forma de versos breves y puntos suspensivos que
insisten en evitar la descarga emocional. Aun los signos de
admiración, en vez de ser una exclamación desgarradora al
estilo romántico, reprimen todo desborde, encierran y reducen
al mínimo el desahogo emotivo; otra vez, al igual que en Bécquer, operan como muro de contención. Machado coincide
con Gustavo Adolfo en el tratamiento de la emoción dentro
del marco de sencillez que proponen sus poemas; en los dos
poetas se esquiva la grandilocuencia.

Otro poema de Antonio Machado que muestra una clara

atención a su maestro sevillano es el X, que forma parte de *Soledades* también:

X. HASTÍO

Pasan las horas de hastío
por la estancia familiar,
el amplio cuarto sombrío
donde yo empecé a soñar.

Del reloj arrinconado,
que en la penumbra clarea,
el tictac acompasado
odiosamente golpea.

Dice la monotonía
del agua clara al caer:
un día es como otro día;
hoy es lo mismo que ayer.

Cae la tarde. El viento agita
el parque mustio y dorado...
¡Qué largamente ha llorado
toda la fronda marchita! (901)

No sólo la temática de esta poesía nos hace pensar en la rima LVI que analizamos en nuestro último capítulo, sino que también la técnica que usa Antonio Machado tiene clara resonancia de la rima becqueriana. Ambos poemas terminan en una queja que no logra romper la pesada monotonía anterior. La sucesión incuestionablemente cíclica de la estrofa tercera del poema de Machado parece desprendida de la primera y cuarta estrofa de la rima LVI de Bécquer:

Dice la monotonía
del agua *clara* al *caer:*
un día es como otro día;
hoy es lo mismo que ayer.

Nótense las correspondencias con la rima LVI:

(1)   Hoy como ayer, mañana como hoy,
¡y siempre igual!
Un cielo gris, un horizonte eterno,
¡y andar..., andar!

....

(4)   Voz que incesante con el mismo tono
         canta el mismo *cantar;*
        gota de agua monótona que *cae*
        y *cae* sin cesar.

En la rima de Bécquer se capta el sonido del corazón: «Moviéndose a compás, como una estúpida / máquina, el corazón»; la imagen y el efecto sonoro de la rima se desarrolla y se transforma en un reloj en la estrofa segunda de «Hastío»:

          Del reloj arrinconado,
        que en la penumbra clarea,
        el tictac acompasado
        odiosamente golpea.

El lenguaje deliberadamente conversacional sería otro punto de contacto entre los dos poemas que acabamos de considerar. Ambos poetas se liberan de los tabúes románticos incorporando a sus poesías vocablos antes considerados no poéticos. Como ejemplo de esto se puede aludir en el caso de Bécquer a la comparación que realiza del corazón humano con «una estúpida máquina». En el poema de Machado el efecto onomatopéyico del «tictac» que reproduce el sonido del reloj acarrea también el tono coloquial [9]. En todos estos detalles mencionados se hace evidente la firme admiración de Antonio Machado por Gustavo Adolfo Bécquer.

En Bécquer habíamos notado un acercamiento a la poesía popular que se lleva a cabo a través de un cuidadoso esteticismo; es decir, es poesía de tono popular pero no resulta vulgar ni pedestre. En este sentido, Antonio Machado es un continuador de esa tendencia que veremos alcanzar su plenitud con los poemas de Federico García Lorca.

Quizás otro elemento que valdría la pena tener en consi-

---

[9] ANDREW P. DEBICKI, *Estudios sobre poesía española contemporánea*, 2.ª ed. (Madrid: Editorial Gredos, 1981). Lo que Debicki dice sobre los contemporáneos está como antecedente en Machado y Gustavo Adolfo Bécquer: «(Pudiéramos decir que este grupo rompe definitivamente con la noción de un «vocabulario poético» particular, y abre camino a la poesía actual).» (48-49)

deración, es la similitud del proceso de la vida de Bécquer con la de Jiménez y la de Machado. Los tres pasan sus años mozos en su región natal de Andalucía y los tres marchan a Madrid con las mismas esperanzas de triunfar, para enfrentar luego las grandes vicisitudes de la existencia en una gran ciudad. Hasta ese entonces Castilla había producido los grandes poetas; con este grupo de andaluces ilustres el polo de la producción lírica cambia de sitio, y Andalucía se convierte en el centro de donde provienen los mejores poetas. No es sólo un lugar de origen lo que comparten estos artistas, sino también una sensibilidad en común, y esto para la poesía es muy importante.

En resumen, existen llamativas correspondencias entre Gustavo Adolfo Bécquer y los dos poetas más destacados de principio de siglo: Juan Ramón Jiménez y Antonio Machado. El simbolismo, la pureza del lenguaje, el cuidado estético son cualidades de la poesía de Bécquer que Juan Ramón recoge y elabora para luego influenciar a Jorge Guillén y otros poetas de la Generación del 27. Un lenguaje coloquial, una emoción contenida pero muy vital, un acercamiento a la poesía popular son atributos de las *Rimas* de Bécquer que Antonio Machado retoma y trabaja, que más tarde se evidencian en García Lorca y otros poetas de su generación.

IV. ECOS DE BÉCQUER EN LA GENERACIÓN DEL 27.

Al tratar al poeta de Sevilla en relación con el grupo de 1927 se hará necesario considerar ciertas simplificaciones. Esta última generación está compuesta de poetas heterogéneos, cada uno de los cuales desarrolla un estilo muy propio. De todas maneras, es posible encontrar aspectos en común que relacionan sus obras tan diversas [1]. Teniendo en mente esto, podemos destacar que Bécquer no sólo dejó su poesía como semilla que germinará en estos poetas contemporáneos, sino que también les legó una poética y cierto estilo con características que reaparecen en ellos.

Gustavo Adolfo pule su producción poética, retoca y cambia; la forma final de sus *Rimas* se obtiene diez años después de escribirlas. Juan Ramón hace algo similar con sus *Obras*

---

[1] DÁMASO ALONSO, *Poetas españoles contemporáneos*, 3.ª ed. (Madrid: Editorial Gredos, 1969). Alonso, hablando de su generación, reconoce la diversidad dentro del mismo grupo: «La variedad es, por tanto, enorme: hay técnicas comunes a estos y a estos otros, pero no una manera formal que defina todo el grupo.» (168) ANDREW P. DEBICKI en su libro *Estudios sobre poesía española contemporánea*, 1981, da una serie de características de los poetas contemporáneos que coincide con elementos presentes en las *Rimas*, los cuales evidenciaremos con nuestro análisis:

Hemos visto que estos escritores combinan una visión de la poesía como creación de valores nuevos con otra que la considera el descubrimiento de lo importante de la realidad; así hacen de lo poético un ideal vital. De ahí arrancan otras características comunes a las poéticas de estos autores: su conciencia artística y su interés en el empleo más adecuado de la forma y de la lengua; su desdén por el sentimentalismo, la retórica, y cualquier léxico particular como válido en sí, aparte de su utilidad en un poema dado; su interpretación final de la poesía como misterio que trasciende a la lógica y a lo pedestre. Estos rasgos comunes de sus poéticas ya los definen como grupo... (55)

completas: escribe y reescribe en búsqueda de la forma más acabada. Siguiendo la misma línea, Jorge Guillén también reelabora su *Cántico* varias veces. Esta conciencia de estilo se origina en Bécquer y se intensifica en sus sucesores. Todos ellos son poetas que publican lentamente[2].

La poesía de Bécquer no representa ninguna clase de preocupación social como la tuvo la romántica. Al igual que Gustavo Adolfo, la Generación del 27 produce poemas desvinculados mayormente de los problemas sociales[3].

Bécquer no se opone particularmente a ningún movimiento, ni la Generación del 27 se gesta como reacción contra algún «ismo» determinado. Bécquer sí rompe con lo trillado y el cliché. En esto, la Generación del 27 es una continuación de Gustavo Adolfo, al oponerse a lo gastado y repetido; todos ellos odian el lenguaje anquilosado[4]. Bécquer desconfía del lenguaje an-

---

[2] A. P. Debicki describe este factor de la lentitud al definirla como característica de la generación de poetas contemporáneos, y que bien se relaciona con el proceso de Bécquer en la creación de sus *Rimas*: «(La lentitud con la que publican libros prueba ante todo su conciencia artística; adquieren primero una «sólida formación literaria», y escriben cuidadosamente sus obras.)» (65)

[3] Dámaso Alonso puntualiza que su generación se conservó, al igual que Bécquer, apolítica en su expresión poética: «No, no hubo un sentido conjunto de protesta política, ni aún de preocupación política en esa generación.» (161). A. P. Debicki también propone que aunque la poesía de este grupo, tal como la de Bécquer, parte de la realidad, está ausente de los problemas sociales del momento:

No hay duda de que en los años 1925-1930 estos poetas no se preocupan mucho de los problemas sociales. Pero sus amplios conocimientos estéticos, su raigambre en lo tradicional y lo popular al mismo tiempo que en lo culto, y sus esfuerzos de crear un arte perdurable no pueden limitarse a un deseo de escaparse del mundo en el que viven. (60)

[4] Dámaso Alonso da rápidamente un panorama de continuidad en la poesía contemporánea de España que bien podría incluir a Bécquer en este mismo deseo de renovar en vez de destruir:

Resulta, pues, que, considerando muy a vista de pájaro el proceso poético español, desde fines del siglo pasado hasta la generación de que hablamos no hay ninguna discontinuidad, ningún rompimiento esencial en la tradición poética. ... Entre el modernismo y el momento de los Machado y Juan Ramón Jiménez, entre éstos y mi generación, entre mi generación y los poetas jóvenes por quiebras más o menos superficiales, pero hay un tejido continuo por debajo y muchos elementos que sirven de laña o ensambladura. ... He ahí medio siglo de hermo-

terior, lo modifica y construye en base a una retórica nueva
que servirá de inspiración para los poetas más recientes.
Ni Bécquer ni los contemporáneos protestan contra los
movimientos anteriores, sino que los motiva el propósito de
hacer poesía nueva. Ninguno de ellos presenta postulado al-
guno; si hay algunas propuestas nuevas éstas nacen de los
poemas que escriben.

Ninguno de los componentes de este llamado segundo
siglo de oro español dejó de reconocer la valiosa aportación
de la poesía de Bécquer como fuente donde se nutre la salu-
dable obra poética contemporánea[5]. Dámaso Alonso, quizás el
crítico más afamado del grupo, comienza su libro *Poetas españoles contemporáneos* hablando de Bécquer[6]. Luis Cernu-

---

sa continuidad en poesía española, continuidad en donde cada
momento cumple con su deber de innovar, pero no siente un
prurito ciego de destruir. (161-62)

[5] CONCHA ZARDOYA, en *Poesía española contemporánea*, 1961, en la
introducción a su estudio estilístico de Bécquer, pp. 21-26, hace un
magnífico recuento de los trabajos críticos sobre Gustavo Adolfo.
Allí menciona que la crítica finesecular menospreció a Bécquer. Luego cita trabajos de los poetas de la Generación del 27 que elogian a
las *Rimas*. Zardoya enumera los análisis de Rafael Alberti (1931),
Dámaso Alonso (1935 y 1944), Luis Cernuda (1935), Juan Ramón Jiménez (1953), Jorge Guillén (1943); así como muchos críticos destacados de entonces que también elogiaron a Bécquer: Benjamín Jarnés
(1936), Guillermo Díaz-Plaja (1936), José María Monner Sans (1938), etc.
Para un recuento completo de nombres de críticos y sus artículos sobre Bécquer vale la pena referirse directamente al comienzo del
libro de Zardoya.

[6] Dámaso Alonso vincula a Bécquer con la Generación del 27:
    —Bécquer, ¿poeta contemporáneo?
    —Bécquer es el punto de arranque de toda la poesía con-
temporánea española. Cualquier poeta de hoy se siente mucho
más cerca de Bécquer (y, en parte, de Rosalía de Castro) que
de Zorrilla, de Núñez de Arce o de Rubén Darío... Bien evidente es esto en Antonio Machado y Juan Ramón Jiménez. Y
tanto como se alejaban de Rubén Darío se aproximaban a la
esfera del arte de Bécquer. Por eso es Bécquer —espiritual-
mente— un contemporáneo nuestro, y por eso su nombre abre
este libro y, en cierto modo, también lo cierra. (9)
Más adelante prosigue detallando la vinculación de la Generación
del 27 con Bécquer:
    ¿quién duda que ese entrevisto trasmundo, muerte o sueño,
nace en poesía española en Gustavo Adolfo? Más aún: al relacionar Bécquer —el enamorado de las cosas de España— su
propia poesía y la popular, ¿no está vagamente profetizando
lo que había de ocurrir en nuestros días, cuando las dos zonas

da, reconocido también como crítico dentro de estos poetas, en sus *Estudios sobre poesía española contemporánea*, concluye su capítulo sobre Bécquer dándole quizás el mayor y más justo reconocimiento, emparentándolo en su función de precursor con Garcilaso, como habíamos apuntado ya en nuestro análisis [7]:

> En efecto, Bécquer desempeña en nuestra poesía moderna un papel equivalente al de Garcilaso en nuestra poesía clásica: el de crear una nueva tradición, que lega a sus descendientes. Y si de Garcilaso se nutrieron dos siglos de poesía española, estando su sombra detrás de cualquiera de nuestros poetas de los siglos XVI y XVII, lo mismo se puede decir de Bécquer con respecto a su tiempo. El es quien dota a la poesía moderna española de una tradición nueva, y el eco de ella se encuentra en nuestros contemporáneos mejores. (50)

Dada la amplia gama de recursos de que disponen los poetas de esta generación, nos vemos en la necesidad de seleccionar. Así pues, en este trabajo se destacarán sólo algunas calas que parecen ayudar a agrupar a estos poetas. Solamente se tendrán en cuenta algunas características aplicables al análisis de las *Rimas*, para luego vincularlas con la producción de ciertos poetas contemporáneos. Además, nos referiremos a algunos trabajos críticos excelentes que ya se han hecho de Bécquer en relación con estos poetas, sin tener que repetir o extendernos innecesariamente. Esta tarea, de aspirar a ser

---

—Bécquer, lo popular— por último se habían de fundir en una sola voz? Cuando se quiera explicar el mejor Alberti —y aún una parte de Lorca—, ¿no pasará por nuestra imaginación, detrás de la idea de la poesía popular —y mezclada con otros elementos—, la sombra de la poesía de Bécquer? Y la voz será remansada y dulcemente dolorida —Manuel Altolaguirre— o nostálgicamente blanca y finísima —Luis Cernuda—, o se encrespará hasta el torbellino, como la del penúltimo Alberti, y más aún, la de Aleixandre. La sombra de Bécquer, más cerca, más lejos, estará siempre al fondo. Y no es que estos poetas hayan siempre pensado en Bécquer, o hayan sentido su influjo, ni es necesario que se pueda probar históricamente una tradición no interrumpida desde Bécquer a ellos: es que viven en una atmósfera, en un clima poético que sólo el genial experimento de Bécquer alumbró e hizo habitable para los españoles. (25-26)

[7] LUIS CERNUDA, *Estudios sobre poesía española contemporánea*, 3.ª ed. (Madrid: Ediciones Guadarrama, 1972), p. 50.

completa y exhaustiva, tendría que ser muchísimo más minuciosa, lo cual no es nuestro propósito. Nuestro propósito es que tras el análisis queden fijados puntos vitales que unen a Bécquer con la Generación del 27, y esto, posiblemente estimule para que en un futuro se amplíen estos estudios. De ninguna manera este capítulo final puede pretender abarcar en forma completa tema tan amplio como interesante. Hechas estas observaciones procedamos a la investigación.

El plan de estudio que proponemos básicamente pone atención a la bifurcación que se establece en la Generación del 27. Guillén y Lorca, quizás los poetas más sobresalientes, son los polos extremos hacia donde se abren las dos direcciones principales del rumbo que toma la poesía española de esos años. Joaquín González Muela, en un estudio estilístico de 1954, ya había observado esta bimembración y polarización; el mismo título del volumen lo indica: *El lenguaje poético de la generación Guillén-Lorca* [8].

Bécquer es el poeta plástico del siglo XIX español, el efecto visual es parte esencial de su poesía. En sus poemas los símiles y las metáforas van creando un mundo poético armonioso. Los «colores» y «la belleza plástica» en manos del poeta componen una realidad que trasciende lo cotidiano [9]. En el juego de metáforas y comparaciones se va creando una sensación de unidad y plenitud que nos hace recordar tanto a Garcilaso como a ciertos poetas de la Generación del 27, por ejem-

---

[8] JOAQUÍN GONZÁLEZ MUELA, *El lenguaje poético de la generación Guillén-Lorca* (Madrid: Insula, 1954). El autor comenta sobre el título de su libro:

El nombre que doy a la generación: «Guillén-Lorca», no me parece completamente satisfactorio, pero tampoco me lo parecen otras designaciones, como «generación de la Dictadura», por ejemplo. Yo prefiero llamarla con los dos nombres más significativos en las dos direcciones más importantes de la poesía de la época. (10).

[9] Debicki define este fenómeno:

Nos hace ver como la poesía nos ofrece significados que de otra manera no pudiéramos obtener, y como nos salva de lo pedestre y de lo rutinario. Pero este punto de vista nos hace pensar en el significado de la obra como algo personal al poeta, como un mundo creado, diferente de este en el que vivimos; la poesía viene a ser una elevación sobre lo ordinario. (34)

plo a Jorge Guillén. Garcilaso de la Vega resulta un precursor
del Siglo de Oro porque ya en sus églogas se manejan los componentes artísticos que harán renacer la poesía española. En
Garcilaso se nota el proceso metafórico que marcha paralela
y simultáneamente a un proceso metonímico que sirve para
integrar un mundo delicadamente balanceado propuesto a
través de las imágenes de los poemas [10]. Es en Bécquer donde
se redescubre esa armonía plástica. Con Bécquer renace la metáfora que luego adquiere importancia central en el modernismo para continuar siendo el eje estético en la Generación
del 27.

Será revelador analizar la rima II en base a estas conside-
raciones. En este poema se presenta estrofa tras estrofa una
serie de imágenes que parecen difuminarse, pulverizarse y eva-
nescerse conformando un mundo etéreo:

II

(1)   Saeta que voladora
        cruza arrojada al azar,
        sin adivinarse dónde
        temblando se clavará;

(2)   hoja que del árbol seca
        arrebata el vendabal,
        sin que nadie acierte el surco
        donde a caer volverá;

(3)   gigante ola que el viento
        riza y empuja en el mar,
        y rueda y pasa, y no sabe
        qué playa buscando va;

(4)   luz que en cercos temblorosos
        brilla, próxima a expirar,
        ignorándose cuál de ellos
        el último brillará:

---

[10] MARIO A. BLANC, «El proceso metafórico y el proceso metonímico en la Egloga I de Garcilaso de la Vega», *Ulula*, 1 (1984), pp. 39-48.
En este artículo muestro con más amplitud, con el análisis detenido de la Egloga I, este concepto enunciado en el texto. Nótese el paralelismo que existe en el proceso metafórico y metonímico de la
Egloga I con respecto a la rima II de Bécquer que analizaremos en
el texto, igual que con el poema «Perfección» de Jorge Guillén que
incluiremos en nuestro análisis.

(5)   eso soy yo, que al acaso
             cruzo el mundo, sin pensar
             de dónde vengo, ni adónde
             mis pasos me llevarán. (402)

Esta serie de imágenes descritas en las estrofas (1), (2), (3) y (4) se transforman en una comparación metafórica en la quinta estrofa cuando aparece el «yo». Pero si las imágenes previas eran vagas, este «yo» de la última estrofa también resulta misterioso. Muy bien podría ser el «yo» que corresponde al poeta, como podría también, más que a un determinado hablante, representar una voz poética:

                   eso soy yo, que al acaso
                   cruzo el mundo, sin pensar
                   de dónde vengo, ni adónde
                   mis pasos me llevarán.

También podríamos considerar un tercer nivel interpretativo para el «yo» de esta última estrofa. Dado que estas primeras rimas formulan la poética del libro, el «yo» de la rima II bien podría corresponder al poema en sí; o también, extendiendo la interpretación, el «yo» podría encarnar la poética, dado que las primeras rimas sugieren cierto aspecto metapoético y autoreferencial.

Teniendo en cuenta, todo esto, la serie de imágenes del principio —que llega a adquirir aspecto metafórico con la última estrofa— resulta ser un proceso que no termina allí, pues es una serie de imágenes que se comparan y conectan con el «yo». En vez de ser una relación A = B como generalmente se establece en un proceso metafórico, en la rima II tenemos una relación con este aspecto A, A1, A2, A3 = B (A corresponde a la imagen de la estrofa 1, A1 a la imagen de la estrofa 2, A2 a la imagen de la 3 y A3 a la de la 4). Esta relación evidencia una sucesión metonímica dentro del proceso metafórico que habíamos descrito en esta rima II.

Pero todo no termina aquí, sino que aun falta explicar un poco más sobre lo que habíamos dejado dicho acerca de los niveles interpretativos del «yo», que en nuestra fórmula correspondería a B. Al diversificarse el «yo» en varios niveles interpretativos posibles, observamos en el lado B de la comparación metafórica la misma transformación hacia una continuidad metonímica que ocurría en el lado A de la relación. De esta manera, la comparación de A = B establecida al principio, en realidad, corresponde a una equivalencia metafórica y metonímica que se cumple simultáneamente y que se podría dejar representada así: A, A1, A2, A3 = B, B1, B2, B3 (B corresponde al «yo» interpretado como el poeta o hablante, B1 al «yo» como equivalente de la voz poética, B2 interpretado como el poema en sí y B3 el «yo» como la poética del volumen).

Estas ecuaciones algo matemáticas solamente nos son útiles para ilustrar los procesos metafórico y metonímico que transcurren en el poema en forma simultánea; de ninguna manera pretenden imponer una precisión rígida a una poesía que se escapa de toda posible definición. Sólo el hecho de pensar que por ejemplo A podría estar vinulada (nótese que no digo igualada) tanto con B, como con B1, B2 o B3; o también se podría seguir el proceso inverso de relacionar B tanto con A, como con A1, A2 o A3, llegándose a crear así múltiples interpretaciones del poema. De esta manera quedan representadas una infinidad de comparaciones posibles que se han creado en la rima II.

Este proceso metonímico de las metáforas parecería estar planteado no sólo en la sucesión estrófica de las imágenes, sino también en la construcción lingüística elaborada en el poema. Por ejemplo, la tercera estrofa nos hace poner atención al encadenamiento metonímico con el empleo de la conjunción «y»:

> gigante ola que el viento
> riza y empuja en el mar,
> y rueda y pasa, y no sabe
> qué playa buscando va;

Bécquer, como lo harían más tarde los miembros de la Generación del 27, no sólo revive la metáfora, sino que con ese conjunto de imágenes que ofrece en los poemas compone un mundo integral. Andrew P. Debicki, en su análisis sobre la

Generación titulado *Estudios sobre poesía española contemporánea*, 1981, describe un poema que bien pudiera pertenecer a cualquiera de esos poetas contemporáneos, como de la misma forma podría estar refiriéndose a la rima II que acabamos de analizar [11]:

> El poema llega a una resolución total mediante la estructuración compleja de sus partes, y de varias visiones parciales: capta así la multiplicidad emotiva, sensorial y conceptual, y muchas veces el sentido paradójico de cualquier experiencia vital. Y al encontrar una forma fija para configurar y expresar la experiencia, evita los peligros de una expresión demasiado personal no objetivada y por lo tanto sentimental. (10-11)

En el capítulo de introducción que titula «Una generación poética» (refiriéndose a la de los contemporáneos), Debicki muestra como el poeta conecta la poesía con la realidad, proceso que otra vez pudiera también estar definiendo la rima II de Bécquer:

> Para sobreponerse a esta limitación del lenguaje directo, el poeta encarna los valores que ha creado en imágenes de la realidad; escoge objetos o experiencias que pueden llevar estos valores al lector con la multiplicidad y coherencia necesarias. (31)

La rima II no es una excepción, sino que traza el camino hacia lo que ocurre en muchos otros poemas becquerianos. En la rima III se presenta una vez más esa enumeración metonímica de imágenes, símiles y metáforas, construyendo una realidad poética autosuficiente. La rima IV insiste en la misma dirección, y el proceso es más obvio con la repetición del «mientras» engarzando la serie de imágenes que van conformando ese canto de fe en la revitalización de la poesía.

En Jorge Guillén se nota el cuidado de la composición de las metáforas y palabras claves que crean un mundo singular con significados esenciales y desprovisto de lo anecdótico [12].

---

[11] ANDREW P. DEBICKI, pp. 10-11.

[12] A. P. Debicki, en cuanto al énfasis que se pone en la creación de un mundo singular, en las páginas 128 y 129, cita los trabajos de Joaquín Casalduero; en cuanto a la búsqueda de significados esenciales y la omisión de lo anecdótico nos remite a J. Casalduero y Ricardo Gullón.

El poema «Perfección» del libro *Cántico* de Jorge Guillén, nos propone la imagen de la rosa como símbolo de la belleza y alrededor de ella se va conjugando un mundo armonioso donde las partes encajan con la totalidad [13]:

PERFECCIÓN

Queda curvo el firmamento,
Compacto azul, sobre el día.
Es el redondeamiento
Del esplendor: mediodía.
Todo es cúpula. Reposa,
Central sin querer, la rosa,
A un sol en cenit sujeta.
Y tanto se da el presente
Que el pie caminante siente
La integridad del planeta. (66)

En el poema se deja ver un proceso paralelo al de los poemas de Bécquer en la composición tanto metafórica como metonímica de una experiencia que nos eleva hacia la perfección estética.

Hemos visto que los poemas de Gustavo Adolfo Bécquer esconden la posible anécdota. Uno de los recursos que utiliza es la indeterminada referencia espacial y temporal. Las rimas escapan de un acontecimiento particular ya que en sus versos no se precisa ni un sitio identificable, ni un momento indicado. Así, de una experiencia posiblemente circunstancial llegamos a una universal. En «Perfección» pasa algo similar; se refiere al mediodía, pero no a uno exclusivamente. El cuadro que se conforma pertenece o se origina en nuestra realidad, pero no se sujeta a ningún punto geográfico posible de localizar a través de los vocablos del poema. Tanto Bécquer como Guillén parten de este mundo, pero en sus poesías damos con una creación que va más allá. Jorge Guillén en su estudio *La poética de Bécquer*, 1943, brinda citas de Gustavo Adolfo donde este asunto es el foco de atención [14].

---

[13] JORGE GUILLÉN, *Obra poética* (Madrid: Alianza Editorial, S. A., 1970), p. 66.
[14] JORGE GUILLÉN, *La poética de Bécquer*, 1943. Como ejemplos extraídos del libro de Guillén se podrían referir las páginas 36, 43, 44,

El mundo poético trascendente logrado en las *Rimas* de Bécquer continúa en las poesías de Juan Ramón; y será Jorge Guillén quien más tarde siga creando en su lírica esa visión poética que une lo concreto con lo absoluto, produciendo la sensación de haber alcanzado una universalidad total. Al igual que en Bécquer, en los poemas de Guillén se mezcla lo tangible con lo abstracto, las experiencias concretas apuntan a significados absolutos [15].

Gustavo Adolfo Bécquer, en 1868, cuando tenía 32 años, que para poeta es una edad relativamente madura, deja compuestas definitivamente sus *Rimas*. Jorge Guillén publica *Cántico* cuando tiene 35 años. Pedro Salinas, otro miembro de la misma generación que todavía no habíamos mencionado, escribe *Presagios* a los 32 años [16]. Dámaso Alonso es también ya algo maduro al publicar sus poemas. Dentro de estos poetas de la Generación del 27 se deja ver en sus poesías una voz poética adulta que tiene, en este sentido, conexión con la de las *Rimas*.

La otra vertiente de la poesía contemporánea va presidida por el genio de la figura de Federico García Lorca. Vivió entre fechas claves (1898-1936) y en este aspecto histórico nos pone conscientes de tres generaciones que realmente forman una continuidad y que conviven simultáneamente; la Generación del 98, la Generación del 27 y la del 36. Ya vimos como Béc-

---

45, 47, 48, 49 y 55. A través de todas estas citas extraídas de los libros de Bécquer se nota una gran dedicación por parte de Guillén en desentrañar el mundo de las *Rimas,* inspirador de su *Cántico.*

[15] A. P. Debicki comenta sobre el foco de atención del análisis que hace de Guillén: Pero los poemas de Guillén que he examinado aquí comunican experiencias tangibles, al mismo tiempo que tratan temas amplios.» (146)

[16] Debicki menciona características de Pedro Salinas que están vinculadas con las *Rimas:*
La amada, realidad e inspiración al mismo tiempo, le permite a Salinas ofrecer un cuadro coherente del proceso poético que tiene en cuenta su aspecto indagador y su aspecto creador... Esto indica que el tema del amor es un aspecto del tema central de la obra de Salinas, el de la poesía. (95-96)
Debicki recalca la presencia de un protagonista-poeta en los libros de Salinas, al igual que sentimos su presencia a lo largo de las *Rimas* de Bécquer. Luego, en las páginas 103 y 104 de su libro, Debicki relaciona a Pedro Salinas con Gustavo Adolfo Bécquer.

quer influyó en la primera, especialmente a través de Antonio Machado y Juan Ramón Jiménez [17]. También vimos que a través de Jorge Guillén influencia a los de la del 27. Con García Lorca, la influencia de Bécquer no se limita a la del 27, sino que abarca a los poetas de la del 36 también [18].

---

[17] BIRUTE CIPLIJAUSKAITE, «Bécquer y Baroja», *Sin nombre*, vol. IV, núm. 1 (julio-septiembre, 1973), pp. 29-36. Este trabajo no sólo emparenta a esos dos escritores, sino que también une a Bécquer con los miembros de la generación del 98. Ciplijauskaite concluye así su análisis:

> Este ha sido no sólo el ideal de Baroja. La preceptiva de los hombres del 98 se opone unánimemente a la ampulocidad superficial. La pauta «¡adentro!», lanzada por Unamuno, expresa la misma búsqueda de la intimidad, aunque menos analítica iniciada por Bécquer. Bécquer les acompaña a través del campo y de las ciudades castellanas; Bécquer les alienta en su insistencia en el ideal. En ellos, así como en Bécquer, está ausente el amor erótico. De Bécquer recogen, por fin, la inclinación al ensueño... (36)

[18] JOAQUÍN GONZÁLEZ MUELA y JUAN MANUEL ROZAS, *La generación poética de 1927* (Madrid: Ediciones Alcalá, 1966). González Muela agrupa a los de la tradición popular: Alberti, Lorca, Diego. Luego destaca a Lorca: «...es el que refleja mejor, con talento de folklorista, esa poesía (y no olvidemos la música) de tipo tradicional.» (13). También vincula a Rafael Alberti con Bécquer: «Alberti está escribiendo, tal vez, sobre un amor perdido y el desencanto de la juventud, y el tono onírico ya hemos dicho que tiene mucho que ver con el de la Rima LXXV de Bécquer.» (16). LUIS LORENZO-RIVERO, «Vivencias becquerianas en Alberti», *Estudos Ibero-Americanos*, vol. I, núm. 2 (dezembro, 1975), pp. 291-98. Lorenzo-Rivero destaca: «Evidentemente es imperativo el tener presente en todo momento, al hablar de poesía, la trayectoria: Bécquer-Juan Ramón Jiménez-Generación del 27. Luego aparecen los poetas más significativos del 36 y posteriores.» (291). Al igual que se podría decir de Lorca y los demás, Lorenzo-Rivero expresa de Alberti en relación con Bécquer: «No se puede negar lo mucho que este aprendió de Bécquer, ni su gran compatibilidad de espíritu, sin que esto disminuya en nada su gran originalidad y maestría artística.» (298). González Muela considera el contacto de Alberti y Luis Cernuda con Bécquer:

> No podremos entender *Sobre los ángeles*, de Alberti, explícitamente dedicado a Bécquer, sin leer cuidadosamente la Rima LXXV, donde el alma, como «huésped de las nieblas», se remonta por espacios desconocidos durante el sueño. Y el título de un libro de Cernuda, *Donde habite el olvido*, está tomado de un verso de la Rima LXVI, con mucho del espíritu de Gustavo Adolfo. (11)

En *Estudios sobre Gustavo Adolfo Bécquer*, 1972, aparece un artículo de JOSÉ LUIS CANO, titulado «La fusión con la naturaleza en Bécquer y Aleixandre», pp. 641-49, donde comienza conectando a Bécquer con todos los poetas contemporáneos. Vale la pena citar el principio

García Lorca retoma lo hecho por Bécquer, y luego por Machado, en materia de la tradición popular. En el libro *Poema del cante jondo*, 1921, Lorca compone poemas de valor musical semejante a canciones: son canciones que se han hecho poemas y poesías que parecen canciones [19]. Mediante la poesía se destaca el valor de la música y el arte en general. «Las seis cuerdas» es un ejemplo de lo dicho:

LAS SEIS CUERDAS

La guitarra,
hace llorar a los sueños.
El sollozo de las almas
perdidas,
se escapa por su boca
redonda.
Y como la tarántula
teje una gran estrella
para cazar suspiros,
que flotan en su negro
aljibe de madera. (191)

Los primeros seis versos ponen atención al sonido que produce la guitarra expresando los sentimientos en el «llorar»,

---

del estudio por el hecho de englobar y resumir nuestras investigaciones de este capítulo:

No se ha hecho aún, que yo sepa, un estudio sobre la presencia de Bécquer en los poetas de la famosa generación del 27, y no me refiero tanto a las posibles huellas, que sin duda, existen, cuanto a la simpatía y admiración profundas que los poetas de aquella generación han mostrado por la figura —el hombre y el poeta— del autor de las *Rimas*. Cierto que en esa admiración por Bécquer les habían precedido los grandes poetas de la generación anterior —Unamuno, Antonio Machado, Juan Ramón Jiménez—. Pero no creo equivocarme al afirmar que la generación del 27 es la más becqueriana de entre las que se han sucedido desde Bécquer hasta hoy. Salinas y Guillén, García Lorca y Alberti, Aleixandre y Cernuda, Dámaso Alonso y Gerardo Diego, Prados y Altolaguirre fueron —y son aún los que viven— becquerianos entusiastas, que han dejado en sus escritos, unos en prosa, otros en verso, testimonios inequívocos de ese fervor por Bécquer. (641)

En la misma página de esta cita José Luis Cano nos provee con una lista extensa de artículos de los poetas de la Generación del 27 que tratan sobre Gustavo Adolfo Bécquer.

[19] FEDERICO GARCÍA LORCA, *Obras completas*, 15.ª ed. (Madrid: Aguilar, S. A., de Ediciones, 1974), I. Todas las citas de Federico García Lorca indicadas en el texto están extraídas de esta edición.

«el sollozo de las almas» y «escapa por su boca». Se produce sonido, pero nace de lo inerte «guitarra», «sueños» y «almas perdidas»; todos estos son ecos de la vida, pero no tienen vida en sí.

En los otros cinco versos los sonidos se acallan en la paciente labor de «la tarántula» que ahoga los gritos y llantos en «suspiros». Ahora no hay sonidos, pero hay vida, indicada en la actividad febril de «la tarántula» y en la imagen del «aljibe» como fuente de agua y manantial vital.

En el poema hay una separación de seis y cinco versos. Los primeros seis ponen atención a lo sonoro, pero están carentes de vida propia. Los cinco versos restantes toman vida, pero no producen sonidos en sí. Las primeras seis líneas bien podrían simbolizar la guitarra, de esta manera se encabezan esos primeros seis versos: «La guitarra», que equivalen a las seis cuerdas del instrumento. Esta interpretación queda respaldada por el título del poema. La guitarra es el instrumento sonoro, pero inerte, tal como habíamos descrito en los primeros seis versos que producen sonidos, pero no tienen vida. Luego, la tarántula de los próximos cinco bien podría ser una metáfora de la mano ejecutora que rasguea la guitarra. Siguiendo la misma línea de análisis que usamos para la primera parte de la poesía, podríamos decir que estos cinco versos restantes corresponden a los cinco dedos de la mano ejecutante con vida, pero no son el instrumento sonoro, sino los que lo ejecutan. Ahora, en esta segunda parte, hay vida, pero no tenemos sonidos. La amalgama de los primeros seis versos con los últimos cinco, de la guitarra con la mano del ejecutante, se complementa para producir la música, el poema y el arte en general.

«Las seis cuerdas» tiene un lenguaje sencillo, pero su cuidado formal y el logro de imágenes tan bien empleadas lo distancian del canto popular corriente; parte de la tradición del cante jondo, pero su elaboración es más compleja, como queda evidenciado en el análisis. Lorca, así como Bécquer, crea poemas de raigambre popular, pero cargados de una alta conciencia estética.

En «Las seis cuerdas» no se destaca el ejecutante, sino la guitarra en sí. En este poema se pone de relieve la creación artística mediante el procedimietno de dirigir nuestra atención hacia la fuente creadora [20]. Y el acercamiento de Lorca muestra correspondencias con la rima VII de Gustavo Adolfo Bécquer:

VII

Del salón en el ángulo oscuro,
de su dueña tal vez olvidada,
silenciosa y cubierta de polvo,
        veíase el arpa.

¡Cuánta nota dormía en sus cuerdas,
como el pájaro duerme en las ramas,
esperando la mano de nieve
        que sabe arrancarlas!

¡Ay! —pensé—. ¡Cuántas veces el genio
así duerme en el fondo del alma,
y una voz, como Lázaro, espera
que le diga: «¡Levántate y anda!» (410)

Las relaciones entre un poema y otro son dignas de destacarse. En vez de una guitarra en el poema de Bécquer tenemos el arpa como instrumento sonoro. En la segunda estrofa se desarrolla el símil de la «nota» (el sonido) «como el pájaro duerme en las ramas» con posible vida, pero no propia. Luego, está «la mano de nieve» que nos hace pensar en la tarántula de la poesía de Lorca. Tanto en un poema como en el otro la música (el efecto artístico) brota milagrosamente. En ambos casos el genio creador ausente proporciona vida, de la muerte se levanta un canto vigorizante. Tanto el asunto como las técnicas, y el proceso de percepción, son similares en Bécquer y Lorca. Se podría decir que los símiles e imágenes de

---

[20] Andrew P. Debicki, en su análisis de «Las seis cuerdas», puntualiza:

No cabe duda: la estilización de la guitarra en «Las seis cuerdas» sirve para destacar el impacto de la creación artística, para ayudarnos a ver la música de la guitarra no como distracción ni como ejercicio técnico, sino como la actividad vital de expresar valores humanos importantes. (230)

Bécquer son algo más directos, pero lo importante en destacar es que en ambos poemas encontramos un procedimiento
muy similar para hacernos dedicar nuestra atención a la creación artística como asunto del poema. Ambos poetas se nutren de los efectos visuales que se unen a los sonoros, ambos
parten de ciertas imágenes que evocan sonidos. En los dos
casos se utiliza un lenguaje sencillo, pero muy cuidadoso.

Veámoslo en el poema «Memento», del volumen *Poema del
cante jondo* de Federico García Lorca:

MEMENTO

Cuando yo me muera,
enterradme con mi guitarra
bajo la arena.

Cuando yo me muera,
entre los naranjos
y la hierbabuena.

Cuando yo me muera,
enterradme si queréis
en una veleta.

¡Cuando yo me muera! (208)

Este poema de Lorca muestra fuerte conexión con la rima LVI de Bécquer:

LXI

Al ver mis horas de fiebre
e insomnio lentas pasar,
a la orilla de mi lecho,
¿quién se sentará?

Cuando la trémula mano
tienda, próxima a expirar,
buscando una mano amiga,
¿quién la estrechará?

Cuando la muerte vidríe
de mis ojos el cristal,
mis párpados aún abiertos,
¿quién los cerrará?

> Cuando la campana suene
> (si suena en mi funeral),
> una oración al oírla,
> ¿quién murmurará?
>
> Cuando mis pálidos restos
> oprima la tierra ya,
> sobre la olvidada fosa,
> ¿quién vendrá a llorar?
>
> ¿Quién, en fin, al otro día
> cuando el sol vuelva a brillar,
> de que pasé por el mundo,
> quién se acordará? (441-42)

Ambos poemas muestran al hablante pensando en su futura muerte. Tanto Bécquer como Lorca murieron jóvenes, y estos poemas parecen presagios de sus fines tristes.

Lorca, en su libro *Canciones*, 1924, crea poemas breves de tono popular [21] que recuerdan al Bécquer de las rimas XXXVI, XLIX, LIV, LVIII y LX; esta última la citamos como ejemplo:

LX

> Mi vida es un erial:
> flor que toco se deshoja;
> que en mi camino fatal,
> alguien va sembrando el mal
> para que yo lo recoja. (441)

Joaquín González Muela destaca muy oportunamente que por sobre los clásicos, la figura de Gustavo Adolfo Bécquer es la de mayor influencia para la Generación del 27 [22]:

> En cuanto a Bécquer, la influencia no se limita sólo a esa afinidad espiritual, sino que es bien visible en Rafael Alberti y Luis Cernuda... (Dámaso Alonso, Gerardo Diego, Pedro Salinas, Jorge Guillén, Luis Cernuda...), y conocieron a fondo los clásicos españoles. Pero la influencia de estos clásicos no es tan directa y evidente comò la de Bécquer. (11-12)

---

[21] FEDERICO GARCÍA LORCA, «Canciones», en sus *Obras completas*, 1974. Lorca, en el volumen de poesías titulado «Canciones», de los años 1921-1924, pp. 273-390, trae poemas breves de raigambre popular, pero estilizados que notan correspondencias con algunas rimas breves de Bécquer.

[22] GONZÁLEZ MUELA, pp. 11-12.

Si Garcilaso, en su breve producción artística, encendió la llama que trajo luz al Siglo de Oro, paralelamente vemos que Gustavo Adolfo Bécquer con su condensada obra poética de las *Rimas* ilumina en muchos aspectos fundamentales la renovación de la poesía española en su segundo siglo de oro. En este estudio se han podido señalar las correspondencias específicas que existen entre la elaboración artística de las *Rimas* y los poemas de los poetas posteriores.

En las *Rimas* late la presencia de un canto popular pero estilizado. Esta vertiente que ofrecen los poemas becquerianos se acentúa en la poesía de Antonio Mahado, para más tarde vibrar con la vitalidad del cante jondo de Federico García Lorca.

Por otro lado, en las *Rimas* se asiste también a una depuración estética, a una estilización de las técnicas poéticas, que vemos ahondarse en la poesía de Juan Ramón Jiménez. Más tarde, este cuidado formal en la expresión artística tiene su punto culminante de elaboración en la perfección anhelada de los cantos de Jorge Guillén.

En las *Rimas* están en embrión las venas poéticas que se extenderán con vigor en nuestro siglo. Bécquer y su producción artística son un hito en el desarrollo más reciente de la poesía española. En el aire vagoroso y extraño de su himno nace un canto renovador, se proyectan rayos luminosos que nutren esa nueva aurora del segundo renacimiento poético español.

BIBLIOGRAFÍA

VOLÚMENES DE POESÍA CITADOS.

BÉCQUER, GUSTAVO ADOLFO. *Obras completas.* 13.ᵃ ed. Madrid: Aguilar S. A. de Ediciones, 1969.

DARÍO, RUBÉN. *Obras completas.* Madrid: Ediciones Castilla S. A., 1953. Vol. V.

GARCÍA LORCA, FEDERICO. *Obras completas.* 15.ᵃ ed. Madrid: Aguilar S. A. de Ediciones, 1974. Vol. I.

GUILLÉN, JORGE. *Obra poética: Antología.* Madrid: Alianza Editorial S. A., 1970.

JIMÉNEZ, JUAN RAMÓN. *Primeros libros de poesía.* Madrid: Aguilar S. A. de Ediciones, 1959.

MACHADO, MANUEL Y ANTONIO. *Obras completas.* Madrid: Editorial Plenitud, 1947.

TRABAJOS CRÍTICOS.

ALONSO, DÁMASO. *Poetas españoles contemporáneos.* 3.ᵉ ed. Madrid: Editorial Gredos S. A., 1969. Vol. 6.

— y CARLOS BOUSOÑO. *Seis calas en la expresión literaria española.* Madrid: Editorial Gredos, 1951.

ALONSO, MARTÍN. *Segundo estilo de Bécquer.* Madrid: Ediciones Guadarrama S. A., 1972.

BALAKIAN, ANNA. *El movimiento simbolista.* Traducido por José-Miguel Velloso. Madrid: Ediciones Guadarrama S. A., 1969.

BALBÍN, RAFAEL DE. *Poética becqueriana.* Madrid: Editorial Prensa Española, 1969.

BARBÁCHANO, CARLOS J. *Bécquer.* Madrid: Ediciones y Publicaciones Españolas S. A., 1970.

BERENGUER CARISOMO, ARTURO. *La prosa de Bécquer*. 2.ª ed. Sevilla: Publicaciones de la Universidad de Sevilla, 1974.

BLANC, MARIO A. «El proceso metafórico y el proceso metonímico en la Égloga I de Garcilaso de la Vega». *Ulula* 1 (1984): 39-48.

BROWN, RICA. *Bécquer*. Barcelona: Editorial Aedos, 1969.

CANO, JOSÉ LUIS, editor. *Gustavo Adolfo Bécquer: Rimas*. 2.ª ed. Madrid: Ediciones Cátedra S. A., 1976.

CARPINTERO, HELIODORO. *Bécquer de par en par*. 2.ª ed. Madrid: Artes Gráficas Benzal, 1971.

CASTILLO, HOMERO, introd. *Estudios críticos sobre el modernismo*. Madrid: Editorial Gredos S. A., 1974.

CELAYA, GABRIEL. introd. *Gustavo Adolfo Bécquer*. Madrid: Ediciones Júcar, 1972.

CERNUDA, LUIS. *Estudios sobre poesía española contemporánea*. 3.ª ed. Madrid: Ediciones Guadarrama S. A., 1972.

CIPLIJAUSKAITE, BIRUTE. «Bécquer y Baroja». *Sin nombre*. Vol. IV, Núm. 1 (Julio-Septiembre 1973): 29-36.

Consejo Superior de Investigaciones Científicas. *Estudios sobre Gustavo Adolfo Bécquer*. Madrid: Sucesores de Rivadeneyra S. A., 1972.

CHADWICK, CHARLES. *Symbolism*. London: Methuen and Co. Ltd., 1971.

DAVISON, NED J. *The Concept of Modernism in Hispanic Criticism*. Boulder, Colorado: Preutt Press Inc., 1966.

DEBICKI, ANDREW P. *Estudios sobre poesía española contemporánea: La generación de 1924-1925*. 2.ª ed. Madrid: Editorial Gredos S. A., 1981.

DÍAZ, JOSÉ PEDRO. *Bécquer*. Buenos Aires: Centro Editor de América Latina S. A., 1968.

— *Gustavo Adolfo Bécquer: vida y poesía*. Madrid: Editorial Gredos, 1958.

DÍAZ-PLAJA, GUILLERMO. *Modernismo frente a noventa y ocho*. Madrid: Editorial Espasa-Calpe S. A., 1951.

ENTRAMBASAGUAS PEÑA, JOAQUÍN DE. *La obra poética de Bécquer en su discriminación creadora y erótica*. Madrid: Gráficas Clemares, 1974.

GONZÁLEZ MUELA, JOAQUÍN Y JUAN MANUEL ROZAS. *La generación poética de 1927*. Madrid: Ediciones Alcalá, 1966.

GONZÁLEZ MUELA, JOAQUÍN. *El lenguaje poético de la generación Guillén-Lorca*. Madrid: Ínsula, 1954.

GUELBENZU, JOSÉ MARÍA, introd. *Gustavo Adolfo Bécquer: Poética, narrativa, papeles personales*. Madrid: Editorial Alianza S. A., 1970.

GUILLÉN, JORGE. *La poética de Bécquer*. Cuba: Ucar, García y Cía., 1943.

— *Lenguaje y poesía: algunos casos españoles*. Madrid: Artes Gráficas Clavileño S. A., 1961.

GULLÓN, RICARDO. *Direcciones del modernismo*. Madrid: Editorial Gredos, 1963.

HENRÍQUEZ UREÑA, MAX. *Breve historia del modernismo*. 2.ª ed. México: Fondo de Cultura Económica, 1962.

HINTERHÄUSER, HANS. *Fin de siglo: figuras y mitos*. Traducido por María Teresa Martínez. Madrid: Taurus Ediciones, S. A., 1980.

JARNÉS, BENJAMÍN. *Doble agonía de Bécquer*. Madrid: Talleres Espasa-Calpe S. A., 1936.

JIMÉNEZ, JUAN RAMÓN. *El modernismo: notas de un curso* (*1953*). Introd. Ricardo Gullón. 1.ª ed. México: Gráfica Cervantina S. A., 1962.

JIMÉNEZ MARTOS, LUIS, introd. *Gustavo Adolfo Bécquer: Rimas, leyendas y cartas*. Madrid: Editorial Magisterio Español S. A., 1970.

KING, EDMUND L. *Gustavo Adolfo Bécquer: From Painter to Poet*. México: Editorial Porrúa S. A., 1953.

KOVACCI, OFELIA, introd. *Gustavo Adolfo Bécquer: Rimas y escritos sobre poesía*. Buenos Aires: Editorial Plus Ultra, 1966.

LEÓN, MARÍA TERESA Y RAFAEL ALBERTI, introd. *El gran amor de Gustavo Adolfo Bécquer: (una vida pobre y apasionada)*. Buenos Aires: Editorial Losada S. A., 1946.

LITVAK, LILY, introd. *El modirnismo*. Madrid: Taurus Ediciones S. A., 1975.

LORENZO-RIVERO, LUIS. «Vivencias becquerianas en Alberti». *Es-

tudos Ibero-Americanos. Vol. 1, Núm. 2 (Dezembro 1975): 291-98.

MONNER SANS, JOSÉ MARÍA, introd. *Gustavo Adolfo Bécquer: Rimas e ideario de sus obras.* Montevideo: Claudio García y Cía., Editores, 1937.

ONTAÑÓN, JUANA DE, introd. *Gustavo Adolfo Bécquer: Rimas, leyendas y narraciones.* 6.ª ed. México: Editorial Porrúa S. A., 1971.

PAGEARD, ROBERT, ed. anotada *Rimas de Gustavo Adolfo Bécquer.* Serie IV, Vol. III. Madrid: Consejo Superior de Investigaciones Científicas, 1972.

RAMA, ÁNGEL. *Rubén Darío y el modernismo.* Caracas: Ediciones de la Biblioteca de la Universidad Central de Venezuela, 1970.

REVUELTA, VIDAL BENITO. *Bécquer y Toledo.* Madrid: Artes Gráficas Benzal, 1972.

RICO, FRANCISCO. *Historia y crítica de la literatura española.* Víctor G. de la Concha. *Época contemporánea: 1914-1939.* Vol. VII. Barcelona: Editorial Crítica, 1984.

RIFFATERRE, MIPHAEL. *Semiotics of Poetry.* London: Indiana University Press, 1978.

RUIZ-FORNELLS, ENRIQUE. *A Concordance to the Poetry of Gustavo Adolfo Bécquer.* Alabama: The University of Alabama Press, 1970.

SANDOVAL, ALFONSO DE. *El último amor de Bécquer.* 1.ª ed. Barcelona: Editorial Juventud S. A., 1941.

SEBOLD, RUSSELL P., editor. *Gustavo Adolfo Bécquer.* Madrid: Taurus Ediciones S. A., 1985.

SPHINZ, ALBERT, introd. *Nineteenth Century French Readings.* New York: Holt, Rinehart and Winston, 1965.

TURK, HENRY CHARLES. *German Romanticism in Gustavo Adolfo Bécquer's Short Stories.* Lawrence, Kansas: The Allen Press, 1959.

Universidad Nacional de La Plata, ed. *Gustavo Adolfo Bécquer: (Estudios reunidos en conmemoración del centenario), 1870-*

1970. La Plata, Argentina: Facultad de Humanidades y Ciencias de la Educación, Universidad de La Plata, 1971.

ZARDOYA, CONCHA. *Poesía española contemporánea: estudios temáticos y estilísticos.* Madrid: Ediciones Guadarrama S. L., 1961.

EDITORIAL PLIEGOS

OBRAS PUBLICADAS

colección pliegos de ensayo

EN PREPARACIÓN